BLOCK PARTY 666

BLOCK PARTY 666

MARK OF THE BEAST

VOLUME TWO

AL-SAADIQ BANKS

Author: Al-Saadiq Banks

Contact Information:
True 2 Life Publications
P. O. Box 8722
Newark NJ 07108

Email: alsaadiqbanks@aol.com
Twitter: @alsaadiq
Instagram: @alsaadiqbanks

www.True2LifeProductions.com

Edited By: Pen 2 Pen
Email: info@pen2penpublishing.com
2261 Talmadge Road Ste. 71
Lovejoy, Ga 30250
For Editing, and Typesetting Services

1

CAMDEN

THE SOUND OF Tupac's, '*The Last Motherfucker Breathin'* blares through the speakers. Skelter mumbles along with the song as she stares out the back window. "Tell me, who will be the last motherfucker breathing?"

Middle Godson passes Skelter the blunt. She inhales slowly, bopping her head to the beat. She exhales even slower. "Woke up with fifty enemies plotting my death. All fifty seeing visions of me shot in the chest. Couldn't rest, nah nigga I was stressed. Had me creeping 'round corners, homie sleeping in my vest," she says a little louder.

She passes the blunt back to her Godson. She never smokes during the day, especially not while working but today she is. Her nerves are shot and she needs to calm them. She just needs to ease her mind to make sense of it all and put together a plan.

On her lap is a 9-millimeter with a 30-round clip attached to it. She grips it tight as she sings along with the song. "Complete my mission, my competition no longer beefing," she says with her lips snarled. "I murdered all them busters now I'm the last motherfucker breathing." She can only hope that it goes like this for her.

Youngest Godson turns the truck onto the block. Skelter looks up ahead with no plan in her mind. She doesn't know exactly what she's come to do but she knows she has to do something. Her enemies have been attacking day and night and she needs to retaliate. She needs them to feel the same pressure she feels on her end.

The block is empty and quiet. Stores are just opening so there's no real action in and out of them. Skelter notices the beauty salon's gate is closed. The abundance of mail overflowing the box is an indication that it hasn't been open.

With Quabo's woman not being around, Skelter isn't sure what else she can touch that will really mean something to him. Quabo is putting pressure on the area, touching any and everything, but she has a different agenda though. She wants to touch that in which is dear to him. She's hoping that will be a big score in her favor and just maybe that will make them simmer down a little. She knows for certain that in war if the enemy has nothing dear to them on the line they act out with no fear because they feel like they have nothing to lose.

"Pull over," Skelter instructs.

She watches an old man who is obviously an alcoholic. He's sweeping in front of the stores, quickly while talking to himself. The man sweeps half of the block, in front of every store that's affiliated with Quabo's brand. He then goes over to the salon and steps into the alley. He picks up the loose trash, throws it in the garbage cans and ties the bags up. While in the alley he confirms what Skelter was thinking when he pulls a bottle of cheap liquor from his pocket and guzzles it down.

He steps to the front of the salon and takes all the mail from the box. He stretches the keychain from his belt buckle. Through the many keys on the ring he goes directly to the one that opens the salon. He opens the door and drops the mail on the floor before closing and locking the door.

He then walks two stores down to the liquor store which is closed as well. He goes directly to the key that fits the lock on the steel gate. He lifts the gate, but never opens the door to the actual store. He does the same thing on the Travel Agency and the Barber Shop and the Laundromat.

Skelter quickly puts it together in her mind. This man has a key to every store on the block and he's in charge of the upkeep. He's obviously the Super. They have a lot of trust in him for him to be a drunkard though. With that much trust, he must be someone dear and close.

"Bust a U-turn," Skelter commands. As the truck is being turned in the middle of the street, Skelter keeps her eyes glued onto the man. He's now in the alley of the Travel Agency, tying the garbage bags that are in the cans.

The truck is stopped short. Skelter forces the door open and darts out. Three giant steps and she stands directly in front of the man, gun aimed at the back of his head. He turns around and before his eyes can stretch open with fear, she squeezes the trigger. *POP! POP! POP!* All three shots to the face before he falls flat on his back. She fires one more out of rage. *POP!* It takes only two giant steps to get to the truck. She jumps in and the truck speeds off.

"Who will be the last motherfucker breathing?"

2

NEWARK

PEBBLES WALKS OUT of her Society Hill condominium and the sight parked in front has her mesmerized. The Purple Rolls Royce truck looks like a picture ripped from an exotic car magazine. If not for her dark sunglasses, the huge chrome grill would blind her. Tony gets out and makes his way over the passenger's side, where he holds the door for her to get in. "Hey lady," he says with a dazzling smile.

Pebbles pinches herself just to make sure she's not dreaming. Tony called her this morning telling her that he would like to have lunch with her one day this week. Pebbles didn't want to sound too thirsty but she put her pride to the side and pushed the date for right now. No way was she going to blow the opportunity to go out with him.

Pebbles slides into the passenger's seat and like hot chocolate syrup, she melts into the buttery, caramel interior. Tony closes the door behind her gently. The smell of expensive leather mixed with cologne creates a beautiful fragrance. The sound of Japanese, female jazz pianist, Keiko Matsui's 'Edge of Twilight' comes out of the speaker, crisp and clear, sounding like an actual concert.

As Tony seats himself Pebbles can't keep her eyes off of him. She's never seen anything like him. He's the perfect gentlemen yet the hood side of him peeks out naturally. A simple white v-neck tee shirt, distressed jeans and Air Jordan Retro 2's, he has Newark written all over him. But driving a half a million-dollar automobile, listening to jazz music just wipes the trace of Newark clean off him.

"You smell amazing," Pebbles says with seductive eyes. "What's that Creed?"

"Thanks," he replies. "No, Clive," he says bluntly.

"Nice," she says with total familiarity. *Damn, $2,000 for a bottle of cologne*, she thinks to herself. "Hmm, must be nice."

Pebbles is trying her best to look unimpressed but it's hard. She's rarely impressed with men because she's seen it all and done it all from a ghetto rich perspective, but this right here is an altogether different level for her. She's played on the Bentley level more than a few times but Rolls Royce is a brand-new game to her. She's sure she can adjust though.

She hasn't been this impressed with a man in a long time. She has to keep her cool just so he doesn't get any fuller of himself. Although she finds his cockiness attractive she doesn't want to contribute to it. She wants to come across as unimpressed with him as he seems with her.

Truthfully she really can't believe that they're actually here. After shooting her shot, he didn't give her much hope. She wasn't crushed though because in her heart she felt she would be patient and eventually get her man as she always does. There's never been a man that she's wanted that she didn't get. This date gives her promise that she still has the touch.

They're just getting in the car and haven't been together three minutes yet and she's already visualized herself having sex with him. Pebbles knows how to play the game but with him she feels he's so far ahead of the game that he will peep it a mile away. Usually a man of his caliber, she would play the good girl role, and make him wait for the sex. Most men of his caliber are turned off by women who come across as freaky whores. So, if interested in them, it's at a woman's best interest to play the innocent, good girl role. That school of thought she calls, Securing the Bag, and in order to do so the woman has to be strategic to lock them in.

The other half of that school of thought is good for nothing; men can get it on the first night with no worries because there's no future in them. It's all in fun and you get up and walk away, never looking back, pretending it never happened. That is, unless it was good, and then you call him back for more when you are in need.

Pebbles plays that game so well but with Tony she will not play. She can spot game a mile away and she recognizes that he has too much game to play around and waste time with him. She would give it to him right now, in the car, this very second, if he told her that's what he wanted. She wouldn't care if he looked at her like a freaky, little whore just as long as he looked at her like *his* freaky, little whore.

Tony pulls up to the traffic light and stops. He looks over to her. "I hope jazz music doesn't bore you. I will put something else on if you like."

"No, this is fine," she replies. "I love jazz music," she lies with a straight face. "So relaxing," she says. She bites down on her bottom lip, while staring in his eyes. Their stares lock until she shakes her head with the *'you just don't know'* look on her face and in her eyes. She chuckles to herself as she thinks of all she would do to him.

She strategically plants her Birkin Togo purse on her lap just so he can see it. She pulled out the Big Girl, as she nicknamed it. She needs him to know that she ain't no regular bitch, she's a part of the $20,000 Bag Club. He has all his toys out on display so she feels it's only right she lets him see that she has some toys of her own. She worked her ass off and saved up for the money for this purse just like she does everything else she has in life. She did have the help of two of her sponsors though.

Tony pays no attention to the bag whatsoever. In fact, it's intentional that he isn't. Her struggling for his attention is humorous to him. He wants to see just how far she will go to make him notice the bag.

The light changes and he pulls off. As he cruises through the intersection, he peeks over and finally gives her what she wants. "Oh, by the way, beautiful purse."

Pebbles looks down as if she doesn't recall what purse she has today. "Oh…thanks," she says casually as if she didn't just do everything except smack him in the head with the purse.

Pebbles peeks over, every few blocks, debating with herself. She has every mind to dive into Tony's lap and blow his saxophone to the beat of the jazz music that's pouring from the speakers. She wonders how he would react. She can't get a full read of him and she's not sure if he would love it or hate it. With a man like him she's sure he's had it all kind of ways so she knows she has to bring her A game and top any and everything that he's had done to him in the past.

Tony slows down and cruises into the parking lot. Pebbles looks around to see where they are. "Please, just give me one second. I have to make this one stop."

"That's fine," she replies. "Take your time. I've set the whole day aside for you."

"I appreciate that," he says as he opens the door. "Be right back."

Pebbles watches Tony until he disappears into the building. She finally can breathe in every sense. She exhales slowly and allows her belly to hang. She's been mindful to hold her stomach in and not let the pudge show. She's been holding her breath the entire ride. She's been on her best behavior, sitting like a lady, and talking like a lady. She lowers the volume to zero. The jazz music is making her sick to her stomach. She needed this pit stop here for a brief intermission to the stage play that she's performing in.

Tony approaches the Security Guard in the lobby. "Good afternoon," he says. "I'm here for Jasmine Hunter. FDA," he adds. Tony has been calling his friend's phone, thinking that maybe her phone was off but every day he gets the same automated message. He has no other way to contact her but coming here to her job.

The guard picks up the phone as he goes down the list of departments in search of the right number. "Is she expecting you?"

"Yes," Tony lies.

"Jasmine Hunter, you said right?" he asks as he reads over the list carefully. "I don't see her on the directory. Are you sure she works here at this office?"

"Yes, for over twenty years," Tony says confidently.

"Let me call up there, maybe she's just not on the list." He places his finger in the air. He speaks into the phone. "Hello, yes, I have a visitor down here for Miss Jasmine Hunter." The guard listens closely with his mouth hanging wide open. "Oh, ok, got you. Thank you," he says before hanging up the phone. He looks to Tony. "You said she was expecting you? They said she no longer works here and hasn't worked here in weeks." He waits for Tony's defense.

"Has to be some kind of misunderstanding. Can you call back up there for me? She's been here for twenty plus years."

The guard picks the phone up and dials. As the phone rings he watches Tony suspiciously. "Hello, Anna. Me again. The guest would like to speak with you. He doesn't believe me and wants to hear it from you." He hands the phone over to Tony.

"Hello, yes, I am a good friend of Jasmine Hunter and I'm trying to get in contact with her. It's extremely urgent."

"Sir, I'm afraid Jasmine Hunter is no longer an employee here."

"What do you mean?" Tony asks angrily. "Did she move to a new location?"

"Sir, that is all the information that I can give you. The status of our employees past and present is confidential. I have to go now. Enjoy the rest of your day."

Tony hands the guard the phone and walks away in a trance like state. First her phone shut off and now to hear this, has Tony baffled. To move so erratic like this is not her style. She would never disappear on him like this. She threatened him with cutting their ties but he didn't believe her not one minute. Something about this whole thing isn't adding up to him.

45 MINUTES LATER

After a long ride down the Turnpike, Tony and Pebbles have finally reached their destination. Red carpet service got them through the process in seconds. Here Tony and Pebbles stand inside Fort Dix Federal Prison. They stand at the door, peeking into the diamond shaped glass. What lies before their eyes Pebbles can't seem to grasp.

There Manson sits just twiddling his thumbs. He looks 50% better since the last time Tony saw him. At Tony's request his hair has been cut, beard shaven and he hasn't been drugged since that day. The look in his eyes is starry, still, but not as bad as he was. His lip smacking and twitching is evident and may be permanent. Tony waited sometime before presenting Pebbles to him. Out of respect for Manson, Tony wanted him to at least look halfway decent.

Pebbles peeks through the glass, stuck in shock at what she sees. She looks to Tony to speak but the words won't come out of her mouth. Tony smiles. "Believe your eyes," he says. "This is no dream. Now, aren't you glad you didn't connect that home-run swing and we would be standing here having to face him, knowing what we had done?" he asks with sarcasm.

"But, but?" Pebbles is quite speechless.

"That newspaper article, stating his death was rigged. He's been here the whole time, hidden from the world."

Rage replaces the confusion on her face. "So, you knew this all the time and never told me?"

"No, I found out this not too long ago. I flew out there to Colorado immediately to confirm what my source had told me. Pulled a few strings, made a few threats, and voila like magic, they got him in front of me."

"But we had a whole funeral for him. You know. You were there."

"Indeed I was there, but let me ask you something? Who identified the body at the morgue?"

"I did," she replies quickly. She goes back into deep thought and now it comes together for her. "But I never actually saw the body," she says slowly.

"What do you mean?" Tony asks.

"When it was time for them to pull the sheet back they kept warning me about how gruesome the sight was. They kept saying it over and over and I just didn't want to see him like that for the last time. I wanted to remember him as I knew him." She stares into space, playing back the day at the morgue.

Tony shrugs. "There you have it. Well, here he is very much alive and in the flesh. I demanded that he be shipped to a closer facility. I also demanded they stop shooting him up with drugs to calm him. He's been through a lot over in that other spot. Beatings and torture."

Tears of sympathy fill Pebbles's eyes. She places her hand over her mouth to keep the cry in. She looks inside the window at Manson and can see the result of the abuse. She's never seen him look so broken.

"I have to be totally honest, even I won't be able to get him free. He will spend the rest of his life in prison. There's no way around that, but in no way do I plan to let this act go unpunished. I plan to publicize this whole situation. Later, I will go over it all with you. I will tell you one thing though. After I blow this open, you will understand the meaning of generational wealth. Your grandkid's grandkids will be wealthy. I put that on everything! Now, go on in and reunite."

Pebbles steps into the room with fear. She's trembling with each step. Manson looks up and shame presents itself. He pokes his chest out with a false sense of confidence that Pebbles can see right through. She hates to see him like this as much as he hates for her to see him like this.

He stands up slowly and they embrace each other. Her touch gives him a shock that hits his heart like he's been hit with defibrillator shock handles to bring him back to life. He hugs her tighter to drain her of the love voltage she has inside. She soaks his shoulder with tears as she squeezes him tightly, recharging him.

Tony watches them through the window, appreciating the sight. It all plays out like an ending scene from a Lifetime movie. If he wasn't so cool he may even shed a tear. He has plans of replacing all their tears of sadness with tears of joy once he claims his victory and makes history. He can picture it clearly.

His vision is interrupted by the buzzing of his phone. An alert is coming through. He holds his phone up to his face and the alert from his bank, stating that the $10,000,000.00 deposit made is now available. He smiles brightly. This text just made it all official.

He still had his doubts about it all, no matter how much Jane Doe reassured him. Now, after seeing the deposit available in his account all doubts are erased. This is real and it's now, go time! He needs five more weeks to build his arsenal and after that the war begins and history will be made.

3

TRENTON

A GROWN MAN riding on a pink, little girl's bike with a pink basket is a funny sight to see and will only be seen in the hood. The even funnier part is the grown man being every bit of 6'5" inches tall. His long legs are pinned up to his chest, riding fast like a clown in the circus. The fact that he's dressed in a pink terry cloth robe and pink furry bunny rabbit slippers makes it an even more hilarious sight.

With his fists balled up he steers the handlebars using his thumbs. In the palm of his left hand, he grips a crack pipe. In the palm of his right hand, he grips three cookies(packets of crack-rock). These cookies are not edible cookies, made from flour, eggs, butter and sugar, that are baked. These cookies are made from cocaine, baking soda and water, and boiled. This man here is known in the hood as The Pink Cookie Monster. He's the neighborhood Flaming Homosexual.

The Pink Cookie Monster dashes out of the projects on the little bicycle. He hits the bell. *Ding, ding, ding!* "Excuse me, 'scuse me!" he shouts. He's in a race to get back to his destination to get back to his cookie smoking. He bunny hops off the curb with expertise and zips across the street.

Just as he reaches the yellow dotted line, the Bronco comes flying down the street. The engine is roaring so loudly, the Pink Cookie Monster doesn't have time to look at it. His main concern is getting out of the street. Just when he thinks he's safe and out of the way, the Bronco hops the sidewalk and smacks him. The ram bar crashes into the bike causing a sound loud enough to be heard from blocks away.

Pink Cookie Monster and the bike go flying in the air. With his hands still gripped around the handlebars, he looks like something from a cartoon where the character is riding a bike on the clouds. Finally he descends and he and the bike smack the ground with huge impact. The bike frame is mangled and so is the Pink Cookie Monster's right leg which stops him from getting right up.

Pink Cookie Monster finally lets the handlebars loose and tries to lift himself up. Just as he gets onto his left knee, he sees a shadow standing over him. He looks up and the barrel of the .357 long nose is aimed at his eye. *BOOM! BOOM!*

The gunman hops into the passenger's seat of the Bronco and the driver speeds off. The Pink Cookie Monster lays in a pool of his own blood. Both of his fists still balled up. Through it all, not one time did he drop the crack pipe or his cookies. Rest in Peace to the Pink Cookie Monster.

MEANWHILE IN CAMDEN

Police have a whole block taped off from one end to the next. Damn near every detective in the city is on this scene. Quabo walks with his head high as Tortura walks right by his side with the phone glued to his ear. Most of their crew is here scattered around the block except for the few men they left to work in Trenton.

Tortura ends the call just as they reach the yellow tape border. He looks to Quabo. "A crackhead or dope-fiend," he says as referring to The Pink Cookie Monster who has just been murdered minutes ago.

They stoop underneath the tape and make their way over to the crowd of police. The closer they get to the crowd the more clearly they can see the old man's body on the ground. There he lies stiffly, one leg crossed over the other. The detectives step toward Quabo and Tortura with intentions of holding them off.

Quabo looks to the detective with respect. "My father," he says pointing to the ground.

"I'm sorry for your loss," the detective says as he steps to the side.

Quabo stands over the body with rage boiling inside. It hurts him to see his father on the ground like a dead dog. The fact that he's been laying here for over an hour hurts him even more.

Quabo looks to Tortura. "They hit the jackpot on this one," he says with his eyes getting watery. "It's funny how we hit two, three, four times a day and this one lucky shot evens the score. No more random, meaningless hits. Now it's time to hit hard. Time to find something she's attached to, something she loves. That will bring her out for sure."

A spark of life creeps into Tortura's eyes. "This is what I've been waiting to do. I thought you would never give me the green light. All that other stuff was only foreplay. Now, it's time to really fuck them!"

4

ROGER GARDEN APARTMENTS

THE APARTMENT IS bare and doesn't even have household necessities. No food on the shelves, no silverware, no pots and pans, no toothpaste in the bathroom. Just a few chairs in the living-room, Rent-A-Center kitchen set, and rolls of toilet tissue and cases of water piled up at the pantry door. This apartment isn't for living. This apartment is the Honeycomb hideout for the drug dealers.

Thick clouds of weed smoke soar into the air, mixed with cigarette smoke and Black and Mild smoke. The smell of sour liquor is embedded in the floors from alcohol spillage. The smell of rotten garbage comes from the row of garbage bags that are filled with old fast food. The only luxury in the apartment is the flat screen television that's on the wall with the X-Box game attached to it.

The young men are gaming and betting. They are putting hundreds of dollars on themselves as they compete against each other. This is a great way for them to kill time since the area is flooded with police right now. These back to back shootings are taking a toll on all of them. They can barely get a cash flow before another shooting takes place.

Also the shootings are running the customers away. If it keeps going at this rate the goldmine they have will turn to fools' gold and all the money will be ran somewhere else.

The sound of the lock opening causes them all to face the door. They all return back to what they were doing once they see who is entering. They all straighten up as well. The jokes and playing around stops. The last thing they want is for this man to think they're enjoying the time away from the block. He's so full of rage right now.

This man known as Triple Threat is one of the biggest sources of income in these projects. All the good dope that has dopefiends coming from near and far is his work. He uses his high-ranking status as a Blood to the fullest. He makes sure his entire line eats and by doing that, he's able to move a major amount of dope. His dope is not only in these projects, but any project or street corner that a Blood in his sect stands on.

He has money but he didn't pay his way to the top of the Blood Organization. He put in work and climbed up the ladder on his own off of his sweat equity. Just as fast as he will press the button, he will put in his own work even faster. And that still applies right now even with him being ghetto rich.

He feels money makes men soft and he refuses to ever let that be his case. Triple Threat is equally wicked with his hands as he is with his gun and that is how he earned the name Triple Threat. He has big money, his pistol game is atrocious and his hand skills are immaculate. Some people call him Triple Threat and others call him Trinity; Three in One.

"Yo, this shit is beyond crazy!" Triple Threat shouts.

"Aye man, one thing for sure, two things for certain," a man in the backdrop says. Triple Threat looks to the man with his full attention. This man who is speaking everybody knows as Old Head. They call him Old Head, not because he's an Old Head, but because he has an old soul. He's been on the streets since ten years old, surviving on his own. His life experiences has him well beyond his years of 26. When Old Head talks, it's in everyone's best interest to listen.

Triple Threat awaits the words to come out of Old Head's mouth but he's busy licking the blunt that he just rolled to seal it properly. He lets the blunt dangle from his mouth as he lights the tip. "This war is bigger than we know," he says before taking a pull of the blunt. "Who-ever behind this ain't for play, play, ya dig me? They trying to prove a point and doing it well. Ya know I know these streets like the back of my hand and this shit is deeper than some typical hood shit."

He holds the blunt between his two fingers high in the air, fancily. "I've been sitting back watching and putting context clues together and something tell me somebody done stung the plug and stung him nice too. For all the bodies this had to be a nice score," he says before taking another pull.

Old Head passes the blunt over to Triple Threat who takes a few back to back pulls. "As a kid, one thing I could do well was put to-gether a puzzle. I may have been in Special Ed all the way up until I dropped out but one thing I could do is put together a puzzle. No matter how big or small the puzzle is, I could put it together. One time I put a puzzle together that had over twenty-five hundred pieces. But that's another story," he says.

Triple Threat hands the blunt back over. "Back to the story at hand," he says as he reaches for the blunt. "Jeezy, Lil Pop, T-Mack and Skelter hanging tough," he says while at the same time, inhaling the blunt. "Jeezy get murdered at the junkyard in Camden for what rea-sons we don't know." His eyes stretch wide open increasing the drama. "T-Mack get burned up in a car and Lil Pop get popped on the street. Only one still left is Skelter." He studies the blunt that he holds before his eyes.

"Boom," he says with a burst of energy. "Murder, murder, murder," he says. "One thing leads to another then, Boom, masked men shoot the spot up, one get left here. Take the mask off, boom, it's a Domin-ican.

"Now, let's put the puzzle together based on all the pieces I laid out on the table. Skelter and Jeezy come up on a jux. Jeezy get killed during the jux. Skelter get rid of everybody else. Now the Dominicans coming through to get back what they are owed. My guess is they must have come up on some powder because if you notice both the Godsons popped out of nowhere with coke."

One of the young men playing the video game can barely pay attention to the game. His attention is on Old Head. This young man is super tight with Middle Godson and hearing his name mentioned sent off an alarm in his head.

Triple Threat speaks. "Makes sense. All this shit ain't no coincidence. I just didn't sit down and put it all together like that."

"I don't expect you to," Old Head says. "That's what you got me for."

Hearing all of this just intensifies the hatred that Triple Threat already has for Skelter. Skelter and him can never see eye to eye because she has her own mind. While everyone else has no problem following his lead, Skelter marches to the beat of her own drum. She also stays in his way because no matter what she always seems to find good dope that gives him a run for his money. She never has enough of the dope to be a real threat to him but she always manages to stay in his way. He's fed up with her right now.

"Well, dig this. That lil bitch fucking up the block. Bringing all kinds of heat. We can't even make no fucking money out here. Bad part is she don't even come through like that so I don't know how the heat falling on us over her. But I tell you one motherfucking thing," he says with rage. "They gone stay the fuck away from here.

From now on, I don't want to see none of the them nowhere around this motherfucker. Got the block all fucking hot and none of us ain't get a piece of whatever score they made. Didn't even offer us a piece of the action. Bottom line is, they can't come out here no more. Fuck that!"

"There's one more piece to the puzzle that I forgot to throw in," Old Head says. "Chapo get his shit knocked off and boom, Blue Blood got coke all of a sudden. My guess is Blue Blood been got the coke from Skelter but Chapo had the coke game in a chokehold so he had to go. Blue Blood ain't been up in years but now he got birds. Go figure," he says before taking another pull.

"Little bitch done made a big-ass mess for us to be back here standing in," Triple Threat says as he's in deep thought. We got some cleaning up to do. On sight!"

The young man on the couch is losing terribly due to the fact that he's texting on his phone instead of concentrating on the game. With one finger he texts, Middle Godson: "LET'S MEET ASAP. AND NOT AROUND HERE. YOU SET THE LOCATION. SUPER URGENT."

"Hey, somebody take over my game," the young man says. He drops the controller onto the couch. "One of my white boys just texted me for a brick. I need that for something." He fast trots to the door. He has to get to Middle Godson before anybody else does.

"Yo, Bleek," Triple Threat says just as the young man gets to the door. "Keep your eyes open and be safe out there."

The young man pulls his shirt up to show his .40 caliber on his waistline. "Absolutely," he says with no sign of worry at all.

5

THE FRIDAY JUMU'AH service is in session in the gymnasium. It's just 10 minutes left before conclusion. The Imaam speaks loud and clearly. "People are not accepting Islam the way they should. Why?" he asks.

He continues on. "In my view, in my experience, one of the main reasons people are not accepting Islam is because they don't want to be like us," he says while shaking his head negatively. "I believe that we are one of the major reasons that people are not coming full force to Islam. Because us... because we are not living like Muslims. As a matter fact, there are a lot of youth that are very impressed with the Western society lives. They want to be like them," he says with a displeasing smirk. "They want to talk like them. They want to move like them. They want to behave like them. Brothers, I'm asking you and I to live like Muslims. Live like Muslims!" he repeats with tears pouring from his eyes.

It's a beautiful sermon and it's no coincidence of the topic he's chosen to discuss. The gymnasium is packed with more inmates than there's been the past few weeks. Smith and his followers fill the back of the gymnasium. He has with him gang members from every Blood sect, Crips, and even Latin Kings. He has inmates from every wing of the prison standing with him. Most of these men were already Muslim but some of them converted just to be a part of Smith's movement.

Smith was told by a liaison that the Imaam wanted to speak with him. Smith started to disregard the invitation but his respect and admiration for the Imaam is what led him here. He figures the Imaam must have noticed the decrease in attendance and now wants to talk to him about them coming back. At this point he's content with having his own movement and really doesn't want to come back.

Right now, he's on a mission to build his congregation. His long-term goal is to stretch out beyond Northern State Prison and start a nationwide prison movement. He figures if he can start a nationwide prison movement, that movement will eventually bleed out onto the streets. He knows it's not going to happen overnight but he's accepted the challenge.

The Imaam raises his voice. "The Prophet says whoever imitates a people he is of them. Whoever imitates the *Kufaar* (disbeliever) is of them."

This is the last straw for Smith. He's heard enough. He knows the Imaam is referring to them, subliminally speaking to them about them. He looks back to his men and signals for them all to leave. His head of security takes the lead and he follows at their heels. The group of more than 50 men follow behind.

"As Salaamu Alaikum, brother!" the Imaam says. "Mujahid, don't leave, please. I would like to speak with you, Insha Allah!"

Smith turns around and the pleading look in the Imaam's eyes forces him to stop. His men stop as well. Smith backs up against the wall, waiting impatiently for the sermon to be over.

MEANWHILE

Baby Manson is in the middle of a meeting as well. In the corner of the Dayroom standing directly in front of Baby Manson is one of the OG's of the sect that Baby Manson is under. This man is known as Lunatic. The OG, Lunatic has three of his men close. They stand around not saying a word, just listening. Baby Manson knows if the OG makes the call the pups will have no choice but to move, but still he stands his ground.

"It's like this," Lunatic says. "The kite came to me basically saying like you on some outside type shit. Like you don't even be rocking with the homies. Like you on some solo shit."

"Dig this," Baby Manson says. "I don't even know how it came back like that because as soon as I touched I checked in and let niggas know who I be. I also let niggas know I was around if I was needed but I'm on some getting my mind right time. I mean, I'm always a call away but I ain't out here on banging time."

Really, Baby Manson wants to tell the man to fuck off but he knows all this is protocol. He fears no man, from the head OG's down to the pups but he does respect the sect that he reps under. He's careful of the words that come out of his mouth because he doesn't want his words twisted. He understands one twist of his words and the OG's over this man will press the button and every man under the sect will be against him.

"I even sent the kite to bruh letting him know, anyway he need me, I'm here. I'm just not in here running around like I'm a Super Blood, you feel me?" Baby Manson can tell the OG doesn't really like his answer but he has to respect it.

"You running around here like a solo act. I'm getting the word that you hitting shit like on some one-man army type time. I respect all that but it ain't got to be like that. You got us. Ain't no *I* in *we*," Lunatic says with a genuine look in his eyes.

Baby Manson knows exactly what this meeting is about. It's not necessarily about him not actively banging with them. This meeting has been called because the word has gotten back to the OG's over him that Baby Manson has the dope and is locking the jail down.

Lunatic cuts right to it. "There's a lot of homies in here starving. The word is you filling other niggas' bellies. Picking and choosing all around the homies while the homies fucked up. You in a position to spread love and you not even doing it. On some G shit, I ain't even tell bruh I heard no shit like that. I came to you first as a man just to hear your logic and reasoning."

"I respect that," Baby Manson says. "I don't got no problem spreading the love though. If niggas want to eat, I got the food. I'm on a mission though and I ain't got no time for games. If I put something on the plate and it don't come back as it should I'm handling it accordingly. Homies or no homies, I ain't got no room for losses."

"And I respect that," Lunatic says. "All I'm saying is you got the food and you got a machine behind you. Use it. That lil back and forth you got going on with the lil nigga, that shit would've been handled if you was locked into the machine. Feel me?"

"Absolutely," Baby Manson replies. He nods his head up and down in agreeance. This is that power that he was planning to get. It was right under his nose yet he wasn't looking at it. Now that it has found him, he plans to use it to the fullest.

GYMNASIUM

Smith sits on the prayer rug in the middle of the gym. More than 50 muslim/gangbangers stand behind Smith with aggressive demeanors. The peace that Islam represents shows on none of their faces. Sitting on the opposite end of that same rug is the Imaam.

Behind the Imaam there stands about 15 inmates. Amongst those inmates are a couple younger brothers but mainly older, die-hard *Salif* (predecessor or forefather, and refers to the first three generations of Muslims) who refuse to pray next to gang-bangers. They follow the school of thought of early Islam and feel like there's no bending on certain issues; with this being one of those issues. These Salaf brothers stand upright, chest out with fiery eyes. They stand behind the Imaam with no fear and ready for war if need be. These brothers fear nothing but God and are willing to sacrifice their lives in the name of this cause.

The Imaam extends his hand to Smith. Smith hesitantly reaches back for him. The Imaam takes further initiative by snatching Smith's hand and squeezes it tightly with love. A bright smile spread across his face. "Brother, I am not your enemy," the Imaam says as he squeezes his hand tighter. "I am your brother. I love you," he says as he crawls onto his knees. "Hug me brother," he says before he bear hugs Smith.

Smith can feel the love in the tight hug but his anger has a tighter grip on him.

The Imaam crawls backwards and sits down. "I love you. This is why I reached out for you. We are sitting here like it's a war in progress but it's not. I don't like this tension we have in here."

Smith looks at the men standing behind the Imaam and fury rips through him because of the way they are looking at him. He's ready to press the button and have them all destroyed but his respect for the Imaam would never allow him to do that.

Smith stands up slowly. "Let's talk over here," Smith says as he points to his left.

The Imaam struggles to get up until Smith lends him a hand. He pulls him onto his feet and they walk to the side, leaving both sides standing at the scratch line. Both sides are equally ready to go. Both standing on what they believe, and neither side willing to bend.

As soon as they are off to the side, the Imaam starts to speak. "Brother, this is not Islam. This is a state of disbelief. Muslims ready to go to war with each other."

"Look at your guys, though," Smith says in defense. "They think they're ready for war too."

"I hear you are holding classes of your own and even giving Friday Jumu'ah service. Each week the attendance here decreases. I have heard that you are using force and placing fear into the men. They have abandoned the Jumu'ah service because of threats on their life. I also hear that you are using that same force and those same threats to have men follow and stand with you."

"Here you go. You always hearing something," he says angrily. "Supposed to be the Super Salafi brothers but they stay backbiting and slandering."

"It's not slander if it's true," the Imaam says with a smile. "I was told you were a gangbanger and I asked you. The proof is right here before my eyes. It was true right? So, maybe the other accusations they are making can have that same truth in them?"

Smith looks away from. "Whatever," he sighs. "I didn't come here to defend myself. I only came here out of respect for you."

"And I respect that more than you know," the Imaam replies. "But let me ask you something. Do you think this here is the answer? You think the solution is to start a sect that accepts a disbelieving lifestyle? What you have going on isn't religion. It's a cult. A controlling of the minds and the people of no substance are looking to be led. I will admit to you that I am amazed by the power of your influence. From what I hear," he says before stopping. "Yes, what I hear is you have hundreds and hundreds of men following your lead in that gang. And I'm sure you can get those same men to follow you in this here movement. You have a cult-like following and they all will follow but let me ask you," he pauses for seconds while staring into Smith's eyes. "My brother in Islam, where are you leading them besides the hellfire? A flock of gangbangers," the Imaam says. "This is not Islam."

"You see a flock of gangbangers. I see a flock of warriors," Smith says in rebuttal. "As you know there were many warriors in Islam. Hamza Ibn Abdul Muttalib (R.A.), the uncle and companion of Prophet Muhammad (pbuh)." Smith says in eloquent recitation. "A mighty brave warrior, the Lion of Allah."

"Are you comparing yourself to Hamza Ibn Abdul Muttalib (R.A.)?"

"La (no), in no way am I comparing myself to the companions. Just clearly stating that there is a place for warriors in Islam."

"I believe that as well," the Imaam says. "But those warriors all understood that there's no God but Allah. Do your warriors understand that? Those warriors also understood that they should only submit to Allah. We worship the creator, not the creations. And none are worthy of praise except Allah. Do your warriors understand the same? Those warriors understood that the blood of their brother was sacred? Do your warriors understand that? To pray with your brother five times a day and kill him in the wee hours of the night is a gravest sin."

The Imaam has a face full of tears as he continues on. He doesn't even bother to wipe them. He lets them drip at a rapid pace. "If your warriors not know that, I pray that you teach them this, my dear brother. For they are not charged with what they not know. And you taking on as their leader, you are taking on a huge responsibility for the sins these men commit without knowing, that you know well of, will be on your back. I pray that you teach them the ways of the Sunnah and not manipulate their minds like so many deviants in the past, ameen! I pray that Allah guides you and these brothers to the right path and you be used as the vehicle to get all the young brothers on the right accord and save them from the hellfire, ameen!"

The Imaam extends his hand to Smith. They grip hands tightly. "Please tell me that you will be here next Friday with all of your men and we can work on you all disassociating yourself with the ways of the disbelievers? Please tell me?"

Smith pauses briefly before speaking. "As a Muslim, all I have is my word and right now I can't give you my word because I have unfinished business in the dunya."

"Well, my dear brother all I can do is pray that your unfinished business is not a sin that you cannot be forgiven for and also pray that unfinished business doesn't finish you. A salaamu Alaikum!" The Imaam walks off, leaving his words bouncing around in Smith's head.

6

EAST ORANGE, NEW JERSEY

DRE SITS DOUBLE parked in front of the masjid as Muslims pour out onto the streets. They are full of life smiling and recharged after hearing the sermon. Now they are off to continue on with their day. Some are back to work and others are off to lunch with their families.

Dre spots Lil Mama in the crowd of women coming from the farthest exit. With her being so short she disappears in the midst of the crowd. Her beautiful custom-made over garment stands out boldly, giving Dre a mark to keep his eyes on. When he loses the overgarment, he looks to the ground where her matching Louis Vuitton sneakers gives him another mark to follow. Dre admires how fashionable she is. Dressed in full Islamic attire yet she makes it look trendy and fashion forward. Her designer sneakers, her bracelets, her necklaces, the precise fit of her overgarment make her stand out but it's her bop, her confident stride that gives her the edge.

A smile covers Dre's face as he watches her walk toward him. She appears to be so happy with her new way of life. He understands that without prison she may have never found religion but he hates the fact that she went to prison for him. It hurts him every time he thinks of the fact that he took away 10 years of her life.

For her to be gone so long it doesn't seem like she's missed a beat. Her mind is sharper than when she left and not stuck in the past. She's determined to get into college and get herself a career. She says she blew a dime but she now has to catch up and she's determined to do so.

Lil Mama steps off the curb, staring into the car. As soon as she sees Dre's face she blushes just as she always does when she's in his presence. Her cheeks turn rosy red. She bites her bottom lip, bashfully, exposing her huge dimples.

She gets in and plops into the seat. "Thank you," she says as she slams the door shut.

"You could've drove here yourself. It's right on the other side of the street from your house, damn near," Dre says.

"I told you I'm not even sitting in the driver's seat. I got five years of parole left and I won't be going back for driving." She laughs goofily. "I told you I could've taken one of those Uber cars but I'm glad you came. I really got something to talk to you about."

The sound of her voice makes Dre super curious. "Something bad? You alright?"

"Yeah, I'm alright. I don't know how long I will be though."

"Huh?" Dre asks. "What that mean?"

"What I have to say may come across as crazy but I have to say it. I just hope you don't get crazy on me after I say it."

"Go ahead and say it."

"First, promise me you won't treat me different after I say it?"

"I promise. Go ahead and say it."

"I know this may come across as crazy but," she says as she intakes a deep breath. "Listen, I'm just gone say it and however it sound it just sound. I just hope you don't judge me."

"Just fucking say it, would you please? You're fucking killing me!"

She takes another deep breath. She exhales. "I need a husband, yo."

Dre looks to her and his facial expression shows that he expected so much more. "That's it? You need a husband? Don't judge you for that? Get you a husband then. You just left the spot with a thousand Muslim dudes. I saw how they were watching you with lust in their eyes," he says jokingly. "You're a pretty, fly, good girl, I'm sure they would marry you in a heartbeat."

"I'm sure they are but that ain't where I'm at. Like, I'm Muslim but I'm different. And I need a different type husband. I ain't looking for no old, nappy, lint in the beard, big belly husband. I'm too fly for that and I ain't attracted to that. I need me a sharp, hip husband to compliment my fly."

"I seen a couple fly ones out there."

"Listen, you ain't getting what I'm saying. You acting slow as shit so I'm just gone put it out there and if you judge me, fuck it. Why don't you marry me and stop playing," she says with all the courage that she's mustered up.

"Huh?" Dre steers the car to the right and pulls into the first empty parking space. "Marry you? Me?"

"Yeah, you," she says. She's on a roll now. She realizes a closed mouth doesn't get fed so she has to open her mouth in order to get fed. "Listen, you took care of me for all those years on the street. You paid my rent, my car note, and always bought me nice gifts. When I fell you kept money on my books and was there for me emotionally. I come home and you hit me off lovely, and again, you give me a car to drive and you paying my rent. You already doing all the shit a husband supposed to do. Well, except, you know," she says embarrassingly.

Dre is speechless. He can't believe the words that are coming out of her mouth. He always saw her as a beautiful, little girl and never let his mind go farther than that. She comes home a beautiful grown woman but still he never let his mind go farther than that. Of course he knew she had a crush on him but all this sounds strange to him.

"But damn like, I always been a big brother to you, had no clue that you saw me like that," Dre says sincerely. "Like, how two people that are not in love gone get married? Well, you know of course I love you and I know you love me, but we are not in love with each other."

Her eyelids flutter quickly. "Speak for yourself. Anyway, in Islam it ain't about being in love. It's about loving your mate and respecting them and wanting the best for them and saving them from the hellfire." She exhales. "Which is part of my problem. Simple as this...I been gone for almost ten years," she says with frustration. "Ten years I haven't been touched by a man. Shit, I was barely getting touched back then but that's a different story. I wasn't off that gay shit when I was away. I wasn't playing that shit at all. But here I am now home and frustrated.

I don't know how much longer I can hold up. I'm trying to do the right thing. I told myself when I got home I was gone save myself for my husband. I been *Deening* hard for all that time and to come home and throw it all away just to fornicate, it ain't worth it and I don't want to do it. But my body is saying something totally different."

Dre stares into her mouth as the words seem to come out slowly. He can't believe that she's actually serious about this. He pulls out of the parking space and proceeds to the destination. He doesn't say a word for minutes. He just replays her words over and over.

Dre double-parks in front of her building. Lil Mama looks over at him. She realizes she just put it all on the line and right now she needs to put the nail in the coffin. A part of her is embarrassed but the other part doesn't care because she meant every word she said.

"You think I'm crazy? Are you judging me?"

Dre really doesn't know what to say. "Uh, nah," he says still baffled.

"Do you love and respect me?"

"Come on, that goes unsaid," he replies.

"Do you want the best for me?"

"More than you know," he replies sternly.

"Then marry me then. Take me as your wife and save me from the hellfire because if you don't, I can see it already. I'm gone get back out here fooling with these niggas and all my future plans and my religion gone fly out the window. Marry me," she says with pleading eyes. "I will make it simple for you. The money you gave me when I touched will be the dowry. I don't need nothing else. Well, I do need something else but we will talk about that once you marry me," she says in a joking manner.

"When I first came home, you said you got me and said you respect me taking the fall for you like that and you gone take care of me for the rest of my life, right?"

"Wow," Dre says, feeling like she just hit him below the belt.

"Those were your exact words, correct?"

"Yeah," he says nodding slowly.

"Well, if you got me, then really get me. If you gone take care of me for the rest of my life, then really take care of me for the rest of my life. Marry me," she says as she gets out. She slams the door shut in his face and walks away.

Not one time does she look back but she can feel him looking at her. She's sure she left a lasting impression on him. She has no shame because she said everything she dreamed she would say while she was locked up. However it goes from here is how it's supposed to go and she has no regrets.

Dre watches her until she goes into the building. He sits there for close to an hour soaking in all she's just said to him. He heard her loud and clear, but still he can't believe it. He's still speechless, just looking into the rearview mirror at himself, opening his mouth trying to force words out.

7

SKELTER AND HER Godsons stand huddle around the young man known as Bleek, listening with all of their attention. He runs his mouth a mile a minute and they are trying to keep up without missing one step. "He was like Jeezy and you must have went on a mission and Jeezy didn't make it back. He think you killed T-Mack and Lil Pop once the move was made."

Bleek pauses, awaiting confirmation. He wonders how much of Old Head's assumptions are correct. It feels crazy for Skelter hearing this information played back to her. She isn't worried about the backlash from them. She's worried about the police getting wind of all of this.

She frowns with a chuckle, trying to keep a straight face to make the man believe none of it is true. "Motherfuckers be reaching boy," she says.

"Then he was like the Dominican that got smashed was sent by the plug," Bleek further says. "He went into this whole spill about how he always been the best when it comes to putting puzzles together. He like, it had to be a coke plug because out of nowhere y'all got the coke," he says while pointing to the Godsons.

The Godsons are not as polished as her and the guilt can be seen on their faces. Skelter speaks quickly to take the attention off of them. "Who was all in the room when all this was being discussed?"

"Shit, damn near everybody," Bleek replies. "We was all in there playing the game. Niggas was barely paying attention, but me, I was all ears, feel me? Especially when I heard big bruh say what he said. He like y'all bringing heat around there and didn't bring nobody in on what y'all scored but bringing the heat to the hood. And y'all fucking up the money because nobody can't eat. Like, he basically banning y'all from the hood, like some shoot on sight type shit."

"What?" Skelter barks. "Did he actually say that out of his mouth?" Her blood is boiling.

"Yeah, his exact words was y'all gone have to get the fuck from around there."

In no way does Skelter take this lightly. She can't when she doesn't take Triple Threat lightly. She has no fear of him but she respects his gangster to the fullest. She also respects his reach. She knows when he presses the button the gangsters come out. The walls are closing in on her. She already has a war on her hands that is a little over her head. Now here comes a potential war with her own hood. She feels like the odds are stacking high against her.

"Oh, and he said ever since Chapo got smashed, Blue Blood stepped in his place. Like, he don't see that as a coincidence and he think y'all behind his murder."

Skelter's heart stops. Hearing this adds more salt to the game. If word that she's behind Chapo's murder gets out, she will have a bigger war on her hands. It won't just be her against her hood. It will be against the most of Trenton.

She inhales a breath of clarity. Her Godsons all stare at her with the same expression as she's wearing. She nods her head and all three of them know exactly what she's thinking without her having to say it. They must move first before Triple Threat gets the drop on them.

8

IN PRISON THERE'S a saying; 'You either come out and thump or play the bunk like a chump.' Some would say that Shakir is one that plays the bunk like a chump. He rarely comes out because he doesn't have to. He has everything he needs right here in his cell and he has a connect in the kitchen that cooks him special meals of his choice.

His days of running around proving himself are over. Furthermore, he believes he should only surround himself with those like him. He feels inside this jail system there are very few like him. So, because of that, he spends most of his time alone.

As he lays back on his bunk, reading his favorite book, '*Think and Grow Rich*,' for the hundredth time, his peace is broken. He looks over and gets pissed off at the sight of Baby Manson standing there. He looks away from Baby Manson and goes back to reading the next line on the page.

"Pardon my intrusion," Baby Manson says humbly.

For a few seconds Shakir continues on reading. Finally he closes his book, plants it down and sits upright. He twists his body around, planting his feet onto the floor. He stands up, staring coldly at Baby Manson. His temples pulsate with anger. His presence alone irritates him.

Baby Manson steps in without invitation. Shakir notices a sock in Baby Manson's hand and his blood starts boiling. He pivots, right foot forward, left foot planted firmly onto the floor. His shoulder blocks his chin. He has one hand at his waist while the other he discreetly reaches for his knife that's tucked in the back waistline of his boxers.

Baby Manson reads his body language but continues on. He extends his hand with the sock in it. "Here this is for you," he says. "I took over a few of your accounts and they won't be needing this anymore. I recovered some of your work just so you won't take a loss all around the board. As far as collecting the money they made already, you will have to handle that."

Shakir snatches the sock from Baby Manson. Right now he's seconds away from sticking his knife in Baby Manson.

"Black, Ice, Swag, Chin, Lil Rico, Mars and Lil Meech, they all with me now. I will be taking over those accounts from here. Whatever they had left is in that sock. I just wanted to give you the courtesy of letting you know what's going on so you're not in the dark."

Shakir is on fire right now. From a gangster standpoint he understands that he's supposed to react right now. He also understands that if he lets this go, he will have a series of problems coming his way. What he does or doesn't do right this very moment, determines the future of his business in this prison.

Baby Manson doesn't like his silence. He didn't know what reaction to expect but the silence is throwing him off. "Talk to me," he says as he tries to get a read on Shakir. "What's on your mind?"

Shakir turns about-faced and walks toward his bunk. Baby Manson feels disrespected as Shakir gives his back to him in disrespect. The fact that he's turned his back, makes Baby Manson feel as if Shakir doesn't feel threatened the least bit. And the fact that he's ignoring him, makes it even worse.

Shakir turns back around and finally he speaks. "Talk to you about what?" he asks with a weird look in his eyes. "You've taken over those accounts. I thank you for recovering the goods for me." Shakir lays on his bunk, picks up his book and starts reading as if Baby Manson isn't standing there. Baby Manson stands in confusion. He's not sure how he should take Shakir's actions right now. Is it threatening or non-threatening?

"Any other accounts I take over, I will try to recover whatever I can," he says in attempt to edge Shakir on.

"No need to," Shakir says with his face still buried in his book. "You can keep it or let them keep it." He finally looks at Baby Manson and for the first time ever Baby Manson notices a look in Shakir's eyes that paints a different picture of him. Shakir stares without a single blink. The look in his eyes is dark with a sneaky wickedness. "Don't worry about it. It's all G."

Baby Manson isn't sure how to take Shakir's words. One thing he learned about old heads is they are sneaky. They are passive-aggressive unlike the younger generation who are always aggressive. He's witnessed firsthand the sneaky antics of the old heads. Prime example is the move Short Fuse made.

Baby Manson refuses to be the next win for the old heads. He will not wait around for Shakir to move on him first. He already has his plan in place. He stares at Shakir with a smirk. If Shakir only knew what was running through Baby Manson's mind right now, he would make his move this second while he has the chance.

9

TRENTON

THE DARK AND raggedy block shows no sign of life except the man walking along the sidewalk. He puffs a Black and Mild in attempt to intensify the intoxication from his pills, and alcohol. It's the end to a highly intoxicating night. The man stops at the most raggedy house on the block.

At the top of the stairs he puffs the Mild like it's his last smoke before going to the electric chair. He plucks the Mild onto the sidewalk and as he goes to turn to the door, a shadow appears to his right. The shadow turns out to be a bandit dressed in all black. He's hurdled over the railing and is now clenching the man by his throat. He cuts off his wind so he can't utter a word. Underneath the mask is Middle Godson and his victim is, Old Head.

Middle Godson places the gun under Old Head's eye bone. "Now, see what you get for thinking? Now see if you can put this puzzle together."

POP! POP! POP! Old Head collapses onto the porch, dead before he lands. Middle Godson jumps over a whole flight of stairs. He races to the getaway car that's awaiting him. The tires of the Nissan Pathfinder screech as it speeds off.

MEANWHILE

Skelter sits in the kitchen of Blue Blood's apartment. Stacks and stacks of money are piled in front of her. She pulls yet another stack of money from the plastic shopping bag. She looks up in between bills to listen to Blue Blood.

"I swear I knew somehow our names would come up in this," says Blue Blood. "Motherfuckers probably was already thinking it but now that this little big mouth, gossiping-ass nigga done put it out there that rumor gone fly like crazy."

"Aye, we can't control what was already said but he won't be running his mouth no more," Skelter says confidently. She grabs her phone from the table and looks at the screen. She scrolls and reads the text. She looks over to Blue Blood. "He's just been shut up permanently."

"Good," Blue Blood says. "But that don't stop the rumor that's gone be traveling. We need to get on this immediately. We can't play with him."

"Absolutely," Skelter replies. "You got any leads on him?"

"Nah, nothing," he replies with despair. "I got my man who may know something though. If anybody know something he will. Don't nothing get past this nigga."

"Well, you need to get him on the line asap." Skelter lays the last stack on the table.

"Count on point, right?" Blue Blood asks.

"Sixty-two thousand, right?"

"Yeah," he replies. "I'm waiting on my man to get with me tomorrow and square me away. He got seventy-five hundred. That will be everything. I told you the boy Chapo was clogging the pipeline. Ever since he left us, shit been wide open. My phone stay busy like an abortion clinic. We were on our way and now we got this shit in front of us."

"And we still on our way. This shit not gone stop us. Just stay on top of your man so we can get this done and over with. Then we can get onto whatever else that's coming our way."

She digs into a bag that's on the table in front of her. From the bag she pulls out four kilos, one at a time, and stack them in front of Blue Blood. "We can't let none of this stop the money," she says as she puts the stacks of money into the bag.

She gets up and throws the bag over her shoulders. She shakes his hand. "Listen, don't waste a second. Hit your man so we can do what we got to do. If he start moving before we do, it's gone be crazy. And really, we don't know how far into this shit he already is so we have to go immediately. This has to get done like yesterday!"

10

SOUTH PHILADELPHIA

A **NARROW STREET,** barely wide enough to be a One Way yet it's a Two Way. On both sides of the street row homes are lined up with no alley space in between; all joined together. At the end of the block, the very last building on the corner, there's a change of scenery. The change is not just in the architecture and design but also the property value. Unlike the rest of the row homes on the block, this is a newly designed, four-million-dollar building. The 10-unit condominium building is a product of gentrification.

This property is still in the production phase. The newly designed building sticks out like a sore thumb amongst the raggedy row homes right next to it. An even bigger eye sore is the group of thugs who are sitting on the steps smoking weed, drinking alcohol and holding a small card game. These young men don't know what the word 'gentrification' means but they do know that they are being forced out of their own neighborhoods for the white people to move in, as they call it. It's happened on so many blocks around them that they now understand the process.

The wealthy buy the property and renovate it, turning the row homes into brownstones and condominiums that the lower-class residents can't afford. They then are forced to move out and the middle-class folks move in. These young men understand the process, but they are holding on. Some of them have been posted up on this corner for 10 years when it was an abandoned row home. Now that it's a newly built condominium building that doesn't mean they plan to move and stop making money here. Just as it is business for whoever bought the property, it is business for the young men as well. Row home or newly renovated condo building...to them, it will always be the Trap House.

As these young men are conducting their business in front and around the condo building, construction workers are handling their business on the inside of the building. The building is 80% complete and they are just adding the finishing touches. The building is beautiful inside and out is worth every penny of the $3,000 a month, one-bedroom apartments. Three-bedroom apartments start at $4,000 a month.

The sound of a diesel engine ticks loudly, drowning out any noise around it. The young thugs sitting on the stoop can't hear themselves talk over the sound of the loud engine. All their attention is diverted to the candy-apple red pick-up truck that is parking across the street from them. The bright red Ford F-250 sitting on extra-large mud tractor tires is a pick-up truck lover's dream.

The paint job is so beautiful and the gloss so high the paint looks like it's still wet. The special Rancho Shocks and elevated suspension kit has the overall height of the truck over eight feet high. Dark tinted windows add mystique. This pick-up truck should be featured in a Monster Truck Show and not cruising through the narrow and congested streets of South Philly.

The passenger door of the truck opens first, and Tony jumps out like he's jumping out of a plane with no parachute. He lands on his feet gracefully and puts together his cool as he walks to the curb. He stands here with his eyes fixed across the street, admiring his latest project. As he looks around at the thugs crowding the stoop he realizes they may lower the property value, but he also respects the game and knows that everybody must eat.

Inside the truck, the driver, Maurice, hits a few gadgets on the dashboard and steering wheel at the same time. A secret compartment slowly drops from underneath the dashboard. Once it's fully exposed, in clear view is a chrome .40 caliber and a black 9-millimeter. Maurice hands the 9-millimeter to the man who sits in his backseat and he then tucks the .40 caliber in his own waistband before closing the secret compartment.

Maurice opens the door and hang jumps from the truck. As he slams the door shut the man in the backseat has already gotten out and is standing next to Tony curbside. Tony walks in the middle of the two men as they cross the street in unison stride. On the left of Tony there's Maurice, standing well over 6 feet 3 inches tall, small waist and broad shoulders, and on the right, he has the other man standing one inch under 6 feet, with 21-inch biceps, chest to his chin with no neck. Tony is dressed like a rock star in designer clothes; these two look like they could be his bodyguards.

The man that is to the right of Tony is fresh out of prison from serving over 17 years for a homicide. He hasn't been home three days yet. This man is known on the streets of Newark as Twelve Play. He earned that name because he has 6 fingers on each hand and those 12 fingers were magical on the piano when he was a kid. Once he got into his late teens he traded in his piano for a pistol and with that pistol he learned to create equal magic as he did with the piano.

Maurice brought Twelve Play into the Federation as one of his enforcers, his clean-up men. He performed his job well until one of his murders caught up with him. Long before Maurice met Tony, Twelve Play lost the case and was sentenced to 30 years to life. Once Maurice met Tony this was one of the first cases he assigned him to.

Tony immediately started finding loopholes and appealed the case. Twelve Play was able to give back almost half of the original time he was given. Twelve Play is home now, and he feels he is indebted to both Maurice and Tony. Without them he would be only halfway done with his time. He spent most of his 20's in prison and all of his 30's. Thanks to them, next month he will be introduced to his 40's as a free man.

The young thugs stop what they're doing and lock in on the men coming toward them. Tony and both of his men read the play as they watch a man on one end of the porch give another man a head-nod. That man then steps closer to the porch, with a clear view of Tony and the others approaching. Street knowledge tells them that the man who was signaled is the one holding the gun and he was signaled just to get ready if need be.

Twelve Play senses danger and he quickly takes the lead. If anything goes left, he will sacrifice himself before allowing Tony or Maurice to be harmed. Maurice discreetly positions his hand just in case he has to draw his gun. Tony looks to the apparent gunman and with holding two peace signs in the air, he speaks. "Peace!"

Tony then looks to the crowd and greets them the same. "Peace, peace, fellas!" Not a single one of them return the greeting, clearly indicating that they are not at peace with them. The reality is they can never be at peace with anyone when they are not even at peace with themselves.

The young men carry on as if they don't see Tony and his men approaching. Twelve Play muscles his way through the huddle, creating an opening for Tony. Maurice is at the end of the line, watching around and not liking what he sees. They make their way up the stairs. Maurice sighs frustration catching Tony's attention. Tony quickly looks to Maurice and can read his mind. He knows how much of a ticking time-bomb Maurice is. "Come on, man," Tony says as he waves Maurice on.

"These motherfuckers don't have no respect," Maurice snaps. "Act like they don't want to move. I know how to make them move though." They step into the lobby of the building which is almost complete. They are smacked in the face by the smell of fresh paint and new marble floors.

"Moe, no need for that. Don't let them trick you out of your freedom. We got eighty investment properties in this city. We about to get more money than them kids can count. That little spot they got out there on the curb is all they got."

What Tony says is true. He and Maurice have properties being developed all over the city of Philadelphia. Maurice started off buying abandoned (HUD) homes for dirt cheap, as low as $5,000 a house. He then would renovate them and drop another $10,000 in fixing them, only to sell them for up to six times what he put into them. It was a beautiful flip and a nice way to clean his dirty money.

He then decided to bring Tony in. He didn't need the financial backing, just wanted Tony in as a partner, understanding that Tony's knowledge of business would be an asset. Tony stepped in and took the game to the next level, just as Maurice expected. Instead of fixing the houses up and selling them for less than $100,000, Tony came up with the idea of putting a couple million into a property and building condos that could create much more financial gain. Right now, they have over 80 investment properties, but the goal is to eventually own all the property their money can buy.

"Twenty-five years ago that was you out there on that curb, but in Newark though," Tony says, reminding Maurice of his humble beginnings. "Long before The Federation, all you had was curbside nickel and dime sales. Look now, all that is behind you. On to bigger and better things. Let them have that shit and pray that one day they get it together and get up off that curb like you did."

Maurice loses his rage and comes to his senses. He remembers exactly where he came from. "You're right big bruh."

The sound of hammers and drills echo throughout the building but a noise that is heard faintly in the background catches their attention. The sound of a baby crying surprises them all. They hope this isn't what they think it is. No stranger to this, they immediately know what is going on. They walk to the back all together and what they see in an apartment that isn't even completed nor live-able enrages them.

They see a whole family set up as if they're supposed to be living here. They have no furniture, just a few blankets lined up on the floor. The head of the family, a middle-aged dopefiend looks at them with a saddened expression. His wife and three small children all stare at them in the doorway.

This is a family of squatters, living here. They've come across situations like this in almost every property they have here in Philly. It's a problem that they can't seem to get around. The hardest thing for them so far has been keeping squatters out of their properties.

Surprising to them, the man steps closer to them with attitude and aggression as if he has every right to be here and they are the intruders. "What's up?"

His delivery infuriates Maurice. "What's up?" Maurice asks angrily. "You got to get up out of here, that's what's up!"

"I been here all week waiting for you to come through so I can kick it with you. Let me talk to you over here," he says with more of a demand than a request.

"Ain't nothing to kick it about," Maurice says. "Like you said, you been here all week but I'm here now so it's over. You got to go now. You know, my heart goes out to your wife and your babies but y'all can't do this here, man."

"Listen man, we ain't got nowhere to go," the man says sternly.

"That ain't my problem," Maurice says aggressively. "You a man like I'm a man. You got to figure it out. But not at my cost though."

The man puffs his chest up with agitation. "Dig man, I'm gone keep it a bean with you."

"A bean?" Maurice asks cluelessly. "What the fuck is a bean?" Maurice asks, getting more angry by the second.

"A bean is a hundred," Tony whispers to Maurice.

"Listen man, I don't understand all that Philly slang. I'm from Newark. Don't keep it a bean with me. Just pack it up and go on, man, that's it."

"I'm gone tell you like this. I ain't trying to impose on you and your investment but I ain't got nowhere to go and I ain't trying to have my family in the streets. I just need a couple days to figure it out and I will be out of your hair."

This man has them perplexed. They can't understand how he can be dead in the wrong for being in here and instead of exercising some humility, he's arrogant. It's as if he feels entitled. The look in his eyes indicates that he's a drug addict but maybe he's on prescription drugs for mental illness as swell. That's the only thing that will explain his response to this matter.

Maurice looks to Tony who has an obvious soft spot for the family. He refuses to let Tony talk him out of throwing the man out. Especially with the way he's carrying on. Had he been humble, Maurice would have probably let him lay around for a few days being that he has a whole family.

But now he refuses to. He knows how this goes. A couple days turn into a couple weeks which turn into a couple months and before you know it, you're in tenant court trying to get a family out that are not even tenants.

"You gone tell me when you leaving my spot? Dig this my man, you gone leave here willingly or unwillingly. The last thing I want to do is embarrass you in front of your family but don't force my hand, please."

The man chuckles with disrespect. Twelve Play has already positioned himself behind the man and is ready to steal him and put his lights out.

Tony notices the vein protruding in Maurice's forehead, and he knows what is soon to follow. He realizes now is the time to step in before things go left. "Easy Moe," Tony whispers. He steps away, wrapping his arm around the man's shoulder. "Let me talk to you out here."

The man follows Tony reluctantly. He and Maurice stare each other down, both looking as if they are ready to jump at each other. Once they step outside of the apartment into the hallway area, Maurice walks over and starts picking up blankets and stacking them into a pile.

The look in the woman's eyes breaks his heart so he tries not to look at her too long. He sees her as helpless and in a tough spot for choosing a loser as her husband and children's father. He looks at her with pity in his eyes. "Hey, I apologize but we can't do this here. Y'all got to get with the city and get some help or something."

The woman has no rebuttal. "I totally understand."

In a couple minutes Maurice has all the blankets and loose items packed into the plastic bags that were laying around. The man comes walking into the room with attitude still flaming. He looks at Maurice and eyeballs him once again. He and Maurice have a stare down before the man looks away with a chuckle. He looks to the woman and the children. "On the strength of you and the children, I'm chilling," Maurice claims.

"You ain't got to chill," the man says. "Won't be the first time they seen me rumble," he says with a smile. He sucks his teeth as he looks Maurice up and down.

Twelve Play in the background, looks over the man's shoulder. With his eyes he begs to be unleashed. Tony notices what is about to happen and intervenes. He looks to Maurice and shakes his head. "Let it go," he whispers.

Tony will never tell Maurice that he gave the man $500 to get a room for him and his family for a week. Maurice will see it as a weakness, but Tony sees it as a black man looking out for his black brother and sister that is in need. He also sees it as preventing a situation that can result in Maurice and Twelve Play murdering a man in front of his family. That will put them all in a bad spot.

It takes the family no time at all to gather their belongings. They exit the apartment and Tony and Maurice follow closely behind. The man talking slick for his entire exit, is making it hard for Maurice to ignore him. Maurice realizes it's the man's pride and ego that has him running off at the mouth. Problem is Maurice has an even bigger ego.

Once the man gets to the porch his vulgar language gets louder because he now has an audience to perform for. "You a long way away from home to call yourself calling some shots!" His shouting catches attention of the all the thugs on the curb and even the people who are walking by.

"Dig nigga!" Maurice shouts as he trails behind the man on the stairs. "It ain't where you from, it's where you at!" The woman stands in between Maurice and her husband with her baby in her arms. The woman and the children touch that soft spot in Maurice's heart again and he stops short.

"Yeah and it's obvious you don't know where you at or who you talking to," the man shouts. "Better ask somebody about me. Sal Strothers…that's the name! Check my resume! I am South Philly! 20th and Tasker! Ozone! Do your homework before you start disrespecting legends!"

Maurice looks the man up and down and quickly identifies the man as some has-been who thinks he's still relevant. "Legend?" Maurice says with a chuckle. He doesn't know what he may have been years ago but today he's just a junkie living in the past. "Nigga, I don't give a fuck about you, your name, your resume or nobody else! Ozone, no zone, don't none of that shit mean nothing to me!"

The young thugs all stand at attention, staring Maurice down. He notices them but at this point he doesn't care about them either. By now everyone in the area is standing around nosily. Everybody loves a little action.

"How the fuck you from New Jersey and eating off the soil of South Philly anyway? You ain't laid nothing down around here to be able to eat off this land! Do you realize that niggas done laid down and laid shit down to be able to eat around here?" The man seems to know all the right things to say to get Maurice to say something to anger all the Philadelphians. He's not just making this a beef between Maurice and him. He's making it seem like it's a beef between Maurice and the entire South Philly area.

"I eat wherever the fuck I want to eat!" Maurice shouts. Tony grabs Maurice by the arm and pulls him along.

"How the fuck you gone make a plate in South Philly without permission from South Philly niggas? Or not even letting South Philly niggas eat with you?"

Maurice snatches away from Tony furiously. "Nigga, I don't give a fuck about South Philly! Yeah, I'm making a plate here. Come take the plate! That's what I want you to do, Sal Strothers. That's your name, right?"

Twelve Play has managed to get away from the porch without notice. He is set up in the perfect spot to get a clean shot at the man. He can shoot him without anybody else being struck. Twelve Play knows he can beat the man with his hands but he rather shoot him down like a pig. Seventeen years later and still he isn't rehabilitated. He loves murder. He looks to Maurice awaiting the signal. Just as Maurice and Tony see Twelve Play, so do the thugs that are scattered along the curb.

One of the thugs wraps his arm around the man and pulls him away. His wife and children follow behind them. They walk down the block with the man turning around every few seconds, still shouting back at Maurice. Maurice can't make out what he's saying but still he's getting more angered.

Traffic is backed up on the block as a Dodge Ram pickup truck holds the traffic up. The tinted driver's window is rolled halfway down, just enough for the driver's face to be seen. Pitch black face, bald head with a huge Bin Laden beard, this man is the typical Philly mold. The man stares at Maurice from behind the window.

Maurice's gangster senses alerts him quickly and he notices the man staring at him. Twelve Play notices him as well. They both focus on the man in the pickup truck. Seconds of neither of them backing down and the man pulls off slowly. Maurice and Twelve Play watch the truck until it's out of their sight. They are not sure how this will go from here but at this point it is what it is and whatever it is, is what it will be.

11

SKELTER RIDES IN the backseat of Blue Blood's pickup truck as they cruise along the dark block. She's been listening to Blue Blood go on and on about the same subject for the entire ride but she's managed to block him out. She has so much on her mind right now and needs to figure it all out. He doesn't even realize that she hasn't replied to him in over 10 minutes.

"That rumor didn't take no time to start surfacing," Blue Blood says. "Dumb motherfucker! I swear I wish his ass was alive so I could kill him again! Three motherfuckers done already came at me talking about what they heard."

Skelter exhales agitation. "It's out there," she says emotionlessly. "What can we do about it? We just gone have to get to that too. Knock this situation down and get right onto the next one."

"I feel you on that," Blue Blood says. "But we have to be crafty with that one. A lot of motherfuckers loved that boy. With that being said, we don't really know where that shit gone come from. We have to think smart. I'm wondering what's the best way to go about it. I'm thinking maybe I should get with Swan and Jubilee and have a sit-down."

"A sit-down?" Skelter asks angrily. "About what?"

"I figure if I bring it to them, we shut all the rumors down. Like, dig, I been hearing some crazy shit out here and just wanted to clear the air."

"Man, listen, if them niggas got that shit on their mind, ain't nothing you gone be able to tell them to change that. Niggas gone believe what they want to believe."

"But acting like we don't hear the rumors is crazy. I figure if we come straight to them with it, at least they know we are aware of what's going on. Like, that will buy us the time we need to make our move."

"I just think it's senseless. We know the rumor is out there, so we move accordingly. I mean, if they want to rap about it, we can rap about it but calling a meeting about it to me is some sucker scary shit."

"You know ain't nothing scary about me. We just can't be out here beefing with our whole city at one time. We can't win. We have to be smart," he says as his focus is directed to the Toyota Camry that's parked up ahead. Blue Blood pulls up and parks directly behind the Camry. He flashes his high beams to signal the driver that it's him.

The driver gets out and walks toward them. Skelter and Blue Blood watch the man as he approaches. It's dark out but his silhouette is that of a tall and slender man. As he gets closer, Skelter notices his attire, khaki pants, flannel button-up peeking from underneath a v-neck sweater and soft bottom shoes. Once he grabs hold of the passenger's door, Skelter can see a head full of grey hair and a face full of salt and pepper hair. To the average eye he looks like the average middle-aged man but still Skelter doesn't trust him. She grips her gun underneath her thigh.

The man gets into the passenger's seat and slams the door behind him. "Peace!" he shouts upon entry.

"Knowledge, Born," Blue Blood sings jokingly. They shake hands. "Peace!" Blue Blood returns his greeting. The man senses someone in the backseat and turns around suspiciously. He looks back and forth at them as if it's about to go down. "Knowledge, that's my niece, Skelter," he says in formal introduction. "Skelter, this is Infinite Knowledge. He's my man, my mentor, like an uncle to me."

"Peace," Infinite Knowledge says with genuine sincerity.

"Aight," Skelter replies.

The man feels the draft coming from her and turns around to Blue Blood quickly. "What's going on, Strength?"

This man is Blue Blood's 'Enlightener/Educator.' He's the one who introduced him to the 5 Percent Nation in Annandale Correctional Facility back in the 90's. He put him under his wing and taught him the lessons. It was during his next bid in Northern State years later where he went off track and got involved with a group of Bloods from New York.

Blue Blood plants his hand on the man's shoulder to reassure his trust. "I got a situation in front of me. A real situation," he adds. "And I have to get ahead of this thing before it come at me full throttle."

"Yeah? Well, you already know if you got a situation, I got a situation. How can I help you?"

"I know don't shit get past you. I need a location on a motherfucker and I know if nobody else don't know where he at, you do."

The man smiles in appreciation. "And who might that be?"

Blue Blood pauses before replying. "The young nigga, Triple Threat."

The man pauses even longer before replying. "Last I known he be in the projects every day, in plain view."

"I know that. I mean, where he where he at? Like where he *live* at?"

"Oh man, I don't know where he live at."

Blue Blood can tell the man is lying. He also can sense discomfort coming from the man. "Knowledge, this me. If you took a lie detector test right now, you would fail."

They both laugh together. The man secretly points into the backseat. Blue Blood nods his head. "I can talk in front of her?"

"Bro, I just told you she like a niece to me. You know I wouldn't bring nobody to you that I don't trust. If you couldn't talk in front of her I wouldn't have asked you in front of her. I practically raised this one and I would put my life in her hands."

"Understood," Knowledge says before going silent. "This the deal," he says slowly. He's still not quite ready to spill the beans. "I know exactly where he at but."

"But what?" Blue Blood asks.

"I've been on that for a minute. I done put a lot of time in on it. I got big plans for that one. I've been scouting the joint for months. I know that's a big score laying around in there. If I give that location up, I'm gone need half of whatever is in there just so my time hasn't been wasted."

Blue Blood looks back at Skelter for her answer. "Honestly, this shit ain't even on robbery time," she says. "This some other shit. You give us the location and we will take it from there."

Knowledge quickly interrupts her. "I can't lose on this one though. I've put too much energy into it."

"You ain't gone lose," Blue Blood intercepts.

"How do I know that?" Knowledge asks.

"Because I'm confirming what she says," says Blue Blood. "You got my word."

Skelter quickly chimes in. "I can send my lil niggas in with you and you can bust the bag down with them. Or I can send my lil niggas in alone and they can bring the whole bag to you. I just want him."

"Oh nah," Knowledge says as he looks to Blue Blood. "Tell her how I roll. I don't fuck with these young niggas. Seen too many of them roll over when them people holler at them."

"Not my young niggas," Skelter says with total confidence. "I didn't raise them like that."

Knowledge turns around slowly. "No disrespect to you, but I don't know you, how you were raised and how you raised them. The only reason I'm having this conversation around you and to you is because of him and the trust I have in him. Normally I don't even talk to or around strangers period."

Skelter notices his transition. He no longer looks like the average middle-aged man. She now sees a gangster in hiding, a master at deception. "And truthfully I don't speak to women unless I'm educating them, romanticizing them or being intimate with them. I don't ask for women's opinions, objectives, or perspective on shit."

Skelter has to play his words back to make sure she's heard right. His words catch her so off guard that she's left speechless. "Again, no disrespect to you but from here on out, I would like to only speak to him about this matter. I ain't second guessing your gangsterism but we on Man-time right now and I only feel comfortable speaking with him man to man. As a matter of fact, can you excuse us for a minute while we continue this conversation?"

"Excuse you?" Skelter asks angrily. "You mean like step out the truck? You must be out your motherfucking mind! You better get out! Who the fuck you think you are? Better yet, who the fuck you think I am?"

"Hold up y'all," Blue Blood says in attempt to diffuse the problem. "We're all family." Blue Blood winks at Skelter slyly. "Nobody has to step out the truck. We all are on the honor system."

With no reply, the man opens the door and gets out. He stands at the door, looking directly at Blue Blood. "When you're ready to holler at me on Man-time, then call me. Also, I trust that what we discussed in this truck tonight will stay in this truck. I love you like a nephew. I have fought on the same side of the battlefield with you but if you put me in an upside-down situation I will have no choice but to stand on the opposite side of the battlefield against you. I will have no choice but to fight just as hard against you as I have fought with you."

Blue Blood is flabbergasted by what the man is saying. "Word, Knowledge? Like that?"

"Yeah, like that. You know I love you, but I don't like the situation you just put me in. You brought a stranger to me and this is where our conversation ends right here. I've already said too much as is. I just pray that what I said stays right here. For all of our sake," he adds. "When you're ready to get with me man to man, holler at me. I would give you my Peace before we depart but I don't know if we are at Peace at this moment," he says before slamming the door shut.

Blue Blood doesn't like how this meeting has gone left. In no way is that man anyone to play around with. The love they have for each other makes Blue Blood believe he would never come for him but one thing he knows for certain is Knowledge is a man of principle and he's seen him murder many men over principle.

"Man, fuck that old motherfucker!" Skelter says with rage.

"Nah, it can't be fuck him," says Blue Blood. "We need him."

"Ok, let's get what we need from him and then it's fuck him," says Skelter.

12

BABY MANSON STANDS, waiting for his door to be bust open, like a track star waiting for the gun to sound off to start the race. He's filled with anxiety. His mind is on business and he just wants to make sure that all went well with his mother and the accounts last night. She didn't answer last night when he called her a few times and that has him alarmed. He wasn't able to sleep a wink last night, worrying about her.

The cell is opened and Baby Manson wastes not a second. He darts out and makes his way along the tier. Inmates pop out of their cells as well and in seconds the tier is packed with inmates. Some going with the flow of traffic, others going against, and some standing still awaiting other inmates to catch up with them.

Up ahead, in the crowd, Baby Manson notices his enemy, coming in his direction. The man looks up and he notices Baby Manson as well. Fearfully, he looks away and turns around and starts walking in the opposite direction. This is exactly how he acts every time they see each other, since the day Baby Manson had the drop on him in the shower. He does such a good job at avoiding Baby Manson that he makes it hard for Baby Manson to get hold of him. Baby Manson has been patient but he doesn't know how long his patience will last.

To the right, leaning against the railing is a young man who appears to be way too young to be in an adult prison. His baby face and his little boy body has him looking more like 12 years old than 22 years old. The man may have an innocent boyish appearance but truly he's a little monster. Baby Face Monster is here on three different charges, all ending with murder. Initially he was fighting a triple homicide beef. The triple homicide opened the back door to another two separate murders. Baby Face Monster walks around the jail as if he has nothing to lose because really he has nothing to lose it. Everyone knows that so they stay out of his way.

Baby Face Monster is so small he's able to not just blend in with the crowd but he's also able to hide in the crowd. From where he stands, Baby Manson doesn't see him yet he's able to see every step Baby Manson makes. Baby Manson standing tall, looks over the crowd. He keeps his eyes on the enemy, up ahead whom has now picked up his step. Baby Manson stretches his neck as he watches the man squeezing in between two men before disappearing. Not paying attention as he walks, he collides into an inmate. As he looks over, he's face to face with the Good Christian who grabs his arm and attempts to pull him closer. Baby Manson notices the knife in the Good Christian's hand, coming at him but he has no time to react.

Out of nowhere, Baby Face Monster pops up, directly behind the Good Christian. He pokes the Good Christian in the side, three times with the quickness. The Good Christian's body caves in with each blow. His own knife drops to the floor. Baby Face Monster pushes the Good Christian back into his cell. Once inside, he goes to work. He pokes, cuts, slash and carves the man. He works his knife with the same expertise of a samurai working his sword.

Baby Manson stands in shock for two reasons. He can't believe how he's been caught slipping. Nor does he understand why a stranger has to come to his defense. He watches as the baby-faced inmate pokes at the Good Christian with vengeance.

Baby Manson feels a nudge at his side. Very edgy and defensive, he looks over. "Keep walking, keep walking," Lunatic says as he passes Baby Manson. Baby Manson follows behind Lunatic. The alarm sounds off and so does the intercom. In seconds, correction officers in riot gear come swarming in from every direction.

The inmates know the routine. They drop to their knees and assume the position, on their bellies, hands clasped behind their heads. Baby Manson lays on his stomach and turns his face to the right and there he is face to face with Lunatic.

"See, all the while you had your eyes on the wrong man," Lunatic whispers. "If you was plugged into the machine you would've known that. Took me no time to get to the bottom of it."

The baby-faced inmate is dragged from the cell by his arms, feet dangling in the air. The Good Christian's blood covers him in entirety. Specs of blood spread across his face like the measles. His t-shirt looks like he spilled a pitcher of cherry Kool-Aid on it and his pants and shoes have globs of blood on them like a painter who paints in blood.

"Based on my word, my lil man sacrificed himself," Lunatic whispers. "He put it all on the line with no questions asked. All on the strength of love and loyalty to the set. A little love goes a long way, feel me?"

13

PEBBLES'S RANGE ROVER is parked in the far corner of the Staples Parking Lot. Inside the Rover, she recounts through a stack of bills as she sings along with the group City Girls, '*Act Up.*' "Real ass bitch give a fuck 'bout a nigga," she says with her lips puckered up. She looks into the rearview mirror admiring herself.

"Big Birkin bag, hold five, six figures," she says as she grabs her purse by the straps, showing the stacks of money that are piled inside. "Stripes on my ass so he call this pussy Tigger." She bops her head to the beat as she licks her fingers to keep them moist for the bills. "Drop a couple racks, watch this ass get bigger." She pops her neck, lips puckered, conceited like. "If his money right, he can eat it like a snicker," she says before biting onto her bottom lip in seduction.

As she lowers her eyes back onto the money she peeps a snow-white 4-door Maserati pulling into the parking lot. The driver of the Maserati spots the Rover and speeds over in her direction. The driver parks right next to her and gets out with no hesitation. The young man reeks of money. The solid gold Cuban link with the huge Maserati emblem is big enough to tip him forward but his iced-out Audemar Piguet and his thick, full, cuff-style bracelet are heavy enough to keep him grounded. He's dressed in designer everything from head to toe.

Pebbles looks at the young man as he walks toward her truck and she can't grasp the fact that this is the same young man that used to spend weekends at a time at her house. The dirty, pissy smelling boy whom she had to make take showers when he spent the night there has matured nicely. The neighborhood kids teasingly called him Dirty James. He has renamed himself, J-Prince.

She realizes how much he's matured and that makes her also realize how old she really is. She always considers herself fly enough to hang out with the young girls, but this right here is a reality check for her. "Damn, I'm getting old," she mumbles to herself.

The young man gets in on the passenger's side. "Hey, Miss Pebbles," he says respectfully. He's just stabbed her in the gut without knowing it. The whole 'Miss Pebbles' just made her feel 10 whole years older than she was already feeling.

"Hey," she replies. "I hope you got a shopping bag because I don't," she says as she opens her pocketbook and allows him to see the money inside.

"Nah, I don't."

Pebbles sucks her teeth. "I may have one in the back. Let me check," she says as she opens her door and slides out of her seat.

She stands in the doorway, pulling her jeans up. Her booty bounces heavily. She bends over to slide her skintight jeans over her thick thighs and her booty spreads as wide as the doorway of the truck.

J-Prince sits back enjoying the eyeful. Seeing her like this takes his mind way back. He always had a crush on her since he and Baby Manson were in kindergarten together. They became the best of friends and he loved to play with Baby Manson but coming to their house on the weekend wasn't just to play with Baby Manson. He loved being in her presence. She would cook breakfast for them in short boy-shorts with no panties and t-shirt with no bra. She obviously had no idea that he even noticed. Probably thought he was too young and innocent to notice but how wrong she was.

One time as they were all at the table eating and his biscuit fell on the floor. When he bent over to pick it up he got a clean shot of her clean shaven cat. Her tiny shorts were like curtains with her lips peeking from behind them. That day changed his life. It was the day he gained appreciation for the female anatomy.

That vision stayed embedded in his mind all the way up until now. For seconds, he allows his mind to go back in the day. He's had so many dreams of having sex with her as a kid. Once he went through puberty those dreams always ended up with him ejaculating in his sleep.

Pebbles drags her wagon as she makes her way to the back of the truck. The young man sits up in his seat, turned around, appreciating the view. He turns around in his seat, quickly before she lifts the hatch open. She returns with a handful of Whole Foods shopping bags. She hands him a few as she closes the door behind her.

She digs into her purse and then hands him seven stacks in total. "He said this the money for the 100 grams you fronted him. Seven thousand, right?"

J-Prince nods his head as he tucks the money into a shopping bag. "Yes."

"And here is another seven," she says as she drops the stacks into his bag. "And another seven." The young man looks at her with surprise. "He says he wants to buy two hundred grams on his own and you match him by fronting him two hundred."

"Wow," the man says in shock. He's never really known Baby Manson to be about his money like this. He doesn't know what has gotten into him but whatever it is seems like the best thing that ever happened to him. "Yeah, I can do that."

"Ok, then my job here is done," Pebbles says with a smile. "I don't get into the rest of that shit. I just handle the money. I ain't touching no dope, driving no dope around, handing nobody no dope. I don't even want to see no dope," she continues to clown. "Hit ole girl when you ready and y'all can link up from there. When he calls, I will tell him you ok'd it and everything is in motion. What day should he be expecting you to call her, just so I can know what to tell him?"

"Tomorrow morning," he says casually. "Really I can do it right now, but I got some other business to handle. Just tell him I will be calling her tomorrow."

"Ok, will do," Pebbles replies. "Now get on out my truck with all that money. My damn blood pressure been up since I first got in the truck with it."

"Alright, Miss Pebbles," he says with the same crooked tooth smile she's known him to have since a little boy. He hugs her before getting out, not wanting to let her go. The smell of her perfume gives him an instant hard-on that makes him feel uncomfortable. He opens the door and gets out. Once he's out, she gets out as well. He walks to his car and she walks to the back of her truck and lifts the hatch. She stands at the back placing the shopping bags in the corner.

The young man drive past her slowly. She turns around and they lock eyes over the half-opened window. The window rolls down slowly. "Miss Pebbles, when are you going to let me take you out to dinner?"

His question takes her by surprise. "When Rahmid comes home we all will go out to dinner. My treat," she adds, hoping that his question was completely innocent.

"No, I'm talking about me and you going out to dinner?" He can't believe that he's asked her this.

"Huh?" She asks with a confused smile.

"Yeah, I want to take you out, just the two of us." Although he can't believe that he's initiated this, he must carry it out because he's already started it. All his life he's waited for this day.

"Boy bye," she says brushing him off.

"Nah, serious," he says. "I ain't no little boy no more."

"Boy, you will always be a little boy to me. That same little boy who used to pee my beds," she laughs.

He smiles embarrassingly. "I don't wet the bed no more. Well, I do wet beds but not like that." He stares at her seductively.

"Little boy, you're smelling yourself now, huh?"

"Please, with the little boy. I'm a grown-ass man. A grown man with a lot of money."

"Little boy," she says with strong emphasis. "That little money you getting has made you lose your mind. I ain't one of those little girls you can run that weak game on. Have you in the poor house," she says laughing hard.

"It will take a lot to have me in the poor house," he says with cockiness.

She shakes her head. "We gone act like this conversation never took place, ok?"

"I was hoping that. This conversation ain't for everybody to hear. From my mouth to your ears," he says with arched eyebrows. "But does that mean I can take you out or nah?" he asks with persistence.

"Go on, little boy," she says teasingly before getting into the truck. Before she pulls off she looks at him one more time. She truly can't believe he just tried her. Young enough to be her son and she looks at him almost like a son, but she has to admit his approach was flattering. She pulls off, leaving him staring at her lustfully.

14

THE PRISON IS on lockdown due to the murder of Good Christian. The inmates are all confined to their cells due to administration fearing the domino effect. If they didn't lock the prison down they're sure retaliation would take place. They have to nip it in the bud before 1 murder leads to 20 murders.

Baby Manson is still in shock about how it all played out. That was a near death experience and if it wasn't for the man stepping up for him, he probably wouldn't be here today. He feels indebted to the man for putting his freedom on the line as he did. What he doesn't know is his freedom was never on the line because he was never going to be free again ever in life.

Baby Manson revisits the words of Lunatic and they make more and more sense each time. That machine as he calls it, is already in working order. He's already a built-in piece of the machine for the rest of his life whether he likes it or not. He just has to stay plugged in and the rest will be history.

Before he was trying to stay away from the foolishness and just get money, not realizing the foolishness will help him to get money. He has decided to use the machine to the fullest. Of the 400 grams he's waiting on, he plans to break off a portion of the work specifically for Lunatic. That portion he will take a profit cut on, giving Lunatic a better price than he's given anyone else. He's just not sure how much he will grant Lunatic at a time as of yet because he's not sure how much of a profit loss he's willing to take right now. The dope he's giving Lunatic has nothing to do with fear and everything to do with respect for what they have done for him.

Baby Manson has calculated and has decided to cut his profit margin in order to leave room for Lunatic to make some money. He may be losing profit but he will be gaining full control of the machine. To him, that makes all the business sense in the world. Right now, his mindset is all about thinking and growing rich.

Baby Manson quickly scribbles on a paper. This is a letter to the G. It reads as follows:

> *My gratitude is on a zillion right now. I'm a man of action and very little words so I would rather show you than to tell you. I'm in the waiting room now but once the doctor sees me and I'm back in good health I will show my gratitude. Send the homie my love when you get the chance and let him know I will be sending my love to him as well. Salute!!*

Just as he's signing his name, the kitchen worker appears. He stands there holding the tray of food. Baby Manson gets up and walks over. He grabs his tray through the slot. In between his fingers he holds the paper which is folded up into the size of a matchbook. "Give this to the homie, Lunatic," he whispers.

The man takes the paper and within their grip, Baby Manson drops a token of his appreciation into the palm of the man's hand. In the crease of the little piece of paper may only be a mere few pinches of dope but to this man it will be more than enough.

He tucks both the letter and the gift he's received and makes his way to the next cell. Before he finishes this meal run he will have received more gifts than a spoiled kid on Christmas Day. He can count on receiving more dope, and food and even promissory notes. A kitchen job is the best job to have because of the many perks. He eats all around the board in every sense of the word.

• • •

On the opposite wing, on the bottom tier, another kitchen worker passes a note into a cell. The man takes the note before grabbing his tray. He's more eager to read the letter than he is to eat the disgusting looking food. The kitchen worker can actually tell him word for word what is in the letter. How does he know? Because secretly he's already read the letter. He's aware that doing so could cost him his life but his nosiness won't allow him to pass a note without reading it.

The things that he's read and that he knows just by reading letters that he passes to the next inmate. He knows all the players and their positions. He knows intimate details about men he doesn't know personally. One of those men is Baby Manson.

The kitchen worker has no clue of who Baby Manson is but what he does know is, whoever he may be, he is in a world of trouble. He knows that Baby Manson is behind the murder of the man on the other wing. He also knows that Baby Manson is about to be next in line to be murdered. He escaped death this time but the next one he won't be able to escape. He knows when he will be murdered, how he will be murdered and by whom. In his mind he holds valuable information that could save Baby Manson's life. Too bad that by revealing that information that would save Baby Manson's life it would cost him his own life.

15

SOUTH PHILLY/6:15 A.M.

TWELVE PLAY STEPS onto the small stoop of the condominium building. Maurice needed him to stay here to prevent any more squatters setting up. He's used to the bare minimum so the Ikea Futon bed, mini refrigerator/freezer, Keurig coffee maker, and big screen television Maurice picked up for him is more than enough for him to survive. In fact, compared to Trenton Prison where he just left, this could be considered the lap of luxury.

He's up bright and early. He's still on his prison schedule and 4 days home will not break habits that he formed over 17 years. The construction crew hasn't even arrived as of yet. The drug dealers haven't clocked in yet either.

Twelve Play holds a cup of coffee in one hand and a newspaper in the other. This is the same morning routine that he performed the last 6,385 days of his life. He sips his morning coffee while reading the newspaper, catching up with his current events. While others may have done their time in the gym or playing card games or whatever else for entertainment, Twelve Play was different.

He spent his time reading books and staying on top of current events just so he would be kept abreast of all that was happening in the world. He knew with him facing 30 years, a lot would change by the time he got back to the streets. The last thing he wanted was to be left behind. He didn't want to come home stuck in the past which is why he was sure to keep up with the rest of the world and their evolution.

Twelve Play sits at the top of the staircase. He lays his newspaper flat on his lap. He takes one long look around the area as he sips his coffee. After complete surveillance of the area he sits his cup on the stoop next to him. Sneakily, while looking around he digs into the middle pages of the newspaper and grips the 9-millimeter. He looks around suspiciously as he removes the gun from the newspaper and tucks it underneath his butt. He then carries on with his morning ritual of reading every line of the newspaper, missing not a single one of them.

MINUTES LATER

Twelve Play, still reading, peeks up over his newspaper and the grill of a vehicle catches his attention. The Dodge Ram emblem on the hood stands out boldly. Sitting at the red light is the Dodge Ram pickup truck from the other day. The front window is so dark it's impossible to see inside.

Twelve Play scoots back so the handle of his gun is accessible. He lays the newspaper flat on his lap to conceal the gun. He looks around as if he doesn't notice the truck. Just as the truck is creeping through the intersection, Twelve Play cuffs the newspaper in one hand as he grips the handle of the gun. The gun is now gripped tightly. He always keeps one in the chamber and he never keeps his safety on. He's ready to go.

He eyeballs the truck down as it passes him. Once the truck passes him, he stands up, with his hands rested behind his back. The gun is in his hand under the newspaper. He watches as the truck's brake lights pop on. Twelve Play looks around to see if any witnesses are in the area. The last thing he needs is witnesses. He lowers the gun to the back of his thigh just as the truck stops.

The window rolls down slowly. The driver clearly sees Twelve Play is ready for action. "You *Mu'minun* (Believer) right?"

Twelve Play nods his head up and down with suspicion. "Alhamdullilah (Thank God)," Twelve Play says still keeping his eyes on the man.

The man smiles pleasantly. "I can spot a believer a mile away. His smile, his mannerisms. True believers got a different look in their eyes. They smell different, you know?"

Twelve Play nods his head and cracks a smile of his own yet he never releases the grip of his gun.

"Aye *Akhi* (brother), I know you got to tie your camel but I ain't on that type time," he says. "I'm on Muslim time." He's making it evident that he knows Twelve Play has his gun on him and ready to go to work. "Is it alright if I get out and holler at you?"

Twelve Play nods his head up and down. "*Na'am* (yes)," he says still showing slight distrust.

The man parks the truck right in front of the building. He gets out and what Twelve Play sees is a Muslim. As much Muslim as he looks, he's still quite fashionable. The man's kufi hangs on the top back of his head. His selvedge, distressed denim jeans are high water, cut off above the ankles, exposing the tip tops of his throwback Jordans.

The prostration mark on his forehead looks like dark ashes on his pitch-black skin. His beard in the light is not as full and bushy as it looked behind the tints. Instead it's patchy and brittle, mostly black with patches of carrot color henna. The smell of uncut Red Egyptian Musk oil reaches the porch long before the man even gets to the curb.

Halfway up the stairs, the man extends his hand for a handshake. "As Salaamu Alaikum! Umar is the name, Umar Bilal."

Twelve Play stuffs his gun into his back pocket with the handle hanging out just in case. He reciprocates the handshake. "Walaikum As Salaam! Abdul Malik," he says in his best Arabic dialect.

"Aye Akhi, about the other day, I ain't want no trouble," the man claims. "I was just breezing through and saw all y'all had going on. Once I saw you, I recognized you as a believer and I ain't never gone watch a believer get oppressed. Once I saw y'all had it under control I boogied on out of here."

Twelve Play listens attentively, trying to figure out the man's angle and why he's even here. He pays close attention as the man speaks. "I heard what it all was about and that's a battle in itself, Akhi. Keeping them squatters out of your shit is a full-time job. I got a couple properties of my own around here. Not on this level," he says as he points to the building. "Some small homes I cop and renovate. That's where I'm headed now," he says as he points to the back of his pickup truck where piles of lumber are stacked neatly.

"As far as main man go," he says as he looks around skeptically. "I ran his name through the wash and rinse and it came out that he some old nigga that used to put it down. Back in the day, he was getting *no telling*(was getting so much money, you couldn't count it). And he was with the dumb shit. Love to hit that bag though. Today he's harmless. I heard he still got a couple nephews running around on that same dumb shit he used to be on.

"I ain't no South Philly bul. I'm from West, but I be all over though. I mean I got a couple properties around here, and a few up North and I got a barber shop up Mount Airy, right by the masjid. Germantown Avenue," he specifies. "West Philly born and raised though."

One thing Twelve Play knows about Philadelphians is they are super geographical. Philly pride is like no other place in the world, not even New York. They will make sure you know that although they are from Philly, their part of Philly reigns over any other part.

Twelve Play still hasn't figured out why the man is even here. He continues on, "I say that to say this, I'm from West but I know the whole Philly like the back of my hand." He peeks around once again. "And trust me when I tell you, ain't nothing greasier than a South Philly nigga. Can't trust them. Not the niggas and not the chicks. Chicks will set you up. If you know anything about South Philly, you know South Philly chicks are not to be trusted. So be careful around here. I know you ain't from around here."

Twelve Play goes on the defense. "I ain't from around here but that don't matter. I'm good."

"I don't doubt it, Akhi," the man replies. "Just saying, keep your eyes open. Y'all down here on money time and they out here on nut time, you feel me? I ain't telling y'all how to run your business but I hired a management company to deal with my tenants. Less headache for me and it prevent that type shit y'all went through. I can plug y'all into the company if you want."

Twelve Play knows not the first thing about business. "I'm gone keep it real with you. I'm here with my brothers. I ain't got no say so in none of this. I will pass the info to them though."

"Yeah, do that. I got so many plugs in this city that I can be a huge asset. Plugged in down city hall so I can get permits pulled and everything. Even got a grant writer who pen game is crazy. Can get all the money you need. Just let me know how y'all can use me. Take my number down and if it's anything I can do for y'all or anything we can do together, keep me in mind."

Twelve Play pulls out his phone with no real interest in doing so. The man calls out his number slowly. "Got you," Twelve Play replies as he pretends to lock the number in.

"I'm out though. Time to make the donuts," he says with a smile. He reaches for a handshake. "As Salaamu Alaikum!"

"Walaikum As Salaam!"

The man trots down the stairs and jogs to his truck. He climbs in the truck and speeds off, burning rubber. Twelve Play watches the truck go down the block. After a 10-minute conversation he still doesn't understand the purpose of the man stopping. He's not sure if his Islam is genuine and he came to him with sincere concern or if he has a different agenda and is using Islam to rock him to sleep. This is a question that only time will answer.

16

PISCATAWAY, NEW JERSEY

TONY CRUISES THROUGH the suburban streets as Dre sits low in the passenger's seat, running his mouth. "Shit blew my mind. I was speechless."

"Yeah, I bet," Tony replies. "What you think though?"

"Shit, that's what I'm here asking you," he says before cracking a smile. "She popped that shit on me out of nowhere. I had no idea she was feeling like that. I mean, back in the day I knew she had a little teenage crush on me, but I didn't never think that deep into it. But ten years later, she here asking me to marry her, is some other shit. The crazy shit is I feel like I owe her that. Like I put that girl whole life on hold."

"You really want my honest opinion?" Tony asks.

"Absolutely," Dre replies.

"As far as you owing her because she did the time, I don't agree with that. That was business and all that comes with the game. I understand your loyalty because I operate on that same system. Charge that to the game. But," he says, holding one finger in the air. "I will tell you this though. As a young dude, I always heard the old heads give the advice of make sure you marry someone who loves you more than you love them. I never really grasped that concept until my divorce. When you marry someone who loves the ground you walk on, it's a different life. You want her to need you like she needs air to breathe. You want her to be so wrapped up in you that she can't imagine living without you. It may sound selfish but it's not. And when you find a woman that feels like that about you, you don't destroy that. You build on it.

In today's time we live in a Reality Television world. Nothing is real. These women are plastic, see through. Their love is based on your net worth and your assets. If you find one that has your back and loves you unconditionally, you got to hold onto her. And I think Lil Mama is that one.

She's already proven the test of time. Ten years later and she's still in love with you. She already showed you that she has your back. She took a fall for you that took her off the map for ten years. Back then, you trusted her with millions of dollars of dope and she never came a dime short. You trusted her with your life.

You say that you are not in love with her, though. I say, I know people that are madly in love and don't have the trust, loyalty and respect you and her have for each other. If you ask me, I think you should marry her because you will never ever find another like her. I say you marry her right the hell now."

Both Tony and Dre share a laugh. Dre sits back digesting all Tony has just said as he stares in a daze. Tony slows the car down and steers into a parking space. As he slams the gear into park he looks at the beautiful house that's directly across the street. This house is where his friend Jasmine resides. At this point he's so confused that he has to have an answer, just for his own sanity. The only thing he knows to do at this time is to walk up to the door and ask for her. But what if her husband answers, what will he say? They don't know each other, but the fact that Tony and her had an affair on the man he has guilt. He would hate to have to shake his hand and bullshit him anymore than they already has.

He has to get to the bottom of this. Before he knows it, he's opened the door and has one foot on the ground. "Be right back," he says to Dre. As he crosses the street he pays close attention to the two cars in the driveway. One is a Porsche truck and the other is a BMW 4 series. This is an indication that both of them are possibly home.

He hates to put her in a situation like this, but he has no choice. He prays she answers the door and not him. He doesn't have a scripted answer for the husband if by chance he answers. He's not too worried though because with him being a bullshitter by profession he's sure he can come up with something quickly on his toes, if need be.

Tony rings the bell with his heart pumping fast and hard. He knocks right behind the ring and to his surprise the door parts. He peeks in. "Hello."

In seconds, he hears the sound of stilettos clicking on hardwood floors. He inhales a deep breath of part relief that it's her and not him. The door opens and he's surprised to see a beautiful, young Caucasian woman, dressed in a business suit. "Good afternoon," she greets.

"Afternoon," Tony replies. "But, I'm looking for Jasmine Hunter." Tony peeks over the woman's shoulder where he finds a Caucasian couple. "I'm afraid The Hunters no longer live here." She points to the lawn where an 'Open House' sign is as clear as day. He doesn't know how he missed it. "The house has been on the market for a couple of weeks now. I've just finished showing it to this lovely couple. You're free to step inside if you like."

Tony steps inside and looks around like a spy. The house is still fully furnished. It's as if they just picked up and left. "I'm not looking to purchase. I'm just looking for my good friend. Do you know how I can contact her?"

"Uh, I'm afraid not. I've never even met Mrs. Hunter. All my business has been with Mr. Hunter. Several meetings about house business and I have yet to meet her." The woman steps close enough to whisper. "Everything is rush-rush with him but I don't know what the emergency is. I've been hired to get the house sold and that's what I plan to do. I can maybe connect the two of you, if you like."

"Oh, no," Tony says. "That won't be necessary. My business is with her. I thank you so much though. Have a great day," he says without waiting for a reply. He exits the house with his mind heavy.

All this is becoming one big puzzle that he can't seem to put together. First, he loses phone contact with her, then he finds out she no longer works with the company she's been with for close to 25 years, and now her house is up for sale. He knows how much this house means to her. This house even means a great deal to him. It cost him close to 50-grand to save this house for her back then when her and her husband were going through financial difficulty.

He can clearly visualize the expression on her face when she made him promise to cut ties with her and she expressed the danger zone he was stepping into. He can't help but to wonder if her disappearance has anything to do with that. Now, he's taking everything she said seriously. He's now worried about her safety.

The suspense is overwhelming. He has to find a way to contact her just to keep his own sanity. He storms back toward the house. There's only one way to find out where she is and that's through her husband. Right now he's ready to contact her husband to get to her or to at least hopefully get the answers he needs. He realizes he will have to explain to the husband who he is. He figures he will he just have to worry about that bridge once he crosses it.

17

YARDLEY, PENNSYLVANIA/10:15 P.M.

THE NISSAN MURANO cruises down the quiet residential street. The Grubhub sign on the roof indicates a food delivery is in progress. A half of a block behind the Murano is an all-black Dodge Charger. The Charger has been tailing the Murano the entire ride here. In the Charger there is Blue Blood and Infinite Knowledge. The person in the Murano doing the deliveries is Infinite Knowledge's wife.

The Murano finally pulls over and parks and so does the Charger. A woman gets out, with both hands gripping shopping bags. She walks up the stairs and rings the bell. She stands on the porch for about 2 minutes before the door is opened.

"Timing is key," Infinite Allah says from the passenger's seat. "Got to give her time to get off the block but not too much time. Got to catch them within a minute or so, so they think maybe it's the driver coming back. In those first two minutes they still are relaxed and off point, not thinking.

"True," Blue Blood replies.

The woman makes her way down the steps and into the Murano. She pulls off with no hesitation. They watch the door of the house being slammed and then they watch the Murano bend the corner.

"Go now," Infinite Knowledge commands as he pulls his ski-mask over his face. Blue Blood pulls up a house away from their targeted house. Infinite Knowledge gets out quickly. He takes complete surveillance of the area as he's walking. Blue Blood follows at his heels, his face covered by ski-mask as well. They both stand on the porch. The man looks at his accomplice with a head-nod before ringing the bell. He hits it 3 times because he knows 3 times to be a sense of urgency yet irritating and the people inside normally get so irritated that they rush to the door.

Just as predicted, the door opens. The woman stands at the door, expecting the Grubhub delivery woman but instead she's faced with two gun-toting, masked bandits. Infinite Knowledge snatches her by her blouse and covers her mouth all in the same motion. Blue Blood rushes inside and closes the door gently behind them.

Infinite Knowledge places the gun to the woman's head and pushes her toward the inside of the apartment. Blue Blood tiptoes behind them with his gun already aimed up ahead. As they approach the doorway, there Triple Threat is, shirtless and in his boxers sitting at the dining-room table. He's busy setting the food out onto plates and not even looking at them stepping into the doorway. He looks up from the table and he becomes stiff as a statue.

He looks at his woman standing at gunpoint. He then looks to the two masked bandits, one coming in his direction. He slowly raises his hands high in submission. Blue Blood pulls a rope and duct tape from his waistband of his step-in. Triple Threat snickers to himself. Until now he never thought it was possible for him to get caught slipping.

Triple Threat puts up no fight at all as he's flung around. Blue Blood ties Triple Threat's hands behind his back, before using his foot to sweep him. Triple Threat falls face first onto the floor, never uttering a sigh or a word. He lays there on his stomach, paying close attention to the men. He's looking for the slightest sign of who they could be. How they found him here is a puzzle to him. He's sure this has to be an inside job; it always is. Not many people know where he rests his head, which brings his list down to one or two that could be behind this.

Triple Threat watches as his girlfriend is brought over to them. Infinite Knowledge grips a fistful of her long hair and yanks her head to the side. Tears drip down her face rapidly. Infinite Knowledge places the nose of the gun onto her temple. "You gone tell me where the money is or you gone watch me pop her top smooth off?"

"Aye man, it's only money and material," Triple Threat says calmly. "You can have it all. No need for no tops to get popped." Blue Blood and Infinite Knowledge are both shocked at his casualness. Even under pressure he keeps it G. Most don't.

"Take me to it," Infinite Knowledge says as he yanks the woman's head harder.

Blue Blood snatches Triple Threat onto his feet while keeping the gun rested on his head. Triple Threat looks at the gun and is tempted to go for it. He looks over at his woman and the look in her eyes makes him cancel the thought. "Which way?" Blue Blood asks.

Triple Threat nods toward the back and the man pushes him in that direction. As Triple Threat is being dragged by the collar he cuts his eye and what he sees sends a chill through his body. A bit of Blue Blood's wrist peeks from underneath the sleeve of his step-in. He immediately recognizes the tattoo of 2 guns crossed at the wrist. He now knows that it's Blue Blood behind the mask.

It all makes sense to him now. He knows this hit has come from Skelter. He will never allow them to get away with this. Revenge is on his mind but first he has to make it out of here alive. He puts up even less resistance, with the hopes that they will let him live. If they do, that will be the biggest mistake they ever made. He looks at the man who is holding his woman and tries to figure out who he could be but he's coming up with a blank.

Triple Threat leads them into the bedroom. He stops at the nightstand. "It's in there." Infinite Knowledge forces the woman onto her knees and immediately starts pulling out the drawers of the nightstand. "Where the fuck is it? Think it's a game?" He aims the gun at the woman and taps the trigger.

"No, no, no, please," she cries as she waves her hands in the air.

"Turn it over," Triple Threat advises. "The money is inside."

The man quickly realizes that the nightstand is really a trick nightstand. He locates the opening and is able to see stacks of money.

"I know this ain't it. I know it's some more. If I look around and find some more, this bitch dead."

"Both nightstands." Triple Threat has more money stashed but he believes the money in the nightstands is enough to make them satisfied. At this point he will give them every dime he has hidden in here just for them to allow him to live. That way he could ruin their lives in revenge.

"Yo, tie that bitch up. We gone search high and low and I swear if I find another dime in here, I'm gone blow your bitch head off and sit it on your lap," Infinite Knowledge promises. Blue Blood ties the woman up as instructed. Triple Threat and his woman sit on opposite sides of the room as they watch the bandits comb through the entire bedroom with tooth and nail, leaving nothing unturned.

They find and pack every valuable into a duffle-bag. The woman watches sadly as they pack away every diamond he's ever bought her. They leave not a single dollar behind, including the rent money that was in the top drawer and three single dollar bills from the change for the Grubhub delivery.

They find over three hundred bricks of dope, close to a kilo of coke, and a few pounds of weed. These are the ingredients of a good robbery. It's a shame the four guns that he had stashed around the bedroom are of no help to him right now because he sure could use the help right now.

Forty minutes passes and for Triple Threat and his woman the twenty-four hundred seconds have felt like twenty-four hundred days. For Blue Blood and Knowledge, it's been a fast-paced adventure with both of them wishing they had more time. Something tells them they could possibly be missing something. The woman continues to whimper but the tape covering her mouth keeps the noise down. Triple Threat with tape covering his mouth as well, sits and watch with fury boiling inside of him.

Infinite Knowledge has both hands filled with goods and is ready to exit. He looks to Blue Blood and gives him the signal that it's over. He then snatches the woman from the floor. He drags her to the doorway.

Triple Threat watches in confusion, wondering where they are taking her. He stands up and runs behind them. Blue Blood grabs him by the neck and flings him onto the floor. Triple Threat looks up at him with rage in his eyes as the gun is aimed at his head. He tries to squirm to get out of the way but there's no way to escape it. *POP! POP! POP!* Triple Threat's face caves in as the hot slugs melt into it. Blue Blood stands over him, feeling victorious; a job well done.

Minutes Later and the Charger rides away into the darkness. Blue Blood looks over to Infinite Knowledge with admiration. "You are a fucking genius. How the hell you come up with this scheme?"

"In the process of delivering food I was finding myself in little hidden towns that I never heard of. Places where hustlers with that bread be hiding, feel me? Big houses with big cars in the driveways and basketball courts and swimming pools in the backyards. I was just working and trying to do the right thing but the crook inside wouldn't let me," he says with a sinful grin.

"Wow," Blue Blood says in wonderment. "I always wondered how you knew where every fucking body lived. I couldn't figure it out to save my life."

"Yeah man, I got a little pad that I write down cars and license plates and the address. Then, for the next few weeks or months, I investigate," he explains. "Sometimes I be in the hood and spot a car that I've seen on my delivery route in the suburbs. They have no clue who I be because if I peep a potential vic, I lay low and let my wife deliver. Just so I don't draw no attention to myself. I only take the suburban deliveries. That's where the money at," he claims. "Ain't no money in the hood. The money niggas out here hiding," he says with a goofy chuckle.

"I call it a part time job and a full-time job all in one. I deliver food at my full-time job and then later on I clean those same houses out at my part-time job. Crazy thing is, I make way more money at my part time then I do at my full time," he says with a serious expression on his face.

Infinite Knowledge continues yapping. "I been on 'ole boy for like three months. I lucked up on it on a humble. One day I pulled up and saw a car with tints in the driveway, so I let the wife go in. I popped my seat back and just watched. No soon as I lay back another car with tints pull up. Who the hell get out but the boy, Triple Threat. Man, I felt like I hit the lottery, the mega million." He smiles, staring in a trance, just remembering the day. "And boy was I right. This was a bonafide come up right here."

He looks to Blue Blood as he sinks into further relaxation. "Him and his old lady love that fast food. Bitch never cook. On Mondays, Chinese food... Tuesdays, Chipotle... Wednesdays, Pizza Hut... Thursday, Chinese Food again, and Fridays, Outback Steakhouse... I know their meal schedule like the back of my hand."

"Damn," Blue Blood says in amazement. Blue Blood is glad Infinite Knowledge is on his team. Without him they would've never had a lead on Triple Threat.

Blue Blood reached out to Infinite Knowledge immediately just to make sure their brotherly bond had not been tainted. Blue Blood apologized to him for bringing a stranger to him. Infinite Knowledge accepted the apology. He respected the bond Blue Blood and Skelter had with one another, but he refused to work with her or her Godsons.

Infinite Knowledge told him the only way he would help them was if Blue Blood was the one who came along with him. Blue Blood has never been a robber or a thief, but he still went along just because he had his own agenda. He's no robber but after seeing the amount of goods they now have their hands on, he would be a fool not to take half.

"I have to admit one thing," Infinite Knowledge says with a solemn expression. "Through all the jobs I've done I never left a motherfucker."

"Huh?" Blue Blood asks, not understanding at all.

"Nah, never," Knowledge says. "I've tied them up, pistol whipped and abused some of them but never murdered a man. I made a pact to myself a long time ago that I would never kill another Black man for money. If I'm supposedly civilized and I kill my brother for money, what's the difference between me and the uncivilized? I mean, the money don't hurt nobody really. They can always get more of it. It's dirty money anyway. But I ain't taking no Black man life for no amount of bread."

Blue Blood has gotten so far away from his lessons over the years and listening to Infinite Knowledge makes him realize just how far gone he is. He remembers a time when his mind worked just like that. Of course, he was in prison at the time and not in the world. To hear Infinite Knowledge tell him this weighs on him. He has so much respect for Knowledge that he hates to be looked upon as a savage by him.

"Indeed, God," Blue Blood replies. "But for the record...I never came here to murder a man for money," he claims. "I came here to murder a man that was on his way to come and murder me."

Knowledge shrugs his shoulders with a more clear understanding. "Well, in that case, say no more. Overstood."

18

ROGER GARDEN APARTMENTS

BLEEK WALKS AROUND to the front of The Projects peeking around cautiously. Both of his hands are tucked in his jacket pocket and both hands have a semiautomatic handgun in them. A total of 22 bullets are at his disposal. He refuses to be the next victim sprawled out on the sidewalk.

As he approaches the tinted-out Bonneville, he looks around even more cautiously. He stops at the driver's door and stands facing the street. He looks up the block both ways, studying the area close and far. He releases the grip on the gun in his left pocket and snatches the door open with his left hand. He allows his right hand to dangle from his pocket, ready to go, as he lowers himself and plops into the seat. He snatches the door closed behind him, starts the car, and speeds out of the parking space like a bat flying out of hell.

TWO BLOCKS AWAY

Tortura sits on the edge of the passenger's seat while Quabo sits in the second row, on the edge of his seat. He's so close it appears that he, Tortura and the driver are all sitting shoulder to shoulder. All three of them have their eyes fixed on the Bonneville. Tortura calculates with perfect timing. "*Ir ahora!* (Go now!)" Tortura shouts. The driver puts the pedal to the metal and speeds up the block. They all keep their eyes on the taillights of the Bonneville. In no way will he get away from six eyes.

After a 10-minute drive, the Bonneville cruises along Clinton Avenue. Tortura and the crew are only a few cars' length behind. Bleek, now, less alert since he left the area, hasn't looked in his rearview mirror in a few blocks. Miraculously, Bleek finds an empty parking spot directly in front of Martinez Bar .

The driver's door swings wide open no soon as the car is parked, Bleek darts out of the car and slams the door shut. Just as he turns around he's greeted by the van with the side doors already open. Two rifles are aimed at his head but only one man jumps out of the van That man grabs Bleek by the throat and snatches him.

Another man jumps out and restrains Bleek's hands. His guns do him no good as both of them are being taken out of his pocket and shoved into the van. As he lands on his stomach in the van, Tortura throws a pillowcase over Bleek's head and ties a rope around his neck. The rope that's tied at the bottom of the pillowcase makes it hard for Bleek to breathe.

Tortura quickly ties a perfect Boy Scout knot around Bleek's wrist. He smacks him one good time in the back of the head with the barrel of the gun. The blow knocks Bleek silly but not silly enough to do something crazy. He lays there afraid to move. Tortura rests his combat boots on Bleek's back as the van pulls off.

Thirty minutes of riding with a pillowcase over your head can seem like an eternity. Bleek tries to control his breathing, and not suck up too much air because he knows his air is limited. He's never been this afraid in his life. The music is blaring loud like they're in a Spanish festival. Every now and then the occupants say a few words to each other in Spanish. That makes him even more afraid because he has no idea what they have in store for him.

The van is finally stopped. The music stops shortly after. The sound of all the doors opening leaves Bleek in suspense. The side doors are slid open and Bleek is dragged out of the van by his feet. He falls face first onto the ground.

One man has one leg and another man has the other. They drag him almost in separate directions, stretching his legs like a wishbone. He's dragged by his feet across a field; every bump, every rock, every boulder, every pebble can be felt. His life flashes before his eyes, yet he doesn't see his ending. But something tells him it's near.

19

THE NEXT MORNING
FORT DIX, NEW JERSEY

SKELTER STUMBLES INTO the room on wobbly legs. Her heart beats hard enough to bang a hole in her chest. Tony contacted her a day ago, and today with no warning, he brings her here to see Manson. Manson requested for Tony to get in contact with her. Manson had no way of contacting her but luckily for him, Skelter had reached out to Tony over a year ago to represent one of her associates for a gun charge. Tony took a long shot and hit the last number he had on her and it happened to work. Skelter has been through a hundred burnout phones since then but she never got rid of the family line.

Skelter is weak enough to faint right now. She feels like this is one of the many dreams she has had of her reuniting with Manson. Two, sometimes three, times a week she dreams about him, dreams that seem so real. In her dreams they ride around and joke and share deep conversations. The dreams feel so real that she hates to be awakened. Times when she's awakened from a dream with him, she quickly attempts to go back to sleep with hopes of picking back up from where they left off in the dream.

Right now she feels like this has to be one of those many dreams but she doesn't know what to do to find out if it's real. It feels real but so does all the other dreams. She decides to just go with the flow and if it's a dream she will just appreciate the moments they share just like she does all the other times.

Manson's smile gets wider and wider the closer Skelter gets to him. He holds his shackled hands high in the air and Skelter ducks low, under them. She wiggles into the comfort of his hug. They hold each other tight, not wanting to let go.

"Is this a dream?" Skelter asks with a crackling voice. "This feels too real. It can't be a dream. Please tell me, is it?" Skelter pleads.

Manson lifts his arms over her head so she can escape his grip. He backs away from her looking her up and down. He smiles at her like a proud father. He looks into her eyes and sees a coldness, a hundred times colder than he's used to from her. The cold, emptiness he sees them is a sign of a dead spirit.

Manson's mouth is becoming dry. Unlike before he wasn't mentally stable enough to even pay attention to it. Now that he's aware of the many side effects, it shames him. He fears the fact that he may never be the same. His twitching and his dry mouth and lip smacking all are traits that may be with him for the rest of his life and that hurts his pride to know.

He rubs his hand over his mouth to cover his lip smacking. He's not sure if she noticed or not but he quickly tries to take her attention off of it. "This is real life," Manson says. "It's a long story and I'm gone fill you in detail by detail."

It takes Manson all of 10 minutes to explain to her what has happened and all that he's been though in the past 3 years. It takes her all over an hour to tell him just 10% of what she's been through in the past three years. It hurts her to know that Manson has been treated like he has been. She knows he's a trooper and she sees that he hasn't been broken but seeing the effects of the medicine and the abuse on him really touches her heart. The weird part is Manson can see the abuse all over her as well and it hurts him the same. He wishes he could have been there to save her and feels like he failed her by leaving her in the world to fend for herself.

Manson feels helpless as he listens to Skelter finish up telling him the complete story of her most recent situation. She tells him every detail from start to finish. She also tells him all the problems it has caused for her and the many innocent people around her. Manson is the only person that she feels she can say this to.

None of the people around her, would she ever admit this to. With Manson, she knows she can be herself. Also, she hopes by keeping it real with him, he will be able to give her the advice she needs as far as how to move from here on out. He's always been a mentor to her and she will never let her pride get in the way of his advice.

"I ain't gone hold you," she says with her eyes locked into his. "You are the first person I admitted this to. Every day I wish I wouldn't have made that move. But I know what's done is done and I can't take it back. Like, I got all them units and can barely move them because all the shit that been going on. Right now, I'm sitting on close to a quarter million in cash and I can't even enjoy it."

Manson is shocked by the fact that she sounds as if she feels like she's not deserving of all that has come her way. "I will be the first to tell you that I stepped in way over my head," Skelter admits. "I don't know how this shit gone end but I plan to die fighting. I refuse to let them catch me lunching."

Manson shows sign of worry and compassion on his face as he thinks of the right words to say to her. "First, let me say I commend you for pulling off a caper of that magnasize," he says. He means magnitude but yet another effect of the medicine. Even smaller words he's forgotten. His vocabulary has taken just as much of a beating as he has.

"But, what did you expect from this? Did you think there would be no consequences? Or were you just not thinking at all?"

"Of course I was thinking. I never make a move without thinking. I just thought I covered all my tracks."

Manson nods his head slowly. "First thing I'm gone need you to do is get you, your sister, and the baby out of Trenton and just lay low for a minute."

Skelter's stubbornness presents itself. "Yeah, I plan to get out of the city but I ain't gone go in hiding. I never hid and I never will! I ain't letting nobody run me away from home, fuck that!"

"What you mean, you ain't going in hiding? This ain't the time for no dumb ass pride!" Manson's aura transitions quickly. "That pride will get everybody killed. I listened to you and all I hear is selfishness. Seems like you're only worried about yourself. Your sister found a way out and trying to be there for her daughter and all you see is he took her away from you?" he asks in disbelief.

"You want her with you and risk her daughter losing her? When the hell did you become that selfish? And, you're so selfish that you would rather stay in the city and lose your life just so people can never say that you got ran out that city? You don't see that as selfish? What about me, your sister, your niece and anybody else who loves you and need you?"

Skelter has been broken down. She can't remember the last time that she's cried but whenever it was, she's sure she didn't cry this hard. She cries tears of pain, pain that goes back over twenty something years. She cries with no shame. Manson is the only person in the world that she will cry in front of and he's the only person that could make her cry like this.

Manson lowers his tone. "You my motherfucking baby. If something happen to you out there and me being here not able to defend you, that would crush the hell out of me." Tears now build up in Manson's eyes. "I already know how this shit gone go. Right now the whole city is about to go against you," he whispers.

"You touched one motherfucker they all loved. You touched another motherfucker they all feared. Now both of those sides will be working against you. And them Dominicans don't have to be the one who bust the move. Somebody close is going to give you up. Trust me when I tell you, the next move will be for them Dominicans to snatch somebody up and they will put the pressure on them until they give you up. Trust me on that!"

MEDFORD NEW JERSEY

Twenty-five minutes away from Camden, and still in New Jersey yet the cities are so completely different. In fact, Medford is nothing like city life. Both are total opposites. Medford is farmland, no different from the plantations in Alabama. Country life that one would never believe exists in New Jersey and is probably one of the reasons why Jersey is named the Garden State.

An old plantation style house sits on acres and acres of farmland. Not another house in sight for many miles. Behind the house is a barn, old and barely standing. The smell of burning fire is in the air and with no neighbors to smell it, it goes undetected. Inside the barn, a huge steel basin has fire rippling violently from it. Over the fire Bleek hangs from a shower rod, completely naked. His feet dangle just a few inches from the flaming fire. His soles are burning hot. He dangles over the fire like a Rotisserie chicken.

Quabo, Tortura and a few other men stand around the fire, watching it all play out. Bleek has been hanging over this fire since last night when he was captured. They left him out in the barn alone until right now. Tortura believes by flame broiling him over night he will be more than willing to cooperate.

Bleek is sweating bullets form the heat. His feet are swollen and hot. His heart pounds with fear. His arm sockets are swollen and painful from hanging but his arms are numb from the blood rushing to his shoulders. This is like nothing he's ever experienced.

Tortura approaches him from one side while another man approaches form the opposite side. The man on the opposite side holds a huge dagger in his hand. He raises the dagger upward near the rope that holds Bleek onto the shower rod. Tortura holds a paper up to Bleek's face. The paper has a picture of Skelter.

"No time for games," Tortura says calmly. "I'm asking you one time and if you don't answer, my friend will cut the ropes and you will fall into the pit of this fire. You will burn alive, hell on earth," he says with a satanic smile. Tortura pulls the tape from Bleek's mouth so he can speak. "Where is she?"

"I don't know," Bleek says loud and clearly.

"*Corta las cuerdas* (cut the rope)," Tortura says, before turning around and walking away.

The man holds the knife to the rope and before he can cut, Bleek shouts out. "I don't know where she is, but I know who does!"

Tortura turns around. He smiles. "Ok, now we are talking. I was hoping you didn't cooperate. I really wanted to smell your flesh burn." He walks over to Bleek. "Talk to me—and fast—or I will roast you like a pig."

FORT DIX

"Trust me," Manson says. "The walls are going to close in on you. Do as I say and you will be ok. Listen and listen carefully. You listening?"

Skelter nods her head. "Yes, I'm listening," she says humbly.

"Go up to my city, Newark," he says. "Do you remember the Crip kid, Vito?"

"Yes," she replies.

"Okay, go up there and find him. You may not remember exactly how to get to his area but I believe once you get there you will be familiar. I need you to get to him and give him my phone number. I got a jack in here that I will give you the number to. Tell him to call me and I will take it from there."

Skelter is confused. She can't believe that Manson is asking her to link up with a Crip. She knows how much he hates the other side and feels maybe the medicine has him really tripping. "You want me to link up with a crab?" Skelter asks.

"Yes, it's the only choice we have right now. Our line polluted. Not one motherfucker I can trust with your life. On the real I'm going to discontinue the whole line and start a whole new one, eventually. And on a bigger note, I been in **communversation** with the head Blue dude and we are in negotiations about something big, real big.

Skelter's heart sinks every time he uses a word wrong. She turns away from him to prevent him from seeing the look on her face. "Like, we talking about putting together a line of our own. Like nothing to do with Cali. A Jersey movement and we stretch out on some whole East Coast shit. He got the power to do it. But that's for another conversation," he says not wanting to get too deep into it right now. "So, like I said, go and find the kid and get me in touch with him. You do that and I will take it from there."

Manson stares through Skelter. "I swear to God I'm glad you got to me just in time. Another week or so may have been too late. You good now though," he claims with confidence. "Get to the boy Vito and I got it from here."

20

NORTHERN STATE PRISON

PEBBLES SITS IN the visiting hall across from Baby Manson. All of the attention in the room seems to be on her. The inmates all watch her with lust while the wives and girlfriends of those inmates watch her hatefully. She can see the arguments being brewed up around her and because of her.

She enjoys the attention while Baby Manson hates very second of it. His jealousy over his mother is like the jealousy of an insecure man over his woman. He's been like this since a small child. They say a boy's first love is his mother and he always proved it to be true. Even as a child he was overprotective over her and would stand in between her and any man who tried to approach her. Nothing has changed in his adult years. It's only gotten more intense.

"I spoke to Jay last night," Baby Manson says. A huge smile spreads across his face. "Nigga crazy, talking about you looking like a whole snack. I told him don't make me kill his ass," he says jokingly.

Pebbles becomes slightly uncomfortable, yet she blushes. "He told you that?"

"Yeah, he was just bugging though. He know better. Look at you like his mother."

Pebbles would hate to tell him what happened and change the dynamics of their lifelong friendship. She also knows James may be killed in the process. Just another secret she will possibly take to her grave. She has so many of them.

"That's a good, good nigga there," he says as he thinks of his best friend in the world. His eyes brush across the room and collide with the eyes of an inmate a few tables over. The inmate can't seem to keep his eyes off Pebbles. Baby Manson's smile is replaced with a scowl. "Fuck you looking at," Baby Manson mumbles. The man reads his lips and turns away quickly.

"What's up?" Baby Manson hears a voice pass their table. He looks up, and to his surprise, it's Shakir. He looks at Pebbles with a familiar look in his eyes. Baby Manson looks over to Pebbles who is obviously uncomfortable.

"Hey," she says rather casually before looking away.

Baby Manson watches Shakir as he makes his way over to the table where his visitor is awaiting. The beautiful girl looks young enough to be his daughter but the energy in between them tells otherwise. Jealousy spreads across Pebbles's face and she can't hide it. Baby Manson senses the weird energy coming from her.

"You know that nigga?"

She waves her hand. "From years ago," she says. "I went to elementary school with him," she says as if he has no meaning in her life. "You know him?"

"I seen him around once or twice," he says. "I don't know him though."

Pebbles sits quietly, hoping he will say more. She feels now is the perfect time to break it all down to him. She watches as Baby Manson stares over at Shakir with hatred. She thinks of the words to say to stop any future problem they may have. She wonders if maybe she should've introduced him to Baby Manson as a childhood friend of hers. Maybe then he would respect Shakir on the strength of her.

She had plans of telling him all about Shakir, until the other day. Finding out that Big Manson is alive changed her plans. She's already decided to continue on with the lie that she's been living the past 21 years. It hurts her to do this, just as it always has but she believes telling the truth now will only make matters worse for everybody.

She exhales a long wind of air. "I have something to tell you," she says as she grabs his hand. The Correction Officer walks over and without saying a word she knows to take her hand off of him. She rolls her eyes with attitude as she removes her hand from his.

"Tell me," he demands. "What's up? Everything alright?" he asks anxiously.

She quickly thinks of the best way to break this down to him. "I got a call from Tony the attorney the other day. We met and..."

A spark lights up in Baby Manson's eyes. "Y'all hooked up?" he asks with a smile. Baby Manson admired Tony from the first time he met him. His style and demeanor was like no other man he ever met. His name rings bells in the prison system like a God. This is the only man that he would be happy if his mother hooked up with. In fact, it would be an honor to him if she did.

"No, boy," she says brushing off the idea as if she has never dreamed of it. "I don't really know how to say this."

"Just say it Ma. Damn, you're killing me."

"Your fa – " She stops from guilt. "Manson is alive."

"What? Ma, you tripping," he says in total disbelief.

"I'm not. I seen him with my own eyes. We went to Fort Dix and I sat and talked to him."

Baby Manson is speechless. "But," he says with no words to follow.

"It was all bullshit. The Feds never killed him. It was all a lie. They had him out in Colorado all this time."

"Alive?" This is the only word that he can force out of his mouth.

"Yes, but he's not the same. The attorney said he will be fine though."

"What you mean he's not the same?"

"His mind not the same. They've drugged and beat him and it's taken toll."

Baby Manson's heart sinks. He thinks of the men that he's seen during his prison bid who have been through the same thing and the effects it has had on them. He quickly pictures his father, his idol, walking around as a '730.' His heart shatters into pieces and the tears dripping down his face is evident proof of that.

Tears pour down her face as well. Seeing her son cry always breaks her heart. She clasps his hands again with no regard for the officer who is watching over her them. "This my son, not my damn man," she barks to the officer.

Baby Manson wipes the evidence of crying from his face yet he wants to break down. The last thing he wants or needs is for these men to see him crying. His sadness turns into rage. He snatches away from her and stands up.

"I got to go, Ma," he says as he kicks the chair from behind him. "I have to let this shit digest." The pain he feels for his father builds a rage inside that he wants to take out on someone, anyone. "I'll call you," he says not able to look her in the eyes. He steps away from her with no further conversation.

"Rahmid," she calls out, attracting the attention of everyone.

Baby Manson stomps across the room like an angry child. The tears drip down her face as she cries with no shame. She doesn't notice the attention on her because all of hers is on her son. She prays he doesn't let his anger get the best of him and he get himself into trouble. All the years of thinking his father, or who he believed his father to be, was dead and now to hear differently has to be mind blowing. She just hopes he can cope with it.

Pebbles stands up from the table and walks out of her way to pass Shakir. She stares coldly at the young girl in her passing. Shakir watches her closely. He knows her like a book and can tell when she's on her shit. He knows all about her jealous streak.

"Call me asap," she says spitefully. She looks the girl over before rolling her eyes. She just wants him to be as uncomfortable with the situation as she was. And he is. She's sure Shakir has some explaining to do. Not only does he watch her leave the room but so does everyone else. The attention doesn't bother her at all. Actually, she lives for it. She switches harder, putting on more of a show for the spectators.

21

NEW JERSEY TURNPIKE

THE HIGHWAY TRAFFIC is light for now and won't pick up for another 2 hours once the afternoon rush hour kicks in. In the middle lane, zipping a few miles over the speed limit is an all-black Brinks armored truck. 25,000 pounds of steel truck bounces awkwardly along the highway. On the inside of the truck it's expected to be guards armed with semiautomatic handguns, guarding hundreds of thousands of dollars. Instead, inside there are 8 criminals armed with semiautomatic weapons. These criminals are known as The Federation.

Maurice sits in the passenger's seat, hiding behind dark windows. He bought this armored truck years ago and rarely has ever used it. Its sole purpose is for war. He has a make-believe company logo posted all over the truck as a decoy. This truck is big enough to hold his entire Federation. Equipped with stash boxes to hide their guns and over 30 peek holes for the guns to be inserted for firing. This armored truck can sit in the middle of a battlefield and not a one of them will have to step foot out of it. They can win a war from inside.

Maurice dials the number on his phone with fury. He listens impatiently as the phone rings. "Pick up the phone," he shouts as he dials once again.

NAPA VALLEY, CALIFORNIA/NAPA VALLEY WINERY

The big and beautiful cottage which was built back in 1735 is still as luxurious as it was back then. The cottage is surrounded by over 250 acres of vineyard. Juicy grapes hang from vines everywhere. In the middle of the vineyard, Tony and Miranda appear to be the models of a wine commercial or advertisement.

Tony's crisp white linen dress shirt is wrinkled with personality. His white linen slacks are rolled up to his ankles stylishly. Miranda is dressed in a beautiful sunflower yellow, flowing sundress. Their matching Panama straw hats make them mesh as a couple beautifully.

Both of them are bare-feet, squashing grapes with each step they take. Grape juice squirts as each toe bursts a grape. The ground blanketed with grape peelings, causes them to slide. Tony holds Miranda's hand tightly as she steps on grapes meticulously crushing each one in her leg's reach. She enjoys the feeling of the grapes bursting in between her toes and sticky grape juice coating the bottom of her feet.

Tony had a free day with no appointments, so he decided to spend some quality time with his lover. Spontaneity led him to Teterboro Airport where he got into his G4 with California as the destination. They arrived here just in time for lunch where they ate at the most intimate family owned Italian Restaurant. Only 8 tables in the entire restaurant and 7 of those were vacant, thanks to Tony.

He paid to have the restaurant shut down for lunch, just for them. After lunch they ended up here in the winery where they tasted every red wine in the building. Both of them are feeling quite tipsy so treading grapes is easy. Their stumbling makes for better treading. The more they stumble, the more grapes they crush.

The constant ringing of Tony's phone agitates him. He stops short and looks to see who is calling him off the hook as such. He sees it's Maurice, who never ever calls him like this. Tony looks to Miranda. "Mama, I have to take this call. Sorry," he says with sincerity. He quickly answers the call. "Yo."

"Yo!" Maurice shouts with rage. "We got an issue in Philly. Shit crazy! I just got the call that motherfuckers done came on the site and forced everybody off. They not letting them work! And they getting violent!"

"Huh?" Tony asks in total disbelief.

"Yeah, like a hundred motherfuckers out there right now. I'm on my way there as we speak. I'm gone tell you like this, these motherfuckers done got up under my skin. They been trying to ruffle my feathers and now they ruffled!"

"Moe, be easy, please," Tony begs. "We got a nice situation going on down there. Don't do nothing stupid."

"I'm only gone get as stupid as they want to get!" Maurice shouts.

"Moe, please just wait for me. I will be home this evening."

"We don't have until this evening. By the time you get here I will have situated it already. I will keep you posted!"

"Moe," Tony says before he gets the dial tone.

Miranda looks to Tony with pity. She can sense that something is wrong. "Everything ok?"

Tony hates to admit this because Miranda warned him about getting into business with his drug dealing clients. He never listens and he always ends up behind the 8-ball. He knows how violent Maurice can be and he's one of the only ones who knows where Maurice's *Off* switch is. Only problem is, he has to be there in person to hit that switch. With him not being present, there's no telling what Maurice will do.

"Babe, is everything okay?"

"Yes," Tony replies.

PHILADELPHIA

The armored truck cruises along Columbus Boulevard. To the left of them is the Delaware River. Beautiful condominiums and tall buildings all line up on this block. What should be fast moving traffic is bumper to bumper traffic on both sides.

Traffic is backed up for 3 blocks. Maurice looks up ahead and notices the reason for the backed-up traffic is the crowds of people that

surround his property. As he looks at the strip mall, which is supposed
to be under construction, not being constructed, he becomes livid. He's
angry enough to do something stupid but he's business smart enough
to refrain. He would hate to destroy all they have built and to mess up
what they plan on building.

"Yo," he says to the driver. "Can't pull up in this truck and let people see us get out of it. Pull around the back block and park on that
One-Way."

Maurice and his men are surprised to see over 50 men pacing all
around the strip-mall. Some are posted along the curb while others are
floating in the parking lot. Seventy-five percent of the men that are
out there are red hair, freckle-faced, Irish men. The other twenty-five
percent may not have red hair or freckles but it's clearly visible that
they are Irish.

When the worker called Maurice and told him what was going on, he mentioned gangsters. This is not what they expected. He
was expecting what he knows gangsters to be, black men with durags,
white tee-shirts and sagging jeans. What is here before him is a bunch
of Irish men in white t-shirts, blue jeans and Redwing work boots.

They all seem to have the same, slick back, under cut with a fade
and cinched beard, just the shades of their hair are different. Some
sandy brown, some jet-black and some ginger red. Every one of these
men are equipped with bazooka sized arms and cinderblock sized
chests. All of them look freshly released from prison. He thinks maybe
this is the Irish mafia that he has heard so much about in the movies.
Whatever it is doesn't matter. They are getting in the way of him making money and he must remove them.

The armored truck is parked and Maurice and his guys all strap
up. They conceal their weapons before getting out. They walk a half of
a block in. As they reach the corner Maurice sees his workers sitting in
the cut, across the street. Fear and despair on their faces.

Ten deep, The Federation stands in a huddle at the corner. Maurice's construction crew runs over happy to be rescued. The foreman in
charge speaks. "I'm glad you're here. As you can see, they won't let us
work."

As the foreman is talking, a short, frail, well-dressed Irish man
approaches. The man, dressed in a 3-piece suit wingtip shoes, and an

applejack hat, looks like a blast from the past, something from the 1920's. As he's walking, he digs into his inside pocket and pulls out a clock that hangs on a string. He muscles his way into the huddle and stands between the foreman and Maurice.

He stares into Maurice's eyes as he places his watch back into his pocket. Three of Maurice's men already have the drop on the man, just in case he pulls anything out of that pocket besides his hand.

"You're the man in charge?" the Irish man asks.

"Yeah," Maurice replies angrily.

"Brick City Development Group?"

"Yes, that's me and my partners," Maurice replies.

"Brick City is Newark, New Jersey, correct?"

Here we go with this geographical shit again, Maurice thinks to himself. "Yeah, yeah, what's up? Who are you and why are you standing in front of me?"

"Strike one," the man says with a smile. "You step into a city and start developing, without knowing the key players of that city. Who am I? I'm a very powerful man. I can make you or I can break you. There's no man in all of Philadelphia more powerful than me. I stretch out all over the city of Philadelphia, but South Philly is my playground," the man says arrogantly.

"You're doing so much development in my playground," the man says as he points to the strip mall. This strip mall has the storefronts on the lower level and ten condominiums on top of the second level. "Over eighty properties attached to Brick City Development. That's a lot of work. You're generating a lot of jobs but that doesn't help my community."

"I don't owe you no fucking explanations but we've helped the community," Maurice says. "Over half my construction crew is from here. We hired from within the city!"

"But you haven't helped *my community*. I checked over all your jobs and not one Irishmen has ever been employed by you. That right there is the reason we stand here in such disarray."

Maurice has to refrain from choking the man. "Listen, I don't know who the hell you are or who you think you are but you ain't stopping nothing over here. My crew is going back to work and anybody who get in the way of that will have problems."

"No, you listen. I don't know how things work in your Brick City but here in South Philly, I call the shots. I can pull the plug on every investment you have developing. If you don't believe me I can show you proof. After I unplug your jobs, I will replug them for you just to show you my power. But then I will want more from you. If I have to go through all that work to prove to you who I am, the playing field will be different at that point. Right now, all I want from you is to put some Irishmen on your jobs and let my people eat with you. No way in the world should all this building be going up under my nose without my people eating with you."

"This sounds like extortion if you ask me," Maurice says.

"You sound like a smart man, if you ask me," the man replies with sarcasm.

Maurice is pissed and shocked at the same time. This is the first time that he's ever been approached with extortion on any level. He's ready to slap the man silly and continue on with their work but he's not sure what damage that will do to his brand. He realizes this is a different level of the game right here and he should step back but his ego is wired differently.

"Listen, I ain't about to be extorted and I hire who I want to hire on my jobs."

"Good, so, hire some Irishmen."

Maurice looks to his foreman. "Y'all go on back in there and get to work."

The crew of workers get up and they walk nervously toward the strip mall. The man shouts to his men in his native tongue. Maurice has no clue what he just said but he sees an aggression on these men that clearly shows they are ready for action. The Irishmen come from every direction and parade behind the construction crew.

"Trust me, this is not what you want," the man threatens.

"Don't tell me what I want," Maurice replies.

"Please, don't make me exert my power," the man says with sincerity.

Maurice looks to his men who are all waiting for his green light to do what they came to do and that is go to war. Maurice then looks to the Irishman. "No, don't make me exert mine."

Maurice's phone rings, breaking the tension. Maurice looks down and sees Tony's name on the display. He answers quickly. "Out here right now. We on our way back to work. Fuck the dumb shit," Maurice says as he looks down at the Irishman.

"Little Irish motherfucker right here talking some Irish Mafia, bullshit that I don't want to hear. I don't know his fucking name and I don't care. No, no need for you to talk to him. Nothing to talk about. We are going back to work and anybody who get in the way of that, then fuck it, it is what it is. Man, fuck that. It started on the street so it ends on the street." Maurice sighs with frustration.

Tony always manages to talk him down. "Here," he says as he passes his phone to the Irishman.

The man snatches the phone. "Hello, McCaulley speaking."

"Attorney, Tony Austin," Tony says loud and clear. Founder of Austin Developmental Group in conjunction with Brick City Developing.

"Tony Austin," the man says, disregarding the attorney part all together. "At the time of this conversation are you speaking as the owner of the development company or are you speaking as the attorney representing the development group?"

"Both," Tony says sternly.

"Well, I will tell you like this," he says as he looks Maurice up and down with a smirk. "I hate involving attorneys in my business. They make a bigger mess of things. So, if you as the owner of the development group would like to come meet with me and discuss our possibilities, then I will kindly allow you to get back to developing. We must sit down and come up with some terms."

Tony holds the phone in silence. For the first time in a long time he's speechless with no come back whatsoever. The level of arrogance this man exerts he has to have some power. Tony is well versed enough as a businessman to know better than to challenge this man without knowing the reach that he may have. "In two days, I can sit with you."

"Ok, fine," the man replies. "Two days from now at this exact hour," he says before ending the call. He presses the numbers on Maurice's phone and locks his name and number in. He passes the phone over to Maurice without even looking at him. He places two fingers in his mouth and whistles loudly. He waves his men on.

He looks over to Maurice. "See how a simple phone call got you two extra days of work? That's the same way a simple phone call on my end can get this job and any other job you have terminated. See you on Friday at the meeting. The dress code is business casual. More business than casual," he says with sarcasm. "No need for a suit but at least put a nice shirt on," he says in a demanding tone. "Good day men!"

22

TRENTON

THE DODGE DURANGO is parked in the Home Depot parking lot, blended in with all the many vehicles. Skelter and Blue Blood occupy the back seats. Skelter listens closely as Blue Blood tells the story of the murder of Triple Threat. He paints the picture so vividly like a master storyteller.

"I hits the nigga, *boom, boom, boom* and we blow the joint," he says very hyped up. "I ain't gone lie though, nigga was prepared for anything. Had all types of guns in that motherfucker. If anyway we would've came in there lacking, shit would've went crazy." He changes his whole tone. "What's the word though? What niggas saying about it?"

Skelter displays a careless attitude. "How I'm hearing, like niggas sick out there, you feel me?" Mad different stories of shit that ain't nowhere near true. As of right now our names ain't been mentioned but I'm sure they will be. No matter what the fuck happens they always find a way to put my name in this shit. Never fails."

"Fuck them," Blue Blood says as he snatches the shopping bag from the floor and drops it on Skelter's lap. "That's money for a joint and a half, forty-eight stacks. I blew through that in two days. This shit coming like the 90's," he says happily. "Oh," he says as he holds up a smaller shopping bag. He hands it over to her.

Skelter looks into the bag and sees neat stacks of money. "What's this for?"

"From the other night," Blue Blood replies. "Boy had over eighty racks in the crib. Mad bricks of dope and some smoke. We bust the bread down the middle and I kept the smoke. I let him have that dope. I don't need that shit leading back to me. That's half of my score right there."

A smile stretches across Skelter's face. This is one of the things she has always admired about Blue Blood; his honor. His loyalty and honor to her is why no matter what she gets her hands on, she always makes it her business to go to him first. He also does the same with her. She never thought twice about what could be in Triple Threat's house, mainly because she now has her own money. The average person wouldn't be willing to cut her in being that she didn't go in with him but not Blue Blood. He has always been a different breed.

"Nah, I'm good," she denies. "Keep it for all the times you held me down while I was out this motherfucker starving." She drops the bag onto his lap.

"Nah," he denies. "We don't do that," he says as drops the bag onto her lap.

She digs into the bag and quickly counts out the 20 stacks. She then separates 5 of them and extends them to him. "Alright then, I will give my Godsons five apiece to hold them down. Nobody ain't been able to eat since all this shit started. My five, you can keep. Just hold it for me, if I ever need you," she says with a smirk. "Let me get on out of here. We need to jump on this highway real quick."

"Bet," Blue Blood replies. He opens the door to make his exit but he stops short. "Oh yeah, I forgot to tell you the boy Rick hit me on my way here, telling me what he heard and this that and the third. He said he overheard Jubilee running off at the mouth and saying he need to rap to you. Said he was gone hit me up to set up the meeting between y'all. I'm telling you, we need to go there and have the sit-down on our own time. If we wait for them to set the meeting up, it's gone look crazy on our end. I think we need to get on this immediately."

"I will think about it," Skelter says with no interest at all. "Hit you when I get back."

ONE HOUR LATER
NEWARK

In the center court of the Project buildings it's as busy as an airport. Addicts come and go consistently. Dealers gambling as they drink and indulge in their drug of choice. The neighborhood children play around and in between all the action. Lots of business is done in the wide open but there's even more business being conducted inside the buildings. The center court is free for all but the buildings are territorial. Certain dealers have a building all to themselves and making an unwarranted sell inside their building can start a war.

For the most part the dope on the outside is the garbage dope and the dealers who sell the garbage dope are like the stragglers and the bottom feeders. Paper-heads, who can get high off anything keep these dealers in business. Inside the buildings are the higher echelon dealers with the high-quality dope. The dopefiends who prefer quality dope know exactly where to go to find it and they know which building has what dope name/stamp. The court is like the dumpster of the dope game so you can either roll around in the dumpster and pick up some garbage, or step into the buildings and elevate your high.

A chunky middle-aged man, shabby in appearance exits the building. He stops and leans against the building as he tries hard to catch his breath. He uses one hand to fan himself. He's faint. He takes a step and falls on his face. Two dope fiends practically step over him to get into the building and two others step around him. Another one exits the building with his nose buried in a bag of dope. With no sense of compassion, not a one of them stop to check on him.

Finally, one of the dealers run over and come to his aid. He leans over and shakes him as if to wake him up. "Skinless," he says as she shakes him roughly. "Skinless," he says shaking him harder.

Skinless is the name all the dealers around here know the man as. They call him Skinless because the whole right side of his face is patchy and scaly. Years ago, he worked as a laborer dropping tar and an accident on a roof while he was high caused him to burn his face with hot tar. Only in the hood does the dealers make up names for their customers and the customers answer to those names no matter how disrespectful or inconsiderate they may be.

A crowd of dealers form a huddle around them. "Skinless." He shakes the man by his arm and when he stops the man's arm flops onto his chest.

An older female, dopefiend runs over. This woman is dressed in a filthy nurse uniform and dirty rundown nurse shoes. She's had on this same uniform for the past 2 months and the dirt stains are a clear indication of that. The black headscarf on her head is so greasy and filthy it looks like leather. The scarf is to hide the nappy, matted down bush of hair she has on her head. Naps and peas lead a trail down her neck, connecting like Tic Tac Toe.

"Watch out, let me work," says the woman. This woman is a staple here in the Projects that everyone knows as Head Nurse. Over 25 years ago she lost her job as a nurse due to her heroin addiction. She believes she's still a nurse and has a chance of getting her job back.

Ironically, anytime any trauma or emergency situation goes on, she just happens to be around. Times that men have been shot, she tries her best to keep them comfortable until the paramedics arrive. She knows just what to do. Thanks to her a few men's lives have been saved. She also writes illegal scripts as well. Head Nurse writes a great deal of the scripts for all the pills that the dealers around here sell and get high off.

She's also known to have the best bedside manners around. Not only does she know how to comfort the sick or wounded, she's known to comfort healthy men as well. Word on the street is that she has the best head in the business. She's said to take her false teeth out and go to work. Her nursing skills and her head game is how she has earned the name Head Nurse. So many of the young thugs and drug dealers had their first sexual favor from her, dating back to 25 years ago. Here today and with her being close to 60 years old, she's still breaking young dealer's virginity.

Head Nurse grabs the stethoscope which is dangling from her neck. She places the buds into her ear quickly. She places the other end to the side of the man's neck. Her face drops sadly. "He's not breathing," she says nervously.

She quickly gets onto her knees and places both hands on his chest. With force she pushes on the man's chest in desperate attempt to pump life back into him. She pushes and pushes and places her ear next to his mouth. She shakes her head in despair. "I can't bring him back." One thing she hates is to lose a patient.

"Another one," a young man sings in D.J. Khaled's voice. All the dealers around laugh with no compassion for Skinless. "That's that Death Before Dishonor," the man says with no compassion at all. He looks on the ground next to the man and where a bag of dope lies right at his head. The young man picks up the bag and reads the stamp. He holds it in the air for his friends to see. "Told you, Death Before Dishonor."

The Death Before Dishonor stamp has claimed 5 lives in the past 3 weeks. Dope cut with fentanyl has been causing overdose cases all over the city. Instead of dope addicts staying away from the fentanyl cut dope, they seem to come looking for it. It's as if the more deaths it causes the more they want it.

A smooth and strong statured man steps out of the building and walks toward the crowd. Walking on the opposite sides of him are 2 men the complete opposite of himself. Both are brolic and rough around the edges. They walk in stride with him, but a few steps ahead of him, guarding his every step.

Head Nurse looks up to the man with tears in her eyes. "Vito, I tried my best but I lost him." Vito knows his stamp has claimed another life. With law officials now charging the dealers with murder when an addict overdoses off the fentanyl, it's always in the back of his head. The show must go on though.

Vito whispers to the man on his side and the man leans over and digs into the dead man's pockets. He quickly retrieves 3 bags of dope. The last thing he needs is for them to find his dope stamp on the man when they find his body. He then gives the group of men a single nod.

Four of the men surround the corpse. Two grab a leg and two grab an arm and they struggle to lift the body from the ground. They carry the body across the court like it's an old piece of furniture. Three other men lag behind them. Once at the end of the field, far in the corner they stop at a dumpster. The seven of them with great teamwork lift the man high and toss him over and into the dumpster. The body flops

BLOCK PARTY 666

onto the pile of garbage and lays there just as garbage. The men all walk away ready to carry on with business.

All eyes are on the Dodge Durango which is creeping into the courts. All the shooters present assume their positions. If by chance the occupants of the Durango are here to violate they will never make it out of here alive. They will be ambushed from every side.

Skelter peeps the set-up in process. She rolls the back window down and waves both hands high in the air, letting them know she comes in peace. "We don't want no trouble," she says to the crowd of men closer to her window. "I'm looking for Vito."

A young man creeps from the back of the crowd with his gun drawn. He peeks through the opened window, trying to see inside the rest of the vehicle. "Who you?"

"Tell him Skelter from Trenton looking for him. He probably won't remember my name but he will know my face. Tell him I met him back when he met Black Manson." The man nudges a kid standing next to him and the kid runs off into the building. The kid exits the building just as fast as he entered it. Vito steps out of the building. This time he has more men with him, three on both sides of him. All six of the men have guns exposed. Vito stares into the truck with squinted eyes.

Skelter pulls her hood off her head and reveals her face. "You get out and tell him to park over there," Vito demands.

"Nah, fuck that," Skelter's Godson whispers to her from the passenger's seat. "We getting out with you."

"No, chill," Skelter replies as she pushes the door open. She gets out and slams the door shut. "Park," she tells her Godson. She walks toward Vito and his men courageously as everyone studies her closely.

The closer she gets the more familiar she becomes to Vito. His posture eases yet his men stand the same. "Oh, what's up, Shorty?" Vito says flirtatiously.

"Skelter," she says coldly. She extends her hand as she gets closer. They lock hands with a firm grip.

"What brings you to me?" Vito asks.

"I come here to bring you a message from my big bruh, Black Manson."

113

"Black Manson is dead. Don't bring me no message from no dead nigga," he says jokingly.

"Black Manson ain't dead," she says without a smile. She finds his words disrespectful. "All that was bullshit. He wants me to give you his number or give him yours so y'all can rap."

"Nah, I'm good. Shit sounding type weird. Y'all already known to be moving around with rats and now this. I'm good, Shorty."

"Skelter," she says again. "Listen, I never moved around with no rats. That ain't what I do. I'm here to bring you the message. If you hit bruh, I'm sure it will be beneficial for you. I know for a fact that bruh solid as a rock. I put my life on it and if anyway he isn't you can take my life."

Vito nods as he reads the genuineness in her eyes. "And I will. Give me the number," he says as he pulls out his phone. "On God, if this shit go sideways any type of way, I will find you and take your life."

Skelter puffs her chest out. "When it comes to Big Bruh, if any way it goes sideways, you won't have to come looking for me to take my life. I will come to you and give you my life."

23

BABY MANSON STARES off into a daze. In his daydream he lives the life he always dreamed of living. He's caught up in Lala land before snapping out of it. Right now he feels as if all his wildest dreams are now possible. As he looks down at the 400 grams of heroin in his hand, he feels like his dreams are now in reach.

He's calculated his total gross as a quarter million dollars once he moves all the dope. Based on the amount of time it took to move the first 100 grams, he estimates his total time for this load to be a few months. Hopefully with his new helping hands it will be sooner. He's eager to get the dope into the Lunatic's hands and see how he works.

He's really starting to believe that jail is the best thing that could have happened to him. Because of prison he's gotten his mind right and thinking of money. While on the streets he never really focused on money because his mother gave him all he ever wanted like a spoiled brat. All he could think of doing while having on the latest sneakers and hottest clothes, was to get into dumb trouble.

Now his mind is on becoming rich. He has no room in his mind for foolishness. He has a few more years left on this bid and he promises himself that after this bid is over he will go home as a millionaire. He also promises himself that this will be his last bid ever.

GYMNASIUM

The Imaam stands at the front of the gym preaching his sermon to the lowest amount of presence ever. Less than 20 men are in attendance. Only a few men yet he speaks as if he is in front of a packed arena. It bothers him that so many of the inmates have chosen to stand along with Smith on this matter. All he can do is pray that Smith's heart is softened and that God guides him to the straight path.

"There will always be others who will make the claim that he became Muslim because he was locked up," the Imaam says with a big grin. "Have they ever thought that Allah may have brought them to jail so they would become Muslim?" He pauses, allowing his message to digest. "Allah makes no mistakes and maybe Allah knows that man would never sit down and receive the message unless he is forced to sit down. Allah says in the glorious Quran that he will bring you back to the place where you remember him the most."

All the inmates listen with their undivided attention except for one. The homie Lunatic sits blended in with the brothers amongst the ranks. He's Muslim but he just considers himself not on his Deen. He hasn't been to Jumu'ah once in all of his 4 years here. His only reason here today is to bring a message to someone.

Minutes later as the sermon concludes and all the brothers are lined up, praying shoulder to shoulder, foot to foot, Lunatic stands at the very end of the row. He goes through the motions but truthfully not a word of what is being said is sinking into his ears or his heart. His mind is on the dope that he's about to get his hands on later today.

"Ameen," he sings along with the congregation. His voice is the loudest of them all for he's the happiest one that the sermon is finally over.

As most of the inmates rush over to shake hands and greet the Imaam, Lunatic catches up with the man he came here to see. They walk side by side in equal stride. They don't greet each other nor look at each other. This man is one of Smith's spies. Smith sends this man to Jumu'ah as his eyes and ears so he can know what is going on. He also uses him as the messenger to get any message to the other wing if need be.

Lunatic whispers out of the side of his mouth. "Tell bruh, everything is everything. Shit going as planned. I got him right where I need him."

Lunatic is speaking of none other than Baby Manson. Although Baby Manson is under Lunatic, under the same sect, Lunatic has chosen Smith over him. What Baby Manson doesn't know is all of this was a big plan to get closer to him. There were sacrificial lambs that were sacrificed without their knowledge.

Once Smith poked up the man that was sent to kill him, he realized he needed another plan. He reached out to Lunatic and the two of them put together a plan. Good Christian was also sent over to touch Baby Manson. They knew when Good Christian was going to make his move because he was instructed on when to make that move. That is how Baby Face Monster was placed at the scene. Baby Face Monster nor Good Christian had a clue it was all a set-up. Both were just following orders from their G, Lunatic. Lunatic masterminded all of this with hopes of getting closer to Baby Manson and it has worked.

"Let him know I have to work this to my advantage and lay my foundation," Lunatic says. "And once I get my feet planted like I need them, consider that done."

24

PHILADELPHIA

TWELVE PLAY LEANS over the rail of the condominium, sort of like on guard. The activity takes place around the spot as usual. The young men carry on with their daily activity as if he's not here. He's figured out how they operate. When one of them is out there alone, they 'Big Bruh, Big Homie, Big Muslim' him with respect but when they all get together in a crowd they don't acknowledge him at all. Once he figured it out, he stopped even responding period. He wants them to clearly see the line that separates respect and disrespect and he wants them to understand that any way they cross that line he has no problem punishing them.

Twelve Play gets an instant attitude when he looks to his left and sees the Dodge Ram bending the corner. This dude, Umar is starting to be a pain in his ass. He comes through sometimes three times a day. He always has the same story of him just checking up on him. Twelve Play has told him many times that he doesn't need any help but that doesn't stop the man from saying it again.

Twelve Play has Umar pegged as a wannabe type of dude who will go to any extent to be down. One thing Umar has proven is he has his hands on everything. He's like the ultimate hustler. Most of the time when he comes through, he has something new up his sleeve.

Overall, he's good to have around. From plumbing work to carpentry work, to light electrical work he does it all. Also, as he's stated, he has connections with the City. Just last week, Inspectors came around pitching a bitch and he just happened to be here at the time. He spit a name out from City Hall and the Inspector eased up off of them. As much as he irks Twelve Play, he's starting to grow on him. Being stuck down here in a land where he knows nobody, the conversation sometimes comes in handy. That is when he's in the mood for it, but today he's not in the mood for it.

The engine roars as the Dodge Ram speeds through the intersection. Umar steers the pick-up wildly into the first open parking space. The way he whips the truck he draws the attention of all the men standing at the curb. He gets out and slams the door. "As Salaamu Alaikum, Akhi!" he yells loudly.

Twelve Play analyzes Umar for a second. He talks like a gangster but one thing Twelve Play learned a long time ago is it's easy to talk like a gangster. Umar moves like a gangster as well. He's from West Philly but he carries it like he's at home comfortably. He leaves his truck running, pulls out wads of money, even leaves lumber in the pick-up while he's been inside the building. He seems to have no worries at all.

"Walaikum As Salaam!" Twelve Play shouts in return.

"Ay Akhi, come here and let me drop a bug in your ear, real quick!"

Twelve Play sighs under his breath before making his way down the stairs. Two men sit shoulder to shoulder on the bottom step. They hear him behind him yet they don't move. Twelve Play refuses to excuse himself for them to get up from somewhere they don't belong. "Yo!"

The men look back at him slowly and take their time getting up. Twelve Play steps over their shoulders with disrespect, not caring where his feet land. One of the men huffs loudly. Twelve Play turns around and looks him up and down.

He stares back at Twelve Play, not backing down until the other young man taps him. "Come on, man." Together they step away from the porch and make their way over to the curb.

Twelve Play continues on to meet Umar in the street behind his truck. They shake hands. Umar grips Twelve Play's hand tightly. "Yo, I just came up on something crazy. You know I always got my hands in something," he says with a smile. "I got Lowes credit. I can get anything no matter what it is. If it's in Lowes I can get it big or small. Hit your peoples and see if they need something. I will take sixty percent of the original price. You can keep the fifteen percent and I will take the forty-five percent. Make a couple dollars for yourself."

"Nah man," Twelve Play denies. "I don't do that. I don't charge my people. They are my brothers."

"I can dig it," Umar says. "But check and see if they need something," he says very anxiously. "Come on Akhi, time is money," he says persistently.

Twelve Play is hesitant. He knows Tony and Maurice have plenty enough money to get whatever they need and don't need to be cutting corners. But hey, he thinks to himself; a penny saved is a penny earned. He dials and waits for Maurice to answer. Maurice answers on the second ring.

"Yo," Maurice says.

"My man here got the Lowes connect. Said anything you need he can get for half price," says Twelve Play.

Maurice translates the message to Tony in the background. Twelve Play can hear Tony talking in the background. "I'm about to put y'all on speaker," Twelve Play says in warning.

"Aye man, what we need ain't no nickel and dime shit," Maurice says. "Let him know we doing big shit. The shit we need ain't a gallon of paint and a carpet."

"You on speaker bruh," Twelve Play says. "He hear you."

"Good," Maurice says. "Check it, shit we need you ain't gone be able to get on one of those little Gift Cards."

"What you need?" Umar asks. "Talk to me. I can get anything."

"I need twenty Hot Tubs for the building over there," Maurice says, believing he's said something impossible.

"Say no more," Umar says.

"The eight seat joints. The ones we need for that building cost 9 grand a piece."

"Ok," Umar says as if Maurice has said nothing at all.

"Yeah, alright," Maurice says. He will believe this when he sees it.

"Give me three days and I will have it. Delivery on me," he adds. "All y'all got to do is have them installed."

"I will tell you like this, if you can get me them tubs for half price I will add a bonus on that for you too."

"Bet. Like I said, give me three days and it's done."

Twelve Play takes the phone off speaker. He's sure Maurice is in as much disbelief as he is. "Yo, I'm gone finish talking to my man. Where you at?"

"Over at this spot called McGillan's Ale House. We will be over there as soon as we done."

"Cool," Twelve Play says before ending the call. Twelve Play looks to Umar. "Yo, you think you gone be able to pull that off? I don't like making promises to my people that can't be delivered. I don't like calling him on no bullshit."

"Akhi, trust me. I will make you a believer." He pauses. "I got you though. I don't play bruh. I'm a man of my word. I'm gone deliver."

"Alright," Twelve Play says, still in disbelief.

"It's still five percent on the table. Forty-five hundred for your pocket, Sheikh."

"Nah, I'm cool. Just keep your word with my brother and that's more than enough for me."

Umar reaches for Twelve Play's hand. "Got you bro. Trust me. I just want to eat with y'all. If I can supply all y'all construction needs at half price, that's a nice plate for me. I'm a hustler baby."

MCGILLAN'S OLD ALE HOUSE

Tony and Maurice sit inside the traditional style Irish Pub. The only black faces in the spot belong to them so they stand out. Although most of the attention is on them, they both sit back cool, calm and overly confident. Their comfort seems to disturb some of the other patrons.

A beautiful young waitress approaches them holding two draft style beers at her chest. Her short haircut is full of big and bouncy curls the color of wheat. Her face covered with freckles makes her look like the poster girl for the Lil Debbie snack cakes. Her perky, cantaloupe sized breast peek from over top, underneath and the sides of the huge mugs of beer that she holds in front of them. The crisp white, ruffled blouse chokes the life out of her boobs. Cleavage spills from her blouse like the foam of the beer spills over the mugs.

"Your mugs are spilling over," Maurice says with a seductive look in his eyes. She looks down at the mugs of beer and her breast, not sure which set of mugs he's referring to. Her cheeks blush a cherry red. She looks away bashfully but appreciative of the comment.

As she plants the beers on the table, she positions herself wherein her breast are in Tony's face but she gives Maurice a close-up of her behind. She's entertaining them both equally. She leans over forward and the mini skirt raises high enough to see her white schoolgirl panties and her lily-white grown woman ass. She looks Tony in the eyes and quickly looks to Maurice, careful not to make him feel left out. "Let me know 'ya need anything else," she says in an Irish accent that both Tony and Maurice find to be sexy. She walks off fast with her skirt bouncing high in the air, white panties showing, vanilla ass jiggling.

"Can't tell me she don't have no Black in her DNA," Maurice says as he studies her curvy and voluptuous booty. He quickly looks away to erase the perverted thoughts from his mind.

"Go on and get her," Tony encourages. "You see how she looked at you. She knows the black man is God," he says jokingly.

"Nah," Maurice denies. "I don't fuck with the Beckys like that. You can have that," he says sternly.

"Oh, prejudice, I see," Tony says with laughter.

"Nah, I'm not prejudice," Maurice claims. "Just preference," he adds. "I rather stick with my own."

"Go on and knock her down one time. Do it for the culture and what they done to our ancestors," Tony says jokingly.

"Nah," Maurice denies sternly. "I'm good."

They look up and the waitress is on her way back over to them. "Look, she coming back for you," Tony teases.

The waitress stands there before them. "Would you like the lunch menu?" she asks. As she stands there they both witness her nipples swell right before their eyes. Her nipple imprints poke their way through the cotton. She looks down and sees them protruding and a look of shame covers her face.

Tony attempts to rescue her from embarrassment. "Not yet, dear," he says. "We are expecting another party."

No sooner than he says that, the expecting party appears at the door. A brolic 6' 4" tall, Irish giant holds the door for McCaulley to enter. He enters, wearing the exact same style outfit as the other day, just in another color. Behind him is another Irish giant. McCaulley looks around and notices the two brown faces immediately. He walks over toward them as his men assume their positions at the table right behind them.

McCaulley takes off his hat, like a gentleman just as he stands before them. "Good day," he says as he extends his hand to Maurice. Maurice stares at his hand before giving him a quick once over. He looks away and lifts his beer to his mouth, leaving McCaulley's hand dangling in the air.

Tony stands up and intervenes. He grabs the man's hand. "Tony Austin," he says proudly.

"McCaulley," McCaulley says even prouder. "It's a pleasure to meet you," he says as he takes a seat. He lays his hat on his lap. "We all are businessmen," he says before looking to Maurice. "Well, at least two of us are," he says with blatant disrespect.

"Listen," Maurice says with aggressiveness. "Before we start this meeting let's get one thing straight. You will not disrespect me and if you do it will take more than those Jolly Green Giants you got over there to get me off your ass."

McCaulley is not the least bit moved by Maurice's threat. "As I was saying," he says to Tony. Clearly, he isn't worried about Maurice. "Time is money and I don't waste much of either one of them. I apologize if my delivery came across as abrasive. I'm no Irish crime boss," he laughs. If you are the intelligent businessman I assume you to be, I'm sure you have done your research on me before coming here. Just as I have done my research on you."

"And you are correct in your assumption," Tony replies.

Tony researched the man thoroughly the past few days and has found out that he isn't just a big mouth. He's a powerful Union Boss who has held a tight grip on all the big construction jobs in the city. He's held this position for 25 years. His Union has over 5,000 members. He also leads the Building Trades Council which has over 70,000 members. All in all, this man is even more powerful than he says he is. He has the power to shut Tony and Maurice down with the blink of an eye. With Tony knowing this he understands he must deal with this man with white gloves on.

"As figured," McCaulley says. "So, being that you have done your research you should know that I'm a fair man who looks out for the best interest of his people. I apologize if my delivery came across as extortion," he says as he looks over to Maurice who looks away from him.

McCaulley continues on unbothered. "In no way is this extortion. This is clearly a method of everybody eating off the plate. As I'm sure you have found out, I am a power source with many connections. I like to plug in where I can. Just as I can be of tremendous help, I can be equally detrimental. I've spent many years networking and building relationships in this city. I have no problem being the bridge between your pipeline but," he says with a dazzling smile. "There's always a but.

But, you have to make a plate not only for yourself but me and my people as well. Most people see me as some power struck individual when all I really am is a proud Irishman who loves his people and always looks out for the best interest of them. And right now, our interest is putting food on the table for our families. Over seventy properties across the city with not an Irishmen on the site of one of them," he says unhappily.

Maurice fidgets in his seat. His anger is bubbling inside of him. If not for Tony he's sure he would've ruined any possible business ventures in Philadelphia. In no way can he tolerate this level of obnoxiousness. Up until now, he's done business his way. This is his first encounter as such and he doesn't like it nor does he know how to handle it.

"Not one Irishman on the job," McCaulley reiterates. "That must change," he says with demand. "Just as I look out for my people, I expect you to do the same. I'm not asking you to hire all Irishmen and take food out of the mouths of your people. I'm asking you to be an equal opportunity employer and put some of us on your employment roster. In return for that, any way that I can be of service to you I am here. Fair exchange, no robbery," he says with a smile. "What do you say?"

Tony pauses before speaking. "I say I have no problem eating with those who help make the plate," Tony says with all sincerity. "In no way, no form, no fashion will I ever be extorted," Tony says with fiery eyes. "But if hiring some of your men and shaking your hand over business increases the size of my plate, I have no problem allowing you to eat off of that same plate.

"Totally respected," McCaulley says with a smile. "I knew you would get the picture. My connections all across the board will be open to you. There will be nothing that you can't do in this city," he says with certainty. He looks to Maurice. They lock eyes in a brief stare-down. "I will help the two of you make a ton of money and hopefully then you," he says pointing at Maurice. "Will get a better understanding and respect for me. We will make a lot of money together." Maurice turns his head away.

"Now that we got that part over," McCaulley says. "Now onto another chapter," he says as he sinks into relaxation. "After doing an extensive background check on you I realize that you can help me in another way. Your body of work is amazing, to say the least."

He looks Tony directly in the eyes with the most humility that he has displayed the entire meeting. "I have some close friends who have a major problem hanging over their heads. A criminal case that not just anyone can handle. It involves the loved one of a very important man. This case effects a great part of my existence which is why I have been careful who I assign to it. My good friend only cares about the future of his loved one. If I can assure the best for his loved one, there's no limit to the doors that will be open for us," he smiles.

"Notice I said us. I'm ready to attach you to this project for two reasons. One reason, after my research I have not seen a better man for the job. You seem to have a love for criminals and that is why you have such a success rate because you go the extra mile for them," he says as he looks at Maurice with his subliminal attack. "And two, I would like to bring you onboard this project to show you the magnitude of business that I have in store for us. I just want to show you that business goes both ways and when I eat, you will eat. I just need to be sure that when you eat, you have no problem allowing me and my people to eat."

"Let's eat," Tony says.

"Are you prepared to take on a case that my future is dependent upon?"

"You've done your research, correct?" Tony asks.

"Yes, I have," McCaulley responds.

"So, knowing what you know about me, has there ever been any case that I have not been prepared for?"

"Exactly what I expected to hear."

25

NEWARK

THE PEARL WHITE Corvette sits parked with the halogen lights shining brightly on the dope flow that's taking place in the courts. The custom leather designed interior is all purple leather. Vito loves the color but he loves his Crip set more. He sits in the driver's seat with the seat laid back as he rolls a blunt. He can barely focus on the blunt rolling due to the distraction on his lap. This is one of the many perks of being The Man. The hood-rats of the area feel honored to be able to get within arm's reach of him. It's an even bigger honor to get within a mouth's reach.

22 inches of Brazilian Weave spreads out across his lap, stopping inches away from one of the biggest booties he's seen in real life. The thick and curvy hood-rat may only be a nickel in the face but she's five nickels in the body department. She slurps loudly and spits and slurps some more. He pulls her skirt up over her back to watch her butt as she pleases him. One look at her spread and he pulls her skirt back down. He fears if he keeps his eyes on it, he will blast off like a rocket and

that he doesn't want to do. He tries to take his mind off of the amazing head job she's giving him and focus on the blunt rolling.

Vito's phone rings breaking his concentration, yet the woman continues on with her lip therapy. "Yo," Vito answers, not recognizing the number.

"Vito," the caller says. "Black Manson."

"Yo," Vito says with no enthusiasm. He sits up and attempts to lift the woman's head from his lap. She stiffens her neck instead. "What up with you?" Vito asks as he tries to pry the woman's mouth off of him. She's locked on him like a vicious pit-bull.

"I know you're shocked to hear from me," Manson says.

"Yeah, real shocked, especially with what I read."

"Listen, it's all bullshit and I can tell you all about it."

"Please do," Vito says with sarcasm. "Dig it, I ain't gone hold you; I ain't trusting nothing about you or this conversation right now. The only reason I agreed to talking to you is on the strength of the shorty. She gave me the word that she stand with you on any and everything. So, with that said if she stand with you and this some bullshit then she will fall for you, feel me?"

Manson's ego kicks in but he realizes he must suppress it under the circumstances. "Definitely and I can prove to you that ain't no bull-shit involved. I can get all my paperwork from my attorney and have it brought to you. I ain't got no rat, stool pigeon in me. I could never roll. I got kids and babies' mamas out there. I would never put them in a position where they have to be embarrassed of me or have to defend me. Spent my whole life building my reputation and I be damn if I destroy it after all I had to do to build it. I'm in here fucked up because I didn't roll, know that!"

Vito listens attentively and the words Manson says speak vol-umes. He still speaks like a boss with no compromising in him. "Yo, check this out. I'm gone hear you out, right?" he says before pausing. He gets caught up in the head for a few seconds. "Because I respect the hell out of you and all you stood for out here in these streets. But if this some bullshit that you're trying to drag me in to fuck me up, I hope it weigh on your conscience for the rest of your life that you fucked a good nigga that held you on a pedestal as one of the realest G's to

ever walk the streets of Newark. Before I take this chance with you…
whatever it is, will you be able to live with that if you fuck me over?"

"No," Manson replies. "Absolutely not! My paperwork will be
brought to you by tomorrow afternoon. My attorney won't even represent a rat. That's public information," he says sternly. "He came and
found me where they had me. I had no clue nobody was ever going to
find out that I was alive and it was all bullshit. Listen, all that you will
find out once you get with my attorney and get the paperwork."

Vito fights back his urge to moan. The young woman feels disrespected that he can hold a full conversation as she's giving Vito her
best head job. Vito sinks in the seat and pumps her mouth as he continues to listen.

"Your big bruh should be hitting you any day now and he will
vouch for me. If you still don't trust me yet and want to wait until the
smoke clears I respect that. Just hear me out now and when my name
clears you can get right on what I'm asking of you. My reason for
getting in touch with you is this," he says before taking a deep breath.

"That lil girl that came to see you is dear to me. Like a daughter. I
had her under my wing for over twenty years. I guided every step she
ever took until now. She has a major situation on her hands down in
Trenton and shit too thick for her to get out of by herself.

Whether you know it or not, I respect you more than you know.
From the first day we met, I saw something in you. That's the reason
why when you came to me on that business, I engaged. I went against
everything I believed at the time by doing business with you. Now, I'm
coming to you for help. I have nowhere else to turn. My line has turned
to shit. I got my little girl out there alone and I can't help her."

"So, you coming to me to come to her aid? No disrespect but
what's in it for me?" Vito asks bluntly.

"More than you know," Manson says. "The reason for all this mess
she's in right now. I'm sure by helping her, helping me, helping us, it
will all be beneficial for you. Also what I am giving to you is a gift
more valuable than money or gold."

"And what is that?" Vito asks.

"I'm giving you one of my most loyal soldiers. Honorable, courageous and trustworthy," he adds. "I'm giving you, my baby. I can't guard
her while I'm in here. I know you can find great use in her and all she

brings to the table. You will never find another man or woman like her." Manson says with confidence. "I only ask one more thing of you."

"And what's that?" Vito asks curiously.

"Whatever you do, don't stick no dick to my baby. When I say baby, I mean baby like my daughter. As long as you don't stick no dick to her she will remain loyal to you and I will vouch for that. But if you stick dick to her I can't vouch for anything that happens between y'all after that point. I promise you my baby brings more to the table than sex. Just don't cross that line and there's no limit to what moves y'all can make together. Understood?

Vito nods his head slowly. "Totally," he replies.

26

THE DODGE DURANGO cruises through the dark streets of Trenton. The truck may as well be floating in the sky because every one of the occupants is high as an airplane right now, including Skelter. Tonight for the first time in years she popped a Xanax. She hates that she's resorted to pill popping but she needs to bring some ease to her mind. She knows pills are her weakness and they bring the worse out of her which is why she stays away from them.

Normally, once she starts pill popping her addictive behavior kicks in and she goes left. Right now she knows going left can get her murdered. She needs to be on point to face any and everything that's coming her way. But she needs to be calm while facing it all. Right now she's on her way to face one of her problems head on. She was trying to avoid it but it keeps popping up in her mind. She's heard it too many times already and she refuses to sit back and wait for anyone to decide to attack her.

Middle Godson sits in the passenger's seat dialing numbers on his phone. He's been quiet in deep thought the past 15 minutes. After getting the automated voicemail once again, he ends the call with anger. He slams the phone onto the floor. "Yo, I'm telling y'all, something not right about this," he says. "Nobody seen or heard from Bleek in days. His grandmother called me last night asking me if I seen him."

He turns around to face Skelter. "You think niggas found out that he told us and we pushed Old Head? That's what I'm starting to think."

Skelter is deep in thought. What he's saying doesn't sound too far-fetched though. That could very well be the case but truthfully she doesn't even care. Bleek means nothing to her. He's just another pawn on the chessboard. Right now, she has some major pieces to deal with.

"What you think?" he asks. He desperately awaits an answer from her yet she shrugs him off with no real regard for what he's saying.

Youngest Godson slows down on a dark and secluded street which is packed with parked cars on both sides. To the right of them is a small Auto Body Garage. In the daytime it's open for auto body and mechanic work. In the wee hours of the night it's an after-hour spot. All the heavy hitters in the town frequent this spot to drink, enjoy women, strippers and regular women, and even gamble.

"Park over there so we don't get blocked in," Skelter advises. "Just in case shit get hectic. Youngest Godson parks where she instructed him to. "Y'all ready?" The three of them all nod in unison. "Let's get it," she says. They get out of the truck and walk toward the garage.

As she stands at the door, she looks at them to make sure they all are on point and ready to roll. She knocks on the door and in seconds it's opened slowly. Behind the door is a familiar face. He's nobody of importance, just a fat nobody who wants to be somebody. The coolest thing he's ever done is bounce at parties. By being a bouncer he feels relevant.

The man peeks underneath Skelter's hoodie and recognizes her instantly. "Oh, what's up," he says as if he's happy to see her. "Come on in, come on in," he says hastily. He holds his hand out to be shaken but she fist bumps him. That's more than enough to make him feel of importance. He quickly locks the door behind them.

The spot is crowded wall to wall, with everyone doing whatever it is they came here to do. Everyone watches closely as Skelter and her Godsons float throughout the spot. The ones who know her watch her because they know her. The ones that don't know her watch her because she's walking through with a hood on her head and they find that to be peculiar.

Real love is thrown her way and so is fake love. Skelter accepts it all the same. She isn't here for the love or the hate. What she's here for, she spots at the other end of the room. Swan and Jubilee are standing around with a bunch of other men and two women. All of them have big red cups in their hands which indicate they all are drinking.

Skelter reads the play as Swan nudges Jubilee on the sneak tip. She continues on toward them but Youngest Godson stops short. He backs up against the wall and keeps his eyes on everything. Skelter stops in front of Jubilee while Oldest Godson keeps walking. Halfway around the turn he stops and backs up against that wall. Middle Godson stands shoulder to shoulder with her.

She taps Swan with her back hand and then with the same back hand she taps Jubilee. "Let me talk to y'all," she says as she leads the way to the back door that she knows to be their office. Jubilee takes the lead stepping into the door first. Skelter is second and Swan is right behind her.

Middle Godson closes the door and backs up against it, guarding where no one can enter or exit. The three of them keep their eyes on everything moving, which is very little right now. Ever since they stepped in, movement has ceased. The tension is heavy enough to tip the building over.

Swan, the tall, athletically built pretty boy, takes the lead. He pulls a chair from underneath the desk. "Take a seat," he offers as he points to the loveseat across from him. He sits down slowly as Jubilee, a short, big belly man with a beard as big as Santa Claus paces behind him.

Skelter sits down and before she lands she has both of her guns exposed. She's drawn them so fast they seem to have appeared out of nowhere like a magician pulling a rabbit out of a hat. She rests her hands on her lap, guns clenched tight. "What's up? What we doing?"

Swan looks at her in a state of confusion. "Huh?"

"What we talking about?" Skelter asks.

"Pertaining to what?" Swan asks.

Skelter keeps her eyes on both of them. Jubilee has stop pacing and is standing right behind Swan. "First, let me say rest in peace to Chop. Second, I keep hearing my name pop up in this. I'm used to my name popping up in shit I don't have nothing to do with. I'm a G about mine and I own up to all mine but that one ain't on me. First when I heard it, I just let it go like whatever but once I kept hearing it, I'm like hold up. Then big bruh Blue hit me, like, yo we should go holler at Swan and Jube because we never know how they feeling after hearing all the rumors."

Swan looks at Jubilee and then looks back to Skelter. Both Swan and Jubilee have the same expressions on their faces. Suddenly Swan's expression changes into a pearly white smile. "This is the first that we are hearing about any of this."

Skelter feels foolish right now. All she's said and to be hit with that reply. She regrets even coming here now. She's has some words for Blue Blood.

Jubilee steps up and takes over the floor. "Nah, we never heard that. We respect you coming here and clearing the air but if we felt like that we would've came and found you," he says with an edge of sarcasm.

"Found me and what?" Skelter questions with the same edge he delivered.

"Bottom line is this…if we thought y'all was behind it this little meeting wouldn't even be taking place," says Jubilee. "Mad different shit been circulating but right now it's all just rumors. Eventually the shit will come out. It always does."

Skelter stands up. She doesn't like how he's talking right now. Swan recognizes her change of demeanor and steps in. He's known to be the negotiator of the two of them. Just because he's the negotiator doesn't mean he's not dangerous. He's just willing to hear a man out and possibly talk it out if possible. Jubilee on the other hand is known to be a ticking time bomb, always ready for action.

Swan positions his body so that he blocks the eye wrestling they're doing. "The reality is the streets always talking and most of the shit don't even be close to the truth. You know how this shit goes." Swan says. "But like I said, we never heard y'all name in this shit until right now. I'm glad you came but do me a favor?"

"What's that?" Skelter asks.

"Anytime you hear anything that me or him supposed to have said please come and check with us. What I'm telling you right now is if we have anything to say about you or y'all we gone say it directly to you and y'all. And I give you my word that if I hear something y'all supposed to have done or said, I will come directly to y'all."

Skelter tucks her guns into her pockets. "I feel that." She pulls her hood over her head. "Now that we got that out the way, I'm out," she says as she walks toward the door.

"If anything more concrete comes up you'll be the first to know. We will find you," Jubilee says. It's evident that he trying to incite her.

Skelter stops at the door and turns around. "I ain't hard to find," she says with a smirk. "But I'd probably find you first."

27

THE STAPLES PARKING lot may as well be Pebbles's office for she handles all her business in it. Right now, she watches as the triple-black extended version Cadillac truck pulls into the parking lot and parks. The Cadillac and Pebbles's Rover have a face off, grill to grill. The 6 foot 3-inch-tall, wide shouldered man gets out and leans against the hood of his truck rather suavely.

"How are you?" Pebbles asks in her fake professional voice. She gets out and prances toward him.

"Fine, love," the man says in a flirtatious, fake sexy, low baritone voice. His head is about to pop from holding in his breath. He looks down to make sure his belly isn't protruding.

"Hello, Tillis," Pebbles says with a huge smile.

He extends his hand. "Gerard," he says. "It's a pleasure to meet you."

Pebbles cuts through the small talk and hands him an envelope. In the envelope there's $5,000. This is compensation for the destruction of the video footage of Baby Manson poking the inmate up. Tillis had to bribe the officer that had the actual tape. He kept $1,500 for himself though.

"Have a good day, Tillis." Pebbles walks away, leaving him stuck in her web. He watches her switch away sexily. He wants to say something, just doesn't know what exactly he should say. He can't let her get away from him like this. He thinks that maybe shooting his shot at her may cause him and Baby Manson to have a problem. Even knowing that he still takes a shot at it.

"That son of yours, boy," he says as he waits for her to turn around.

Pebbles opens the door and climbs into her truck. The waistline of her skintight jeans lower as she steps inside, exposing at least two inches of butt naked ass crack and booty meat. Pebbles spots perversion in his eyes as she sits down into the seat. "Yes, I know he's a handful."

"I got him though. I always try and drop some jewels on him. I don't know if he ever told you or not."

"No, I'm afraid not. Your name never came up. I thank you though. Enjoy your day, love." Pebbles rolls the window up and pulls off.

MEANWHILE

Baby Manson and Lunatic stand across from Baby Manson's cell, both leaning against the rail. Baby Manson didn't invite him inside because he's picky about who he invites into his home. His mother always told him the home is sacred and not everyone should see the inside of yours. Instead of bringing Lunatic inside he's taken the risk of transferring the drugs through a handshake and hoping no one peeped it.

Lunatic is angered right now but concealing it well. He was expecting Baby Manson to give him more dope. He was hoping it was enough to put him on his feet and have him well ahead of the game. The little bag of dope in the palm of his hand, which is small enough to be able to form a tight fist around is not what he expected.

"What is this though?" Lunatic asks with squinted eyes.

"That's fifty of them," Baby Manson says.

"Oh alright," Lunatic says while getting angrier by the second.

"Just give me back two hundred dollars," Baby Manson says. "Just trying to give you extra room to breathe," he says with innocence and sincerity.

Baby Manson has given Lunatic 50 box pieces which is actually about 3/4 of a gram. Lunatic can resell that box piece for up to $15.

Normally, Baby Manson sells a box-piece to a customer for $7 to $15 but he's showing love to Lunatic by selling it to him for $4. He figures that way Lunatic has room to pass it onto another dealer and still make a profit. This cuts Baby Manson's profit in half but still he makes a profit so he's cool with that just as long as it moves quick. He understands that it's all in the flip and the faster it moves, the better.

Lunatic really feels like he's been disrespected. He cracks a cheesy grin. "I ain't gone lie to you this ain't really what I was expecting. I mean, I'm appreciative at the end of the day but this kind of threw me for a loop."

"How so?" Baby Manson asks.

"Like, I'm thinking I'm really about to stretch out. I had it all lined up. Everybody just waiting on me," he claims. "Like, this right here I can give to like one nigga, feel me?" Baby Manson is silent. His eyes and his body language indicates that he doesn't appreciate Lunatic's ungratefulness. Lunatic reads the body language and takes it as Baby Manson not backing down the way he's used to people backing down. He decides to change his approach.

"On the real, I'm a grown ass man and I thought you was a grown ass man. Like, I'm thinking you *had it* had it and we could make some power moves but I see it ain't like I thought."

Baby Manson picks up on his verbiage and realizes he's reaching right now trying to see how much work Baby Manson actually holds. He stays silent, understanding the more quiet he is the more Lunatic will talk and reveal his true hand. "It's either that or you trying to lil nigga me, like spoon-feeding me."

Lunatic's anger comes from him expecting Baby Manson to hit him off hefty and he could carry on his move and keep it pushing from there. He would be killing two birds with one stone. He would be carrying out the hit for Smith and making a come-up of his own at the same time.

"Lil nigga you?" Baby Manson asks. "That's how you see it? I thought I was showing love. Testing the water and seeing how it goes. We ain't never done business before and honestly I don't know what your hands call for. What, I'm supposed to do drop the motherload on you, not knowing how it's gone go? Wasn't even about spoon-feeding you. It was just dropping that on you to get the ball rolling."

Lunatic is highly angered right now. He's trying hard not to show it because he doesn't want Baby Manson to get on to him and start watching himself around him. He needs him comfortable in order to get all he can get out of him. Right now he sees it will not be as easy as he expected it to be. He also sees it's going to take more time than expected.

"Pardon me, beloved," Lunatic says. "My bad if I came across as ungrateful. I was just expecting to go super hard straight out the gate. But hey man, I just want you to know I appreciate anything you do for me and lil bruh and the set. And I need you to know that I'm here for the long haul."

It's at this moment that Lunatic realizes he was thinking small minded and there's a much bigger picture in front of him. He has quickly decided to be patient and play the waiting game. In this waiting game, the winner will take all. He plans to take everything from the bottom up to the top. Baby Manson is only the bottom. Lunatic plans to get close enough to him to figure out his whole operation. He wants everything from the names of the people that hold his accounts, to his main trustee on the outside that holds his money, to the dope plug who he gets the work from.

"We can take it from here and grow together." His words come across as genuine. He and Baby Manson shake hands with a firm grip. "Now let's build and get money," Lunatic says.

"Absolutely," Baby Manson agrees.

28

VITO AND SKELTER sit in his Corvette. From where they are sitting they get a full view of all the action that's taking place in the courts. Skelter's Godsons have the same view for they are parked right next to them. Drug sales are made every three-seconds. The hustle and the bustle is equal to that of the World Trade Center.

"All checked out well with the Bruh," Vito says. "I talked to him a few times and he told me what he need from me but he also told me that you need something from me. I'm curious to know what that is."

Skelter is hesitant to open up to Vito at first but she trusts Manson enough to follow his lead. "Bottom line is this, I got my hands on some fire right now and I'm having a little difficulty shaking it because of the other problem that Big Bruh spoke to you about."

"Fire what?" Vito questions. "*Heron?*"

"Nah, soft white," she replies. "Powder."

Vito's eyes bulge from his head. "Yeah? Like how much?"

"More than enough," Skelter replies.

"Check, I ain't trying to get all into your personal business and shit but you got enough to put on a block or two or?"

"I got enough to sprinkle on this whole city," she boasts.

"Listen, that powder hard to come by right now. If you got it like that. That is not a problem. With the right number we can take over the city. And of course I can break it down out here and eat crazy off of it. What you letting them go for?"

"I need thirty a joint. That's really the lowest because it ain't just me," she lies. "She doesn't want him to think she's all alone in this. She trusts Manson's judgement but the truth of the matter is he's not out here with her. She has to use some of her own mind as well.

"Not bad, not bad," Vito says as he stares off in a daze. He recognizes that thirty is a big boy number. The best number he's heard on that side is thirty-two. He's heard of people paying up to thirty-eight, even forty dollars a gram.

"Let me ask you," he says as he looks over to her. He stares into her eyes and for the first time he really looks at her. He notices her beautiful hazel eyes, her creamy skin tone and her pretty tulip shaped lips. She has to be the prettiest gangster he's ever seen. **BOING**, it's as if he's been struck by cupid's arrow.

He shakes his head to erase the thoughts that are racing through his mind. Manson's words echo in his head clearly but he can't take his eyes off of her. He places his hand over his eyes to break them away from her. Skelter notices his weird behavior and watches him closer.

"Let me ask you," he repeats again. "What's the best you can do for me? Like thirty a great number but what if I come to you with a nice bag. Let's say like 250. Could I get them for twenty-five apiece? I mean I ain't got no problem helping you at the thirty but if you can let me get like ten of them at twenty-five that will be love."

Skelter thinks it over. He's asking her to take a fifty-grand loss in return for his help in which she needs dearly. She realizes she must give some to gain some. "Like I told you, it ain't just me but I will take the loss off my end just so you can do what you trying to do. On some G shit," she says. "I'm coming to you opening my whole hand up. All I ask is you be fair with me."

"Check this out," he says. "The respect I got for the Bruh is astronomical. He love the shit out of you but he trusted me with you. My word and reputation means everything to me. The fact that he trust me with his heart over all the motherfuckers in the world that he know, that's a big deal to me.

Out of all the Bloods he knows, he put you in the hands of a Crip. That's some different shit right there because I know how much he hate Crips," he says with a smile. "On everything, I will never do anything to fuck that up. Put your feet up because I got you from here. He told me you're his heart and I'm gone protect you as such."

29

A HUGE TRACTOR trailer blocks up the narrow street, clogging traffic. Traffic is backed up for miles forcing drivers to reroute. Twelve Play stands on the curb proudly as the jacuzzis are being carried into the building. He not only found a truck driver who would deliver the hot tubs, he also hired a team full of junkies to carry them in.

Maurice on the inside of the building supervises as the tubs are being brought into the building and put into the bathrooms of each apartment. He's surprised Umar was able to pull it off. He's not sure how he did it but he's sure if he can do it again and again they can save a lot of money.

It takes the junkies almost no time to bring in every one of the tubs. The tractor has pulled off and all is back to usual. Twelve Play and Umar walk through the lobby of the building. "Now, hopefully you will believe in me," Umar says proudly. "When I say I'm going to do something, I do it," he says while awaiting praise and admiration.

"Hey, that all comes with being a man. Our word is all we got."

Maurice meets them at the end of the lobby. "You pulled it off I see. Is this unlimited or a one-time deal?"

"I got this connect on deck at any time," Umar explains.

Umar has enough Muslim oil on for twenty men. He has the entire lobby lit up. Maurice's nose twitches, awaiting a huge sneeze that just won't come out. He looks to Twelve Play, wondering how he can stand up to it. Twelve Play has gotten used to his overuse of oils. Also, in prison he's met men who use even more than this so he's immune to it.

"Ok, check," Maurice says as he pulls his Gucci backpack off his shoulder. He unzips it, digs inside and pulls out a brown Gucci shopping bag. He hands it over to Umar. "That's the 90 grand you requested." Umar looks into the bag and sees stacks and stacks of new, crisp one-hundred-dollar bills that look like they are hot off the printer. "You can count it right here if you want."

"No need bruh, I take your word for it. I will count it up later."

"How soon can I put in another order?" Maurice asks greedily. Maurice rubs his hands over his nose. His eyes water.

"Right now," Umar says with a smile.

"Listen, we got a ton of properties here and in a bunch of other cities and states. All those properties need shit. If you can get us what we need, you will make a lot of money."

"My goal," Umar says with a huge smile.

"Ok cool," Maurice says. "Give me a day or two and let me put together an order and bruh will holler at you," he says while pointing to Twelve Play. "I don't know how heavy you can go at one time but this move we just made is peanuts compared to the next order."

"Listen, you just make the order and I will make sure I deliver. However I have to get it done, I will."

"Sounds like a plan," Maurice says. They shake hands. "Two days," Maurice says as he walks away back toward the stairs. He looks down at his hand and the smell of oils smacks him in the face. He holds his hand in the air with agitation, knowing this smell will be on his hand all day.

Finally the sneeze comes out full force. It doesn't stop after one. A back to back to back sneeze fest takes place. His sneezing echoes throughout the entire building. Umar has left a huge impact on him.

Twelve Play walks Umar out of the building and to his truck. "Hey Akhi, I can't walk away with a bag like this without giving you something. "Let me give you something man. I understand you didn't want to eat off your folks but let me feed you off my plate," he says as he opens the passenger's door. He lays the bag on the seat and digs into it. He counts through a stack of hundreds until he counts out a hundred and fifty of them. "That's fifteen racks. You're not eating off him. You're eating with me."

Twelve Play takes the money gratefully. "Solid bruh," he says with gratitude. "I appreciate you. Twelve Play cuts his eye at the corner where he sees Tony's Mercedes G-Wagon pulling up. Tony hops out as cool as usual, dressed in a business suit. He acknowledges Twelve Play and salutes him. Twelve Play reciprocates the salutations as he and Umar continue on with their conversation.

Tony meets Maurice in the lobby and Maurice takes him for a tour throughout the building, showing him the hot tubs in the apartments. "You know all good things come to an end," Maurice says. "I say we drain this shit dry before it runs out."

"I'm with you," Tony says. "If we can save a couple hundred grand, we up," Tony says, grinning from ear to ear. "What about Twelve Play? You put a couple dollars in his pocket?"

"Nah," Maurice says. "I took care of the boy for twenty years." Maurice is attempting to be humorous but Tony doesn't find it funny at all. Maurice notices Tony's distaste for the joke. "But nah, that's my man. He ain't on it like that."

"Give the boy ten thousand and I will give you five back when I get back," says Tony. "I know that's your man but we can't starve him while we eat. I know you know this but I'm gone say it anyway. You got to feed the wolves. You can't eat in a wolf's face and expect him not to get hungry. I like everybody around me to eat. Money makes the world go 'round. You got to feed the wolves, and not out of fear, because I'm a wolf my damn self, just in sheep's clothing," he says as he flicks the lapels of his suit in a playful manner. "Let the boy make a couple dollars though."

Maurice feels like a creep after hearing Tony say this. "Nah, I was just bullshitting. I was gone hit him off," he claims.

"Cool, let me get on out of here. I scheduled the flight for 2:30 and it's now 2:30," he says as he shakes his head.

Tony rushes to his car. He throws a peace sign in the air to Twelve Play who is walking toward the building. "Peace Big Bruh!" Twelve Play shouts at him. Twelve Play walks to the steps where the young men have already assumed their positions, around the stoop and two sitting on the stoop. Twelve Play stops in front of the two men, expecting them to get up but they don't. They continue on with their conversation as if he's not standing there.

Without thinking, Twelve Play snatches both of the young men by the collar. With Herculean strength he lifts them both from the stoop and flings them out of his way. "Y'all ain't gone keep playing with me," he says with no sign of the rage that he holds inside.

Both of the young men come at him as if they want to rumble. "Come the fuck on, I will destroy both of y'all together." They want to but they are hesitant. "Come on," he says with an evil grin. In seconds, five other young men surround Twelve Play. Maurice who is just happening to be coming out of the building sees the commotion and in one giant leap he's busting through the crowd. He stands side by side with Twelve Play.

The seven young men look at the two monstrous sized men, planning their attack. They realize it will be give and take. One or two of them may have to be sacrificed in order to get to them. Neither one of them want to be the one or two of them who are sacrificed though.

Maurice gets the party started. He reaches out and grabs the closest man to him. One hand on the young man's collar and the other gripping the crotch of the young man's pants, he takes him uptown and earth slams him on his back. Another young man comes charging him and he does the same to him. He throws a wild bolo at a young man who is watching in amazement. The young man is knocked to the ground.

Meanwhile Twelve Play is going gorilla crazy. With his forearm pressed against the man to hold him against the wall, he beats blood out of the young man's face. As a man tries to grab him from the back, he bends down slightly and when he lifts himself back up he bangs his head into the man's face with the impact of an explosion. Maurice and Twelve Play shoulder to shoulder seem to be outnumbering the seven men.

Twelve Play, like a mad man reaches out with both hands and grabs the closest man to him. He holds the man in the air, three inches off the ground. He leans his head back as far as he can and like a boomerang his necks snaps forward. He head-butts the man and knocks him out cold. He lets the man go and the man drops to the ground.

The young men are outweighed, outsized and out of their fight league yet they are not giving up. It's an all-out rumble. So focused on the destruction of their opponents, Maurice and Twelve Play don't see the young man bend the corner and scale the wall. His hand tucked underneath his shirt, gripping a .357 revolver. Out of nowhere appears Sal Strothers, the squatter. He meets the young man halfway. The young man hands him the gun and he creeps closer to the Battle Royal.

Anxiousness rips through his body. He's been waiting for this moment ever since the day he was thrown out of the apartment. He creeps behind Twelve Play who is standing over a young man, stomping him into the ground. He aims the gun at Twelve Play's head and just as he's about to pull the trigger he gets hit with a blow that knocks him into tomorrow. His neck snaps to the left before he topples over. He falls to the ground and the gun escapes his grip. He lays there knocked out, snoring.

Umar grabs the gun from the ground and aims it at the man's head. He squeezes the trigger. *CLICK. CLICK. CLICK.* The gun is jammed. Another young man who has just arrived at the scene sees Umar with the non-working gun in his hand. All the action has ceased. Maurice and Twelve Play both have their eyes on Umar, a stranger, who was apparently ready to put in work for them.

"Oh, y'all want to play with guns?" the young man says from across the street. Alright bet!"

30

BABY MANSON IS in the Big Yard doing his daily workout regimen. He goes from the pull-up bar to burpees to push-ups and sit-ups. Throughout his entire workout, his father has been on his mind heavy. All he can picture is his father walking around like one of the jailhouse crazies. It breaks his heart at the thought of it and it makes him want to bring pain to someone every time he thinks about it. Right now he's using it as fuel to drive him to work out harder.

He drops down from the bar and as he takes a minute to catch his breath he scans the yard. Everything seems to be as peaceful as it can be on a prison yard. Lunatic stands out amongst the rest of the men as he's greeting another inmate. They stand shoulder to shoulder, backs against the wall. Baby Manson assumes it's a move in the making.

He has to admit that Lunatic is on his job. He moved the first batch of work in a day and a half and is now on his second batch. Baby Manson increased the load. Lunatic claims he will be done with that today. Baby Manson sees it as Lunatic trying to prove his worth and depending on if he keeps it up at this pace, Baby Manson will have no choice but to hit him big.

Across the yard, Lunatic is making a move alright, but not the kind of move Baby Manson is thinking. Lunatic listens attentively as the man whispers to him. "My lil bitch is best friends with the lil nigga

Weebie's chick. Lil Weebie be getting the smack from Baby Manson. My lil chick know almost the whole operation because she be right there with her when they busting the move."

"Word?" Lunatic asks.

The man nods his head up and down, lips puckered. "Word. My lil bitch said his bitch be handling the money. Said he got some old head, big booty bitch. Said the face ain't really all that but the body crazy. Said you can tell she eating. Pushing that big Rover, shoe and pocketbook game crazy. Boss bitch she said."

"You think she the plug?" Lunatic asks.

"I don't know. She might just be handling all the nigga money, feel me?"

"Absolutely," Lunatic says as he stares across the yard at Baby Manson whom isn't paying them any attention at all.

"My bitch said they be meeting like every two weeks and Lil Weebie bitch be giving the ugly old head bitch like twenty-five hundred," he says as if he's said a lot.

Lunatic thinks hard before speaking. "It's either one of two things. Either she's the plug or he taking care of that bitch, hitting her crazy."

"I can see that," the man says.

In jail, just as on the streets, everything is embellished, and the truth is stretched making everything appear bigger than it is. With that being said, the moves that Baby Manson is making appears to be bigger than life.

"I mean the nigga is going full throttle," Lunatic says. "Maybe she ain't the plug," he says. "But damn, nigga buying Ranges and shit from prison," he says with hatred. All this just makes the little dope he's given him seem even more disrespectful.

"Aye yo, check," Lunatic says. "This what I need you to do. See if they can get the old head bitch name. And take that license plates down too. We got to track this bitch down. If she ain't the plug, I'm sure she can lead us to the plug."

"Say less," the man says as he shakes Lunatic's hand. "I'm gone get my lil bitch on the case immediately."

31

INTERNATIONAL AIRPORT IN DUBLIN
3:52 A.M.

TONY EXITS HIS jet, stiff and fatigued from the long six-hour flight. It's a few minutes shy of 4 A.M. here but back at home it's only 11 P.M. His mind and body knows the difference. Usually at this hour, he's somewhere smoking a cigar, decompressing after a long day of work.

Tony is hand in hand with Miranda as they strut through the airport. He brought her along for the experience. Like a tourist, Tony finds himself admiring everything. To his surprise there are pictures of all famous Irish Americans on the walls throughout the airport. Former Presidents Ronald Reagan, John F. Kennedy, current President, Donald Trump. To his surprise there are even pictures of Obama. He's shocked that they show so much love for Americans. They make their way to Customs which is so different from what he's used to. This is the only country he's ever been to where you have to clear customs in that country instead of before departing in the States.

His thoughts about them loving Americans changes as soon as he stands before the Customs Agent. The man's face reddens as Tony steps in front of him. "Passport," he demands. He reads it over, studying it closely as if he's sure something isn't right. Finally, he hands it back to Tony. Tony finds it disrespectful that he has not looked him in the eyes like a man as he asks for his paperwork. "How long do you intend to stay?"

"Twenty-four hours, I guess," Tony replies.

"You guess? Don't you have a return date and time?" he asks sarcastically.

"No," Tony replies with the same amount of sarcasm. Tony cuts his eye over at Miranda. The Custom Agent handles Miranda with nothing but respect.

"So, no return flight? What airline did you fly in through?" he asks with suspicion.

"My own private charter," Tony says as humble as he possibly can.

"Your own charter?" the agent asks as he looks into Tony's face for the first time. He looks him up and down first and then with a frowning face he shows his disgust for Tony. "What is your purpose of this visit?"

"Business."

"Would you like to explain this business?"

"No, not really," Tony says casually.

At this point the agent is ready to take Tony in the back and check him out thoroughly. "What is your occupation?"

"Attorney," Tony says showing no respect at all.

The agent changes his mind. The last thing he needs is a lawsuit filed against him for racial discrimination. He already has a few complaints against him. "Have you ever been here before?"

"Never," Tony says, not even looking in the man's direction. He keeps his eyes on Miranda who has been cleared and is now waiting for him.

"Who is your point of contact?"

"Christy Kinahan."

The agent looks at Tony with the expression of one who has saw a ghost. He swallows a lump of fear and his mouth moves to speak but no words come out of it. Finally, in a high-pitched voice he's able to form three words. "The Dapper Don?" he asks, hoping he's heard wrong. "Christy, the Dapper Don, Kinahan?"

Tony is not certain of all of this. "I only know him by Christy Kinahan."

"Sir, I do apologize for any inconvenience I may have caused you," he says. "Please forgive me." He grabs Tony's hand as if he's ready to kiss the ring but he sees no ring to kiss. He places Tony's backhand up to his mouth and kisses it. "Again, I do apologize, kind Sir."

Miranda watches with surprise. She has no clue of why the man is carrying on like this. Tony looks over to her with a shrugging of his shoulders. "No problem," Tony says as he pries his hand from the man's grip.

He turns around walking away like the Don that he is. He's playing it cool and calm but he does realize the man that he's here to see is probably the biggest deal that he's ever been called on by. He hopes he's granted this opportunity to work with him. This situation coupled with the other two major cases he has in the kitty will cause the biggest splash of his career. These cases will certify him as a big deal internationally.

12:12 A.M.
SOUTH PHILLY

Inside one of the condos, all the traces of a small party is evident. Bottles of champagne, D'Ussé, Ciroc and even bourbon whiskey are scattered along the granite countertops. May look like a party but it isn't one. The 10 men that are lounging around sipping alcohol are all members of Maurice's Federation.

After the scuffle they had earlier today, Maurice decided to call on his army. It's not that he thinks it's a major beef. In fact he believes it to be light work but being here on foreign soil he can't take any chances. He made the call and his men made it here in less than 2 hours. They all came through the back doors so no one could see them. The Philly natives made a threat of coming back and Maurice plans to be ready when they do.

"Aye Twelve," Maurice says. "Go on out there and see what it's looking like." Twelve Play has been carrying on as he ordinarily does. It's nothing out of the ordinary for him to go out on the stoop in the late hours of the night when he can't sleep. Normally there's always someone out there but tonight there isn't. He's been out there three times already and it's a ghost town. It's been like that ever since the beef earlier.

• • •

Umar cruises through the South Philly streets with his mind heavy. He still can't believe how quickly things went left earlier. The day was going great. He just made a $90,000 score and seemed to have found his way into some more money in the future with them and then the nonsense started.

He feels partly at fault of things going to the next level, that is if they do go to the next level. It was a simple scuffle that went left. Once the man aimed the gun at Twelve Play's head it forced him to react. No one seemed to have noticed the gun at Twelve Play's head. All they all saw was him standing over the man and the gun jamming up in his hand.

Right now he's just going through to take a look at how things are looking around the area. He's parked his truck and is driving one of his squatters, an old beat up Malibu with dark tinted windows. As he creeps through the intersection he sees a silhouette on the porch. The silhouette is that of a monstrous sized man. Not many humans are this size so he figures this has to be Twelve Play.

Twelve Play sees the tinted vehicle coming down the block. He stands upright and turns his body on an angle to make himself a smaller target to hit. All the while he's already drawn his .40 caliber and has it concealed at his side. The closer the car gets, the higher he raises his gun, but still it's not visible.

Umar peeps the movement and rolls the passenger's window down so he can be seen. "Akhi!" he shouts. "This me Akhi!"

Twelve Play recognizes the voice and stands at ease. He tucks his gun as Umar parks in front of the building. Umar gets out. "As Salaamu Alaikum!"

"Walaikum As Salaam!" Twelve Play replies.

"Akhi, Allah is Akbar," says Umar. "Something told me to come through and check on you and here you are out here late at night. Come on Akh," Umar says as he stands on the ground, looking up at Twelve Play. "I ain't trying to tell you what to do but it's like you out here taunting them. They gone have to react Sheikh. This thing gone end badly.

Look, you just getting home fresh off a damn near twenty banger and you out here on front line ready to do it all again. These lil niggas out here ain't worth it. They fleas, Akh. Don't let them trick you out of your freedom. I said it once and I'm gone say it again. Tell your folks to get with the management company and let them handle this shit."

Twelve Play realizes Umar is right but his stubbornness is in the way. "I'm gone run it pass them but this right here still got to get handled. Ain't no way around that. We ain't pressing the button but if they press it, we gone PLAY."

"So, you ain't pressing the button but you just gone stand here and taunt them?"

"I ain't taunting them? I'm just doing what I've been doing, coming out here and enjoying my freedom."

"Freedom that you're about to lose again, Sheikh. You with the Money Team, man. Y'all doing big things. Don't let these bottom feeders fuck that up for y'all."

It all starts to sink in despite his stubbornness. The last thing he needs is to sit down for another 20 years. "You're right," Twelve Play admits. "Also, me and my team thank you for what you did earlier."

"No worries, Akh. I mean, that's your team and all but I did that on the strength of you. I'm always gone stand with the Believers. Whether we come from the sandbox together or we just meeting like we did, if a Muslim is in need, I'm here. Plus, I had to protect the money," he says with a big smile. "Shit, one hit and I scored 90 grand. We about to make a lot of money together. I ain't letting them fuck that up."

They share a laugh. "Now go on in and get some rest Akhi. Let me get on out of here." They shake hands and give the salaams. Twelve Play goes inside and Umar pulls off.

As Umar nears the corner, he sees two men walking around the corner suspiciously. As he passes them he notices their familiarity. It's the man he knocked out earlier and the young man who passed him the gun. They both take a glance at the Malibu but pay very little attention to it. Their focus is up the block. Both of them stretching their necks, looking up ahead. Umar doesn't like the look of this. He decides to circle the block just to see what they are up to.

Both of the men cut in between the condo building and the neighboring house. They stop at a small window. This window leads to the basement, where the heating and boiler system is. The squatter, Sal Strothers pulls out a tiny spark plug from his pocket and tosses it against the small window. He tosses it three times until it shatters into tiny pieces. Using his elbow he bangs an opening in the glass.

The young man pulls a string of four t-shirts tied together from his waistband. Using a cigarette lighter he lights the t-shirts. He waits for the fire to catch on before he tosses the t-shirts through the window on the floor. Sal Strothers pulls a Poland Spring squirt bottle from his pocket. He sticks his hand inside the window and squirts the gasoline onto the burning t-shirts. They both watch like firebugs as the flame gets bigger and bigger. Once they are satisfied with the size of the fire and are certain that the flame won't die and will only increase, they take off running.

From where is parked he gets a bird's eye view of what is going on. Through the alley he can see the lights coming from the burning flame. The men run out of the alley and make a right. They stop running once they hit the corner.

Umar starts his car up and bends the corner behind them. He strategically follows them without their notice for half a block before he parks his car and gets out on feet. He walks fast paced on the opposite side of the street until he's closer. He cuts across the street diagonally. He draws the strings of his hoodie tighter as he picks up a trot.

The men turn around and notice someone creeping up on them but it's already too late. Umar throws three shots at them. *BLOCKA! BLOCKA! BLOCKA!* The younger man's body jolts before doing a complete tumble and rollover. Once his rollover is complete, he's looking upward at Umar. *BLOCKA!* The hot slug tears through his face before frying his brain.

Umar takes off behind the other man, Sal Strothers, who is running with a limp. Umar tracks him down like a K9. Once he gets within an arm's length of the man he reaches out and snatches him by the hood. He yanks him backward as he plants the gun against the man's head. *BLOCKA!* The man collapses like a lifeless bag of bones. Umar plants his foot in the center of the man's back before he fires one more shot into the back of his head. *BLOCKA!*

Umar trots back to his car. As he turns the corner he picks up his phone and starts to text Twelve Play. 'CLEAN THE HOUSE JUST IN CASE COMPANY STOP BY.'

Umar spins the block. As he hits the corner he sees the block packed with nosey neighbors surrounding the building. Once he gets closer he sees Twelve Play and the others in the alley with fire extinguishers in hand. The fire has increased dramatically. They fight it fearlessly like trained firefighters. Umar is shocked to see so many of them. Twelve Play didn't even let him in on the secret that he had all of his men in place. He doesn't take it personal though. Well, maybe he takes it a little personal.

Twelve Play notices the Malibu in the middle of the street. He and Umar lock eyes. Umar lifts his gun for Twelve Play to see. He then swipes his hand across his throat as a signal that it's over. Twelve Play stands in a confused state. He thinks back to the gunshots he heard a few minutes ago and puts it all together. Umar can tell by the expression on Twelve Play's face that he understands what he's saying. He places his phone against his ear, as to say 'call me' before he pulls off.

Twelve Play stands in a trance. He owes Umar more respect than he's given him. Just meeting him and he's already proven more loyalty to him than dudes he's known all of his life. It takes a lot to impress Twelve Play but right now he's impressed.

32

HAROLD'S NEW YORK DELI

DRE HAS BEEN avoiding Lil Mama but that hasn't stopped her from putting the full-court press on him. Last week he made an excuse on why he couldn't pick her up from Jumu'ah but today she wasn't taking no for an answer. He picked her up 20 minutes ago and now they are sitting across from each other over plates with Pastrami sandwiches stacked 2 feet high. Lil Mama is barely eating for she has been talking ever since they sat down.

"Listen, I ain't tripping off nothin' else you want to do or whoever else you may want to be with," Lil Mama claims. "I ain't locking you down in no type of way nor am I trying to stop anything else you may want to do. I'm just trying to be married and protect myself from the hellfire," she says sternly.

Dre is shocked at her words. "So, you gone sit here and tell me that you don't care if I got other chicks?"

"Yes, that's exactly what I'm telling you," she says with a straight face. "Honestly, you marry me, I'm gone make it where you don't need another chick for nothing," she says cockily. "But if by chance that after how I take care of you in every aspect, if you still got the energy or the desire for another bitch, then be my guest."

Lil Mama is surprising her own self right now. All the years that she's been holding back but she refuses to hold back any longer. Also, his running away is giving her the heart to go harder. "I'm Muslim Dre. In Islam, it is permissible for the man to have more than one wife. I believe in Allah for real and if Allah says it's permissible then who am I to go against that?"

She's giving him no way out. Anyways, after his talk with Tony, he really isn't against the idea. Just right now he's not totally sure about it. "Lil Mama," he says as he notices the change of expression on her face. "I mean, Halimah. I'm an old ass man though. I'm 51 years old and you not even 31 yet. I got twenty years on you."

"More reason for you to marry me. Soon you will need me to wipe your ass, bathe you and push your old ass through the park in your wheelchair," she says humorously. "Sike, but yeah, you twenty years older than me but you don't look a day older than me. Still looking like a young nigga."

Dre is quite flattered. "Thanks."

"No need for thanks, you know you the shit. Don't play with me," she says in a joking manner. "That time when you said, 'but we not in love with each other', I let you say it and all but." She pauses for seconds trying to build her heart up. "That ain't the case. Before I went away it was an innocent young girl crush. While I was away it evolved into love. I knew it then but I just had to see for myself when I got here. I had to be around you in order to confirm what I already knew."

"And what is that?" Dre asks.

"I'm not only in love with you...I'm madly in love with you. If you tell me right here right now that you don't love me, I will leave you alone about it."

"You already know I love you."

"Well, marry me then."

Dre sits in silence. "I have to keep it real with you. Shit ain't right. Shit ain't been right for a minute. I'm out here trying to find a plan to put some money together."

Lil Mama sighs and leans in closer, "Let's figure this shit out together. Together we will make it right. I'm sure of that. You know we are a perfect team.

"I can't deny that," Dre replies.

"Listen, we can do something small, just me, you, the Imaam and a few witnesses. Mr. Austin can stand in as my Wakil(guardian.) I don't need no ring or nothing."

"Got damn you make it so easy. What if I tell you I'm with it but just need you to hold up for a second? I'm about to take a trip to Honduras and when I come back I'm gone be straight. Then I will marry you."

"I would say no; why don't you marry me before you go to Honduras because tomorrow ain't promised to none of us. And God forbid anything happen, at least my dream of marrying you will be fulfilled. And when you do come back from Honduras we will be straight together and work as a team to build on whatever it is you have planned for *us*."

Dre is speechless. After seconds of just staring at her he finally speaks. "I don't even know what to say."

"Cool, then just say *yes* and I will do the rest."

33

TEMPLE BAR DISTRICT-DUBLIN, IRELAND

TONY AND MIRANDA walk through the streets of Dublin holding hands like the two lovebirds they are. It's raining cats and dogs out but no one seems to mind. In fact very few are even using umbrellas. Rain is likely in the forecast every other day so the people of Ireland are quite used to it and it stops nothing.

Tony tries hard to not look like a tourist but it's not easy. This area is like the Times Square of Ireland. The locals rarely visit this area yet and still it's extremely busy. It's live and festive every day of the week.

The streets are immaculately clean. Not a sign of a homeless person is anywhere in sight. One of the things that amazes Tony is the cops do not carry guns. They are only equipped with a nightstick and a can of mace; not even a taser gun.

The sound of Bagpipe music blares loudly. Tony guides Miranda off the curb and onto the brick road. The road is quite slippery from the rain so Tony is careful to hold her hand tightly. The building in front of them is a tourist attraction; a brick building, covered in beautiful Christmas style lights. Before going into the Pub, Tony and

Miranda stand and watch the man playing the bagpipe. People River dance to the tune. It's not long before Tony and Miranda join in.

TEMPLE BAR

Miranda holds the huge Mug of Guinness up to her mouth. She takes a cute sip and places the mug onto the table. She traces her tongue over her foam mustache. Just as she takes another sip a drunkard Irish man walks over and stops at their table. He staggers back and forth. "You have to suck through the head. Yep, yep, that's it. Uhmm, hmm."

Miranda stops sipping and looks at the man with disgust. Tony jumps off from his seat and snatches the drunk man by his collar and flings him. The man stares at Tony with confusion. "All I said was suck the head."

Tony darts at the man but a waitress steps in between them. "Sir, he means the foam. We call it the head. You need to get through the foam to get the beer," she says in translation.

"Oh," Tony says with a goofy look on his face. He looks to the drunkard man. "Sorry man. Have another round on me."

An hour later and Tony is finally engaging in his purpose of actually being here. Miranda sits in the booth alone next to them. Tony asked her to excuse herself while he handled his business. Tony and the infamous Crime boss himself sit across from each other. He had the bar shutdown minutes ago for his own safety precautions. Right now the only people present in the bar is Tony, Miranda, The Dapper Don and his four bodyguards. Of course, the bar staff are present, waiting on them hand and foot.

Tony can very well see why this man has earned the name of the Dapper Don. He will admit that this man is almost as dapper as himself. Even the Don's bodyguards are dapper. All four of the huge, oddly shaped men have on perfectly tapered suits. One stands at the front door, one stands at the entrance of the restrooms, one stands at the door which leads to the kitchen and the other stands at the back door. Tony is impressed with the strength and power this man has. Everything evolves around him.

The waitress lays their plates in front of them. Tony looks down at his plate and tries to keep a straight face as he looks at the dark colored, pork sausage. He looks up at The Don. "Sir, I do apologize but I don't eat meat," he says respectfully.

It's not that he doesn't eat meat, he just doesn't eat pork. He's learned that pork lovers take offense when you tell them you don't eat pork. Tony feels he may take it better if he says he doesn't eat meat period. He agreed to Black and white Pudding only out of respect, trying not to insult the Don. He didn't want the pudding either. Why they've brought sausage to him he has no clue. "I thought you mentioned pudding."

The Don looks at him without blinking an eye. "Black and White Pudding is sausage, oatmeal, milk and pig's blood."

Tony's stomach does a back flip just hearing of the concoction. The Don slices the sausage in half to show him the inside and Tony becomes nauseated, yet he keeps a straight face. "I do apologize but I am vegan," Tony lies.

"Fine," he says as he slams his napkin onto the plate and pushes the plate away from him.

"I apologize," Tony says with all the humility he can muster up. He knows how people of other countries are about their food. "Please eat?"

"Too late," The Don snaps. "My appetite has already been ruined. Let's get on with our business."

Tony slowly pushes his plate away from him for the smell is turning his stomach. He lays his napkin neatly over it. He can't take the sight of it any more than he can take the smell. He gives The Don his full attention.

"No disrespect but of all the high-power attorneys in the world and McCaulley sent a Negro. You must be one bad negro."

"You know, it never fails, whenever someone says no disrespect, what follows is usually disrespect."

"I meant none whatsoever. Is negro an insult? What should I call you colored, Black? You are African right?"

"To answer the latter question, I am Black. I'm not one of those Blacks that wishes he was white. I'm one of those Blacks who is as proud of his race as you are proud to be Irish."

The Don's eyes pop open widely. "Oh really, that proud?" he asks with evident sarcasm.

"Yes, that proud," Tony replies with his own arrogance. "And in reference to your first statement. I'm not one bad negro. I'm one bad attorney. Probably the baddest attorney of this lifetime," Tony says boastfully. He was trying to play the humble role but that rarely works for him. Now he has to go back to what he knows.

"Oh, and since we started off wrong anyway, let me tell you, I'm not one of those black men who loves pork either. Actually, I hate pork. I'm no vegan. I just hate pork," he says with a wise grin. "Now that we have put it all on the table let's start from the top."

The Don likes the spunk and pizazz that Tony displays. "I'm just interested in what you think you know of me. Everyone has this opinion of me before they meet me. I'm curious what your opinion is."

"I have no opinion," Tony claims. "I only know what the media says about you. Well, I have to be honest, I had never heard of you until McCaulley mentioned you to me and then I started my research."

"Is that so?" The Don is in shock. He was under the impression that everybody in the world knew who he was. "What is it you think you now know, based on your research."

"Again, I only know what the media says. The media says, you and the Monk are the heads of two crime families and are at odds. You've been feuding since 2015."

"No, incorrect," The Don says. "Me and the Monk have never been at odds. It's the generation under us that can't see eye to eye. Just unfortunate that we are old now and it's their energy that fuels the families."

"The media also says that in this feud if there is a winner and a loser, you are the winner."

The Don blushes, trying hard not to show his teeth. The Don is the head of the Kinahan Crime Family and Gerry 'The Monk' is the head of the Hutch Crime Family. The Monk's nephew, Gary Hutch was working for the Kinahan Family and had fallen out with them. He tried to kill Daniel Kinahan (The Dapper Don's son). Gary Hutch was accused of being an informant.

The Monk paid The Dapper Don 200,000 euros to spare Gary Hutch's life. The Dapper Don and Gary 'The Monk' agreed that Gary

Hutch could live and nothing would happen to him as long as he kept his mouth shut, did nothing, and stayed out of the way. The Kinahans reneged on the deal by killing Gary Hutch anyway. They also demanded another 200,000 euros. They stated they wanted certain members of the Monk's family to leave Ireland or they will wipe a whole lot more of them out. The Monk took this all personally and refused any further sit-downs.

Four months later, the Hutch family hit back. It was at the Regency Hotel right before a major boxing match at Dublin's Regency Hotel. Two men stormed in wearing fake police uniforms and brandishing AK-47s. Two more attackers were already inside the hotel, one disguised in drag as a woman. A fifth man, also in fake police uniform, stood guard outside while a getaway driver waited to speed them away. This led to the deadliest gang war to ever take place in Dublin. The families have been feuding ever since. It's been said that the Kinahan family has the upper hand because while both families are striking, the Kinahan's attacks are more impactful because their murder victims are key members of the Hutch family.

Tony listens with open ears and wide-open eyes as the Dapper Don tells him things he rather not even know. Tony now realizes the criminals he's represented who he thought were vicious have nothing on these crime families. The kingpins and gang bangers he has represented who call themselves gangsters are merely street thugs compared to these men.

• • •

Today has been strangely quiet and peaceful in front of the building. None of the young men have stepped foot on the block. The workers have been able to get in and out of the property in peace. Maurice and his men are still in the building staking out, just in case the men decide to attack.

Twelve Play stands out on the porch next to Umar. The silence and absence of the men is what throws them off and they don't know how to take it. Both of their heads are swiveling, keeping their eyes on everything as Umar speaks. Twelve Play has a new level of respect for Umar after what he did last night. He could have easily kept going as if he didn't see a thing but instead he took it upon himself to handle the matter. Not only is Twelve Play impressed, so is Maurice.

Maurice steps out onto the porch. He looks at Umar with respect as he reaches for his hand. "Much respect," Maurice says.

Umar nods his head and lowers his head humbly. "There was no way around it. I stood over him and didn't finish the job," he whispers. "I had to finish it."

"But you put it all on the line from the start and you didn't have to."

"I did what was right, simple as that."

"Respected," Maurice says as he walks around to the alley. His priority right now is to hurry and get any traces of the fire erased. Luckily there was very little damage done. The last thing Maurice needs is for Tony to find out about any of this, which is why he has no plans of telling him.

"Really though, we can't sleep on this shit," Umar says. "Nobody know where it came from but everybody knows what happened prior to it. This thing can only go one of two ways. Now, they will either **back up**, understanding that nobody ain't playing with them or they will **turn up**," he says with wide eyes. "I just think y'all need to fade to black for a minute and let shit die down. We got too much money to get to be going to war with broke motherfuckers."

Maurice steps out of the alley. He looks up to Umar. "Hey, as soon as my partner get back we will be putting in another order, a much bigger order. Oh, and bruh said you got the number to a management company. Before you break out, get that to him, please."

"Smart move," Umar says.

· · ·

"So, what is that you want from me?" Tony asks.

"We are in need of family representation. We may be winning the war but we are losing badly to the justice system," he says with defeat plastering his face. "I'm sure you're wondering why he's chosen you. With all the attorneys we have here in Ireland."

"Uh no, never crossed my mind," Tony says arrogantly.

The Don cracks his first smile of the night. "Here's the deal. With this feud being so high profile everyone is aware of it. People who have nothing to do with it, regular common people, have even chosen a side. This affects us in the media as well as in the courts. We can't get a fair trial. Judges already have their own agendas based on the side they have already chosen."

"Understandable," says Tony.

"So, when it comes to hiring an attorney we must be sure that we are hiring one who honestly has our best interest at heart. One who is not working for the other side, working against us as the last attorney was. Sadly, he drowned at Bray Beach a few weeks ago," he says with no real sense of compassion.

Tony can read in between the lines and is sure the attorney didn't drown. He was drowned. "How unfortunate," Tony says with his face indicating he understands well.

"Very," the Don says. "Our attorney before him was burned to a crisp in his automobile. Faulty wiring," he says. "And then there was the one before him, he was on a seven-case losing streak. It all ended with him accidentally falling in his bathtub and dying. He couldn't win for the sake of losing. And there was one more before him who was assassinated by the Hutch's."

Tony's mind is scattered right now. All that he's hearing is having an effect on his thought process.

"The countless death threats our attorneys receive is unbelievable," The Dapper Don says. "Could you ever represent a family that has so much death surrounding it?"

"All depends on the lifestyle that's provided by representing a family that has so much death surrounding it. Money isn't everything but it does make life worth living."

"I take that as a yes or a strong possibility?" Tony shrugs as if he's unsure. "When did you plan to go back to your country?"

"Tonight, right after this meeting," Tony replies.

"Well, how about you stay another day so we can go over all the financial details. I can have you flown back to the U.S in my chartered jet," he says, believing he's said something impressive.

"Thanks, but I flew here on my own private jet," says Tony. The Dapper Don is astounded. "Yes, I have my own jet. I told you I'm no regular negro. I'm different from anything you have ever seen on CNN. I'm a different breed. I don't fear death any more than I fear life.

I got two more hours before my jet is scheduled to depart. That means you have an hour and a half to work out the numbers and present them to me for my approval. I will give you one chance to convince me. Come up with a number that you believe is fair in comparison to who I am as an attorney.

The dollar value you present to me will let me know just what you think of me. At that time I will respond yay or nay. I will not compromise, negotiate or barter. The dollar value you set will tell me where we go from here. So with that being said, I will step away and give you a few moments alone to think."

34

MIDDLE GODSON PULLS up and parks across the street from Trenton Police Department. He looks over to the older woman in his passenger's seat. "No disrespect Mrs. Barbara but I can't go in there. I don't do police."

"I understand baby. I thank you for driving me here though. I'm losing my mind," she says. "Can't eat, can't sleep," she says sadly. "This ain't like him to just disappear without telling me something. And like Tanya said his car is parked at that bar which means that was the last place he was at. She said she was in there until they closed that night and she didn't see him. He never came in there. What you think may have happened?"

Middle Godson is as confused as her. "I don't know, Mrs. Barbara. It can be anything. Maybe he locked up and he just got lost in the system." Middle Godson has a few things that he thinks could have happened. He thinks Bleek could have easily met with someone at the bar and got in the car with them and took his last ride. He can never tell the old woman that though. "Just got to file that missing person report and see what they come up with."

"Yes, and pray that he's alive and in one piece, amen!" she says as she opens the door and gets out.

Middle Godson ducks low in his seat, not wanting to be seen in front of a police precinct. In no way is that a good look for a gangster. He pulls out his phone and dials Skelter just to make sure she's ok. He listens as the phone rings until the automated service comes on. He dials again and again and gets the automated service each time. He doesn't like this.

Skelter never ignores their calls. He immediately jumps to conclusions, thinking the worse. He knew better to let her go to Newark alone but she insisted. He dials several more times and still gets no answer.

EDGEWATER, NEW JERSEY

Vito's bedroom is immaculately decorated which is quite shocking for a gangster bachelor pad. No Ikea furniture in his apartment, just luxurious handmade pieces from Hellman Chang out of New York City. The theme and concept of the bedroom was inspired by a bedroom he saw in the movie, *Sex in the City*. He did his research and found out the designers of the furniture and went from there.

His bed, made from solid wood, has an expansive sloping headboard, an oversized, low-profile platform, and Hellman-Chang's trademark twist in the aprons. Its sleek shape and flowing lines scream luxuriously. The platform low on the floor, but the mattresses are stacked so high one has to climb onto them just to lay down. His nightstands, his dresser and every other piece of furniture is made in the same wood yet no design is the same; a bunch of beautiful pieces with no uniform.

All the paint on the walls is Ralph Lauren. Suede finish lavender paint is the primary color on all the walls. Splashes of lavender to purple rainbows accent the walls beautifully like a piece of art. Purple borders hold it all together. The carpet which is a lighter shade of purple balances it all out. Vito has invested over $80,000 into this bedroom just to make it his peace away from the streets. He calls this room Grape Heaven. The green street sign which reads 'Grape Street' hangs over his door, representing his Set.

Vito steps into the bedroom, shirtless, with sagging white Givenchy sweatpants. Tattoos cover his whole torso like an easel covered in ink. The zipper scar that extends from underneath his navel up to the middle of his chest is a result of his near-death experience seven years ago when he was shot down. The small hump on his shoulder is a result of when he was shot three years ago and the slug was never taken out. It just protrudes from his shoulder.

The scar that starts at his right bicep and extends across his chest diagonally is a result of a bar fight that led to him being cut. Three hours of surgery and 400 stitches was the aftermath of that. With all the abuse his body has been through he still looks to be in great shape. He's thin and small framed but ripped up like a Mexican boxer.

He walks over to the bed where Skelter lays, sound asleep. As he gets within several feet away from her she pops up, with her gun already drawn. "Hold ma, be easy," he says as he stops dead in his tracks, with his hands in the air. She looks around in somewhat of a shock until it all comes back to her.

She must have dozed off after counting through the money. She started off sitting at the foot of the bed and has no clue how she ended up in the middle of the bed in a fetal position. She can't believe she actually slipped like this and fell asleep around a complete stranger. The room is so tranquil and serene that it was almost impossible not to fall asleep. Add in the fact that she's been barely sleeping the past few weeks. Here, so far away from home, she feels safe.

She looks Vito up and down on the sneak tip and although she will never admit it, she finds him to be attractive. His war scars covering his body is more attractive to her than his physique. He turns his head, looking across the room and she's able to look at him closer without him knowing. She notices a razor scar on his face that starts underneath his temple and swerves around to his cheek. It's an ugly scar but in no way does it take away from his pretty boy appeal.

He stands in front of her drying off his hair with a towel. "All the money was there, right? Two hundred and fifty-thousand?" he asks as he tosses the towel onto the nightstand. He grabs a bottle of cologne from that same nightstand and sprays it into the air, over his head. He stands still allowing the Bond No.9 cologne to drizzle onto his body like a rain shower.

Skelter turns away from him, for her own sake. "Here," she says as she shoves a duffle-bag to him. Her eyes are now drawn to his beard.

The bright lamp behind him shines brightly on him causing the beads of baby oil to dance throughout his jet-black beard. "My apologies for falling asleep in your bed," she says with embarrassment. "Been ripping and running," she says in her defense.

She feels so vulnerable right now. She still can't believe she actually fell asleep in a stranger's bed; a stranger from the other side. She hates herself as she thinks of the fact that it could have easily went another way and she would've never awakened from her sleep. He could've murdered her and got away with 10 kilos of cocaine. She definitely would've gone down in history as one of the dumbest criminals ever. If Manson found out about this she's sure she would never hear the end of it.

Although he's a complete stranger something about him feels different. She's not sure if her trust for him has everything to do with Manson or if it's his own vibe? Or maybe both? Whatever it is he makes it easy to trust him. She just hopes he doesn't gain her trust only to cross her big in the end. This is a chance that she has no choice right now but to take.

"No worries, Shorty."

"Skelter," she says in correction. There's nothing she hates more than to be called Shorty.

"Skelter...my bad," he says as he pulls one of the kilos from the duffle-bag anxiously. He walks over to the dresser, staring at the brick in his hand. He grabs a pair of scissors from the dresser and uses them to unwind the tape covering the kilo. "Damn that shower brought me back to life." His shower is bringing her life right now as well as she stares at the beads of water bubbled all over his back. His tiny size 28 waist evolves into wings that resemble a flying eagle. His broad shoulders are perfectly sculpted. He's so easy on the eyes that she has to pry her eyes off of him.

"I been grinding like a motherfucker," he says. "I had the same shit on for like four days, no bullshit," he says as he peeks over his shoulder at her with a grin. Skelter sits there pretending to be very uninterested in his small talk. "Got damn, this that shit right here," he says as he analyzes the work. "Yo, I'm about to light their ass up. I fuck around and can put a half on everyone," he says with greed in his eyes. "I'm ready to get out here and get on my job!"

He grabs a hoodie from the closet and puts it on. There he stands in all pure white. Skelter grabs the duffle filled with money and starts walking toward him. He leads her through the living room. The sun greets her face almost blinding her. A wall of glass, looking onto the balcony, overlooking the Hudson River is a beautiful sight.

"I didn't even show you the view," he says as he leads her to the window. She follows at his heels. He presents the view to her. The unimpressed look on her face in no way matches what she feels inside.

Skelter is afraid of nothing else in the world but heights, but strangely being up here on the 22nd floor brings her no fear at all. They're just a stone's throw away from Manhattan. Clear, full view of the Hudson River, George Washington Bridge and the New York City skyline all in one eyeful. This has to be the most amazing sight she's ever seen. She could only imagine going to sleep and waking up to this view and how rejuvenating it would be.

"Beautiful right?" Vito asks as he appreciates the view. "I barely stay here. One may think I'm wasting five thousand dollars a month on rent on an apartment I barely stay at," he says as he enjoys the view. "But every time I look out this window, it's worth every dime." No matter how many times he looks out there he always finds something he didn't notice before.

"Check, I know you got a lot of shit going on down there and getting no peace and quiet. You are welcome to come and lay low here until you relocate. You, your sister and the baby can come. I don't even be staying here like that."

Skelter feels transparent as she listens to him speak. She hates that he knows all of her business. She's baffled by Manson running his mouth like that. She wonders if it's a part of his mental illness that has him like that.

She also hates the fact that she thinks he may believe that she's hiding in fear. "Listen, I don't know what Big Bruh may have told you but I ain't in hiding. I'm in my city, showing my face every day. He wants me to hide but that ain't happening," she says with rage covering her face.

"Calm down, Shorty. I mean Skelter. I don't think you're hiding. I just know that Bruh asked me to take care of you and that is what I plan to do. I accepted the job and now you are my responsibility. He grabs both of her hands as they stand face to face losing themselves in each other eyes. "I got you from here."

Skelter feels weird inside. She snatches her hands away from his. He digs himself and realizes the hand touching was not gangster at all and may have been a bit too much. "I'm gone keep my word that I gave to Bruh, in every aspect. Some parts may be harder than others," he says while shaking his head. He sighs, "Uhmm, uhmm, mhmm... but trust me, I got you."

35

TRENTON

IT'S PITCH DARK behind Roger Garden Apartments. The drug activity has come to a halt because of the tension in the air. Middle Godson paces around in circles with a gun in each hand. A bunch of men are lined up against the wall and a few are scattered around all standing stiff with nervousness. It's not that they are in fear. It's just that he has the drop on them, his guns already drawn. The odds are totally against them. A wise man knows how to pick his battles. Right now, it's his game and his rules.

Skelter leans against the Durango, hoodie on, both hands in her pocket. She's keeping her eyes on the crowd. Her other two Godsons stand in the backdrop quietly watching. They are giving Middle Godson the floor to do whatever it is he wants. He has something on his chest that he must get off.

"I'm feeling like niggas know where my man is at," he says as he stops and looks at the men on the wall. "I swear I'm feeling like niggas know something, they just ain't talking. Niggas acting like he don't count, not even giving a fuck that he missing."

One man has the heart to stand up for the crew. "Ain't nobody say he don't count. Niggas ain't detectives," he says like a wise ass. "What we supposed to do, go on a worldwide manhunt and find him?"

"Nah, I'm just saying this ain't no regular shit and niggas don't seem to be giving a fuck about my man that I thought was all our man. But I get it though. Niggas on some every-man-for-himself shit out here, always been. Niggas done put their lives on the line for the hood and then after all the years of putting it down, niggas can say fuck you and turn their back on you, just like that. I get it."

He's in his zone now and letting it all hang out. Skelter is hoping he doesn't incriminate himself and them while he's in his zone. She's ready to intervene but that would seem guilty as well. She knows how emotional he can get when he's off the pills. She keeps her fingers crossed, hoping he contains himself.

"Bleek put it down for the hood and niggas gone act like he ain't missing? That's just some weird type shit to me."

"Been a lot of weird type shit going on that niggas ain't been speaking on," a man says in the backdrop.

"Well, speak on it then," Middle Godson says as he walks toward the man, clenching both guns tightly. The man watches the guns closely, not looking Middle Godson in the face. "If you got something to say, say it."

The man continues on with no fear. "I'm just saying niggas been getting smashed for weeks now and nobody ain't saying why or nothing. Old Head got smashed, even Big Bruh, still nobody saying nothing concrete. Just a bunch of rumors on what niggas think. Bleek missing, nobody got nothing concrete on that either, just a bunch of rumors."

The man has more to say than expected. He's letting it all go. "Do we charge all this shit to the game, like shit that just be happening in the hood? Or do niggas lay shit on the table on what they know and we put all that shit together and start figuring out what the fuck going on out here? You said everybody on some every-man-for-himself shit out here. Wasn't always like that. For the most part niggas out here always got together when it was time to put in work. Lately motherfuckers seem to be on some secret, greedy time shit and that's why other niggas is looking out for self."

Middle Godson is bothered that he seems to have no filter on what comes out of his mouth. He can read in between the lines and knows for certain that the man is speaking about them. "Seems like you got a lot on your mind. A lot to say," Middle Godson says. Seems like you know how niggas moving and how niggas thinking so I'm gone tell you like this," he says as he steps closer to the man. "On the Set, if I find out you know anything about where the fuck Bleek at, I'm taking yo ass off the map. And that goes for anybody else that know anything about where he at. But since you the new spokesperson for niggas and expressing how niggas feeling and thinking then you gone be the first one I take the fuck up out of here!"

The man sees the seriousness in Middle Godson's eyes and decides now is not the time to put up a rebuttal. His pride won't let him bow down completely though. He stares Godson in the eyes with a grin as he nods his head. His look alone could really get his head knocked off right now and Middle Godson is two seconds away from doing so but he realizes the trouble he will put himself by doing it like this.

He decides to walk away before he does something stupid. With no further conversation, he gets into the passenger's seat. Skelter and the other Godsons get in behind him. And the truck is driven off. As Youngest Godson busts a U-turn Skelter rolls the window down and grips her gun tight just in case one of them is feeling risky and decides to take a few shots at them. As they clear the area with no gunfire sent at them, Skelter rolls the window up.

The man said a mouthful and what she learned from him tonight is everybody knows exactly what's going on. This thing runs deeper than she knew. Before seeing this for herself she already felt like it was them against most of the Projects. Tonight, she's found out that it was even more people against them than she thought. Right now, she's certain that it's the whole projects against them and Godson may have just made it worse.

Skelter breaks the silence. "I wish you wouldn't have drawed on niggas and not pop off," she says while staring out the window into the night. "You know the rule, when you pull it out, you got to bust it. By not busting it, you just opened up a whole 'nother can of worms. But hey, what's done is done now. We just gone have to move forward and make our next move stronger than your last move."

36

SHORT HILLS MALL

PEBBLES HAS BEEN ripping through the mall, blowing money fast. Baby Manson insisted she go and buy herself something nice and she has. She doesn't feel guilty spending his money because he now has tens of thousands tucked away in his savings. She's still mindful not to go too hard though.

As she's standing in the line at Louis Vuitton she looks over her shoulder at the doorway where two young girls enter. Pebbles and one of the girls exchange smiles, acknowledging each other. The girls tour the store, just looking at things they wish they could buy.

Pebbles steps up to the cashier who greets her with a smile. "Hello Miss Boone," the cashier says. She spends so much money here that they know her by name.

"Pebbles is suffice," she says. The cashier is her age and calling her 'Miss' makes her feel so much older.

"Ok, Pebbles," the cashier says as she lifts the first item to be scanned. At the sound of the name, the two young girls look at each other with devious looks on their faces. They slowly make their way closer to the counter. They pick up a pocketbook here and a shoe there just to make it look good but really they are ear hustling and being nosey.

The woman first rings up the pocketbook. The Ocean Blue colored City Steamer PM handbag rings up at $10,600. Pebbles cringes as she reads the numbers on the cash register. Her son told her to buy herself something nice but she's not sure if he meant this nice. "Shit, he owe me, all the sacrificing I've done, raising him all by myself," she mumbles to herself. She's attempting to justify spending his money so foolishly.

The woman then scans the sneakers. The Archlight sneaker boot rings up at $1,170. Pebbles doesn't even flinch. "Your total is twelve thousand, five hundred ninety-three dollars and ninety cent," the woman says with a cheesy smile.

"Sheesh," Pebbles mumbles under her breath. She wears an emotionless, 'this is what I do face' as she pulls out stacks of money from her pocketbook. She unwraps the rubber bands off the G-stacks before laying it on the counter. The cashier has to call two co-workers to help her count through it all.

The two young women are no longer pretending to not be watching. In fact, they stand in the middle of the floor outright watching. It takes all of 20 minutes for the employees to count and recount the money. The cashier places the money into leather caches and lays them on the side.

"Thank you, Miss Boone. I mean, Pebbles. Have a great day."

The 2 young girls look at each other at the sound of her name.

"You have a great day as well," Pebbles says. She makes her way to the door and the young girls step along with her. As they're walking one of the young girls steps closer to Pebbles. Now shoulder to shoulder in stride, the young girl sneakily drops a plastic shopping bag into Pebbles big shopping bag.

"That's three thousand," the young girl says. "It's five hundred left on the back end. He said tell you he can get it to me tomorrow if that's ok with you?"

"It's fine," Pebbles replies with limited conversation. She in no way wants the woman to get too familiar with her which is why she keeps her words to a minimum. Their business is over so there's nothing left for her to say. She cuts to the left without saying a word, not even a bye.

Both of the girls watch as Pebbles is on the escalator. "Damn, Miss Boone is a rude, ugly bitch," one of the girls says in a joking manner. It's really an inside joke as the young woman puts emphasis on the name.

"No, Pebbles," the other one says sarcastically. They crack each other up. Their mission of finding out her name is complete. Finding out her name was easy. Now the hard part will be finding out her whereabouts. Or maybe it won't be hard at all.

37

COLUMBUS BOULEVARD, SOUTH PHILLY

THREE TRACTOR TRAILERS are lined up in the parking lot of the strip mall. Dope fiends are in the trailers and standing outside of the tractors. All of them are busy at work. In the tractors there is over $300,000 worth of Lowe's goods. The items in the tractors include tools, lumber, paint, tiling, carpet, sinks, toilets, and lighting. He also has another 15 hot-tubs for another condo building they are working on. Umar has delivered every single item they put in for. He's even added in some items they didn't order but thought they would be in need of.

On the inside of the storefronts, men are hard at work. The sound of power drills, power saws and hammers create a harmonious tune. The workers are the perfect mix of Blacks and Irishmen, now that they have partnered with McCaulley. Everybody working in peace, working toward the same goal, everybody eating off the same plate.

Maurice and Umar stand in a room that will soon be the back office of one of the storefronts. The table-saw in between them has stacks of money on it piled up to their chest. A drug sniffing k9 wouldn't have to sniff this money to tell it's drug money. The bills are crinkled and some are even missing corners. The faces are badly worn and some bills even have blood stains on them. Blood money is the best way to describe it. You can look at it and tell it's been scraped off the ground. If the Presidents on the bills could talk, the stories behind each of them would be gruesome. Maurice dug deep in the crates for this money. They didn't pull the money out of their joint business account. Instead he pulled this money from his own stash and Tony will pay him back in a check. The perfect way to clean up this dirty money.

Maurice counts through the money quickly because for the most part it's already in thousand-dollar stacks. He just had to add a few thousand from his pocket to top it off. Maurice slides the stacks of money over to Umar 10 stacks at a time. Once he pushes the last batch over to him, he speaks. "That's a hundred and fifty-six right there," he says as he looks down at the 4 different receipts. He quickly calculates the numbers in his head and it comes out to $312,800.00. He counts through the loose bills in his pocket. He hands a hefty stack over to Umar. "And that's four hundred dollars."

Umar sucks his teeth and waves his hand. "Man, I ain't worried about no four hundred dollars."

"I ain't gone argue with you," Maurice says as he shoves the money back into his pocket. "You only got to tell me once."

Umar laughs as they reach over the table and shake hands over the deal. "Pleasure doing business with you, my brother," Umar says.

"Oh, we just getting started. Got a big project over by the Schuylkill River we start working on in two weeks and we gone need everything from screws and bolts on up."

"Aye man, as you can see whatever you need, I got you," Umar says. He starts shoving the stacks of money into a duffle-bag.

"Appreciate you," Maurice says. Umar looks up and they lock eyes like men. "About the other night, just wanted to salute you. That was real shit."

"Bruh, that was nothing," Umar says humbly. "I know good folks when I see them. I just did what any other real motherfucker would do. This ain't a Philly, Jersey thing. This a real nigga thing. It's more of them fake niggas than us real niggas which is why us real niggas have to stick together."

"Aye, well, we together now. And we gone get money. I appreciate you more than you know, man. If you ever need me, I'm here," Maurice says.

"Appreciate that bruh and the same here," Umar replies. As he packs his earnings into his bag, Maurice's phone rings.

Maurice excuses himself before stepping away and accepting the call. "Yo?"

SCOTCH PLAINS, NEW JERSEY

"Yo, Big Homie, I'm in Scotch Plains in this strip mall," says the man on the other end of Maurice's phone line. "I just met my man at this little restaurant and you will never guess who I'm sitting here looking at right now," the man says as he sits in the driver's seat of his BMW.

"Who?" Maurice asks angrily. He's not one for the guessing game.

"Please, big bruh, just one guess."

"Come on man," Maurice snaps.

"Your heart," the man says teasingly. "Lil Bit."

Maurice's heart drops. "You bullshitting?"

"Big Homie, you know I would never play like that. I'm sitting right here looking right at her."

Maurice's mind works faster than his mouth. He stutters trying to get all his thoughts out at once. He hasn't seen Lil Bit in over 10 years now. Back when he ordered the hit on her, it took him months to find out that it wasn't fatal. It's like she fell off the face of the earth for years without a trace. Over the years there has been people who have reported that they think they saw her but no real proof.

"Are you sure bruh?" Maurice asks desperately.

"I'm positive bruh. I'm sitting close enough to touch her if you know what I mean. And I'm strapped," he says muffled enough just in case unwanted listeners are on the phone.

Lil Bit has just left out of the nail salon. Now her and a ten-year-old little girl stand in a Rita's Ice line. She obviously is at ease and not thinking about hiding because she hasn't looked over her shoulder one single time. She seems completely comfortable.

"She by herself?" Maurice asks.

"Nah, her and a little girl," the man replies. "Looks just like her. Has to be her daughter." Hearing mention of a daughter plunges through his heart the same way it did years ago when he first found out about it all.

Lil Bit grabs the water ice for her and the little girl and they walk away. She walks to the Infiniti Q80 and opens the passenger's door for the little girl to climb in.

"Big Homie, what you want me to do? She's leaving."

"I don't want you to do nothing but put a tail on her. That's it, no more no less," he says, letting him know not to make a move on her. "I need to see her myself. This shit personal."

Lil Bit backs the big truck up and zips out of the parking lot. The man gives her time enough to get out of the parking lot before he pulls out of his parking space and peels out of the parking lot behind her. "I'm on it Big Bruh."

38

THREE LEVELS LOUNGE/NEWARK, NEW JERSEY

THE V.I.P. SECTION is lit. Vito and his crew are more than 30 deep. The back of the club is like a big Crip reunion. The beautifully designed club is in the newly developed section of downtown, across from Newark's prized Prudential Center. Just a few blocks away, walking distance is the gang-filled Pennington Court Projects. This club is like the backyard to those gangbangers from Pennington which makes it heavy Crip occupancy.

There are old non-active Crips, young active Crips, wannabe Crips, mothers and fathers of Crips and Crip lovers all out for the cause. One of the homies just got released from prison yesterday after doing a decade and a half. That calls for a celebration. With so many Crips in the building, the non-Crips and regular civilians are walking on eggshells.

The back of the club near the V.I.P. section is on tilt because most of the people are back here. The women stand near the velvet rope, doing their sexiest dances with hopes of being invited inside. Others stand there, pretending to not pay attention but they have those same hopes of being invited in. The bottles are flowing non-stop with enough Ciroc and champagne for everybody in the club to wet their whistle.

When Vito is in the building the dynamics of the club changes. It's as if a celebrity is in the building. The women and men watch him in awe of the infamous legend. They want to see how he acts and even how he walks. To be close enough to hear him actually talk would be an honor. Overall Vito handles the attention like a Don and doesn't let it go to his head. It's his lil homies that let his attention go to their heads.

When he's in the building they can't help but to show off. They throw their weight around a little more when he's around, showing off for him. They pray for Vito to have the smallest issue with someone so they can stand up and take matters in their own hands. It would be an honor for them to put in work for the Big Homie and be recognized by him. They will do anything for his recognition and that is why everybody in the club right now is at risk.

Vito sits in the booth with his back against the wall, laid back. Right next to him is Skelter. She feels like she sticks out like a sore thumb being the only Blood in the cipher with close to 50 Crips. The fact that she's an out of towner makes it even worse. Still she plays it like a G despite her slight discomfort.

While sitting here, a thousand thoughts rip through her mind. She's been watching the whole time she's been here and she notices how differently Trenton and Newark operate. She also sees how everyone seems to mesh together, regardless of the set they represent, the flag they represent or even the side of town they are from. Everybody seems to be able to be together in one room regardless of it all. It makes her wonder, if they all can get together in one room like this, then why is the murder rate so high?

It appears as if everybody here gets along. Everyone greeting each other with smiles and hugs. They're buying each other drinks and pouring drinks and passing them out of the V.I.P. section to the common folks. She's never seen so many bottles popped in one section. It's like a scene from a rap video. She watches as the drinks and the fake love flow in abundance.

Vito looks over to Skelter. What he sees before his eyes is not the gangster chick he's gotten used to seeing. Tonight, she's without her hoodie, her skullcap and her Timberlands. Tonight, she has her hair out and is even wearing lipgloss. She replaced her Timberland boots for some Chanel sneakers. The suede motorcycle jacket matches her sneakers perfectly. Fitted jeans reveal her curvy but petite frame and her fitted tee-shirt exposes the beautiful breasts she so desperately tries to hide. Tonight, she's even carrying a purse and wearing perfume. Tonight, she's all woman.

The smell of her perfume smacks Vito in the face and draws him closer to her. He is really digging her as a gangster but as a woman his desire for her is overwhelming. "You shouldn't be enjoying yourself so much," he says jokingly. Skelter cracks a half a grin.

Vito had to beg her a dozen times to come. The only reason she came is because she's trying to build a solid business relationship with him and in order to do so she's trying her best to compromise. She doesn't want him to think she's just using him. She's totally against partying but in this case she's partying with a purpose.

"Thanks for coming out though," Vito says graciously. "I can tell this ain't your wave."

"At all," she confirms. "I haven't been in a club in over ten years," she says.

She positions her Chanel purse on her lap at the perfect angle. With it already unzipped she can dig right into it and grab her gun if by chance she needs to.

"I can tell. You super uptight," he says teasingly. "I really just wanted you to come out so you can see how we do it on the other side. The other side of the Garden State as well as the other side of the color chart. Plus, I got some business I want to run pass you. Loosen up and try to enjoy yourself. We can talk business later."

TRENTON

Middle Godson steps onto the porch. He turns around and locks the door. As he walks down the steps his attention is on his phone in which he scrolls and scrolls, just out of habit. He peeks up every few steps on his way to the Buick LaCrosse that's parked in front of the house. Just as he grabs the door handle, he notices a speeding blur through his peripheral.

He looks over and to his surprise a speeding vehicle is coming toward him. He backs up against his car to get out of harm's way not realizing the harm is meant for him. It's all happening so fast right he has no time to react. The passenger's door flies open before the Bronco gets to him. He grabs his gun from his pocket, aims at the truck and fires. BLOCKA!

A shot is fired back at him. BOC! He's struck and the bullet cracks his humerus bone in half. The vibration causes his whole arm to shimmer. The nerves in his arms down to his hand twitch uncontrollably causing him to lose his grip of gun. It falls out of his hand and he quickly bends over in attempt to get hold of it.

BOC! Another shot is fired at him. This time his kneecap is shattered into four pieces. He can no longer hold his weight on it, so he tips over.

Two men hop out of the Bronco and leap toward him. They snatch him from the ground and drag him into the Bronco. The Bronco speeds off at top speed. Tortura doesn't waste a single second before he gets to the abuse of Middle Godson.

THREE LEVELS LOUNGE

The lights have just flickered on and off. This is the part that everyone hates. The party is over. Now is the time for all the scary dudes to get a head start out of the building. You have two types of scary dudes. The ones that want to get out before the goons get out and the other kind that stays in the club for as long as he can to give the goons time to leave the parking lot.

Minutes pass and now the club lights are on. People are making their exit. Some take their time while others rush hastily. A few men stand around with women shooting their last attempt at getting them to leave with them. For those who have invested a few dollars in drinks for women, it's now time for them to cash in on their investments. Last call really means it's time to wrap it up and seal the deal for the woman you've been working on all night. If by chance that deal isn't sealed by the time the lights come on, you have a very small window of time to work on your plan B chick.

Vito and the crew make their way out of the V.I.P. section. They march through the club like an army; the purple army that is. People get out of their path long before they get near. About a dozen men lead the pack all in a single file. Then there's Vito and Skelter who are side by side. The 12 men in front make an opening, a clear path for Vito and Skelter to walk through with ease. The 20 men behind them have their eyes on everything to make sure no one tries to bust a move on Vito.

Vito has his hand around Skelter's shoulder in a protective manner. She tries to wiggle away from him but he pulls her closer and holds her tighter. The way he's been overprotective with her tonight makes her feel uncomfortable because he's treating her like a lady. The strange part of it all is the girlie part of her actually likes it. It's the gangster in her that hates it.

Skelter is enjoying the protective treatment from Vito so much that she moves from underneath his wing. He looks to her with a smirk. "I ain't trying to treat you like a girl," he says. "I'm just holding you close like a homie," he says with a dazzling smile. Mid-stride, a human collision takes place. Vito and a man bump chest to chest. The man's drink splashes out of his glass all over Vito's cocaine white sweatshirt.

Vito looks down and his shirt is covered in Hennessy. He looks down further at his white spiked Louboutin sneakers which are also covered in Hennessy. His night is now ruined. He looks up at the man slowly with rage burning through his eyes and before he can say a word to the man, the man speaks out.

"Damn motherfucker," the drunkard man says as if he's not in the wrong. He's too drunk to even give a fuck. "Watch where you going, damn!" the drunk says with aggression. "You owe me a fucking drink."

Vito looks at the man, surprised, to say the least. Vito's goons rush in and form a tight circle around the drunkard. A man squeezes inside the circle and grabs the drunk man by the collar. "Sorry bruh," the man says fearfully. "Please don't mind him, he's drunk." He looks to the drunk. "I told you, you had too much to drink," he says in fear of his friend's life.

"Fuck that! I ain't that drunk," the man slurs. "He owe me a fucking drink."

A few of Vito's goons rush in and they practically throw each other out of the way to be the one who gets hold of the drunkard first. The drunkard is slammed against the wall with an elbow pressed against his neck. All Vito's men gather around, ready to duff the drunkard out.

"Please, don't, please," the other man begs before he's snatched out of midair. He's slammed to the floor so hard, the floor shakes. He looks up helplessly just as several boots are raised in the air, ready to be dropped on his head.

"Yo," Vito shouts. All his men look at him like a trained dog does his master. He shakes his head no to them all and they all stop at his command. Vito looks to the sober man on the floor. "You need to stop hanging with him. He will put you in a bad spot. You need to fuck him up in the morning for almost getting you duffed out."

Vito looks to the drunkard. "You better learn some fucking manners. If you can't control your liquor you need to stop drinking. You fucking with a nigga that can fuck up your whole existence. Tonight you get a pass," Vito says as he grabs hold of Skelter. He leads her out of the circle and makes his way to the exit like the Don that he is.

As Vito and Skelter get to the door the goons all step in front of him and exit before them. Once they see the coast is clear he's given the signal to exit. People are scattered all around, not ready to end the night. Through the many people swarming around, Vito quickly spots his men in their positions as they should be. He has 5 of his men posted like a five-point star in front of him. Each of the five men stands at their point, gun in possession, watching the scenery and prepared to go if need be.

Vito and Skelter are in the center of the tightly formed circle. They are escorted to the Audi truck that awaits them at the curb. Vito holds the door open for Skelter like a gentleman. Once Skelter is in, he climbs in behind her. The Audi pulls off with a string of vehicles following it. Skelter is in somewhat of an amazement. She's never seen power exerted like this.

Vito reacts to all of this as normal life. He looks over to Skelter. "Now about that business," he says. "Dig, I put my Master Mixer on the work I got from you and that shit is high power. I only put

250 grams of cut on a joint because I wasn't sure how it would stand up. Come to find out the shit is like that! That little bit of cut didn't change shit. So, this is what I'm thinking," he says as he taps her knee with his backhand. "First of all, I ain't counting your pockets but do you have another ten of them?" Vito asks.

"Why, what's up?" she asks. She's not quite willing to open her whole hand to him. She feels she has already given him too much trust as is.

Vito looks up ahead, paying close attention. "Hold up, one-second," he says as the Audi comes to a stop. He opens the door and slides out, pulling Skelter along with him. He peeks around cautiously.

Behind the Audi the line of cars have stopped as well. Vito leads Skelter to the Range Rover that is double parked beside them. He opens the door and climbs into the Rover. The Rover pulls off and the Audi and every other car pulls off behind it.

Vito picks right up from where he left off. "I figure like this. We can take ten of the units and put a whole joint on a whole joint. I can get my hands on a kilo of procaine for two thousand dollars. Looks just like fish-scale and burns like it and everything," he claims. "They just can't get high off of it. You figure we smack a joint of the procaine on a joint of the raw. So, now one turns into two. Ten joints turn into twenty joints.

I will give you the thirty you asking for but we can sell them for dirt cheap like twenty-five a bird," he says with intense facial expressions. "The quality will be so-so but niggas won't give a fuck because they will be so busy chasing the low number. Number chasers don't give a fuck about quality," he says as he sways his finger from side to side.

"They are more interested in a number. Nobody will beat our number." Skelter is soaking in the lesson he's giving her. "You figure twenty joints at twenty-five a joint, that's a half a million. I give you your three hundred and we deduct the forty thousand for the cut. We are left with $160,000 to split. It's a win-win situation because you getting the exact number you were originally asking for. The bonus is, you're getting an extra eight thousand profit on every joint."

Skelter listens with all of her attention as he fast talks. The slick, fast talk turns her on. She's impressed with his mind. She just can't let him out-slick her. She's sure with him being from the North part of Jersey and her being from the South part he probably thinks she's slower and less sharper than him. Because of that she's paying closer attention to every word he spits.

They've driven another ten blocks without realizing due to them being in so deep of a conversation. The Range Rover Stops and Vito busts the door open. He leads her to a tinted-out Suburban that's awaiting them in the intersection. He pulls her close, guarding her as they make way to the Rover.

He opens the door and allows her in first. They get in and the Suburban pulls off. The string of cars behind them speed off as well. Skelter doesn't understand the game of musical cars they've been playing but she asks no questions pertaining to it. She does have a question for him though. "How long do you think it will take to shake the twenty joints though?"

"No time flat," he replies confidently. "I got a crazy pipeline. My city, Jersey City, Patterson, Passaic, and Elizabeth," he says. "That's just to name a few. Anywhere there's my kind at, I can push the work through," he says as he grabs hold of the door.

Five blocks later and they get out of the Suburban and gets into a 5 series BMW that awaits them. Skelter peeks behind and realizes the string of vehicles have decreased. There are only 5 cars left in the line. The BMW pulls off and they ride in silence. Each car they get in rides longer than the car before it. Skelter's replays all he's said. She hopes that it's as simple as he says it is. If it is, she's looking at one hell of a profit margin.

Skelter has been so caught up in thought that she didn't notice that Vito has fallen sound asleep. His head rests on her shoulder as he snores like a bear. The fact that he's fallen asleep around her speaks volumes. She gets away from that thought as she deals with the reality that she's in a car with a half a stranger on her shoulder and a total stranger in the driver's seat.

As she stares up front her and the driver lock eyes in the rearview mirror. That look in his eyes has slime-ball written all in them. She has no clue of who he is and where they are going. She thinks of how this could go bad. It's obvious that Vito trusts him but that is always how it goes. It's always the one you trust who takes you out of here.

Skelter and the man lock eyes once again in the rearview. As soon as he turns his head, she reaches under her sweater and grips her gun. She slides her gun in between her thighs, never letting the handle go. If he has any other plans he will be in for a rude awakening.

Three right turns and two left turns followed by a twelve block straight shot, the driver finally pulls over. "Vito," the driver shouts while looking into the rearview. "Yo, wake him up," he says.

Skelter nudges Vito with her shoulder while still maintaining her grip on her gun. "Vito," she says into his ear.

Vito snaps out of his sleep and looks around cluelessly. Once he realizes where he is, he gathers himself and forces the door open. Just as they are getting out of the BMW, Vito's Corvette pulls up on the side of them. The driver gets out and runs to the passenger's side. He holds the door open for Skelter to get in, while Vito gets into the driver's seat. The man slams the door shut behind Skelter and Vito pulls off.

Skelter looks into the mirror and notices that all the cars except for one go into their own direction. One car follows them closely. This system he has set up for his protection almost makes him untouchable. No one can ever ambush him because with the constant changing of cars the enemy would not know what car he's in. If one decided they wanted to take the chance and attempt to ambush him they would never make it out alive.

As Vito drives, Skelter looks over at him with admiration. She loves how he moves. She really can get used to being around him like this. He carries himself like the G's used to. Manson is the last man that ever taught her anything. Ever since he fell, she's been out here playing the role of a man and leading and educating men.

Vito, he's so different from what she's now gotten used to when it comes to this new wave of men. She's always been attracted to power and Vito displays it in every sense of the word. She's so in awe of him that she's second guessing if she should stay at his apartment tonight. It's not that she doesn't trust him. She doesn't trust herself alone with him.

Vito parks next to Skelter's rented Durango inside of the huge parking garage. Skelter gets out and to Vito's surprise she walks toward the rental. "What's up?" he asks.

"Shit, got to get on this road," she says.

"Knock it off," he says. "It's too late to be driving. Just chill until the morning," he suggests.

Skelter stands at the door, looking over the hood at Vito. The look in his eyes has her ready to give in but she knows she will regret it in the morning. "You can sleep in my bed and I will sleep in the guest bedroom."

Vito's persistence is making her weak. She has to turn away from him just to continue to stand her ground. She climbs into the truck and backs out, not looking in his direction again. She knows if she looks, she won't be going bye-bye.

39

HOURS LATER/TRENTON

SKELTER STARES AT a bullet hole in the Buick Lacrosse's door. Streaks of blood are splattered on the door underneath the bullet hole. The puddle of blood on the ground sends chills through her spine. She studies the amount of blood and in her heart she wants to believe that this little bit of blood doesn't mean life ending. But in another sense she's seen instances where there's been very little blood and the person was killed on the spot.

She has to back up against the car to brace herself. She looks up to the sky to keep the tears from falling. The last thing she wants is for her Godsons to see her crying; even though the both of their faces are covered with tears. She has a saying 'if I cry, what the babies gone do?' She knows there's a possibility that if they see her cry they will lose their minds and do something stupid. Right now there's no room for stupidity and mistakes.

"Yo, somebody had to see something," Skelter says as she looks around at the neighboring houses.

"It had to be late as shit though because we were playing the game up until like three," Youngest Godson says.

"And then what?" Skelter asks.

"I fell asleep," he replies.

"Me too," Oldest Godson says.

Skelter thinks of where she was at that hour and instantly she feels guilty. At that time she was riding around with Vito and his crew. She feels like it's her fault because she should've been here for him. She feels like if she wasn't up North Jersey this would've never happened.

"I bet y'all was high as shit too, right?" Skelter asks. She's now trying to place the blame on them instead of herself. "So fucking high, y'all don't hear gunshots ringing off in front of the house," she says as a tear of guilt trickles down her face.

"Damn, you blaming us for this shit?" Middle Godson asks.

"I ain't blaming nobody. Ain't no time for blame. We have to fig-ure out where the fuck he is."

"I'm about to go through and hit everything up," Oldest Godson shouts. "That had to come from one of them."

Skelter is almost sure this is a hit from the Dominicans. If it is a hit from the Dominicans she doesn't know the first move to make to get to the bottom of it. It's easier to blame it on the hood. That way she can make a move and let out some of the pain.

"I'm with that," Skelter agrees. Truly she knows this isn't the an-swer, but she must do something.

MEDFORD, NEW JERSEY

The sound of roosters crowing breaks the peace of the farm. Inside the barn, there is no peace. The sound of an old and loud generator roars loudly. There's no real use for the generator but to drown out the sound of the screaming and shouting.

Bleek and Middle Godson are strapped down on two separate, old hospital stretchers in the middle of the floor. These stretchers obvi-ously have been through some real trauma based on the bloody soiled mats and the blood streaks all over the metal and the wheels. They look like they could have been used in a World War of some sort with all the wear and tear on them.

Middle Godson lays there weak and fatigued from the untreated gunshot wounds. The loss of blood has caught up with him. Infection has already set in and the pain from the wounds gets worse by the minute. He's a bloody mess. The smell of his own blood is nauseating.

Tortura stands in between the stretchers at their feet. "We are going to play a game," he says with a big smile. "I'm going to ask you a question," he says while pointing to Godson. "And your answers right or wrong, falls on him," he says before pointing to Bleek.

Tortura holds up a picture and walks closer to them. He holds the picture to Bleek's face. The picture is of a man whose limbs have been cut off and all he has left is a head and a torso. The blood and exposed cartilage is no sight for a weak man.

"The last time I played this game. This is how it ended," says Tortura. Bleek cries even harder after seeing this photo. Tortura then holds the photo for Godson to see. "In this game you are the controller," he says to Godson. "Now, let's begin," he says as he looks over his shoulder. One of his men meet him at the bottom of the stretcher. In his hand he holds a power saw.

He hands the saw to Tortura who wastes no time at all. "Ok, first question," he says like a gameshow host. "Where is the girl? You only get one answer and you must answer in ten-seconds. Ten, nine, eight," he counts slowly.

"Please tell him, please," Bleek pleads as he sobs with no shame. He knows his life depends on it. The torture that he has received has broken him down.

Godson looks at Bleek with hatred in his eyes. To think that he was ready to go to war for Bleek and here it is Bleek rolled on him. That pill is hard for him to swallow. He's heartbroken to say the least. This is something he could never forgive Bleek for.

"Five, four, three," Tortura counts.

"Please," Bleek cries.

Godson sniffs hard accumulating all the mucous he can. He then hog-spits in Bleek's face. "Fuck you."

"One," Tortura says before turning the power saw on. He walks toward Bleek with the saw roaring. Bleek screams at the top of his lungs before Quabo walks over and gags him with an old blood-stained tow-el. Bleek cries with his mouth stuffed.

Tortura stands over Bleek with wickedness in his eyes as he plac-es the saw on Bleek's shoulder. The blade is sharp and with very lit-tle pressure the saw tears the skin. The sound of the blade ripping through the skin is a sound that will flip a weak stomach. Blood squirts from Bleek's shoulder like a water fountain. Tortura actually enjoys the blood splashing in his face.

Godson turns his head, not able to watch. The sound of the saw cutting through through the bone sends chills through Godson's body. The blade slows down as it reaches the thicker part of the bone and then it speeds back up as it gets to the other side. The snapping of the bone sounds like the snapping of a tree branch. The saw finally stops.

Tortura grabs Bleek's detached arm from the stretcher and throws it across the room like an old dog bone. Seeing Bleek's bloody arm lay-ing on the floor makes Godson sick to his stomach. He closes his eyes, just to block it out but he can't erase the visual. He also can't erase the sound of Bleek's screaming.

"Second question," Tortura says as he grabs hold of Godson's face and turns it so he's facing Bleek. He wants him to see the results of him not answering the question. "Ready for the question? Where's the girl? You got five-seconds, this time. Starting...now! One, two," he counts.

Bleek looks at Godson with pleading eyes. He has very little en-ergy left in his body. What lies before Godson's eyes is so unreal. It's hard to believe they are actually here going through this.

"Five," Tortura says. "Time is up. Where's the girl?"

Godson turns his head with no reply. The power saw starts up im-mediately and the sound of it cutting through the skin is coupled with the sound of Bleek grunting as he attempts to take the pain like a man. Godson keeps his eyes closed tightly. He opens his eyes, hoping it's all a nightmare but realizes he's really living this nightmare.

40

GERMANTOWN AVENUE, PHILADELPHIA

IT'S THE BEST day of the week for the Muslims, Friday, the day of Ju-mu'ah Prayer. Umar brought the big toys out today for the occasion. Today he's not driving in his raggedy work truck. He brought out his play truck today. The money green, Bentley Bentayga truck with the saddle color interior catches the attention of all the Muslims standing in front of the Masjid.

Surprisingly, he finds a parking space not too far from the entrance. As he's parking he continues on with his conversation with Twelve Play who sits in the passenger's seat. Umar invited Twelve Play to come pray with him. Twelve Play only accepted the invitation because he felt obligated to do so. He feels like Umar has done more than enough to prove himself. He couldn't tell him no. Also, he feels bad that he hasn't been to the masjid since he's been home. All his years of praying for his freedom and now that he's been granted it, he hasn't stepped foot in God's house once.

"That shit crazy though," Umar says. "Like real gangbangers?" he asks with disbelief. "Like Cali gang-banging?"

"Yeah," Twelve Play replies.

"Like, how y'all let that happen though?" Umar asks.

"Aye man, when it first started we thought it was a fad. The rap boy had been hanging out over in Cali with Suge and them and he brought it to Jersey and it picked up. It was sprinkled here and there, spread out and before you knew it, it was wide open and out of control."

"That would've never happened in Philly," Umar says with certainty.

"You can't say that," Twelve Play says. Philly pride strikes again, Twelve Play thinks to himself. "Really, how could you stop it?"

"I'm saying, there have been cases where young boys tried to get it started in Philly but the Muslims jumped on it immediately before it got started. Like, oh hell no!"

Umar slams the gear in park. He grabs his oil from the middle console and pours more than too much into the palm of his hands. He adds the finishing touches by running his hands and fingers in his beard and over his thobe. He grabs the bottle and offers it to Twelve Play who refuses. Umar already has put enough on for the both of them.

Umar digs back into his middle console and pulls a 9-millimeter from it. He tucks the gun into the pocket of his thobe. Twelve Play is surprised. "A strap in the masjid?" Twelve Play asks.

Umar leans into the backseat and grabs hold of a leather bag. He looks over to Twelve Play as he pushes the door open. "In Newark y'all got Bloods against the Crips. Here in Philly we have the Muslims, our own brothers against their own brothers." Twelve Play shakes his head sadly.

Twelve Play looks Umar over and he's shining like new money from head to toe. Twelve Play is surprised by Umar. He cleans up well. He would never imagine him to be so flamboyant. Any time that he's seen him he's been in work clothes. To see him shining like this and riding like this is a huge shock to Twelve Play. He's not sure if it's the Real Estate or all his scamming, but one thing for certain business must be booming.

The dye has Umar's beard looking jet-black and full. The last thing he would need is rain to start falling and the dye to drip onto the beautiful white Egyptian cotton thobe. The super 160 material of the thobe clings to him, revealing his muscular frame. Under the thobe he has on distressed jeans that are cut off at the middle of his shin like capris. On his feet he wears Gucci thong sandals, exposing his manicured toe nails. The distressed leather messenger bag that he has strapped across his chest has him looking like a reflection of what artists have declared as Black Jesus; without the woolly hair. He's looking very holy until you look at the diamond fluttered Patek Phillipe on his wrist.

That same Patek Phillipe catches the attention of every brother they approach and pass on their way to the masjid. All the brothers stare at the two unfamiliar faces. The looks in their eyes are not that of love for fellow Muslims. Twelve Play and one brother lock eyes and neither one of them back down. Finally, Twelve Play breaks the ice by giving salaams, letting the brother know that he comes in peace. "As Salaamu Alaikum!" Twelve Play shouts loudly.

The man looks away without returning the greetings. This happens a few more times until he gets the hint. He looks to Umar. "I thought this was the city of Brotherly Love?"

THIRTY MINUTES LATER

After a short but impactful sermon, the service is over. Now Twelve Play hopes that his prayers are answered and they make it back to the truck in one piece. He made the prayer, not out of fear. He made the prayer because truthfully he would hate to have to slaughter one of his brothers for transgressing. In Islam, it's stated that the blood of a Muslim is sacred and to kill a Muslim is a grave sin. Judging by the looks and the actions of some of these brothers, Twelve Play isn't sure if these brothers have read that chapter.

It's a long way back to the truck. The sidewalks on both sides of the street overflow with brothers in huddles and some posted up against the walls. Twelve Play and Umar clearly are the center of attention. Umar is the real focus though. The blinging watch on his wrist is like a target. Twelve Play now understands why Umar brought his gun inside with him. He's also wishing he would've brought he's with him as well but he never thought he would possibly need a gun to go worship. He's worshipped in the prison system and even in there was no comparison to the threat he feels here.

They make it to the truck without a situation. "Alhamdullilah," Twelve Play mumbles under his breath. Twelve Play looks to Umar who seems to not realize the danger it appeared as if they were in. He pulls out of the parking space and everyone watches as the truck cruises away slowly.

"Bruh, you should've told me to bring my gun too," Twelve Play says in a joking manner. He's dead serious though.

"Nah, no need," Umar says. "When you are in my city, I got you. Just as I would expect you to have me, when I'm in your city."

Umar reaches into his messenger bag and pulls out stacks of money. Twelve Play is shocked to know that he had all this money on him. He's starting to think either Umar is super reckless or he's just plain retarded. Umar drops the stacks onto Twelve Play's lap.

"That last move I made with your folks was over a bean(100), fifty in cash," Twelve Play says. "That's fifteen cash for you. Got nothing to do with your folks. I know you got a thing about not eating off them. So eat with me Akhi. You connected the dots and made it possible so how can I not let you eat with me?"

Twelve Play nods his head. "Much respect."

"Ay, Akhi I just want to thank you for accepting the invitation and coming here with me to pray together. They say you never truly know a man until you have traveled with him, eaten with him, and prayed with him. You have traveled with me here. We have prayed together and now we are on our way to eat together. After that we both can rightfully say, we truly know each other. May Allah continue to guide and protect the both of us and grant us success and help us to build a strong brotherhood, where we build and make more money than we can imagine, and protect us from the Hellfire while we get this money, Ameen!"

Twelve Play has never heard a prayer quite like it but it doesn't sound bad at all so he agrees. "Ameen, ameen, ameen!"

41

2:47 A.M.

TORTURA, QUABO AND two of their men exit the barn. Tortura and both of the other men both have huge garbage bags in hand. Quabo follows behind them empty handed. In the back of the barn there's a whole farm.

It's the middle of the night and the farm is still as lively as it is in the daytime. One pony runs around while two horses kind of drag around lazily. The chickens in the coop wander around clucking. The most active animals of all are the pigs. In total there are fifteen of them in the pen. The huffng and snorting can be heard loudly.

Tortura climbs onto the wooden gate. He turns the garbage bag upside down and allows the contents to fall onto the ground. He reaches back and grabs the bags from the other men, and one by one he dumps them over the fence as well. The body parts of Bleek and Godson lay in a pile, still dripping blood.

The arms still have the hands attached. The legs have been cut into two parts, from the thigh down to the knee and from below the knee down with the feet still attached. The torsos have been cut into three pieces. The necks lay separately.

The pile looks like what you would see in a slaughterhouse when a lamb or a cow has been sacrificed and chopped up into small parts, ready to cook. Only difference there will be no cooking. These pigs will eat the meat raw, piece by piece. The only thing they will not eat are the skulls because of the bones. Middle Godson and Bleek's skulls will be easier to discard of than their whole bodies which makes their mission of disappearance be 95 percent over once the pigs start to feast.

Doesn't take long for the pigs to realize that an early breakfast or a late dinner has been served. They all make their way over to the pile and grab a body part to gnaw on. Smacking, heavy breathing and snorting sounds break the peace of the night as the pigs get rid of any trace of Bleek and Godson's physical existence. Tortura watches with a sense of satisfaction despite the fact that he got no information out of them. Godson held his ground and never gave Skelter up.

After Bleek's body was chopped up he eventually bled out and Tortura started working on Godson. He gave him more abuse but more time to give in. He sawed his body parts off in smaller pieces, hoping the torture would make Godson break. Through it all, Godson did shed a bunch of tears but he did not shed a single word. He held it down with loyalty and honor.

Tortura looks to Quabo. "Back to the drawing board."

42

BABY MANSON AND Lunatic stand in the corner of the dayroom. Lunatic hands Baby Manson a stack of receipts of transaction. Baby Manson looks at the receipts, counting up the total. The receipts are the proof that Lunatic has had his people on the outside wire the money into Baby Manson's accounts as well as record of the account to account from the inside. The receipts total in at over four-grand.

Lunatic feels as if he has proven himself and decides to apply some pressure on the matter. "As you can see, I'm stretching out. The little work you be giving a nigga be flying like crazy. I got these niggas working overtime, feel me? If I had more I could move more. Like, I don't know what the workload looking like on your end but if I had like a hundred grams I know I could maneuver the V," Lunatic says as he tries to sell himself. "Like, let me break it down myself and stretch out on my own. Instead of being governed, feel me? Just a lil freedom to color outside the lines, dig me?"

Baby Manson sits back, just listening. His silence makes Lunatic speak more. "A few of my lil homies told me they be colliding with other niggas you hitting. Like head-on collisions, you dig? On some real shit, some of these niggas ain't even worthy of being able to say they have access to you. That's what we here for," he says in attempt to make Baby Manson feel like a bigger man. Baby Manson can spot his game a mile away.

"You won't even have to see these lil non-descript niggas. You can fade to black and never be seen. Whatever you got coming in, you can drop it on me and let me maneuver the V and I bust back at you when it's over. Meanwhile, you squeaky clean on some out the way type shit, just doing your workout shit," he says with a smile. "You know you some big back, brolic stay on the pull-up bar type nigga," he says with a smile. "You can pull up all day and all night, resting assure that money gone come back extra right, feel me?"

• • •

Across the dayroom, Shakir and one of his associates sit across from each other over a chessboard. The young man cuts his eye over at Baby Manson and Lunatic without them paying notice to him. He smirks as he nods his head. "Shit be crazy," the man says.

The man has broken Shakir's concentration. "What's crazy?" Shakir asks.

"It be crazy when you on the outside looking in but you got somebody in the inside who be giving you the scoop."

"Huh?" Shakir asks, having not a clue of what the man is speaking about.

"Like you on the outside and on the outside shit look one way but on the inside shit ain't nearly what it look like from the outside."

"What the fuck is that, a nursery rhyme?" Shakir asks. "Fuck are you talking about."

The man nods his head in the direction of Baby Manson and Lunatic. "From the outside looking in, you see niggas building and making moves. But really it ain't what it seem. What it really is, is one nigga trying to get in and destroy what the other nigga is building."

Shakir's whole mind is off the chess game now. He's more interested in hearing what the man is talking about. "Yeah? How you figure that though?"

"I don't figure," the man says. "Like I said, from the outside looking in shit look one way but from the inside, shit ain't what it seem. I can read the play clearly because I got the inside scoop."

"And what's that?" Shakir asks nosily.

"Bruh, you know me. I ain't on no gossip type time and I know you not either so I can share it with you. My mouth to your ears though because I don't need trouble with niggas, feel me?"

"Indeed."

"Lunatic working it on Baby Manson," says the man.

"Working it?" Shakir asks.

"Yeah, him and Smith in cahoots with each other," he further explains.

"But I thought Lunatic and the other nigga is under the same line and Smith under something different?" Shakir asks. He has very limited knowledge of the Blood breakdown but he knows that much.

"Exactly," the man replies. "But who can get closer to you than a person you trust? Smith little plan wasn't working with him sending dudes from the other side to touch Baby Manson so he got Lunatic to come on board. Him and Lunatic under the different Sets but they from the same hood."

"That shit stupid as shit to me and don't make no sense," Shakir says angrily.

"But it's the way of the world so you need to educate yourself about it so you can be in the loop. How can you move around these niggas and not understand their movements and how they operate?" the man asks.

Shakir knows that makes perfect sense but he refuses to ever admit it. "Fuck all of them motherfuckers," he says.

The man continues on. "It ain't really fuck them though, bruh. They control shit. But that's neither here nor there right now. Like I was saying, shit be different," the man says firmly. "Like today ain't like the old days of banging. Niggas hood come first no matter what set you under or what color you banging, feel me? Like niggas obligations to their hood is priority over the Set. Got me?"

"I guess," Shakir says. He's irked with it all and the only reason he's listening to it is because it's at his best interest to do so. "But get to the point though," he says hastily.

"Bottom line is this," the man says. "Nigga Lunatic baiting Baby Manson in for the lil nigga Smith. Lunatic and Baby Manson eating together but Lunatic only trying to rock him to sleep so he can sting him heavy before he make his move on him. Murder him and Smith gets what he wants and Lunatic gets in position. It's a win-win, bottom line, point blank period."

Shakir despises Baby Manson but hearing this bothers him. He knew Baby Manson wasn't smart enough for this game. Now he has put himself in a bad position. He really has no way of warning him except to tell Pebbles. A part of him wants Baby Manson to find out the hard way but if Baby Manson is murdered and he knew what was going on and didn't tell Pebbles he wouldn't be able to live with himself.

"Big young dummy so smart he stupid," Shakir says.

"Yeah, his days is numbered and he don't even know it. Lunatic working him here on the inside but got niggas working on the outside trying to track down the plug. They already know who control his bank. They said his bitch running the point guard for him. Bitch playing hella hard with fifty-thousand-dollar pocketbooks," he says, stretching the truth to make it sound more juicy. "Bitch living like a reality TV bitch. They thinking she might be the plug. If she not the plug, she definitely know who is the plug."

"Yeah?" Shakir asks. His heart is heavy hearing all of this.

"They just trying to find that location and once they do it's a wrap." Shakir tries to remain cool and calm but his mind is running a marathon. "It's only a matter of time and he will be out of your way for good," the man says with a smile. "The clock is ticking."

43

SKELTER AND HER Godsons zip through the streets in a stolen Charger they had stashed away for the perfect occasion. They ride in silence yet they hear so many voices in their heads. It's amazing how Youngest Godson can drive with so many drugs in his system. Right now he has more drugs in him than a pharmaceutical company.

Ever since the news of Middle Godson he has increased his dosage. Right now he has 10 Roxy's, 5 jars of Snot and 2 Zanax sticks in him. He's spent about $600 for this dose. Such an expensive high and he doesn't realize one day a single bag $5 bag of dope will be the replacement for it. He's too young, high and foolish to realize that today's cool drug users evolve into tomorrow's junkies.

Oldest Godson sits in the passenger's seat with a bill in his hand. Inside the bill he has 2 Roxy's crushed into powder form. He sniffs the powder like a vacuum cleaner. He's well beyond popping the pills and waiting for them to get into his system. He prefers sniffing them or chewing them so they go directly to his bloodstream. That way he gets instant gratification.

Skelter sits in the back, super focused. Despite all that is going on around her, her full concentration is on tracking down her Middle Godson. The Adderall she's taken has her mind sharp and focused. The ideas she has of where he could be and the possible scenarios she has put together in her head are as keen as a detective. She may be too focused because some of the thoughts she's having of how it could have went down is like scenes from the Twilight Zone.

One thing for certain she's already accepted the fact that she may never see her Godson again. She hasn't told the other two how she feels because she doesn't want to crush their hopes. She's sure he's been captured to use him to reel her in. She's also sure that Bleek must have given him up. What's she not sure of is if her Godson will roll on her. In the streets she's seen the strongest men break down. Although it would break her heart if she found out he rolled, she has to deal with the reality that men roll every day. All she can do at this point is change her movements just in case he has given up any information.

All these thoughts in her head, yet she hasn't told her Godsons any of them. They are fired up, believing the hit had to have come from their own because of the ill vibes the other night. She will let them use that anger to fuel their engines to get this job done but once they make the movie, she will have a serious talk to them. She hates to have to break their spirits.

They bend the corner and as soon as the Projects are in sight, they all start to pull their masks down. The masks are pretty much senseless because they are sure everyone will know it's them behind the masks. They don't care if they know. They just don't want the police to know.

Over the years they have had many arguments within the Projects. Some of those arguments led to fist fights and a few shootings but never did she think she would see the day when it's her against the whole Projects. But today, that day has come.

The Charger creeps into the court before speeding toward the group of men. Some run for cover while some stand in shock. Two of the men have an altogether different plan. They both draw and start firing relentlessly at the Charger.

The sound of metal against metal can be heard as the slugs rip through the body of the Charger. The front windshield caves in. Youngest Godson leans over for cover while Oldest Godson ducks low. Youngest Godson slams the gear into reverse and without looking behind him, he mashes the gas. The Charger speeds backwards as one of the men runs at them still firing.

"Look where the fuck you going," Skelter says as she peeks behind them. She sees he has no control of the car and fears them crashing. "Lift your fucking head up!" she shouts.

Skelter quickly hits the power window button and as soon as the window is halfway down, she squeezes her body and the rifle through it. She sends a dozen rounds from the A.R. just to back the man up. The aggressive sound of the rifle stops him in his tracks, giving Skelter time to sit on the window and brace herself. She rips another dozen at him, this time with more accuracy than the first. The man takes off, running for cover.

"Fuck!" she says as she ducks back into the car. She's now more enraged than she was when she came here. Youngest Godson busts a wild U-turn and speeds away. "Oh, ok, them pussies wanna play, huh?" Skelter shouts. "Now it's about to get more interesting. Let's play!"

MEANWHILE A FEW BLOCKS AWAY

Blue Blood is in the middle of a move when a series of gunshots ring from not too far away. "Got damn," the passenger says. "Somebody letting that shit go. Let me hurry before the police be all over this motherfucker," he says as he flicks through a few bills.

Blue Blood, now uneasy is watching all around. In between peeks, the passenger manages to draw a revolver and place it against Blue Blood's temple. "Hand it here," the man demands.

Blue Blood flashes a grin. "Word is bond? Wow," he says as he peeks over at the man. Blue Blood can't believe he's being played like this especially by someone who knows him. "It's in my inside pocket," Blue Blood says. "Aye man, you didn't even need a gun. All you had to do is ask me and I would've gave you whatever you wanted or needed. This drug shit don't mean that much to me." Blue Blood is trying the passive aggressive tactic.

"Shut the fuck up," the man says aggressively. "I don't want to hear that shit." He searches the middle console and under the seats quickly. Blue Blood sits laid back and calm. He needs this to be over with. The faster this is over the faster he can get on with his retaliation.

The passenger quickly retrieves the package with 250 grams of cocaine in it but he doesn't stop there. He checks every pocket Blue Blood has, collecting money and another smaller package of cocaine. The man takes one quick surveillance of the area before squeezing the trigger. Boom!

Blue Blood's head bangs into the window. He then aims at Blue Blood's chest and fires two more times. Boom! Boom! The man jumps out of the truck, slams the door shut and takes off to his car that is parked in front. He pulls off nice and calm, drawing no attention to himself whatsoever.

Blue Blood can barely see through the blood that pours from his head, and drips down into his eye. Everything around him plays dreamy like. The ringing in his ears comes from the sound of the gunshot damn near bursting his eardrum. He gasps as his windpipe fills with blood. Surprisingly he feels no pain.

He sees the headlights of a car coming toward him. If he can just get their attention he could get help. If not he's sure he will die here. As the headlights get closer, he tries to lift his hand to grab the door handle. He looks down and just like in a dream, where you think you're moving, but really you're not, his hand is still on his lap.

Surprising to him the car is slowing down. Blue Blood's head is too heavy for him to move so he just cuts his eye to the left. The car cruises by super slow. The window slides down slowly and Jubilee stretches his neck, looking into Blue Blood's truck. He's obviously making sure the job has been done. The spotting of Jubilee makes it all make sense to Blue Blood. Swan and Jubilee are behind the hit.

The blood is now filling Blue Blood's lungs, making it difficult for him to breathe. Blue Blood manages to grip his cell phone that is sitting on the seat. He's not sure if he really has the phone in hand or it's just a figment of his imagination. On his call log he sees Skelter's name and he presses it.

The phone rings for what seems like an eternity before going to voicemail. "Jubee," he gasps. "Jubilee," he says a little more clear. It becomes harder for him to breathe and he feels himself going in and out. Eventually he starts to be out more than he's in.

ONE HOUR LATER
CAMDEN

Skelter isn't happy with the turnout they got back in The Projects and needs some gratification. She's decided that tonight she's tripping on everything. Any beef that she's been sitting on, anything she's been feeling like moving on but hasn't, tonight is the night. The move back at the Projects was just the beginning and this move here is something that has to be done for the hell of it.

Skelter watches the entrance of the bar with great focus. The bar is letting out and the patrons are exiting in packs. Dominican, Mexican and Puerto Ricans swarm the area. None of these people have anything to do with the beef but Skelter feels somebody has to pay for her Godson. She just needs some kind of payback right now just for her own fix.

"Now," Skelter shouts.

Youngest Godson mashes the gas pedal and the Dodge Charger takes off like a rocket. In twelve-seconds they're in front of the bar and just as Skelter is raising up out of the window, a police car turns the corner. Skelter caught red-handed, gun in hand, her and the driver of the patrol car lock eyes. Skelter ducks back into the car. "Go, go, go!" Youngest Godson stomps the gas pedal and the Charger takes off with the speed of lightning.

The cop hesitates with nervousness. His partner gets on the walkie talkie, calling in for backup as the driver busts a U-turn and takes off behind the Charger. The Ford Taurus stretches out and catches up with the Dodge Charger. They're not bumper to bumper but the Charger is in clear view.

Skelter turns around and sees the cop car catching up. "Yo, they on our ass," she says nervously. "Yo, step on it."

"I got it, I got it, don't worry," Youngest Godson says. He's cool and calm.

The horses in the Ford are kicking in and the cop car gets closer. Skelter thinks desperately. "I have to back them up," she says. With no further delay she pops out of the window and sends a couple rounds at them to back them up. She expects to back them up but Supercop in the passenger's seat has other plans. He holds his gun over the roof of the car and sends three shots in their direction.

"Oh shit," Skelter says as she ducks for cover.

The sound of sirens seem to be coming from every direction. This tells them that the chase is about to get intense. Youngest Godson knows he has to get a lead on this car before the others join in. The headlights of the Taurus illuminate the interior of their car. The police car is close enough to bump them right now.

Youngest Godson looks around, totally unfamiliar with the area. He knows not the ins and the outs of the city. He's traveling on foreign land, not knowing shortcuts or dead ends. Up ahead he sees lights flashing from a few blocks away. The last thing he wants to do is go in that direction and they cut him off. He makes a quick right turn and the police car behind them does the same.

He makes a quick left and as he does, Skelter bangs a hole in the back window with the rifle. Just as the cop car turns behind them and gets right back on the bumper of the Charger, Skelter sticks the nose of the rifle into the hole in the glass and squeezes. The bullets banging against the cop car sounds off loudly. Oldest Godson dives into the backseat next to Skelter. He squeezes the trigger of his handgun and the whole back window of the Charger shatters outward. Glass particles fly everywhere.

When they look up they are happy to see the cop car falling back. Behind that car is a long string of police cars. Up ahead, Pennsauken police are at the borderline waiting to greet them. They have a roadblock of cars set up with police set up on both sides, guns in hand. Youngest Godson makes a quick left to avoid them. Camden Police are gaining on them.

"Yo, I don't know the area," he says frantically. "If we don't get out of this car we gone get caught."

"Getting caught is not an option," Skelter says sternly. "Turn right here."

Youngest Godson goes against his better judgement and does as he's told. Up ahead is another Pennsauken Police roadblock. This time there's no place to turn. He looks behind and there he sees a string of Camden police bending the corner behind them.

"This it y'all we gone have to bail right now," he says as he slams on the brakes and pushes the door open. He dashes out of the car.

Skelter and Oldest Godson dash out as well and follow behind Youngest Godson. Youngest Godson cuts through the alley and hurdles over the small fence. He sprints through the yard before climbing over the next gate. The pit-bull in the next yard forces him to detour and hop over the small wooden fence into the next yard. He stops because he needs to catch his breath but the sound of the sirens force him to start back running. Sirens roar all around them. It sounds as if they are trapped with police from every angle.

"We have to split up," Skelter says to Oldest Godson. Youngest Godson has already broken away from them. "See you on the other side," she says before running in the opposite direction of Youngest Godson. Oldest Godson sprints away on a path of his very own. All of them are taking a different paths but their goal is the same. All have high hopes of making it home, safe and sound.

44

MASJID AHLUS SUNNAH/EAST ORANGE, NEW JERSEY

DRE AND LIL Mama stand face to face, staring into each other's eyes. The Imaam stands in front of them, while three men whom all serve as witnesses surround them. Their marriage ceremony has taken all of three minutes. "At this point, I pronounce you as husband and wife," the Imam says happily.

The tears pour out of Lil Mama's eyes. She feels like she reached one of her milestones. Throughout her bid she pictured this so many times. It was a dream of hers that she wasn't sure if it would ever come true. One thing she knew was she was going to express her feelings toward him and she did.

She can't stop the tears from pouring. Dre wipes her face with his hand. To see her happy like this makes him happy. He can't believe that he's actually gone through with this. He tossed and turned with the idea but as he really thought about it, no other woman that he's been in a relationship with has ever shown the amount of loyalty to him that she has.

Tony's words stayed playing in his ear as he debated with himself back and forth. At this stage of the game he agrees that love is highly overrated. He's seen couples that are madly in love with each other still able to cheat on one another. Here it is he and Lil Mama were never a couple, yet she took care of him and had his best interest at heart. He's taken care of her the past 12 plus years. They've always been self-less when it comes to each other. He just hopes this marriage doesn't change them.

The factor that tipped the scale when it came to his decision mak-ing was him feeling he owed her this being that he is the reason so much of her life was taken away from her. He will never be able to get her all those years back but he will do his best to make all the rest of her years' worth living. He still feels as if he was somewhat rushed and pressured into this. For every reason he came up with for them not to get married, she came up with more reasons why they should.

He told her he wants to get back on his Deen first before they get married. She told him it would be easier for him to get back on his Deen if he had a wife. He told her he would marry her when he came back from his trip and she told him coming home isn't promised to him. She begged him to marry her before he goes just in case, God forbid something happened and he didn't make it back. She told him all she ever wanted to be for the past ten years was to be his wife.

The words that broke him down were. 'For ten years hopes of one day being your wife is what kept me strong. God forbid something happens to you before I become your wife. I would be twisted and all those years of hope I held onto would be in vain." Lil Mama said those words to him not even an hour and a half ago and those words led him to picking her up and driving straight to the masjid to marry her.

"He who findeth a wife has found a great thing," the Imaam says to Dre. "I pray that Allah protects this union and you help each other into Paradise, Ameen!"

"Ameen," Lil Mama mumbles under her breath. Little do they know she's in Paradise right this very moment. It's not every day that a young girl marries her childhood crush.

The Imam is long winded. He continues on yapping away as Dre keeps peeking at his phone which is ringing off the hook. Tony has called over ten times already. The Imaam notices Dre looking at his phone and catches the hint.

"Well, I'm not gone hold you two up any longer. My door is always open for y'all if you are need of advice. Allah says," he manages to utter before Dre shakes his hand, cutting him off.

Dre knows if he doesn't stop him now he will not be able to. "Thank you," Dre says. He nudges Lil Mama. She thanks the Imaam and gives Salaams before they make their exit.

As they exit the masjid, Lil Mama grabs hold of Dre's hand. It feels weird, holding his hand like this. She's all warm inside like a young schoolgirl when she sees her crush. As Dre holds the car door for her she feels like a princess in a fairy tale book. Although nothing about her wedding was as lavish and fairytale-ish as she dreamed it to be, she's still as happy as can be.

Lil Mama sits with her back propped against the window. "I'm married," she mumbles under her breath over and over trying to make herself believe it. "I'm with my husband," she says to herself. "Nothing in here cooking for my husband," she mumbles under her breath. In her head she's holding full blown hypothetical conversations and all of them evolve around her husband.

She watches her 'husband' as he speeds through the city hurriedly. He even runs a few red lights. He's pressed for time. If Tony leaves him behind and he doesn't get to Honduras, his big plan is ruined. He drives like his life depends on it because it really does.

As Dre turns onto Lil Mama's block, he sees Tony's car pulling off. He rests on the horn like a maniac. Tony's brake lights come on and Tony slams the car in reverse. Dre quickly parks. He hands Lil Mama the keys.

She looks to him with sadness covering her face. "You're not going to come upstairs and consummate the marriage?"

"Consummate?" Dre asks.

"Yeah, consummate." She makes an O with her left hand and with her right hand she pokes her index finger through the O. "Consummate. You know the marriage not valid until we consummate."

"Listen, we can consummate when I get back. If I blow this trip I'm done. This like my last hope right here. Let me just do what I got to do and when I get back we can do all the consummating you want to do. Ten years of consummating," he says as he leans over for a kiss.

This is the moment she's always dreamed of. She leans in slowly, wanting the kiss to be perfect. She's practiced this kiss in her head so many times. For Dre it feels weird at first for him to be leaning in for a kiss on the lips. That is until she slides her tongue into his mouth and lays it on him.

She takes total control as she's done so many times in her dreams. She places her hand under his chin and gently forces his head back before diving into his mouth tongue-first. All the years of looking at her like a niece, a little sister or even a daughter have just flown out of the window. She now solidifies her new place in his life. Right now is when any doubt he may have had about marrying her have flown out of the window as well. The sound of Tony's horn breaks up the tongue wrestling debut. Lil Mama pulls her face away from his and wraps her arms around him tightly.

"Got damn," Dre says. "You been holding that in forever, huh?"

Lil Mama smiles devilishly. "Oh, that ain't nothing," she says before placing her mouth against his earlobe. "Wait until I put this Halal pussy on you." Her hand drops on his lap and she feels what is now hers. She gropes his stiff erection while looking into his eyes. "You sure you don't want to come upstairs and let me handle that for you, real quick?" she asks with no shame.

She has no reason to hold back any longer. He's her husband now and she feels the limits have now been lifted. She's free to express her thoughts, her needs and her desires. Her grandmother told her years ago a woman's obligation to her husband is to keep his stomach full and his balls empty and that is what she plans to do.

"I got to get going. This trip right here is everything. Once I get back life, shit going to be real different for us, like the old days. Just hold that for me," he says as he looks down into her lap.

"I held it for you for ten years already. A couple more days ain't nothing."

45

CAPITAL HEALTH REGIONAL MEDICAL CENTER/ICU

AFTER LAST NIGHT'S adventurous string of events, Skelter woke up to the news of Blue Blood being shot. It took Skelter almost three hours to make it home from Camden. Both of her Godsons made it back before her. All three of them went their separate ways and had to figure it out on their own.

Last night was by far one of the scariest situations either of them has ever been in. Police sealed off the entire city. Flashing sirens blared and blazed for miles and miles. A helicopter even flew overhead. There was a point where Skelter laid under a car for what seemed like a whole day but was more like thirty minutes. In the end she ended up a popping out of a backyard not too far from the Benjamin Franklin Bridge. She then flagged down a cab to bring her on home.

Skelter stands bedside just staring down at Blue Blood. Seeing him hooked to these machines sends her in a rage of fury. She can't stop looking at his head that is swollen three times the size as a result of the bullet he's taken to the head. Eight hours of surgery and they have done all they can do but what they can't do is say he will come out of this coma. Instead they are almost sure he may never.

Both of Skelter's Godsons stand at the foot of the bed. With no connection to Blue Blood, they aren't saddened the least bit. Skelter on the other hand has real history with Blue Blood. As a child he fed her and her sister when their mother was strung out on crack.

At one time he was like the Uncle to the entire neighborhood. He fed the kids whose parents couldn't feed them. He's kept lights on for families just so they wouldn't have to be in the dark and in the cold. He's paid rent for families.

He's even paid for funerals of the neighborhood junkies and crack addicts. Whether their death was caused by drug overdose or natural causes Blue Blood was there for them. All around the board, Blue Blood is known as a good dude. For Skelter to see him laying here like this it hurts her. It hurts her more to know that he's laying here because of her.

Skelter activates her voicemail and listens to Blue Blood's message for the one-thousandth time. Last night in the middle of her chase she was too consumed with getting away to answer his call. This morning she listened to the message and couldn't figure out what he was saying. He slurred as if he was drunk and she charged it off as that. After the phone calls started pouring in about him being shot, she then put it all together.

She still doesn't know the entire story of how it all went down. No one does or at least, no one is saying what they know. That leaves Skelter to try and put the pieces together herself. The details really don't matter at this point. All that really matters is the two culprits that are behind it.

Skelter limps past her Godsons, barely able to walk. Her ankle has swollen as result of a fall she took last night during the chase. As they stand at the elevator Skelter whispers barely audible enough for them to hear her. "They know the Chapo hit came from us. They lied to me that night because we had the drop on them."

Skelter's Godsons listen attentively as she speaks. "They're old and sneaky and thought they could move in the dark. Wherever they are right now, they know we are coming and they know we are not going to play around with them," she says. "They know they gone have to come full throttle now.

The elevator's doors open. "Rich niggas think different," she says as she steps into the elevator. They step side by side her, never taking their eyes out of her mouth. "They move different," she says. "They like to move in silence and get away with their dirt so they can live another day to enjoy their money. We have to force them out of their level of comfort and that is make them do what they really hate to do."

"And what's that?" Oldest Godson asks.

"Make them dance in front of everybody," Skelter replies. "Niggas with money and shit to lose cringe at the thought of playing in the wide open. We must force their hand where they have no choice but to move in broad daylight. They're not used to that. They're uncomfortable with that. They fear that and that is where we will win the war."

46

EL PARAISO, HONDURAS

A **FOUR-HOUR FLIGHT** landed Tony and Dre flew into Tegucigalpa, Honduras, where a bus awaited them. To go from a comfortable private flight to an extremely uncomfortable bus ride was a big downgrade. They've gone to being stretched out comfortably, just the two of them, to sitting cramped up shoulder to shoulder with complete strangers. The old, school bus must have no shocks left because it takes every bump in the road the hard way.

The best part of the ride is the complimentary cigars and beer. The 24 passengers are thrown around the bus like they're on a ride in an amusement park. As they ride over humps, they damn near bang their heads on the ceiling of the bus. With no air conditioner the heat inside the bus is on Hell. The heat mixed with the thick cigar smoke is enough to strangle them.

As uncomfortable as the three-hour bus ride has been Tony has still found great appreciation in it. The scenery outside is beautiful to him. Dirt roads, acres and acres of tobacco farms with workers in the field picking tobacco. Tony just loves the ambiance of it all. Tony looks to Dre who is such an unhappy camper right now. He hates the smoke, the bus and the trip itself but he's bearing with it because he has his own agenda.

"You know," Tony says. "As I look out in those fields and see them out there picking tobacco it triggers off a bunch of other thoughts. Looks no different from the people picking coca leaves or picking opium in the poppy fields." Tony looks out into the fields where men, women and even small children are picking from the tobacco plants. "I wonder how many of these cigar company owners are drug kingpins, just washing their money through these cigar companies? Just look out there it's the exact same business model. They're not fooling me. I know dirty money when I see it."

Dre has no interest in cigars, the tobacco farms or anything connected to them. His mind is somewhere totally different right now. Being here in Honduras is half the battle. The hardest half of the battle is now out of the way. Now the rest he's assuming will be easy.

A beautiful Honduran woman stands at the front of the bus. "We are now arriving to the resort. I assure you this will be the ultimate experience for you. I have action packed plans for you for each day that you are here with us. I hope to tire you out in a good way," she says with a huge smile. "I hate to be a kill joy or party pooper but I must warn you about this." She pauses before dropping the bomb on the visitors.

"Honduras is the poorest and most economically unequal country in Central America," she says sadly. "With two-thirds of our population living below the poverty line, including 20 percent in extreme poverty," she says with great emphasis. "Extremely high crime rates are fueled by this lack of economic opportunities. While the vast majority of crime victims are Hondurans, foreigners can be affected, hence targeted due to perceived affluence. They believe that all Americans are wealthy and because of that belief it makes you, the Americans, prime targets for crime."

She puts on a false smile. "No worries though. We have with us two of the best armed guards in the business," she says as she waves them on. The two men appear to be big enough to tip the front of the bus over. Together they have to weigh close to a half of a ton.

"This is Gordo and this is Romeo. They will travel with us to every destination of the trip. All we ask is that you do not move without the group. And please do not leave off the premises. Your safety is our biggest concern. As you are making your exit off the bus, we will have a waiver for you to sign. The waiver simply says that if by chance you abandon the group and some crime is committed against you, we can't be held liable."

The passengers are now tense and afraid. Tony breaks the silence by humming a tune loudly. With his best impersonating voice, he says, "You unlock this door with the key of imagination. Beyond the door is another dimension. A dimension of sound, a dimension of sight, a dimension of the mind. You are moving into a land of both shadow and substance of things and ideas. You've just crossed over into The Twilight Zone." All the passengers laugh it off but the fear is still evident on all of their faces.

47

QUABO AND TORTURA cruise around Trenton. It's pretty much back to the basics and fundamentals for them. With no real plan and no real leads, they really are just free-styling, not knowing what their next move will be. At worst case scenario they will grab up a few others that could possibly lead them to Skelter but right now they are drawing a blank.

"Yo," Quabo says as he points up ahead. On the same side of the street as them they spot the walk that only one man in the world has. The limp, hop walk can be spotted miles away. "There goes our man, No Toes." Tortura snatches his gun from his waistband.

As they pull up they notice something different about No Toes. They quickly realize the dirt and grunge on him is no longer there. He looks like a new man. His beard and mustache are trimmed neatly and he has a sharp haircut. His skin is no longer dark. He appears five shades lighter. From head to toe he's all new. If it wasn't for the walk they wouldn't recognize him.

The van slows down alongside of No Toes. He cuts his eye sneakily just out of normal reaction. As much of a new man as he looks to be, he still has a past behind him. All the stealing and dirt he's done is still lingering behind him so he's always on point.

When No Toes recognizes the face inside the van, he damn near shits himself. His nerves get the best of him and he doesn't know what to do. If he could run and get away from them he would go for it. Instead he's stuck here, having to face the music.

He raises his hands high in the air. "Yo," he says as if he's happy to see them. "Where y'all been?"

It's him who hasn't been around. After witnessing firsthand the gruesome murders that Quabo and Tortura were committing it was like an epiphany for him. In his heart, he felt like he was about to be next on their list. With no money to escape, and no place to escape to he did the next best thing. He enrolled himself into a drug detox program. In the program he was able to hide from them and kick his dope habit at the same time.

It was a great thing but now half of the greatness is over. Here he stands in front of what he was running from. It's now time to face the music with no monkey on his back. Standing here in front of them and not under the influence of drugs makes it scarier. Before he saw them as serial killers but the drugs helped him to overlook it. Now standing here sober, he can't overlook it and sees them for exactly what they are.

He stands still, petrified. Quabo slides the door open. "Get in," he demands.

No Toes takes baby steps toward the van. "Hurry the fuck up," Tortura shouts. No Toes picks up his pace.

He stands curbside, trembling like a leaf yet he tries to play it calm. "What's up? How y'all been?"

Tortura snatches him out of the air by the collar and drags him into the van. Quabo closes the door and the driver pulls off. Tortura flings No Toes into the seat. "I saved your ass so many times and you made me look stupid," Quabo says. "I told them you were trustworthy and we could depend on you. If I would've known you would run and hide and turn your back on me I would've let him kill you back then." He leans closer to No Toes. The way I am about to let him kill you now."

"No, please. I didn't run and hide. I was in the detox program, trying to kick the habit. It was getting the best of me. I've been addicted to drugs and alcohol for thirty of my forty-five years living. I had to do this for myself. Please, understand."

Quabo shows no compassion and this is usually not his way. He's so frustrated with this whole situation that hearing this story falls on deaf ears. "Well, you should've checked in with us and told us what you were doing. Instead of having us think you ran off on us. You had an obligation that you didn't keep. Here it is all that time and we still haven't found the girl."

"But I did keep my obligation," he claims. "The day that I checked myself into the detox, right before I checked in, I'm wandering around and guess what I luck up and find?"

"I'm not guessing shit," Quabo says.

"I saw the girl coming out of her house."

Quabo is all ears. "How do you know it was her house?"

"It was her, her baby and I guess the baby's dad. They were on their way to the laundromat."

Tortura sits on edge, just waiting for the word to blow No Toes' brains out of his head. Quabo shakes his head and Tortura flies off the handle. He shouts some vulgarities in Spanish as he throws a small tantrum. He's wanted to kill No Toes long ago and today he felt as if he was right there, ready to get what he's been longing for.

"You better hope this is what you say it is," Quabo says. "Because this is the only thing that will save your life."

48

TWELVE PLAY AND Umar stand in front of the building. All is quiet but they both have their antennas up. The young men are posted up in front of here but surprisingly they haven't been sitting on the porch. They move around Twelve Play and Umar as if nothing has happened. Not a word of the fire or the double homicide has been mentioned, not even a sign of Homicide detectives. It's as if the murders never happened. The silence of the young men makes both Twelve Play and Umar uneasy. They are sure the young men have plans on retaliating, they just know not when.

Umar double takes as a new model Tundra pickup truck comes down the block. He waves his hands high in the air to get the driver's attention. The driver looks over and slams on his brakes. He pulls the truck over close to the curb. The back of the pickup has enough sheet-rock to tip the truck over.

The driver, a short and pudgy Mexican man in his late 30's gets out of the truck wearing a big smile. "What's up Ese, what's up Homes," Umar shouts jokingly. Umar excuses himself and walks away from Twelve Play. He and the Mexican meet at the pickup truck. Twelve Play pays them no attention as they partake in a brief conversation. He keeps his attention on the group of young men.

As Umar was walking away, Twelve Play happened to have caught one of the young men giving some type of signal to the other. The young man the signal was given to, caught the signal and then snuck away from the huddle. Twelve Play watches the young man as he walks toward the corner. Twelve Play steps onto the porch, back against the wall. Without being noticed, he grabs his gun from his lower back and holds it behind his back, arms folded. He pretends to be paying them no attention at all but his eyes are on everything moving.

Umar runs over with excitement in his eyes. "Yo, that's my man right there. Be having his hands on everything. Right now he got a shit load of sheetrock. I don't know if you know but sheetrock goes for twelve dollars a sheet. I ain't gone hold you, he only want four dollars a sheet but I got to tack mine onto that. I just want two points for it. Six dollars a sheet is still a number unheard of. Get your folks on the jack immediately because I know they can capitalize off this." Twelve Play dials Maurice quickly.

MEANWHILE

Maurice's phone lays on the passenger's seat ringing but he ignores because he's busy staking out like a private eye. He's been sitting here parked in this same place for close to ten hours. His stomach is growling from hunger and he's filled five Poland Spring bottles with piss. He refuses to leave here without getting what he came for.

There's only one person in the world that has the power to bring the stalker out of him. For this person, stalking is not new to him. He's stalked her many times in the past but it's been a long time. As he sits here he remembers all the times in the past that he's done embarrassing things in the name of love for this individual. It's when she crossed the line to the point of no return that his stalking was not in the name of love. It was all in the name of war.

He still hasn't gotten over the pain that she caused him. He feels like he lost his family behind her and for her to go behind his back with another man, was a hard pill for him to swallow. The way she crossed him caused a pain that he may never get over. It was a sense of betrayal that he had never felt. Ten years later and he's still as enraged now as he was back then.

Maurice finally grabs hold of his phone which has been ringing back to back for the past five minutes. "Yo, yo," he says in an irked tone.

"Sheetrock for six dollars a sheet, is that a good number?" Twelve Play asks.

"That's a fucking amazing number," Maurice replies excitedly. Suddenly the door of the small one-family house opens and Maurice's heart freezes. A little girl steps onto the porch. The little girl is so beautiful yet his rage and jealousy won't let him see it. Looks like a mini version of his used to be lover.

"Moe," Twelve Play yells into the phone for the third time. "You hear me?"

A familiar face comes out of the house next. The face is the same but she's put on about 50 pounds. Maurice is happy like a proud father to see Star looking well. He practically raised her like his own daughter.

"Moe, you need it or not?" Twelve Play asks. He's becoming agitated.

"Yeah, yeah," Maurice finally answers. Rage burns through his pupils as he sets eyes on Lil Bit who comes out of the house and leads the way down the stairs. She's still as beautiful and youthful looking as she was when he first met her twenty plus years ago. He's so angry with her that everything about her makes it worse, including her beauty.

His heart beats like a drum and his palms get sweaty. Venom bleeds from his eyes and steam flies from his ears. The rage he held for her ten years ago has come back alive this very moment like brand new. "Yo, I will hit you back in a little while," Maurice says before ending the call.

Maurice waits for Lil Bit to get away from the house. He has to time it perfectly so she can't run back in the house nor lock herself in the truck. Right before she gets to her truck, he pops out of his truck and fast trots toward them. The little girl notices him first. His energy scares her. She stops in her tracks and walks behind Star in attempt to hide. Star looks up and she stops, startled. Lil Bit happens to look up just as Maurice is stepping onto the curb. Her face goes pale as a ghost who has just seen a ghost.

Out of normal reaction based on their last encounter, she takes off frantically. She runs around to the front of the truck, fearing for her life. She ducks down, expecting to hear the shots ring. Once she hears no shots, she peeks up, looking for him through the windshield of her truck. Maurice like a madman runs toward her.

"Moe, no!" Star shouts angrily.

Lil Bit runs around the truck while Maurice stops in his tracks, trying to figure out how he can corner her. The little girl cries, not knowing what any of this is about. Lil Bit and Maurice are now on opposite sides of the truck, looking at each other through the windows. Maurice wishes he could jump through the glass and snatch her by her throat.

Star runs over to Maurice. In defense of her big sister she pushes him with all of her might. "Maurice, you better go!"

The little girl cries harder, snapping Maurice out of his zone. Now with a clear head he looks over to Star and notices that she has a box cutter in her hand. The look in her eyes and her body language tells him that she is ready to use it. It stuns him to see a girl he raised and provided for ready to come for him.

The violent rage in him eases and embarrassment settles in as he looks at the little girl who is obviously afraid for her life. She looks at him with fear as if he's a monster. Maurice looks through the passenger's window at Lil Bit who has even more fear covering her face. He stands here feeling like a cold-blooded sucker. The fact that he has two women and a baby afraid for their lives makes him feel horrible.

"Maurice, leave," Star threatens as she grips the box cutter tighter.

"I just want to talk to her," he says softly. "She owes me that at least."

"She don't owe you shit after what you had done to her," Star says. "You better be lucky she didn't have you locked up forever. That's what she really owe your ass!"

Star's words rip through Maurice's heart. "Amber, let me talk to you," he says in his most gentle voice.

Lil Bit peeks around the truck, exposing only the left side of her face. Maurice can't help but to notice the laziness of her left eye. Her eye twitches and waters uncontrollably as a result of the shooting. His heart sinks as he sees this.

The little girl runs around to Lil Bit and grips her around the waist. Star stands at the hood of the truck defensively. "Maurice, will you just leave?" Star begs. Her begging isn't in fear. It's more like her begging because she can no longer control her urge to cut him.

Maurice looks to her with sadness in his eyes. "Star, I've been there for you your whole life and you treating me like a stranger?"

"You treated my sister like a stranger. Left her to die like a stray dog on the street."

Maurice has no words to defend himself. The truth hurts him. He looks away from Star with shame. "Amber, can I please talk to you?"

"Maurice, there is nothing for me and you to talk about. What's done is done," Lil Bit replies with sassiness. "You're upsetting my daughter. Can you please just leave?"

"I'm not leaving until we have a conversation," Maurice replies.

"Well, I'm going to have to call the police," says Lil Bit.

"Wow, you fuck with the police, now?" Maurice asks sarcastically. "Things have changed."

"Yes, a lot of things changed," Lil Bit snaps back. "On February 18th, 2009 my life," she says with sarcasm. "All I thought I knew about you, about life, changed. I don't know you anymore and I don't trust you to talk to you, to be near me, near my home, near my sister nor near my daughter. You do remember what you had done to me right in front of my daughter, right?"

Those words are like a dagger being driven into his heart. "I don't have nothing to say, Amber," he says as he walks away with his head hanging low. He turns around. "I know you will never forgive me for it but please just hear me out one day. Not today, not right here. I will meet you anywhere in the world to have this conversation, even the police precinct if that makes you comfortable. Just think about it please."

Maurice looks to Star. "Star, you are like a daughter to me. I know you can never forgive me but still I apologize. I love you as I love my own daughters." Star turns away, rudely.

Maurice looks to the little girl. "I'm sorry, lil pretty girl. I promise I will not hurt you. No need to be scared." The little girl rolls her eyes. Maurice looks to Lil Bit. "Anywhere in the world," he says. "Just name the place and I will be there. I won't be able to move on with life until we sit down and have this conversation. Please?"

49

THE EVENT PLANNERS of this trip made sure to utilize every second of the day. The guests all get together during breakfast and from that moment on, their action-packed day starts. Tony never thought he would ever be tired of smoking cigars but right now he is. While eating breakfast they smoked. After breakfast they smoked. During their tobacco picking tour, they smoked. During lunch and after lunch they smoked. During their cigar tutorial they smoked. Right now, Tony is all smoked out, yet he's still smoking.

Tony lounges in the pool area of the resort. In Honduras this resort is considered well beyond 5 Star but in the States it would be the equivalent of a cheap Motel 6. In 2019, yet it looks like something from a scene from the movie, Scarface. Palm trees, broken statues and barely working waterfalls surround the pool. Around the pool area, thick cigar clouds float into the sky.

There are mainly Caucasian American men on lounge chairs, laid back blowing smoke rings. There are also a few happy couples smoking together. The main attraction of the resort are the few drop dead gorgeous women that are scattered around. Those women are compliments of Rocky himself.

Beautiful young women serve drinks and cut cigars for the patrons while the older, more mature and refined women lounge around sipping drinks and smoking cigars. Those women are on the payroll. They have been hired to entertain the American men however they choose to be entertained. These women are not here to just blow cigars. They are here to blow anything the American men may want blown.

Tony looks at his watch and realizes it's less than fifteen minutes left before the next engagement. Their next engagement will be without the group. It's not a part of the tour. Tony and Dre will be having dinner with Rocky Patel at his favorite restaurant.

Tony dragged Dre around all day and Dre hated every second of it. The moment they got back to the resort, he stormed up to his room and Tony hasn't seen him since. He complained about being tired so Tony just let him get his rest. He hates to awaken him but he doesn't want him to miss the dinner date with Rocky.

Tony walks up the stairs to the second floor. He stops at the door right across from the staircase and he taps on it. He gets no answer so he taps harder. Still no answer so this time he bangs on the door. Tony looks down the hall where he sees Rocky coming toward him.

"Tony!" Rocky Patel yells happily. "Let's eat. I am starving." He wraps his arm around Tony and guides him down the hall. Tony figures Dre must be sound asleep. He will let him get his rest and catch up with him later.

MEANWHILE

Dre quietly closes the gate of the resort behind him. He wears a look of guilt as he looks around to see if anyone is looking at him. He feels like a kid sneaking out of his house after curfew. He walks away slowly, expecting to hear someone come running after him. He feels like an escapee with his heart pounding in fear of being caught. The rules of no stepping off of the resort alone have been specified more than a hundred times yet and still he's stepping off the resort alone. He picks up his stride.

He's amazed by the poverty. He catches the attention of almost everyone, sticking out like a needle in a haystack. As he approaches the people, they hold their hands out, palms up, begging. He watches as a father practically forces his two young daughters to run over to Dre.

The two little girls, no more than 8 years old stand before him speaking in their native tongue. Dre can't understand a word of what they're saying but he knows it has to be begging. Seeing the look of hunger in the girl's eyes breaks his heart. He pulls out a stack of money and hands them both a crisp twenty-dollar bill.

The girls look at the American money in amazement. They run over to their father shouting loudly. Whatever they're shouting has all the people in the area now looking at Dre. The man looks at the bill like he has just hit the lottery. He runs over and thanks Dre with much gratitude. His daughters follow behind at his heels. To Dre it's only a lousy twenty-dollar bill but that same bill converted to Honduran money, both girls have the equivalent of 487 Honduran dollars.

The man follows behind Dre, constantly thanking him. He even bends down in front of Dre and ties his sneaker. Dre tries to respectfully step around the man but the man is persistent. He's eagerly trying to earn himself a twenty-dollar bill. The man is causing Dre so much attention and he hates it. He quickly pulls the money from his pocket and peels off another twenty. He hands it to the man who starts to thank him all over again. Dre plants his hand on the man's shoulder. "You're welcome, now stop. That's enough," he says sternly.

The man can't understand the language but he reads Dre's body language and his eyes and can tell Dre is getting angry. He bows his head one last time before he takes off. Even when he runs away all eyes are still on Dre. More beggars run over to him and more people watch. Throughout the many eyes that are on him, six eyes stand out.

Three young men are walking ahead of him and the middle one keeps looking over his shoulder at Dre. Game recognizes game and Dre spots this game instantly. In town or out of town, a thug is a thug, just a different dress code. He can tell by their movements that they are up to no good. Now Dre fully understands why it was specified that they should never move around without the bodyguards. A whole separate world on the outside of the resort and no soon as you step into that world it hits you full force.

Now he's out here alone and it's about to go down. He needs to get to his destination and has no clue of how far it is away from here. He doesn't even know who he can ask. He continues walking as he pretends to not be looking at the three young thugs. He doesn't want to make a sudden movement and speed up the process of what he knows they are planning to do.

Suddenly Dre spots something that can possibly save him. The old, beat up, 1972 Plymouth is parked curbside about a couple hundred feet away with a sign that reads, *El Taxi*, is looking like a lifesaver for him right now. Dre picks up his pace and the young men slow down, trying to allow him to catch up. One of the men starts cutting over.

Dre makes a strong cut and snatches the back door of the Plymouth open and dives in. He slams the door behind him, smacks the lock down. The three young men walk over to a building where they post up. Defeat covers their faces as they pass around a single cigarette butt, all taking one pull apiece.

The driver, a man in his early 40's has a more trusting look than any of the men he's passed on the streets. "Hola," the driver says with a smile.

"Hola," Dre replies. "Looka this, my friend," Dre says as he pulls a folded paper from his pocket. He hands the paper over to the driver.

The driver reads quickly. "San Matias, no problemo." He turns around to face Dre. "Maybe two hour," he says. "One, five, hundred," he says while writing the numbers in the air.

Dre doesn't understand. "One or five hundred?"

"One, five...fifteen hundred," he says.

"Fifteen hundred, got damn!" He quickly pulls out his phone and goes to the currency converter app. He realizes fifteen-hundred lempiras equals not even sixty-two American dollars. And that's with the driver cheating him by telling him it's a two-hour ride when it's only an hour ride. Dre looks up from his phone. "Ok, no problem."

The driver hangs his hand out. "Pay first," he says loud and clearly in perfect English. Dre pays and the driver pulls off. Dre looks over to the three thugs who all look like they just lost their biggest payday. Dre taunts them by smirking.

Dre looks up and notices the driver staring at him in the rearview. The driver quickly looks away. Dre tries hard to find a comfortable spot on the old and worn out seat but instead he finds springs sticking up, busting through the blankets that cover it. He stares out the window looking to see all that Honduras has to offer and that seems to be very little. He looks at the people and they all have the same look on their faces. The look of no hope, no opportunity and sheer desperation. As he sits here he can't help but to appreciate the red, white and blue. The poverty that he sees makes him understand why America is the best place to be.

Dre notices a traffic jam up ahead. As the cab stops at the light, Dre shakes his head in despair. The sound of the door handle causes Dre to look over. To his surprise a man quickly gets in and slams the door shut. "Yo," Dre says before looking down and noticing a revolver in the man's hand. Dre, so focused on the man in the backseat with him, doesn't see the man opening the front door until he's in the car and turned around in his seat looking at Dre. The man jams the revolver to Dre's side.

Cool and calmly Dre responds. "The money in my front pocket," Dre says to the man in the backseat. "Take it," he says as he looks at the man in the front seat.

"We no want little money," the man with the gun says with a heavy accent. A huge smile spreads across his face. "We need you come with us. Sit back and relax. We no hurt you. Only you make us hurt you."

50

A GROUP OF men stand in front of a variety store. This store is another one of Swan and Jubilee's many businesses. From variety stores to clothing stores to auto mechanic shops they have their hands in a little bit of everything. If there is any money in Trenton, they want some of it, whether it be legal or illegal. You can total up all of the earnings of their legal businesses together and still they don't amount to ten percent of their illegal earnings.

Swan stands with his back facing the street as he holds court with a group of men. He stands there in deep conversation as the group of four men listen with their undivided attention. "It's like this," Swan says as he looks to all the men in the group. "Until our people learn to separate personal feelings from business we will always be behind. Money has no discretion...it goes to anybody. Shit ain't personal! It's so much money out here in the world just flowing around. It's easy to get your hands on some. Now if you can't get your hands on none, now that's some personal shit right there," he says as he chuckles.

He cuts his eye over his shoulder before speaking and when he does he notices a tinted out Cherokee creeping down the block. His gangster senses kick in telling him something isn't right with the jeep. He can feel it in his gut. Just as he goes to spin around and keep his eyes on the Jeep, the back window rolls down. A 9-millimeter hangs from the window just as the front window is rolling down. The extended clip drapes over the front door. Both guns are aimed directly at him.

"Yo!" Swan shouts as he gets low. He pulls the man next to him down to the ground with him. They hit the ground in the nick of time before the shots start ripping rapidly. The other three men flee the scene in different directions while Swan and the other men crawl around on the ground for safety. Car glass shatters and so does the glass window of the store.

The backdoor opens and the masked up Skelter hops one leg onto the ground before she hears. BLOCKA! BLOCKA! She cuts her eye in the direction of where the shots have come from. To her right she finds Jubilee standing in the cut with both hands wrapped around his gun. He peeks around a van, just waiting for an opening to fire again.

Skelter sends five back at him to give herself enough time to get back into the Jeep. Jubilee backs into the alley and sends two back at them. Skelter sends a few more out the window as the Jeep is speeding off.

"Damn, where the hell he came from?" Youngest Godson asks.

"I wanted to stand over the bitch ass Swan and put eight in his face!" Skelter shouts angrily. "Damn!"

"A whole waste of a car and everything," Oldest Godson says.

"It ain't no waste," Skelter says. "We made them pussies come out to play. Forced their hand like I wanted to. Fuck all that hiding in the dark shit. They used to putting money on niggas' faces and never having to get their hands dirty. We all about to roll around in the mud, fuck that!"

51

DRE SITS ON the edge of a small twin-sized bed with his forehead in his palms. This has to be the craziest situation he's ever been in. He's confused at the entire ordeal. He can barely hear himself think on the count of the man laying in the twin-sized bed next to his who is snoring loudly. He doesn't understand how the man can sleep so peacefully under these conditions.

There's a tapping on the door before the sound of keys jiggling, then the clicking of the lock. Dre watches the door as an older woman comes in carrying a tray of food. Behind her there's a young, tall and strong man holding a M16 rifle in his hand. The man stops at the door as the woman continues on toward Dre.

"Your food, Señor," the woman says with respect as she lays a plate of rice and beans on the nightstand. She then lays a glass of water, a glass of orange juice, and a slice of cake on the nightstand as well. She bows her head at Dre which confuses him even more. These have to be the most respectful kidnappers in the world. Even the gunmen use the word Sir and not one time did they even attempt to manhandle him.

The woman then walks over to the other bed where she awakens the sleeping man. She lays his food on the nightstand next to the bed. She bows one more time before leaving the room. The gun toting man leaves right behind her.

Dre's throat is as dry as the desert but he refuses to touch anything they've brought to him. The man sits up on the edge of the bed trying to get himself together. When his back is turned, Dre takes a quick look at him. The man is black as tar with a bald head and ripped up with tattoos all over his arms. He looks like he may have some street in him.

He reaches over and takes a sip of the water before picking at the food. Before taking a forkful of beans and rice he looks over to Dre. "You can eat the food. It's ok, no poison," the man says. Dre is surprised at his Spanish accent.

He looks up at Dre while chewing his food. "Are you an actor or a model?"

This question catches Dre off-guard. "Nah, why you ask that?"

"No disrespect but you're a handsome man. Nice hair, white teeth, pure skin. Thought maybe a model. Maybe they think you are a model too."

"What is this about? I don't understand," Dre asks.

"It's about money," the man says with a smile. "In Honduras, kidnapping is big business. I knew this and still I get caught up." He has to laugh at himself. "I have two beautiful girls with me at the bar and we drink and drink and boom, I end up here," he says with a smile. "They set me up. Everybody work with the kidnappers. People walk the streets hunting. Even the police work in this business," he says as he shakes his head at the thought.

"I don't know if the women were working all the time with kidnappers or if they find out who I am and contact the kidnappers."

"Who are you?" Dre asks curiously.

"I'm Alfredo Martinez. I play for the Detroit Tigers. Pitcher," he adds.

"Damn," Dre sighs. "So, how long you been here?"

"Only two days," he replies. "I put my people in touch with the negotiator and they come up with a number. Now my people will get the money to them and they will let me go."

"Not to be personal but what kind of number are they asking for?"

"They try to get one million but my people meet them at five hundred thousand." Dre can't believe his ears. "They check out who you are and from there they put together a number. It's business. You see they take care of you. They feed you and let you bathe, like a vacation. They have no need to try and hurt you. They just want the money. Yesterday, one Russian get unruly, they punish him severely. Just do what they say and you have no problems."

The lock turns over and the door opens. Dre sits up alert as a middle-aged Hispanic man comes into the room. He's the best dressed man he's seen in all of Honduras. He has the aura of a scammer, or a fraudulent real estate broker. "Hey Andre," the man says as he holds Dre's wallet open reading from his license. He holds his hand out for Dre to shake.

Dre looks at his hand with disgust before staring into his eyes. Dre's temples pulsate with rage. He has to refrain himself from punching the man in the face. If he thought he could get away with it he would but at this point he doesn't need any more trouble than he already has.

"Andre, you have a point of contact? A phone number to whom you would like me to contact? I will be negotiating for you. I need to let them know you are here with us."

Dre can only imagine how Tony will react once he hears this. He will be pissed that Dre left off the resort and will want to know why. He has no choice though. "Yes, my attorney," Dre says, thinking this will scare them off. The man doesn't even blink. "Attorney, Tony Austin," he says before calling out Tony's phone number. The man pulls out his phone and quickly starts to dial.

MEANWHILE

A huge penthouse with a panoramic view overlooking a 150-acre golf course, and a beach. The sound of Punta music is so loud it shakes every window in the penthouse as well as the glass doors that go out onto the balcony. Punta music is a fast tempo music created with drums, keyboards and electric guitar.

In the middle of the floor, Tony has the most beautiful woman in his grip. The woman is dressed in a sexy bikini with her beautiful body and bronze skin complexion fully exposed. He has his arm wrapped behind her neck, holding her close to him. In one hand, he holds a glass of whiskey. His other hand he uses to hold the woman's hips as they dance in sync together.

Her waist is almost non-existent so he's forced to poke his fingers into the softness of her side just to keep her close. Her hips sway from side to side. He turns his head to the side to blow some smoke from the cigar that he has dangling from his mouth. The whiskey and the cigar has him feeling just right.

The woman steps away with a mean two-step. She stops, allowing Tony a full view of her rear. Her perfect, heart shaped behind sways side to side, enticingly. The thin string of her G-string bikini does a disappearing act after each hip sway. The stilettos elevate her calves, making them look even more amazing. With the five-inch heels she still doesn't crack the five feet mark.

The best part of it all is that there are 10 more equally as gorgeous as she is and some are wearing even less clothing than she is. All the beautiful woman are spread around the room, trying to get Tony's attention. With Tony being the only man here besides Rocky, it's hard for him to entertain all the beautiful women, but he sure as hell is trying.

The woman bends over and backs it up on Tony. She plants herself directly on his bullseye. She winds her hips slowly. Tony winds right along with her, following her rhythm. He holds her hand and lifts it in the air as they grind each other with a perfect flow. Just as things get heated, Tony's phone vibrates in his pocket. He immediately thinks of Miranda who he shamefully hasn't thought about since he got in the penthouse. His phone vibrates consistently.

"Got damn, women's intuition," he mumbles to himself.

As much as he hates to end the fun he has no choice. He slowly pulls away from the woman and he eases away. He grabs his phone from his pocket. To his surprise it's not Miranda. The call is from an unknown number.

"Hello?" Tony answers, irked but curiously.

"Yes, Mister Austin, this is Alejandro Fernandez. I have your client and brother, here and he would like to speak with you." He hands the phone over to Dre.

Dre hates that he has to tell Tony this. "Yo bro," he says with no enthusiasm.

"What's up bruh? What's going on?"

"Some dumb as shit bruh. I'm alright though. I'm sure they gone tell you what to do from here."

"Where the fuck are you? You done got arrested?"

"Shit, damn near worse. I don't know bro, just talk to the man. But yo, I need you to look up my man, Javier Caliez in San Matias. I know his family has a big nightclub out there. That's all I know. Get with him and let him know I'm here and in trouble."

"That's it," the man says as he snatches the phone away from Dre. "Yes, Mister Attorney, he's in our custody and he will be fine until we make the arrangements and we can do what has to be done to get him turned over to you. Let me go over a few things and see what is what and I will call you in a day or so. Get your checkbook ready!"

52

PEBBLES PULLS INTO Staples parking lot and she quickly spots the white Maserati parked in their normal meeting spots. She parks right next to it. She looks into the mirror and appreciates herself before grabbing her newest purse from the passenger's seat. As she's getting out she notices the juiciness of her thighs oozing out of the tight boy shorts she's wearing. She closes her trench coat to keep the weapons concealed.

As she's walking towards the Maserati she intentionally allows the trench coat to blow open so J-Prince can get an eyeful. Once she thinks he's seen enough, she closes it tightly. He watches her with the same boyish lust in his eyes that he's had since a kid.

Pebbles drags her feet like the Ugg boots weigh a ton. Her trench blows open once again and flares in the wind. J-Prince looks her over from head to toe. His eyes get caught up in the high beams of her nipples that are cutting through the cropped t-shirt. He's amazed at how such a tiny waistline can evolve into such enormous hips. The boy shorts grip her camel toe, making it look like a big fist in a boxing glove. Her brick-house thighs transition into curvy and toned calves.

He enjoys the show until she pulls her coat together like curtains at the end of a theatrical event. She gets into his passenger seat. "Boy, don't look at me. I know I look crazy. I just threw anything on to come and meet with you. I was in the house relaxing."

"No worries, I enjoy seeing you no matter what you got on," he says with charm.

Pebbles turns away from him so he won't see her blushing. She hands over seven stacks consisting of all hundred-dollar bills. "That's seven thousand for one of the hundreds you gave him. He says the other half he will have for you in a couple days."

"Cool," he replies as if he's not even pressed about the money. "You figured out a date yet?"

"Date?" She has not a clue of what he's speaking about.

"The day me and you gone sit down over dinner," he says while staring out of his window. "Or lunch," he says as he turns and looks out the front window. He turns to face her and stares deeply into her eyes. "Or breakfast after spending the night together after dinner. The choice is yours."

Pebbles busts out with laughter and spittle flies from her lips into his face. "Little boy you better stop while you're ahead. Before I take you up on that offer and take all your little money. Don't you know a bitch like me will ruin your life?"

"First of all, I ain't no little boy," he says defensively. "And secondly, it's impossible for anybody to take all my little money because my money ain't little. The way my bag is set up, it's gone be around for many years to come. I'm operating on a different frequency right now, a different wavelength. Vibe with me."

"Boy, bye," she says as she opens the door.

"Hold up," he says as he takes a stack from the pile. "Here, get yourself a nice dress to wear for our date. FYI my favorite color is teal. I would love to see you in anything of that hue."

Pebbles looks down at the money and she appears to have been insulted. "See, now I know you got me fucked up. I ain't one of them lil ass girls you be playing with. Ain't shit I wear can be bought with this lil bitty ass money. I can see how right I am…A chick like me will break your little piggy bank."

"Oh, in that case, here," he says as he hands over every stack in his lap. "This should do it. And whatever you don't spend, hold it for a rainy day."

"I don't worry about rainy days babe. Chick ain't never been scared to get wet," she says before getting out. "Oh, and I hope you didn't think I wasn't gone take your lil money. You offered it so I'm taking it."

"I insist. It ain't nothing but money and it's plenty more where that came from."

"Little boy, you obviously don't know what you're doing. I'm the hood version of Cleopatra. This pussy has started wars." She looks up to the sky. "Lord, forgive him for he not know that I will change his life, make him question his whole existence."

She slams the door and walks away with the super sexy switch, knowing that he's watching. The way her rear thumps under her coat sends chills through his body. He feels as if he's gotten a tad bit closer to his goal. Just with her making mention of her pussy makes him feel like she could possibly be thinking of giving him some. Also the mention of her pussy makes him believe the mother/son relationship is now over.

He plans to be patient and take it slow. Having her is a fantasy of his and he will not be satisfied with himself until he lives it out. He realizes he has some more time and work to put in but he's never been afraid of hard work and he has nothing but time. He plans to be patient and walk her down, chipping away at her a little at a time until he breaks her down and she finally gives in.

MINUTES LATER

Pebbles cruises along Roseville Avenue as she talks on the phone via intercom. "He's doing fine just ready to get home. He asks about you every time we speak. He still hasn't grasped the fact of it all. He has so many questions. I just wish y'all could talk. I'm mindful of what I tell him because I don't be wanting him to blow up in there and get in trouble.

He got some lil shit going on in there. I don't know what it is. I don't be asking because I really don't want to know," she lies. "All I know he be sending me money every now and then."

"Oh yeah?" Manson asks.

"Yeah, he told me to ask you if you need something."

"If I need something? Tell him I'm in jail so of course I need something. I need everything. That's a dumb ass question."

Pebbles is taken aback by his response. She quickly tries to change the subject. "Oh, I talked to your lil friend, the attorney."

"Tony." Manson replies.

"Yeah, he working hard on your case. He said this shit gone be big. He talking millions. It seems like he's really out here working. Not sure if he's working for you or for his own financial gain."

"Aye man, either way is cool with me," Manson says. "He already did more than I would expect from him. He really don't owe me nothing so whatever he do is a plus."

Just as she reaches the security booth of her Gated Community, the automated service speaks of sixty-seconds remaining for them to talk. She hopes he isn't calling back because she is tired of forcing conversation anyway.

"You calling back?" she asks as if she's looking forward to it. The security guard recognizes her truck and raises the arm for her to enter. She waves at him flirtatiously.

"Nah, I don't have a lot of minutes left and this dickhead officer is on shift so I will hit you later, feel me?" He's signaling that he will call her from his cell phone later.

"Yes, okay. I will be waiting. Love you," she says as she counts the seconds down in her mind, waiting for the call to end.

"Love you more," he says in a nick of time before the call is shut down.

Double-parked on the street, a few hundred feet outside of the gate is a tinted-out Buick Regal. Pebbles been followed here by the Regal without notice. The occupants watch Pebbles' Range Rover cruise pass the security booth and bear to her right. Her truck disappears after the turn. They may not know exactly where she's gone but they do know that she's in the vicinity. Now for the other half of the battle and that is figuring out how to get past the security.

53

TONY STEPS INTO this office and is greeted by a young and pretty, plus sized woman. As he looks at the beautiful woman he realizes how famished the country has to be because she's the first woman he's seen with some meat on her bones. Tony looks around at the cheaply furnished office which is operated as a third-party insurance brokerage company.

Behind Tony is Gordo, the bodyguard that has been assigned to him if he decides to leave the resort grounds. Tony steps up to the woman's desk. She looks up at him with a pleasant smile. "Alejandro Fernandez," Tony shouts.

"Uh, I'm sorry but Mr. Fernandez is having lunch right now. Do you have an appointment?"

"Fuck an appointment," Tony says angrily. "Where is he, in the back? I will go and let him know that I'm here." Tony storms off, walking toward the back office. Gordo has a look of hesitation, yet he follows behind Tony.

Tony bangs on the door. He doesn't get a reply as fast as he would like so he pushes the door open. He sees the man sitting at his desk, eating lunch. He has a stack of papers that he's reading through as he eats.

Tony storms up to his desk. "Attorney, Tony Austin," he shouts with pride. The man not once looks up from his food or his papers.

"Are we going to handle this legally or are we gone handle this shit like gangsters?"

The man looks up slowly. He looks at Tony as if he's a peon. "Coincidentally, I was just looking over the paperwork my secretary just sent me. Your brother, an ex-felon seems to be not worth much." He looks Tony up and down from his designer clothing, fine Italian shoes and his watch and he sees dollar signs. "Before you rudely interrupted me, I was just putting together a fair number. But I'm glad you did come storming in here uninvited because after seeing you I realize I was about to cheat myself." The man places the pencil behind his ear. "I think we can let him go for let's say, one hundred-thousand."

"Motherfucker, are you crazy! Listen to me, you got twenty minutes to let my brother go."

"Is that how business is handled in the United States? You walk into businesses and scream obscenities and the world moves from there? Or is that because you are a big-time attorney and that is what you are used to?" he asks with a calm demeanor. "Well, that is not how things work over here."

He points to Gordo with disrespect. "And you know better! I can't believe you allowed this man to talk you into walking in here uninvited. He's going home, maybe. But you have to live here." Gordo nods his head in a bow of submission.

He looks back to Tony. "A hundred grand and I will get your brother to you unharmed."

"I ain't giving you a fucking dime!" Tony bellows. "For one, I know for a fact that Americans are supposed to be off limits because of the alliance our countries have. I'm almost sure your scouters assumed him to be from the Philippine Islands. He's part Filipino, part Black American.

That's neither here nor there because my last resort is to go about this legally. I know your country is behind this. This is the business that fuels your economy here. The police, the government and everybody in between all work together in doing this. Check this out though," Tony says as he pulls out two phones and holds them in the air in each hand. "In this phone I have all the political and government contacts that I need to get him freed. And in this phone, I have the contacts to get this handled the gangster way. Which phone you want me to use?"

The man wipes the corners of his mouth with his handkerchief. "I don't care which phone you use. You can utilize the numbers in both phones if need be. Get the contacts from both phones to put up fifty grand apiece. Just as long as you come up with my hundred. Until then we are just wasting each other's time."

"Okay," Tony says as he turns around and walks away. "Have it your way."

54

BABY MANSON IS on the pull-up bar pulling up as he listens to the man in front of him cry his blues. The man, a middle-aged, ex-bank robber is one of the more respected old heads in the jail. Baby Manson and him have never held a conversation of any substance which is why he's shocked that the man is even having such a personal conversation with him.

"The insurance all twisted up and he out of medicine. Pop can't get another refill until next month. Pop 87 years old, living on his own, struggling like a motherfucker. I'm in here feeling like less than a man because I can't even help out."

Baby Manson watches the man closely, trying to get a read on him. In the prison this man is known as an extortionist. One thing prison has taught him is extortion isn't how it's depicted on television wherein a man in a trench coat walks up and demands you drop the allotted cash in the bag. A more real-life perspective of extortion is a case like this, wherein a man cries the blues and begs for help with no shame. Once he gets that help he brags to others that he forced the money out of you. Never admitting that he begged and sold his soul to get it.

"Lil bruh, if I didn't really need you I wouldn't have come to you. You're my only resort."

"First of all, don't lil bruh me," Baby Manson says sternly.

"I apologize. I meant no disrespect. It's just a figure of speech."

"Yeah, to you," Baby Manson says. Baby Manson takes the lil bruh seriously because it's usually said when someone who barely knows you play on you. "You have to earn the right to lil bruh me," Baby Manson further adds. "You ain't my big brother. You never fed me. You didn't raise me and you never schooled me on nothing."

"I respect that," the old head says humbly.

"But how much is it that your father need for his medicine?"

"A hundred and twenty dollars," the man replies.

"Dig this," Baby Manson says. "I'm gone give you the money for your pop's medicine but understand this," Baby Manson says as he steps closer to the man. "I'm giving you the money from the kindness of my heart. You didn't press me or finesse me out of the money. And if I ever hear anything similar to that... on the Set, I will crush you."

"Hell no, man! Word is bond to Allah, I would never do no sucker shit like that. You're doing me a favor from the heart why would I say some goofy shit like that?"

"I know how some of you old heads think. Just want you to know I ain't with it."

Baby Manson stops talking when he spots 3 officers walking through the yard. He spots Officer Tillis lagging in the back, moping along. The other two officers have their gloves on which means they are here to handle business. All the inmates are on alert, wondering who they are coming for. Once the officers pass you can see the relief on the inmates' faces.

Baby Manson jumps up on the bar, as if the officer's presence causes him no alarm. It's when they surround him that he becomes seriously alarmed. His heart pounds harder as the officers shove the old head to the side and close in on him while he's still on the pull-up bar.

"Bryant, come down," says the angry officer. This officer for some reason hates everything about Baby Manson. The hatred is mutual though.

Baby Manson lets go of the bar and allows his body to drop. Before his feet can touch the ground the angry officer tackles him onto the ground. With force he starts to pat baby Manson down.

The first thing that comes to his mind is the stabbing. He wonders how they got wind of it if Tillis claims he got rid of the tape. Baby Manson looks up to Tillis with a burning rage. Tillis looks away from Baby Manson and diverts his attention to the officer.

"Take it down," Tillis says. "He's not resisting."

The officer ignores Tillis and continues on with attitude and aggression. He flings Baby Manson onto his back and damn near breaks his shoulders out of the socket as he places the handcuffs on. He drags Baby Manson onto his feet by the cuffs. He flings him around and shoves him.

Baby Manson looks to Tillis with confusion. He's hoping for Tillis's help. Tillis shakes his head and lowers his eyes. He shrugs his shoulders basically stating he's helpless in this matter.

Halfway through the yard, Tillis takes Baby Manson into his own hands. He handles him more gently, allowing Baby Manson to walk on his own instead of shoving him. All the inmates they pass wonder what type of trouble he's gotten himself into. A lot of the inmates are cheering silently while the ones who know him are sympathetic.

"The fuck is going on?" Baby Manson whispers to Tillis.

"Somebody dropped a slip on you, saying you're planning to escape."

"Planning to escape?" Baby Manson is baffled. This sounds absurd to him.

"Yeah, we know it's bullshit but we still have to move on it just to cover our asses. Whole detailed letter explaining your conversation with them and how you will use your Blood influence to force people into helping you escape."

"What? Are you serious?"

"Dead ass," Tillis replies. "Somebody want you out of here for whatever reason." Just as Tillis makes the statement, Baby Manson's eyes brush across Lunatic who stands in the cut. Baby Manson double-takes and locks in on him. Lunatic's expression on his face doesn't match the look in his eyes. Something tells Baby Manson that Lunatic could be behind this. Just yesterday he gave Lunatic the biggest package of them all.

He fronted him 20 grams, of loose, not packaged in box-pieces. As requested he gave Lunatic freedom to package it as he may. Sure, he cut his profit down by doing so but at that rate he still 6 times the money that he pays for the gram. He left enough room on the plate for Lunatic to still double while still making a decent profit for himself. Off of the 20 grams Lunatic can score anywhere $11,600 to $21,600 before paying Baby Manson the $8,400 he owes for the work. Now, with Baby Manson out of the picture, there's nobody to pay and he walks away with $20,000 to $30,000 all for himself.

"What a coincidence," Baby Manson says to himself. He sends Lunatic a hateful glare before turning to Tillis. "Now what, though?" Baby Manson asks.

"You go to lock up while they investigate. Depending on what comes out of the investigation, you either get back to regular or you get shipped out of here.

Baby Manson's mind starts to race. He's sure this situation is going to set him back dearly. Just being in lock-up will affect his business. He's sure the money will have been chipped at by the time he gets back to his team. If he's shipped out he could possibly lose everything. He's sure that was Lunatic's plan. With him being shipped out, Lunatic walks away into the sunset happily. In no way does he plan to let Lunatic get away with this.

55

TONY STORMS INTO the office, just as the secretary is packing up, ready to leave for the day. "Don't mind us. Your shift is over. Go on home," Tony says sarcastically. The secretary watches as four men who she immediately recognizes, walk in behind Tony. They follow his lead into the back.

Tony pushes the door open with no respect. The Negotiator looks up from his desk with agitation. Tony has managed to get under his skin but he will never allow him the privilege of knowing that. "You got my money?"

Tony chuckles. "Didn't I tell you I wasn't giving you a dime?" The four Honduran men step into the office and gather around Tony. "I told you I had two phones with two different types of contacts in them. My political ties and my gangster ties. I decided to use my gangster ties."

The Negotiator's face turns to stone as he recognizes who these men are. These men are part of the infamous Madriaga Cartel. Tony came in contact with them back in 2015 when he represented one of the heads of the Cartel. In Virginia, one of the head members was caught trafficking more than a thousand kilos of cocaine. Tony wasn't able to beat the charge for him but he was able to get him a very minimal sentence for such a hefty charge.

The absolute head man of the Cartel, Madriaga himself, steps in front of Tony. He speaks directly to the Negotiator in Spanish. His tone reeks of disrespect and aggression. The Negotiator hates that he's being shown up in front of Tony but he will never step out of pocket when it comes to this family. The Negotiator has some vicious men that back him but his men are nothing like these guys.

Madriaga realizes how rude it is to speak in Spanish when Tony doesn't understand all that he's saying. "Listen, I never get involved in your business unless it involves one of mine. This man here is one of ours. He's a very dear friend of ours. Call whoever you need to call and have his brother delivered to me. We will be sitting right here until he arrives," Madriaga says as he takes a seat. He signals his men to sit as well. The Negotiator is pissed but still he gets on the phone.

ONE HOUR LATER

The Negotiator sits in rage, feeling like he's been chumped by Tony. He hates that Tony witnessed him back down as he did. He's made the proper calls to all the parties involved and explained the situation to them all. As much as they hate the idea of letting one go they understand that it's necessary in order to keep the peace.

A tapping on the door is followed by the entrance of two monstrous sized men whom are escorting Dre into the office. Dre spots Tony's face first and upon his entrance he lowers his head in shame. Tony walks up to Dre. "Come on man. Let's get out of here." He looks at Dre with disappointment. "You messed up a great night." He shakes his head as he walks off.

He stops short and turns around. "But I'm glad you did. Whew, I was all the way out there in the matrix," he says as he replays the private party with all the beautiful women. "Let's get on out of here. Maybe it's not too late. But hopefully it is." He's torn like a dope-fiend who knows dope is no good for him but he just has to have it.

As they exit the building, Dre hears a familiar voice. "Pretty boy!"

Dre looks to his left and there he sees his reason for coming here. Javier, the tall and slender man in his early 40's is dressed modestly with just a pair of jeans, a crisp white tee and a cheap flipflop on his feet. He looks quite modest. The brand spanking new convertible 850 that he's sitting on has nothing modest about it.

Dre did 10 years in the Feds with Javier. They were as thick as thieves in prison but lost contact when he was released and got deported back here to Honduras. Tony's top priority was getting in touch with his Honduran connection to get Dre out of the mess he was in. Once he did that he then got in touch with this man as Dre requested.

Dre and his man, Javier meet each other halfway. They share huge smiles before embracing each other like the two long lost friends they are. "You ok?" Javier asks with genuine concern. "What the hell are you doing here?" he asks with a smile.

"Looking for you," Dre replies.

As Tony rides in the car service, Dre rides with his man, Javier. This is the most luxury that Dre has seen since he's been here. His man driving the brand-new convertible 850 is confirmation that not everyone in the country is dirt poor. It also gives him some hope that his traveling here was worth it.

"How the hell you end up in that situation?" Javier asks. "I never ever expected to see you again. Your attorney came to the nightclub demanding he talk to me. My people were on edge and so was I. I told them to find out what he wanted and he mentioned your name. Blew my mind," he says with laughter. "Why the hell are you even here?"

"Fucking crazy shit, man," says Dre. "I came here with my man to a cigar event but I don't give a fuck about no cigars. My goal was to get here and find you."

"And you did," Javier says with a smile. "I'm glad you did."

"Shit, me too," Dre replies.

"What's the deal though? Talk to me."

"Bruh I ain't even gone beat around the bush with you. "I'm fucked up!" Dre says with no shame. "Been fucked up for like five years now and I need a fucking boost."

Javier can see the hunger in Dre's eyes and he doesn't like it. "Fucked up how? You too good of a man to be fucked up? No way people are supposed to allow you to be fucked up. What kind of boost you need? Money?"

"Nah bruh, you know me. I don't ask for no money. I make my own money. I just need something to make the money with. It ain't really all about the money. Even with money you still need a line."

"That's it?" the man asks arrogantly. "That's your problem, work? That's what you want from me?"

"Yeah, if you can stand it." Dre is slightly ashamed to be all the way here in another country begging. "I hate that we haven't seen or talked to each other in ten years and our first time seeing each other, I'm here asking you for a favor."

"Well, I hate that you see it like that," Javier replies. "Because I see you as a brother and as my brother anything I can do to help you get it back together, consider it done. Fucked up is a bad place to be and I never want to see my worst enemy like that. So imagine how I feel to hear that a man like a brother to me is fucked up. You let me know exactly what you need and how much of it you need to get your knuckles off the ground."

"Well, first and foremost, I think you know exactly what I need. And I need enough of it to tear a whole state up. If you can do that for me, I will get my money up to buy enough work to tear several states up."

"Well, I'm in the best position of my life so I'm prepared to give you enough to fuck up more than a bunch of states, straight out the gate. A money problem is only a problem when nobody around you has money. That's not your case which means you don't have a problem."

56

THE NEXT DAY

TONY LOOKS THROUGH a photo album of pictures and samples of the man's work. Javier has brought Tony and Dre to his tailor. He stands next to Tony expecting him to be impressed by the pictures of various suits the tailor has made. Ninety percent through the album and Tony is yet to see anything that impresses him.

"He's the best custom suit maker and tailor in the country," Javier says. "He's been dressing me ever since I first started making my own money." Javier points to a picture in the album. "That's head of one of the biggest cartels in our country," he whispers. "That's the world famous, Emilio Sanchez, soccer player," he says with great pride. "And that is our President, Juan Orlando Hernandez," he says pointing to the picture of the tailor putting the suit jacket onto the President.

Tony nods his head very unimpressed like. All he sees are a bunch of bland suits in the most horrendous colors and the cheapest fabric. Both Javier and the tailor are looking at Tony waiting for some type of response. He hates to tell the truth but the truth is all he knows.

"No disrespect but this isn't really my speed," Tony says as humble as he can. "I must admit, your taper game is immaculate though. Such a keen eye for an old man," Tony says jokingly. Tony looks to Javier. "I appreciate the gesture but this isn't for me."

The old man takes offense. He pulls his spectacles from his eyes. "You come into my house and disrespect me like that? Do you know I am the best tailor and suit maker in all of the country? I make what the people like. The people of Honduras no like show-off like you," he says as he points to Tony's suit. "Who make a that suit," he says as he flips Tony's lapels disrespectfully.

"Paul Stuart," Tony replies proudly. "Phineas Cole Collection," he adds.

"That's a shit," the man shouts. "With my eyes closed I make a better suit than that. Come follow me," he demands. The old man leads them into a wide-open room filled with rows and rows of fabric. Suits of every color, every design, wrap around all walls of the room.

"You pick out the fabric and I guarantee I will make you a suit that will make you never wear that suit again."

Tony walks around breezing through the suits and he has to admit he's impressed. Tony lifts a pinstriped, double-breasted suit from the rack. "What's the number on something like this?"

"Four thousand, eight hundred and eighty-six," the man says without batting an eye.

Tony analyzes the suit. First, he checks the stitching and he automatically determines that the suit is fully hand-stitched as opposed to half hand-stitched. He then checks the construction where he notices the jacket is fully canvassed and not fused, meaning the jacket has three layers; the fabric on the outside, the lining and a layer of canvassing on the inside that gives the jacket its body.

Tony finds the jacket flawless and worth every penny of the four grand that he's asking for the suit. Tony picks another suit and just for the sake of price comparison he asks the price. "And this one?"

"Every suit on the rack around the same price, give or take a few dollars. Four thousand, eight hundred to five-thousand," he says.

Javier steps in between Tony and Dre. "You do know he's speaking of four thousand eight hundred lempiras, right?"

Tony has forgotten all about that. "So, how much is that in USD?"

"About two hundred dollars," Javier replies.

"Tony has to fight to contain himself. He doesn't want the old man to know how badly he's cheating himself. In the States these same suits would cost five grand in United States Dollars. Tony believes this is too good to be true. He's sure there has to be a catch. "What about if I want custom? I don't wear anything off the rack."

"Same price," the old man replies.

Tony walks a little further, doing more examining. He's like a kid in a candy store. "We have struck gold," Tony whispers to Dre. "These suits can be sold back home for $2,500 apiece, easy. And that's a low number."

"Yeah?" Dre asks in slight disbelief.

"Yeah, I'm about to put this old man to work and I suggest you do the same."

Minutes pass and Tony stands in front of the mirror as Javier takes his measurements. "Break right there, an inch over the wrist bone," Tony advises. "I like to wear cute little watches. And I want surgeon's cuffs(functioning buttons) on all of them. None of those decorative buttons."

Tony has picked out the best fabrics, nothing under Super 160. He's given the old man strict details for his suit designs. He's eager to see the man's finished product. He has big plans depending on how these suits look once they're done. All together he's ordered 10 suits.

For Dre it didn't take too much persuading. Dre and the old man are having a sidebar conversation. "So, how fast can you make me twenty-five suits?"

The old man's eyes stretch wide open before the reality of the amount of work sets in. "I only have me and my wife. That's thirty-five suits. That can take some time."

"I don't have time though," Dre explains. Dre peeks over at Tony before whispering to the man. "Mine is priority. My suits will be for business purposes and his is for personal use. Feel me?" Dre asks. "Ok, check this out. What if I give you six grand USD for the suits and another six grand USD for you to hire more manpower. Can you get me the suits in two weeks?"

The old man has never made twelve-thousand U.S. dollars at one time in his whole career. He can't let this get away from him. "I can't make any promises but I will try my best."

"No," Dre snaps. "Try harder than your best. If you can do all I need you to do we will make a lot of money. You hear me? A lot of money!"

The old man looks to Dre with happiness. "I'm looking forward to it."

The only thing Dre sees from this point on is dollar signs. The lack of money flow he was experiencing will soon be over.

57

NORTHERN STATE
D-UNIT/LOCK-UP

OFFICER TILLIS STANDS before Baby Manson with a long and saddened face. Baby Manson can tell by his expression that he has bad news for him. "You're being shipped out."

"Fuck," Baby Manson says as he stomps like a kid. He catches himself before indulging in an all-out temper tantrum.

"I tried to defend you but my Lieutenant wasn't trying to hear it. I got some good news for you though. I found out who dropped the slip on you," he whispers. Baby Manson is barely interested because he believes he already knows who did. "Carter," Tillis whispers.

Baby Manson's neck snaps hard enough to get whiplash. "What?"

"Yes," Tillis says with certainty.

Baby Manson thought for surely it was Lunatic. To find out that Carter, which is Shakir, is a total shocker. "Motherfucker," Baby Manson grunts.

With him being Shakir's competitor it makes perfect sense. He believes Shakir dropped the note on him to get him out of the way. He figures Shakir knew he wasn't prepared for a war with him so he took the coward route. What he doesn't know is Shakir really dropped the note on him to get him out of the way in attempt to save his life. For the sake of Pebbles, it was the only move he could think of, in saving her son's life.

Baby Manson thinks quickly. He runs over and grabs a pen and a pad. He scribbles quickly. He quickly walks back over to Tillis and hands him the folded note. "Just one more favor," Baby Manson says. "Can you pass that to Bennett for me?"

"No doubt," Tillis replies as he walks away. "They should be coming to get you in any minute."

As soon as Tilis is out of sight, Baby Manson walks over to the cot and falls onto it. He has to put the pillow over his face to muffle the sound of his crying. Things were just starting to really come together for him financially and now this. He was standing on a goldmine and now all that he's built has been destroyed.

Over 220 grams of dope in the hands of inmates that he will never see again. Over $150,000 down the drain. It's a sad day for Baby Manson but will be a great day for others. Shakir won't be one of those others who will have great days before them. Baby Manson will make sure of that.

F-WING

Smith stands in the dayroom listening to the young man that stands before him. "I just got the word that the boy got sent to lock up yesterday. He might be getting shipped out. He was planning to escape."

"Escape?" Smith asks. "That don't even make sense." He goes into deep thought and becomes furious instantly. "He escaped all right. This motherfucker done escaped me again. I can't believe this shit. The boy Lunatic played me."

Smith nods his head angrily. "Lunatic had his own agenda. He wanted that motherload. Now if the fuck-boy get shipped out, Lunatic walks away in the sunset with a bag of money and smack. Meanwhile my shit never got handled. At least that's what he thinks," Smith says as he flashes a sinister grin.

Smith continues on, getting angrier by the second. "He will never enjoy whatever money he got out the deal. The minute fuck-boy is shipped out, the spotlight is on Lunatic. I want him dealt with the way we deal with traitors.

The young man nods in agreeance. A young man who is hungry and ready to put in work to climb the ladder of G status. Only one thing is on his mind and that is one day getting that letter G. Knocking off Lunatic will get him a few steps higher on the ladder. "Got you big bruh. You can count on me."

C-WING

Shakir does his time, either reading on his bunk or playing chess. This moment he's playing chess with his chess partner. Playing chess with this man keeps his game sharp and at the same time he keeps his ear to the streets. Shakir keeps him close because he seems to know everything.

"Aye yo, I forgot to tell you, boy Baby Manson got sent to lock up yesterday. You heard?"

Shakir shrugs him off, never looking up from the board. "How would I know? You know I don't be fucking with niggas."

"Yeah, somebody dropped a note on him saying he was planning to escape." Shakir keeps his eyes on the board just to prevent the guilt from showing on his face. "Don't matter though because they got all the information they need already. They know the bitch name and where she live and everything. Supposedly they caught her making a drop off to a nigga in a Mazi and then they followed her right home. She live in Society Hill," he says with bugged eyes. "You know rent in there like ten-thousand a month," he says in his normal exaggeration. "So, you know that bitch eating."

Shakir can't hide it yet he tries. He knows for certain that he has to be talking about Pebbles because he knows she lives in Society Hill. He already knows it's her but he has to ask just to be sure. He prays it's not. "What's the bitch name though?"

"Pebbles."

Shakir goes into a slight trance while her name rings in his head over and over. He can't believe that she's allowed her son to drag her into this mess. Just when he thought the problem was over, it gets worse. He can't imagine this ending well. He has to get to her before it's too late.

D-UNIT/LOCK-UP

Officer Tillis fakes a yawn with a wide arm stretch as he's walking. Within the stretch he stuffs the note in between the tiny crack in the door. He peeks through the small window so Short Fuse can see him and then he walks off. Short Fuse walks to the door and grabs the note. He opens and quickly reads Baby Manson's scribe to him.

He's angered by the fact that Baby Manson is being shipped out. He was looking forward to them building a bond. He likes all that Baby Manson stands for. Usually he stays away from the younger inmates but something about Baby Manson made him break his rule. The way Baby Manson was willing to defend him on the yard meant a lot to him. Now that he's asking for a favor for him he feels obligated to do so. The fact that Baby Manson has put a price on Shakir's head is even more of an incentive to do what Baby Manson has asked of him. He would've done it on the strength but the money is just an added bonus.

C-WING

Shakir holds the phone with rage bubbling inside of him. The automated service connects the call. "Hey," Pebbles says in her fake sweet voice.

"You got to be the dumbest bitch alive, you know that?" Shakir says.

"Excuse me?" Pebbles doesn't believe his tone.

"You heard what the fuck I said. You one dumb ass bitch."

"Your mother a dumb ass bitch!" Pebbles snaps back. "Call me another bitch and watch I hang up on you and never answer for your dumb ass again in life."

"What the fuck would make you get involved in that dumb ass shit your dumb ass son got going on?"

"First, you disrespect me and now my son? Bye, Sha."

"Yo, yo, don't hang this fucking phone up. You the mother, so why would you allow him to get you involved?"

Pebbles isn't necessarily mad that he's called her a bitch or even a dumb ass bitch. She's been so many of those in her life that it doesn't even phase her. She's really surprised that he knows what's going on. "What the fuck are you even talking about?"

"You know what the fuck I'm talking about. The other day you didn't meet with a dude in a white Maserati?"

"What?" she asks as if she's clueless.

"Don't fucking what me, yo," Shakir says with rage. "You left there and drove straight to your house in Society Hill."

Pebbles now realizes the severity of it all. She realizes now is the time to stop the games. "How you know that?"

"Every dumb ass Blood in here know that. They know your name, what the fuck you drive, where the fuck you live. And they think they know that you are the boss of the construction company," he says using code.

"Huh? What you mean, Sha?"

"I mean that motherfuckers are planning to come to the job site and take all the supplies. They want all the lumber, tools and every-thing."

"I don't run no construction company. I don't have no supplies," she says. The fear can be heard in her voice.

"Well, these little dumb motherfuckers don't know that and they coming for you. You gone need to move from Society Hill. I don't know how you gone do it. Rent it out to somebody or something. And get out that dumb ass Range Rover. It's hot as a firecracker right now. Get you a little hooptie and get low. Let me figure out a way to get your dumb ass out of this shit. Dumb ass bitch," he mumbles.

Pebbles accepts the name calling without defense. For one she needs him right now and for two she feels like the dumb ass bitch he refers to her as.

Paranoia has her feeling like she's being watched right this mo-ment. Just to know that the other day she was watched and followed without her knowing gives her the creeps. Her trembling legs cause her to walk across the parking lot clumsily. One heavy twist and the heel cracks in half. She is so afraid that the broken shoe doesn't bother her. She kicks the pumps off and walks across the lot barefoot.

She peeks around fearfully. Every car that rides pass her causes her concern. She looks at her truck as she approaches it and is second guessing getting into it. She stops in the middle of the lot and looks around slowly before getting inside. "Fuck this shit," she says as she pulls off.

It's a long ride home. Her eyes stayed glued in the rearview mirror the whole time. It was all good just yesterday but the tables have turned on her. It's always good when the money is coming in but this is the other side of the game. One small move and one can easily end up on this side of the game. Pebbles never considered herself to be in the game, but now thanks to Lunatic a bunch of gangbangers see it differently.

58

QUABO AND TORTURA sit on the edge of their seats like they are watching an action-packed movie. They've been sitting here since the wee hours of the morning waiting for some action and now here it is, finally. This all seems too good to be true. All this time they've been on the prowl looking and never once have they been this close.

To see the girl that they have been hunting all this time brings out a rage that is unexplainable. The anger and the pain that she's caused brews fury inside of them. Men have died because of her and not to mention the money Quabo has lost. Right here, right now, they are finally able to get their revenge.

Quabo and Tortura have no idea that Skelter has an identical twin sister. With them not knowing that there's no way they would ever believe they have the wrong woman. They watch as she steps out of the house onto the porch, cradling the baby against her bosom. They're just waiting for the perfect time to make their move.

She leans to the side, holding the baby on her hip as she locks the door. She carefully whisks down the steps. She steps outside the gate and just as she does the roaring of a speeding engine can be heard approaching. She quickly turns to her left, just as the Bronco hops onto the sidewalk. The passenger's door and the back door pop open simultaneously and Tortura and another man jump out one behind the other.

Quabo watches from the backseat as she stops abruptly. She turns to face Tortura and his accomplice and out of nowhere the sound of gunfire from an assault rifle rips loudly. Bullet holes zip through the baby's body, leaving holes like Swiss cheese. She drops the baby to the ground and the A.R. 15 is now fully exposed and aimed at the men. She continues to fire relentlessly.

She keeps them at bay as vehicles swarm in from every direction, surrounding the Bronco. She ducks low to the ground and cuts through an alley for safety. She disappears and once she's out of harm's way the sound of gunfire rings loudly. It's quite obvious that it's not one, two or even three guns are being fired. A wide-open gun battle with over two minutes of consistent firing.

The men surrounding the Bronco all look the same with purple bandanas covering their faces from the face down and skull caps on their heads. The gunfire stops. One-man steps on the baby with no regard or compassion for life. He only has one thing on his mind and that is Tortura who is laid out on the ground, not able to move. Tortura looks up to the man with blood gushing out of his mouth, ounces at a time.

Even under these losing circumstances Tortura manages to maintain his devilish grin. The man dumps two bullets into Tortura's face. At the same time Tortura kills over, a few feet away another shot seals the death of one of Tortura's men. Not a second in between the back door is being snatched open. A gunman leans in where Quabo is lying there hiding on the floor in between seats. The man places the gun at the back of Quabo's head and squeezes. Quabo's body folds over before he lays flat on the floor, stiff as an ironing board.

The gunmen hop into their vehicles and speed off. As the cars get to the corner, they all split up in different directions. Back at the scene of the crime a police car pulls onto the scene. Just happening to be patrolling the area and they run into this. Had they turned onto the block three minutes earlier they would have had to work for their money today.

The two officers hop out of their car quickly. The female officer screams at the top of her lungs as she sees the baby on the ground, wrapped up in the blanket, face up. "Oh, my God, a baby," she shouts as she leans over to check the pulse. She quickly finds out it's a baby doll and tears of joy replace her sadness. She throws the doll to the ground and runs over to Tortura who she knows is dead even before she gets over to him.

"I need an ambulance," the other officer says as he stands at the back door of the Bronco. "Hurry," he yells.

Blood pours from the back of Quabo's head as he lies in between the seats. Blood is pouring over his face but his eyes have a sense of alertness in them. He's still, with his head weighing a ton. He can feel his brain pulsating. He fights to breathe as the cop keeps him comfortable. "Just take it easy and breathe," the cop says. "You're going to be all right. Just breathe," he says in a soothing voice. "Are you with me?" the cop asks.

Quabo nods his head slowly. He grabs hold of the cop's hand. He doesn't have the energy to talk but he squeezes the cop's hand as a reply. He digs deep for strength. He's a fighter and has no plans of his story ending like this.

"I got to hold on," Quabo mumbles to himself over and over. He squeezes the cop's hand tighter and tighter. The tight grip he has lets the cop know that he has a lot of life left in him.

59

TONY HAS ONLY been away from the grind for a few days and things have piled up like he has been away for weeks. He drove straight to the office from the airport and got right to work. Right now he has two meetings in process at the same time and a third one on the way. He sits at his desk going over two separate stacks of papers. Maurice stares out of the window in silence before he starts pacing circles. The tapping on the door diverts their attention. The door opens and the secretary holds it for Lil Bit to enter.

Lil Bit walks in nervously. Tony stands up to greet her. "Hey, long time no see," he says genuinely. He quickly notices her twitching eye but tries to overlook it.

Lil Bit's only reason for coming here is out of fear. She knows how persistent Maurice can be and she doesn't want to live in fear of him popping up at her house again. She doesn't trust being alone with him and she doesn't trust him around her house. She figured the only way to get around that is by coming here. She knows the respect he has for Tony and she hopes that respect is enough to prevent him from doing something crazy.

"I'm going to leave you two alone," Tony says. "I have two other clients to meet with," he says as he walks toward the door.

"No," Lil Bit says as she darts behind him. "That was the whole reason for meeting here so you would be here. Don't leave me in here with him."

Tony can sense the fear in her and wonders what could have instilled so much of it into her. Tony knows nothing about any of their drama. He's never known Maurice to be a woman abuser but something about all of this has domestic violence written all over it. He knows for certain that Maurice hasn't seen Lil Bit in years because he asked about her a few times. That means the fear she has of him has been embedded in her for many years.

Maurice walks toward them and as he gets closer, Lil Bit steps further behind Tony. She hides behind him, not allowing him to move without her. Sadness rips through Maurice's heart. He's never had a woman this afraid of him. "Yo, you doing all this for nothing," Maurice whispers. "I just want to talk to you. Just me and you."

"Nope, I don't trust you."

"You don't trust me?" Maurice snaps. "My loyalty was never in question. I'm not the one who back-doored you and went to see the plug and fed the competition."

"Maurice, that was the biggest mistake I ever made in my life and I cry over that mistake all day, every day literally," she says as she traces the tears that drop down her face. "Every time I look in the mirror and see the tears dripping, I think about the day you had me shot in the head and left to die on the street in front of my newborn baby."

Tony has heard enough. He looks at Maurice side eyed. "I refuse to listen to another word of this shit. This personal and y'all need to deal with it as such."

"If you leave, I'm leaving," Lil Bit says.

"Moe, I'm gone act like I didn't hear a word of this shit," Tony says. He's quite disturbed. "I don't want to hear anymore. Anyway, I got things to handle. Give me your word that when I walk out of here she will be good."

"Come on bruh. What you think I'm on?" Maurice is embarrassed by it all.

"Man, at this point I don't know," Tony replies with sarcasm. "Ain't my business though. I'm just concerned for her safety. Right now, she here as my responsibility and I want her safe. Simple as that. Got me?"

"Absolutely."

"Listen," Tony says to Lil Bit. "I can promise you will be okay in here."

"Okay," she replies. "Only if he go over by the desk and I will stand here. And the door has to stay open."

Maurice walks toward the window with his head hanging in shame. Tony grabs her hand and squeezes it for reassurance. He makes his exit, leaving them all alone. Tony walks to the back to his intern's office. Dre sits there scrolling through his phone when Tony walks in and drops a binder on the desk in front of him.

"If you go through the folder you will see the accounts of a bunch of people that you don't know. Every day I listen to you talk about being broke and you complain that I'm not listening. I always listen but never take the conversation seriously because I know you're not broke."

Dre looks up with an expression of skepticism. "What you mean?"

"As your brother sent me hundreds of thousands at a time, I had a job to do. A hard job at that," Tony says. "I had to find accounts to put the money in. I had to contact associates of mine that were interested in making a little money on their money.

If you pay close attention you will see 529's— college funds. Some worth five-hundred thousand," he says. "Mutual funds, money market accounts, trust funds. You name it, it's in there. Some of the funds can't be touched for another seven years. A couple of them you can cash out in three months.

Look at the first four documents. Each form is an account of two hundred and fifty grand apiece, and they all mature within a two-week period. A hundred and five days – tops – you will have a million in cash and you out there in Honduras chasing some drug money shit," Tony says. "You have a portfolio worth over seven million dollars. And that is after my associates have taken their cut."

Dre can't believe the words that are coming out of Tony's mouth. He flicks through the documents. The only thing that registers to him are the dollar amounts. Everything else he has no clue of what it means.

"You don't have to sell drugs another day in your life, thanks to your brother. You and him made the money ten years ago. Now you just have to be patient and wait for the return on your investments. As I said, the first million will be in your hands in three and a half months. Another week later, a buck fifty coming through," he says as if it's pennies.

"Another week, three hundred thousand is due to hit. In the next two years I believe you will have cashed out about two point five million. Another seven years, you will be have cashed out close to eight million. I have all the legal work sealed and documented. No way you can lose, period."

Dre is in awe. Tony stares at him quietly as a smirk spreads across his face. "Yo, not for nothing," Tony says. "But I just have to say this. I remember back in '07 when we first met and bruh was trying to convince you that I was solid and you were determined to believe that I was a snake who was cheating bruh and only out for the money."

Dre looks away shamefully. Tony continues to pour it on. "All I ever wanted to prove to you was that I always had his best interest at heart. I didn't know you but you were his brother and he loved you so I showed that same love to you. Fast forward, over eleven years later and here we stand. I love you like a brother just as I love him. I must ask you this though. Did I prove your brother right and you wrong or did I prove your brother right and you wrong?" he asks jokingly.

Dre smiles. He's shocked that Tony knows of he and his brother's personal conversations pertaining to him. "You proved him right and me wrong a long time ago, bruh. I always think about that and wish that there was some way I could tell him that he was right about you. He knew it all the time. I just need him to know that I now know it too. That's one of the many conversations I wish I could have with him face to face."

The door opens and the secretary holds it open for the guest to enter. Dre and Tony's heart to heart conversation is interrupted. A tall and athletic built man enters the room. He diddy-bops his way into the office with a stride as cool as a 70's pimp.

"Suave, my man!" Tony yells. The man glides across the floor. A sparkling smile spreads across his face as he gets closer to the desk. "Boy, you the coolest motherfucker I ever seen in my life," Tony compliments as he reaches for a handshake.

"Knock it off," Suave says modestly. "You know you the coolest motherfucker in the world. But I will take second place," he says rolling his head around with conceit. He grips Tony's hand tightly. "Good to see you big bruh."

"Good to be seen," Tony replies. "Suave, this is Dre. Dre, this is Suave."

Dre stands up to properly greet Suave. Suave looks at Dre with a familiar look on his face. Dre, Dre?" he asks as if he's star struck. "I've heard so much about you from your brother. It's truly an honor to finally meet you."

Dre blushes modestly. He shakes Suave's hand. "Thank you," he says humbly.

"Dre, this is the man that connected the dots and introduced me to bruh," Tony says. "The history we made is all due to him."

Suave looks to Tony with hunger in his eyes. "I hope y'all got some good news for me."

"It's all lined up," Tony claims. "Got your parole being switched up here within the next week or so."

"Good to hear," Suave says with excitement. "Can't wait to get out of Delaware. I haven't had nothing but bad luck since I went down there fifteen years ago. The biggest mistake of my damn life."

"Your apartment is ready," says Tony. "Your license came back three days ago."

Tony hands a paper over his shoulder to Suave. Suave reads the paper with excitement in his eyes. He's happy to get a fresh start in life. His life has been all downhill ever since the shooting charge he caught in 2003.

Coming home 3 years later and finding out about his woman's infidelity set him back further than the 3-year bid. He took off to Delaware with hopes of getting over her and changing his life. He had no plans of never going back to Jersey, never going back to the drug game and never ever going back to prison. Boxing was going to be his new hustle.

Fighting on an undercard at Madison Square Garden had him believing that he was on his way. That is until he received the purse of a lousy two grand for a televised fight. Didn't take long before he found himself fighting a different fight. He broke his promise to himself. He went back to Jersey and he went back to the drug game and after close to a 5 year run, he went back to prison.

He was set up and got nabbed with a kilo of cocaine and a gun. Tony miraculously made the cocaine disappear but the gun stuck to him like glue due to his prior shooting charge back in 2003. Now, he's fresh home, not even 3 months in off a 7-year prison bid. Now, all he wants to do is the right thing and he believes that will be easy because he's with the right team. Tony promised him when he came home he had something for him. He's home now and ready to put together the pieces of life's puzzle.

"Got the contracts ready for you to sign," Tony says as he hands another stack of papers to Suave.

"Dig," says Tony. "I got your first ten fights lined up already. All easy work. In three years I will have you at 20 and 0. All paid for, 1st round knockouts. You won't even have to break a sweat. Once you're 20 and 0, you become a contender and that's when we will see what you're really made of. That's when the real fights come in."

"Listen, man y'all ain't got to pay for these fights for me," Suave says. "I can really fight," he says with cockiness. "Put me in there with real fighters and I guarantee you I still get us to that 20 and 0 mark!"

"I don't doubt it," Tony says. "But you ain't no spring chicken though. You're thirty-eight years old. We pay for the fights, a grand here, two grand there. We spend about fifty grand out of pocket to build your whole career. Then our first title fight, it's a million on the table for us. At that point our job is done. Now it's your turn to work. All you got to do is go out there and get that money."

"Damn, a million sound damn good right about now!" Suave shouts.

"As I said," Tony reiterates. "You ain't no spring chicken. Being a World Champion is a long shot. It's probably way too late in the game for that. But we can score a few M's along the way."

"I'm with that," Suave replies. "Only thing, I ain't got three years to be running around this motherfucker broke until we make a hit."

"And you won't have to," says Tony. "We are prepared to pay you a salary of six hundred dollars a week and the apartment over the gym you can live for rent free. It ain't a lot of money but you getting paid to show up in the gym. Twenty-four hundred a month just to come to the gym and break a sweat. The little money you make with the first twenty fights you can keep for yourself, with the exception of paying your cut-man and promoters. We don't need a dime off it. Things will get greater later and that's when we all eat."

"All sounds good but what about my clause I asked to be added into the contract," Suave questions. "I ain't just no workhorse," he says with emphasis. "Or no pit-bull in a dog fight. I'm a businessman as well. I need the option of being brought in as an equal partner once I get my bread up."

"It's all right there in the contract," Tony says. "Read it," Tony demands. "You will be signed to IronFist Management which is me and the Book Writer. The Book Writer is also signed on as your trainer," Tony informs. "And you have an open-door policy to come in as a partner on any of your fights as well as any other fighters that we sign in the future.

"Read it for yourself," Tony suggests.

"Big Homie, if you say it's in there, then there's no need for me to read it," says Suave. "I trust you with my life. Where's the pen and where do I sign"

Tony hands Suave the pen and he gets to signing his life away on the dotted line.

"Check it out," Tony says as Suave is signing away. "Them little peanuts that will be on the table for the next three years ain't enough for nobody to live off but we got a plan to get some better money in the meantime."

"I'm all ears. That's what I'm about, money."

"We gone make the money," Tony says confidently. "That's what this thing is about, everybody eats! Let no man around us starve!"

• • •

The tension between Maurice and Lil Bit has lightened. Maurice was certain that if he could get her ear, face to face, just them he could get through to her. Maurice and her stand face to face. He grips her hands tight. His face is covered with tears and so is hers.

"I think about you all day, every single day," says Maurice. "I taught you to never let emotions get in the way of business and rational thinking but I did. When I lost you, I lost my foundation. I haven't been right since. I know you will never be able to forget what happened but I hope you can forgive me," he says as he pulls her closer.

Lil Bit doesn't put up any resistance. Their bodies are close together and she stares up into his eyes. He places his thumb in the corner of her left eye to stop the tears from flowing. He plants a soft kiss on her eyelid.

"I know this is going to sound crazy but can we start all over again?" he asks with desperation. "Or better yet pick up from where we left off. At the point where you said to me that I chose to marry another woman over you. Let's go back to that point right before I made that decision to marry the other woman. This time I will make the right decision. Then we can fast forward and skip all the other shit that happened in between. Is it worth a try?"

"Maurice, I don't know if I can ever trust you again."

"I'm not sure if I can ever trust you again either but I'm willing to give it a try. Are you?"

Instead of replying, she just stares into his eyes. A man who hired someone to kill her yet she still has a soft spot in her heart for him. She realizes how crazy that even sounds and she also realizes how crazy she would look to anyone who knows the story. She knows the answer but for some reason she can't force it out of her mouth.

Maurice steps back, still holding her hands. He can't let her go. At this moment he could hug her forever. "Answer me. Are you willing to give it a try?" Lil Bit stares at him with a blank expression. He digs deeper. "Marry me? Not today, not tomorrow," he says. "I will give you time to find forgiveness in your heart, first. And then you can marry me?"

60

DRE DRAGS HIMSELF into the apartment lazily. He locks the door and drops his suitcase. He turns around and is shocked to find Lil Mama, on her knees, completely nude in front of him. He pushes her back gently yet she wiggles out of his grip and backs him up against the door. She unzips his pants and digs inside for her prize. She wastes no time in presenting her oral presentation.

They say oral sex is better when it comes from a woman who enjoys giving it. If that's the case, Lil Mama must really love giving oral sex because she's doing a great job. In fact the job is so amazing, Dre can barely stand up to it. His legs weaken at the slightest touch she gives him. He plants his hand on her forehead and tries to pry her off of him but that doesn't work. She shakes her head like a vicious pit-bull snapping at him violently.

The pleasure is too much to deny or reject so instead he decides to give in. She hits notes on the trumpet that lift him off of his feet higher and higher. Excitement has him standing on his tippy toes with the expertise of a ballerina. One hand on the top of her head he guides her as he uses the other hand to rest his weight on the wall.

She now has his full attention and takes this time to do all the tricks she has been waiting to perform. Those lonely nights in her cell when she would sneak and read Zane novels just to help her release. In jail she never masturbated for pleasure purposes. She only masturbated to maintain her sanity and ease her sexual frustration.

She was a young girl with raging hormones, and while most of the inmates turned to other women, she vowed that she would never. So it was just her and Zane's, Sex Chronicles whenever she felt like going there. Her masturbating while reading never ended well for her. Just left her to fall asleep even more sexually frustrated. It was those nights that Dre came into her dreams and helped to relieve her frustration. There were a many a nights that she woke up with wet panties and a fast beating heart.

And now here she is. For all those years she only had Dre when she was sleep in her dreams. Right now she has him while she's wide awake and she will not take a second of it for granted. She plans to compile all 10 years of her dreams into this one session.

They've worked their way through the foyer into the living room where Lil Mama has slammed him on the loveseat. He leans back as she sits straddled over his lap, facing him. She rides nice and slow as she stares into his eyes. Just the actual thought of what is taking place right now is enough for her to orgasm. She's had a many wet dreams that went exactly like this. His chinky eyes staring at her, the smell of his cologne, his touch, all seem so familiar.

Ten long years of deprivation. She wishes this moment could last forever. Her body jolts and goosebumps swell all over her body. She's reintroduced to feelings that her body has forgotten all about.

She runs her fingers through the curly locks of his hair as she slow grinds on him. She leans forward, arching her back as she wraps her hands around his neck. She glides up and down on him with slow, wet and slippery strokes. Her back arches more so he can slide deeper inside her. She stretches her torso to get an even bigger arch and it's there that his manhood and her G-spot meet for the first time. The rhythm of their bodies is so harmonious and natural, not forced.

The slightest movement of her hips creates another level of intensity. He reciprocates strokes of equal tempo. He grinds with deep slow strokes as he leans in and latches onto her bottom lip with his front teeth. He bites down on her lip gently, as the strokes get faster and faster, and not so gentle. The stroking of her G-spot becomes more intense.

The feeling so pleasurable, the teasing only makes her angry and more horny. She bounces up and down hard and fast. The sound of her ass cheeks slapping against his thighs is like music to her ears. She holds her breath as he enters her, inhales as she glides along and she gasps for air as she lands.

She stops bouncing and slows up the tempo. She holds onto his neck and allows her body to drape backward. He and her both look down and enjoy the peep show, of him sliding in and out of her. She looks up and they lock eyes. "You see what this halal pussy do?" she asks with seduction in her eyes.

Dre leans over, mouth first and he plants soft kisses all over her breast. A burst of energy jolts through his body, bringing him onto his feet. Lil Mama holds onto his neck tightly as he drills her as hard and fast as he can. Their bodies collide. Her moaning incites him to drill faster and harder.

He stops suddenly, just appreciating her wetness. They lock lips and kiss passionately. She winds on him slowly and he reciprocates. They grind to the beat of the same drum that plays in their heads.

He carries her across the room, their bodies still glued together, his key jammed deep into her lock. He stops at the recliner where he drops her. With force he snatches her by the hair and pulls her onto her feet. He bends her over the arm of the chair, ass up and her face buried in the cushion. She loves that he's now taking the lead as he has done in some of her dreams. She just goes with the flow, allowing him to do whatever it is he chooses, giving herself to her husband.

She's now bent over the arm of the sofa. She peeks over her shoulder at him. "Fuck me," she commands. He mashes her face to the pillow and with the other hand, he grips her waist. With no hesitation he gives her what she asked for. He pounds hard and digs deep. He's in awe of the masterpiece of an ass that lies before his eyes. Her sunshine, yellow ass ripples with every stroke. He pounds faster, using her ass as a trampoline. He rides the waves, holding her waist for reassurance.

She looks back at him. "Baby don't look at it," she warns. She is well aware of the power of her ass. "You can't look at it." He disregards her warning. With each stroke, her ass, so big and soft, it ripples like a tidal wave. He rides the waves, up and down and until he starts to feel seasick. With no warning, he blows his load. He tries to hold on but his knees buckle. Lil Mama looks back at him. "I told you don't look at it. You didn't listen. Now look," she says teasingly.

Dre backs up onto the couch where he collapses. His heart beating like he's seconds away from cardiac arrest. Lil Mama sits on his lap running her fingers through his hair. She's so *horngry* for him. For her, that was only the appetizer. "You ready for round two?"

"Round two?" he asks in a high-pitched voice.

"See," she says with a smile. "Now that's that old man shit we not gone do."

61

SKELTER DESERVES AN Oscar for the role she just played in that movie. Playing stunt double for Helter was ingenious on her part. She realized how risky it was to put herself in harm's way like that but it had to be done. She knew it was the only way she could reel Quabo and Tortura in.

None of this would've been possible had it not been for No Toes. He found himself stuck in between a rock and a hard spot and he really didn't know what to do. The fear he had of Quabo and Tortura is really what made him make the move he made. Deep in his heart he felt they were going to end up killing him anyway. In order to save his life he had to come up with a plan of his own.

It took a lot of courage for him to go against them and tell their plans. One morning he hung around until he saw Helter leaving the house. He went up to her and introduced himself before telling all the details. Helter immediately got Skelter on the phone to come meet No Toes. It was then that Skelter came up with the bright idea to play stunt double and pretend to be Helter. With the help of her new alliance with Newark's Purple Army as she calls it, the mission was a successful one. Well, at least she thinks it was successful. She has no idea that Quabo is in the hospital undergoing surgery. He fought for his life as he waited for the paramedics, but he won the fight.

It's almost 11 P.M. and the city seems to be sleeping. Skelter and her Godsons have just come back out since the incident earlier today. They just picked up No Toes, who sits in the backseat across from Skelter. "Again, I thank you for pulling us up," Skelter says.

"Aye, it was the right thing to do. I would never sell my people out for no damn *Doe-minican* motherfuckers. One thing I learned back in the dope game is the *Doe-minican* don't give a damn about nobody but the *Doe-minicans*. I ain't gone lie, I used them for their free dope though."

Skelter sits back just allowing him to run his mouth. She realizes the more he talks the more he tells on himself. Her reason for picking him up is because something he said earlier didn't add up.

"I was thinking about something you said," Skelter says. "The first time we met you said the Dominican motherfuckers pressed up on you with a picture and they offered you dope to tell where you seen me, right?"

"Yeah but I told them I had never saw you before," he lies with a straight face. "But then that day when I was walking and I saw your sister, I kept looking like damn I know that face from somewhere."

Skelter runs her hand across her forehead trying to ease the stress that's been built up for months. She opens her eyes and looks at No Toes. "Then you never seen them no more until the day you got out the rehab, you said, right?" No Toes nods his head. "But what about the time when you said they paid you dope to be on lookout in front of the Projects?"

"Damn, that slipped my mind. You're right. That dope will make you forget a lot of shit," he says with a cheesy smile.

"Just like it made you forget that you said one time they gave you twenty something bags to go in the back to see if I was back there?"

"Yeah, I wasn't gone tell them if you was back there though. I was just playing them for the free dope."

"Oh ok," Skelter says as she nods her head. "Did it slip your mind that the only reason they knew where I was from is because you told them?"

"Listen, I ain't gone lie. I'm clean now and off that shit. I made a lot of mistakes while I was out there on that shit. While I was in the rehab I told myself once I got back into the world I would try to right all my wrongs. I'm starting with a clean slate and I'm starting right here. No lies, just straight truth.

He raises his right hand high in the air, as if he's about to testify. "I told them where I had seen you before. I was dope-sick and needed a hit to get right. I wasn't thinking for the future. I was thinking for the moment. They were offering free dope and I needed dope. I never really had plans of telling them if I saw you. I was just playing the game."

"The truth is always better than a lie," Skelter says with a fake smile. Her smile transitions into stone. "You realize how many people got murdered around there because the game you were playing? For free dope you brought the heat to us and people got murdered. Do you know that my Godson was captured by them and still to this day we haven't heard from him? We're sure he's dead but we may never find his body."

"Nah, I didn't know that." No Toes shakes his head with a guilty sadness covering his face. "Once I realized how serious shit was getting, I wanted out and that is why I signed myself into the rehab."

"To get away from the game, the mess you had already made, huh?"

No Toes has no defense. "I mean, I didn't know what else to do, I'm sorry. I fucked up. I can only blame it on my illness. I'm an addict."

Skelter draws her gun and grips it on her lap. "I can dig it." She looks into the rearview and her and Youngest Godson lock eyes. She gives him an eye signal to pull over.

No Toes looks at the gun and realizes this about to end badly for him. In a desperate attempt to save his life, he speaks. "Please, don't kill me. I apologize for the problems I caused but I was sick. I started shooting heroin at thirteen years old. I've been getting high for thirty-four of my forty-seven years of living. This is the longest I've been sober and not under the influence. I got a month clean. This a new life for me and I just want to live it." He looks down at the gun. "Please," he begs.

Skelter stares into his eyes, gripping her gun tightly. The rage from her Godson losing his life is taking over her. She raises the gun in the air and No Toes closes his eyes, to avoid seeing it coming. Expecting to hear the boom, he peeks one eye open.

Skelter waves the gun in front of his face. "Get out," she commands. No Toes is scared to move, expecting to be shot from the back. "Hurry the hell up before I change my mind." He opens the door and gets out quickly. "You've been spared. You got your second life. Use it wisely. If I catch you out here back on that shit I will take you out of your misery. Now get the fuck out of here."

"Thank you," No Toes says with tears crawling down his face. "Thank you."

62

11 P.M./THE DUNGEON-NEWARK

ON A RAGGEDY and deserted block the silhouettes of three men bounce off the walls. Creeping through the dark and narrow alley is Tony and Suave. The foul smell of urine is in the air. This warehouse building and the single-family house to the right of it are the only two buildings standing on the entire block.

Leading them through the alley is Tony's good friend and personal security for the night, Ali-Wop. Ali-Wop aka Big Muslim, is as dark as the night, standing at 6'5" and weighing 250 pounds. His bald head and big beard adds to his intimidating appearance. He leads them by a few steps. The further they get into the alley the darker it gets. They stop at a steel door at the back of the warehouse.

Tony dials on his phone and the receiver picks up quickly. "I'm at the back," he says into the phone. In seconds, the heavy steel door creaks loudly as it opens.

As they enter the building, the smell of sweat smacks them in their faces. Loud cheering can be heard echoing through the hollow hall. The screaming and cheering gets louder as they approach the end of the hall. They step into the room which is dark and gloomy, with little to no light. The room is packed from wall to wall. A boxing ring is in the center of the room, with many men surrounding it. The men all have stacks of money piled in front of them which is a clear indication that they are gambling big.

Liquor is sold from a makeshift bar in the back of the room. Raunchy strippers, dressed in sexy lingerie work their way through the crowds. Lap dances are sold to the cheapskates and the perverts for twenty bucks, while sex is on the menu for the ballers, starting at two hundred dollars. Weed, pills and any other drug one can think of is being sold as well. All in all, there's a lot of money changing hands in here.

Men from every angle of street life are in this room. Hustlers from lower level to the big dogs, murderers, stick-up kids, gangbangers and addicts are present. All of them occupying the same space, breathing the same sweaty, stinking air. Tony can feel the attention on him and his crew. The leather duffle-bag Ali-Wop holds is what they really are focusing on. It's as if they have sniffed the money through the bag. Inside the bag is a whopping $150,000.

Inside the boxing ring there are three men who all appear to be junkies or addicts of some kind. One of them is the acting referee. The other two are dancing around the ring banging each other up. Seeing the two men swing wild haymakers with no true art form is quite comical to watch. This doesn't look like a boxing match. It looks more like a drunken bar fight. They're breaking every rule in boxing.

A few wild bolos and the crowd is going wild. Everyone jumps up and down with excitement as one of the fighters is backed up against the ropes and getting pounded on. "That's right," shouts one man. "That's right! He beating on him like he stole something!"

As the man sits on the ropes with his eyes closed, taking massive abuse, he drops his hand down and rips a clumsy looking uppercut from down yonder. The uppercut crashes into the opponent's chin and lifts him off of the canvas about 2 inches high. He flies backwards in the air for a few steps before falling onto his back. The crowd goes wild. "Yeah, yeah!" Loud snoring can be heard from across the room.

"He's out," shouts the referee as he waves his hands in the air. Cheering from the winners and shouting of vulgar language floods the room as money exchanges hands. If one had to estimate this bout had at least $10,000 riding on it.

Once everything dies down and all the money has been transferred from hand to hand another bout is about to begin. The two men standing in the ring now are both over 300 pounds. Neither of them appear to be in any type of physical shape. Diabetes, High Blood Pressure and Heart Problems are what they look like. Instead of boxers, they are built like Samoan wrestlers.

Tony feels eyes burning through him. He looks across the ring where he quickly notices a group of thugs staring at him. Their shifty eyes tell their story. No money in front of them which means they're not gambling. No drinks in their hands, no blunts in their mouths and no half naked women on their laps, means they are not spending money. Most likely they have none to spend which means they are here for something else.

Tony nudges Ali-Wop with his knee, just to make sure he peeps the group of men and keeps his eyes on them. "I'm already on them," Wop says. He looks in every direction except theirs but he most definitely sees them. He looks over Tony's head as he speaks. "They're not the only ones watching. We got eyes all over the room but I'm on their ass. Trust me bruh."

The announcer speaks. "In the red corner coming straight to you from Bradley Court, we have Heavy D! And in the blue corner coming straight to you from Pennington Court we have Dirt McGirt." Loud clapping sounds off. "I will give y'all a few minutes to place your bets before we begin." Money starts flowing throughout the room in abundance.

Al-Saadiq Banks and his brother Naim step up and greet Tony, Suave and Wop. They all make their way into the back to get ready for their bout. Tony makes sure to take the long way, the scenic route so everyone can take a look at Suave. They all study Suave closely so they will know if they should bet on him or bet against him.

Suave is wearing an oversized trench coat. Under the coat he's dressed in khakis, a flannel shirt and penny loafers. Reading glasses top off his nerdy appearance. This whole disguise was all Tony's idea.

He's dressed like a square but something about his walk confuses the people. His bop doesn't match the outfit. The trench coat prevents them from seeing his frame. He doesn't look like much of a threat but the confidence his crew displays also throws them off.

The secret conversations can be heard as they pass. Almost everyone they've heard sounds as if they're going to bet against him. Tony's hoping they all bet against him. The more the better because he plans to accept all bets.

11:45 P.M.

Suave is dressed and ready to rumble. Showtime is at 12 Midnight. He's the Main Event. He's dressed like an Olympic boxer in all Adidas gear from head to toe and his body is ripped like one too. Thick vaseline coats his face to prevent cuts. His shoulders are greased up as well. He has enough oil on his body to fry in the Sun.

He paces back and forth to alleviate the butterflies that are floating in his stomach. He bites down on his mouthpiece to break it in and clenches his fist and bangs the gloves together to break in the leather. He's having a hard time getting himself together. His nerves are a wreck. He hasn't been in the ring in years. In prison all he was able to do was jog the track, no boxing. He knows his cardio is A1 but he's not sure what his fight game is like.

He thinks maybe he should've trained a few weeks before getting in the ring but when Tony told him he had a way for him to make a few dollars, the hustler in him kicked in. Financially he's hurting right now but tonight he will fix that. Tonight's purse is $50,000. He only gets a third of that but $16,000 sounds real good to him right about now.

This purse is so big because his opponent is the grand champion. This man, Marvin 'Magic Touch' Green is a 56-year-old, veteran of the boxing game. He's earned the name Magic Touch because his hands are so fast. He's been fighting since he was a young child. As an amateur he dominated his weight division. He holds the record for being State Champ for 12 years straight. He's a Golden Glove and Diamond Glove Champion. He's also three-time National Champion.

He made it to the Olympic Trials but due to the politics of the game he was robbed of the opportunity to be an Olympic contender.

He didn't allow that to stop him though. He went further on to dominate the pros. He's won almost every fight he's had in life yet there's only one fight he couldn't win. That fight is the battle he's had with crack. He fought that battle most of life until it finally beat him.

In the corner of the room Saadiq holds the focus mitts for Suave to warm up and shoot his combinations at. After a few punches Suave starts to loosen up and knock the rust off his joints. He throws picture perfect combinations. His punches against the mitts sound like fireworks popping off loudly. All the attention is diverted from the fight that's going on to them over here warming up.

A frail and scruffy looking man steps up and just watches them work. After a few minutes, the bell rings and all the attention is now on them. The frail and scruffy man finally speaks. "He ain't never gone be able to hit me with that slow shit. I will be all over his ass like a typewriter! Bddd, bdd, bddd," he makes the sound of keys of a typewriter being pressed. He throws a series of punches in the air.

Laughter fills the room. This frail and scruffy man is Marvin Magic Touch Green, a living legend that Suave has heard so much about. In every gym in Newark and even in every jail in New Jersey his name rings bells.

11:57 P.M.

The time has finally come. Suave stands in the corner of the ring. Saadiq stands up close and personal, in Suave's face, staying tapped into his mind. He gives him a pep talk as Naim massages his shoulders. Tony stands right underneath them on the floor while Ali-Wop stands behind them, keeping his eyes on the entire room.

Suddenly the mood of the room changes when a tune from the 80's, an Oldie but Goodie Classic seeps through the speakers. *"Tricks with cards are easy to do. And tricks with hearts will cast a spell on you. Cause I'm your Magic Man, yes I am."* Everyone knows this is Magic Touch's theme song. This song plays during his introduction in every fight. They all sing along word for word. *"On stage and lights, I'll dazzle your eyes. And later on that night, I'll make you realize, I'm your Magic Man...yes I am."*

Magic Touch comes running out of the back with his old, dirty, wrinkled boxing robe on. The boxing shoes on his feet have at least a million miles on them. They have holes in the sole and are turned over. Magic Touch dances around, firing punches in the air as his entourage follows behind him. The men he's with make up what the hood calls the Money Team. The majority of the dope, coke and weed on the streets of Newark comes from this team.

In this Underground Boxing Circuit, Magic Touch is their pride and joy. They've been crushing the competition all year. Competitors have come from all over New Jersey, even New York and Philly. Magic Touch has earned them hundreds and hundreds of thousands of dollars. He's scored lots of money for the people that have bet on him as well. He's a cash-cow for many.

As Magic Touch moves around, his skunk juice is sprayed. The smell he leaves behind is a mixture of funk, sweat mildewed clothes, feet and sour mop. Suave holds his breath, wondering how he will be able to bear with the smell while moving around in the ring with him for 3 rounds. He can only pray they don't get into body clenches.

Magic Touch hops into the ring and runs around 3 times before he gets into the center of it and starts to do the signature crackhead dance. The crowd rolls with laughter. The commentator invites them both to the center and he introduces them. The bets start rolling in immediately.

Suave and Magic Touch meet at the center of the ring. Suave is ready to get it on yet he is a tad bit nervous being in the ring with this legend. He knows he can't play around with him. He may be an old crackhead but Suave respects his body of work. His addiction has nothing to do with the knowledge and expertise he has of this game.

Magic Touch stands face to face with Suave. Only a foot and a half distance separates them. He stands here shirtless, exposing his bird chest. His ribs poke out like a starving Ethiopian child. Suave looks into Magic Touch's old and weary eyes. His eyes tell a story of past and current drug abuse. He smiles and one tooth hangs on for dear life.

He looks a complete mess but the smell that comes from his body and his mouth is far worse. Suave holds his breath as Magic Touch breathes in his face. "Young boy, I'm a legend in this game! You should've done your homework before you came here and put your life in danger! You better ask about me. I will make your career disappear before your very eyes, like magic. What you need to do is walk away while you still got the chance because when that bell go ding, ding, I'm gone destroy you. You will never be the same after this fight."

All his shit talking is to excite the crowd and make the bets pour in. Suave looks him in the eyes with no sign of emotion. He just snaps his neck from side to side, stretching his muscles. They're off to their corners where they wait for the bell to ring.

The bell rings and both men work their way to the center of the ring. Suave watches as Magic Touch sets up his stance. His stance is like no stance that Suave has ever seen. His body is twisted on an angle. His chin is tucked securely behind his shoulder while his left hand is glued to his thigh. His right hand is held up high, close to his ear. It almost looks as if his glove is a pillow and he's sleeping on it.

All of a sudden, like a flash of lightening he leaps at Suave with a tight knit left hook. Suave is caught by total surprise. The punch crashes into his ear, sending a sharp pain down his ear canal. His legs buckle.

"Whoa!" The crowd cheers as they wait to see if he's going to fall.

Surprisingly, Suave leaps back at Magic Touch and fires a double right hook combination of his own. Magic Touch catches the first hook with his glove and slips the second one. He pivots on his axis and looks at Suave with a smirk.

Magic Touch stands still for a couple seconds before shooting a fast, left hand that bangs into Suave's nose. Suave steps back with confusion. He didn't see where the blow came from. Magic Touch changes angles, by spinning on his axis. With just the slightest movement, he's on an altogether different plane.

Just a small movement for Magic Touch yet Suave has to turn his whole body around to find him. He fires a stiff jab to keep Magic Touch away, just to buy enough time to figure something out. Magic Touch slips the jab with ease.

Magic Touch quickly looks into the audience. "This gone be easy, y'all." He turns back to Suave even quicker.

"Don't wait on him," Tony says. "You first!"

Suave fires a quick jab. Magic Touch slips to his right, just enough for the jab to miss him. Suave then fires a left hand and Magic Touch slips to his left. Suave fires a hook and Magic Touch simply bends at his knees and slips it. Magic Touch stands almost face to face awaiting Suave's next attack. Suave is rusty and he can feel it. His timing is off. His speed is not there and his reaction time is delayed.

"Suave, do you!" Saadiq says. "You're showing him too much respect. Box!"

That is exactly what Suave needed to hear. He bounces on his tippy toes for a few seconds with his hands dangling at his side. A quick jab comes out of nowhere and crashes into Magic Touch's forehead. Suave quickly turns that jab into a right hook that lands under Magic Touch's eye. "Oooh!" the crowd cheers. Suave loads up to finish off with a straight left down the pipe but just as he's setting up, a left uppercut rips at his chin, snapping his neck back. Briefly he's staring at the ceiling. He quickly gathers himself. He looks in front of him only to find Magic Touch not there. He's disappeared.

Suave cautiously peeks to his left, looking for Magic Touch but Magic Touch appears to his right. Just as Suave looks to his right his eye is greeted by a left jab. The left jab transforms into a left uppercut before transforming into a short left hook. Suave takes the punishment like a man. He fires a right hook of his own in exchange but Magic Touch slips it and gets out of the way.

Magic Touch pivots and appears directly in front of Suave again. As soon as he stops he fires a straight right hand that lands in between Suave's eyes. Magic Touch keeps the glove in front Suave's eye as a crafty way to blind him. With his glove blocking Suave's view, Magic Touch bends at his knees and rips a left hook to Suave's body. The hook caves in Suave's midsection. He grunts in pain, not able to conceal it.

The pain incites Suave's rage. He fires an overhand left that clobbers Magic Touch on top of his head. His knees wobble until the left uppercut stands him straight up. The crowd goes wild. Suave tries to finish him off with his trusting right hook but Magic Touch slips it and saves himself. For the rest of the round the two of them exchange evenly, both testing the chin of the other.

The bell rings and Naim flings the stool under the rope. Suave sits down and Saadiq stands in front of him. Saadiq squirts water in

Suave's mouth while Naim rubs Suave's shoulders to keep him nice and loose. "Come on baby boy," Saadiq says. "You waiting too much."

Suave listens attentively. His team believes in him and he doesn't want to let them down. He feels like everything is on the line right now. He would hate for his team to lose faith in him. He's made a promise to himself that he's never going back to the streets so he has no plan B. This boxing thing is everything for him so he must box as such.

"You got to box," Saadiq says. "He ain't gone stand there and let you hit him. Put some pepper on it and stop throwing two and three punch combinations. Throw six and seven. You will never hit him with basic combinations. Be creative. Get on your toes. You're too flat-footed. His fight is toe to toe. He's the slip master. Get on your toes and make him dance with you."

"I got him," Suave says confidently. "I just needed to work out the kinks. I ain't been in the ring in four years," he says in justification of his subpar exhibit.

The bell rings and they get right back at it. Suave has switched his whole style up and it seems to be working. He's been bouncing around so much that Magic Touch is forced to change up his style. They've been dancing around exchanging blow for blow with each other. They're touching each other almost equally but Magic Touch is still beating him on the scorecards. He's the favorite so he can never be beat when it comes to the cards. In order to beat him he has to be beaten!

Only one minute into the round and Suave notices that Magic Touch isn't fighting with the same spunk and enthusiasm he started with. Because of that he's now able to touch Magic Touch more. Magic Touch has been taking shots that have been a shock to everyone. Shots he would normally see coming a mile away, he's getting tagged by. It's as if he sees the punch coming but he doesn't have the energy to get out of the way.

Magic Touch's bloody nose and his split eye is a result of him being tired and worn out. He's so fatigued he can barely defend himself. He stands in the center of the ring with his hands held high as Suave literally punches through his defense. He eats the combinations, not firing a single punch back of his own.

The more tired Magic Touch becomes the more energetic Suave becomes. It's as if he's taking the power from Magic Touch's battery and storing it in his own battery. Suave bounces around vibrantly while Magic Touch stands in one place with a false confident expression on his face. He may have everyone else fooled but Suave can see right through his mask. He's out of gas.

The commentator sings into the microphone. "It's getting, it's getting, it's getting kind of hectic." The crowd is not humored for too much money is on the line. Suave drops to his right and rips a right hook onto Magic Touch's chin. The blow takes a huge toll on Magic Touch. He bangs Magic Touch's abdomen and Magic Touch grabs the pain in his gut. Suave raises up and fires a right hook, left uppercut, right hook combination. He concludes the combination with a straight left to the chin bone.

Suave stares into the eyes of his opponent and is shocked to find him still standing after that combination. He quickly fires again, jab, left hand, right hook, left hand, right uppercut. He concludes this combination with a strong right hook. He bounces away while staring at Magic Touch who is miraculously still standing. Suave is amazed how he has shot his best work at him and he just stands there.

Magic Touch stands with his hands glued to his side. He has no energy left to lift them. His arms weigh a ton right now. He musters up the energy to lift his arms and wave Suave on. "Come on," he says with a grin on his face. "Don't go nowhere."

Suave can look in his eyes and tell that he has no fight left in him. He's bluffing and hoping Suave doesn't come over and finish him. Suave runs over and just as he fires, the bell rings. Magic Touch leans back in a nick of time. "You lucky, boy," Suave says with disrespect before turning and walking away.

Suave sits on the stool, trying to get his breath together. He refuses the water. He's hype, full of energy and ready to get back to work. He's in his zone now.

"Listen, we got him," Saadiq says. "You're doing good but right now we need great. He's tired. All the ripping and running and getting high with no sleep has caught up with him. He's out of gas. He's never had to fight past the first round. He usually puts his opponents down first round."

Saadiq smears more vaseline on Suave's face. "Listen to me. That motherfucker is higher than giraffe pussy, right now. He's coked up. The head shots are not even phasing him. They let him get coked up before the fights so he's numb. Look at his mouth twitching...he been smoking. Later for the headshots. Beat the body and the head will follow."

Tony chimes in. "It's a lot of bread on the table. Let's get that money." The bell rings.

A young man standing ringside peeks around suspiciously before stepping away. At the corner of the ring he leans in close to a young man and whispers in his ear. The young man looks directly across the room at Tony as his ear is being whispered into. The man eases away and exits the gym.

The other man that was left behind is now looking across the room at another man whom no one would ever know they were together. They lock eyes and speak telepathically before the man looks over in Tony's direction. Tony happens to look up and him and the young man lock eyes. The young man looks away, not out of fear, but not wanting to make Tony aware. Tony looks to Ali-Wop and they now speak with their eyes. Tony nods before turning is focus back to the fight.

A minute passes and Suave and Magic Touch are two-stepping in the middle of the ring. Magic Man appears to be slightly rejuvenated. In a quick flash, Magic Touch fakes to his left with a half of a step. Suave moves to his right, encountering an explosive right hand to his midsection followed by a left hook to the kidney. The kidney shot knocks Suave slightly off balance. He stumbles a few steps before regaining his balance.

Suave fakes a jab up high and digs a left hand straight to the body. Magic Touch growls with pain. This motivates Suave and reassures him of what Saadiq has told him. Magic Touch smiles and Suave recognizes that smile as an indication that he's hurt. Suave goes in for the kill. He fires a left to the head, followed by a right hook. As Magic Touch defends his head, Suave drops down and rips a left uppercut into the center of his gut.

Magic Touch folds over, holding his midsection. Suave rips a quick left to the rib cage, switches his weight to his right and bangs another shot to Magic Touch's midsection. Magic Touch stumbles backwards holding his gut. Suave jumps dead on him, not giving him time to get it together. He bangs Magic Touch's body consistently and abusively. The crowd goes silent. Magic Touch growls with agony after each blow.

He tries to grab hold of Suave's arms to clench him and stop the abuse but Suave pushes him off. Magic Touch stumbles onto the ropes. "Yeah! Yeah!" Tony shouts. All the angry men turn to Tony and look at him with rage. Tony continues on anyway. He thinks of all the money that is on the line and he has to cheer him on. "Bang that body!" As Magic Touch sits on the ropes helplessly, Suave does just as he's instructed.

"This some bullshit," an angry man shouts from the back. Right now there are so many angry faces in the building. A bunch of sore losers they are. Sore losers with guns though; a recipe for disaster.

Magic Touch has been hurt. He drops his hands with an ill look on his face. His whole face caves and Suave jumps back in the nick of time before Magic Touch throws up in the middle of the ring.

"Call, Earl," an instigator shouts from the back of the room.

The room is in an uproar. The crowd goes wild as Magic Touch is bent over throwing his guts up. The referee stands over Magic Touch, asking if he wants to continue. As much as he hates to do it, Magic Touch shakes his head, indicating that he does not. The referee waves his hands high in the air. The fight is over. The crowd goes wild, throwing chairs into the ring and flipping tables over. From the looks of it, the only one's betting on Suave is his team. The rest of the gym seems to be taking this not so well.

MINUTES LATER

Suave stands in the center of the ring as the belt is being handed over to him by Magic Touch. Magic Touch's face has defeat written all over it while the faces of his entourage have anger and rage on them. The anger is the result of the huge purse they have lost on him tonight and the rage comes from him losing this belt. Their big money fights with him are over until he works his way back up the ladder to be a contender.

One man obviously saw something in Suave because he bet on him, not even knowing him. His face is full of happiness. "Now, what you have to say?" the man teases. "Popped all that shit and he beat on you like a baby!"

Magic Touch looks over. "Aye man, he supposed to beat me!" he shouts defensively. "I smoke coke all day long! Ain't no secret, I smoke!"

"Oh, now, you admit to being a crack addict, huh? Whatever, nigga! Just give the man the belt and get yo' coke smoking ass outta the ring!" the man says jokingly.

Magic Touch's entourage does not take the jokes lightly. They've lost a great deal of money tonight. As Magic Touch stands here without the belt, they now see him for what he is; a crackhead. Without that belt he has no value to them nor society. In a matter of ten minutes he's gone from a cash cow to worthless. Like an old horse who no longer has value, tonight he just may get taken out back and be taken out of his misery.

THIRTY MINUTES LATER

As Suave is getting dressed, Tony hands him a bag. "That's the whole purse," Tony says. "Fifty-grand," he says as if it's nothing. "Me and the two good brothers decided that we will eat off the next one. Go on and do what you need to do."

Suave looks at Tony in disbelief. "Damn, that's what's up Big Homie."

"We on again next week," Tony says. "Keep fighting like that and you gone get your money up real quick! You're the Underground Champ after one fight. Defend your title and the money gone come. This will keep us busy until the real money start coming in. We gone rule this underground circuit and eat off it while we slowly but surely climb that ladder in the real boxing world." Tony fist bumps Suave.

Tony hands the duffle-bag to Ali-Wop. They walked in with $150,000 and they are leaving out with $220,000. "This bag looking a lot heavier," Ali-Wop says with a smile of uncertainty.

"Exactly," Tony replies. "And now the hard part will be getting the hell up out of here with it.

Ali-Wop pulls a Desert Eagle .44 Magnum from his waistband. Tony looks at the 12-inch barrel, which looks very exaggerated like a gun from a cartoon. Ali-Wop raises the gun in the air. "Oh, that ain't gone be hard at all! We will go out the same way we came in, in peace. Or somebody ass will be tore into pieces."

63

DAYS LATER

THE MERCEDES G-WAGON pulls in between Umar's Dodge Ram pickup and Maurice's Toyota Tacoma pickup truck. Tony hops out of the Mercedes, Maurice and Twelve Play hop out of the Toyota, and Umar hops out of the Dodge. They all come together in the middle. Tony shakes Maurice and Twelve Play's hand, never once looking at Umar for they have never been introduced. The few times they've been around each other Umar has talked over and around Tony as if he wasn't even there.

Twelve Play feels the tension and takes it upon himself to ease it. "Y'all two haven't formally met, right? Mr. Austin, this is Umar. Umar this is Mr. Austin. Tony and Umar shakes hands but Umar brushes him off, not even looking at him. Tony pays very little attention to the fade and continues on with his conversation with Maurice.

They all follow behind Umar who leads them to the entrance of the small and raggedy, brick building. Scattered around the building are a bunch of raggedy cars. A couple beat-up pickup trucks, an old dump truck, a bunch of forklifts and a cement mixer truck. None of the personal vehicles nor the equipment trucks are up to date yet it's obvious that everything is in working order and getting worked.

Umar rings the bell and the buzzer sounds off. He snatches the door open and upon entrance he acknowledges the beautiful Spanish secretary. "He's in the back," the woman says.

Umar leads the group to the back and he knocks on the door. "Come in," says a male voice.

They step inside and the Mexican man is there to greet them all. He shakes all of their hands with the utmost respect. "These are my folks I told you about," Umar says as he points to Maurice and stops at Twelve Play as if Tony isn't standing there. They're doing big business here in Philly and *New-ark*. Strip malls and high rises," he says with praise. "They right here so let me shut up and let them tell you," he says with a cheesy grin.

Maurice intercedes. "So, he says you can get unlimited sheetrock?"

The Mexican man continues to walk without turning around to face Maurice. "Yes, I can." He stops short at the door and he points inside a huge room filled with stacks and stacks of sheetrock.

"Impressive," Maurice says. "But I'm talking way more than that."

The Mexican man steps into the wide-open room and stops short right past the doorway, allowing them all to step inside. "How much do you need?"

"I'm talking twenty-five to thirty-thousand sheets," Maurice says boastfully.

"Wow," the Mexican man utters. "That's a big order. All things are possible though. Just may take me some time to put together an order like that."

"How much time we talking?" Maurice asks. "We have a bunch of projects in the production stage. We need to get this going as soon as possible. I got a check with me for two-hundred thousand, if you can deliver today."

"It would be impossible for me to deliver thirty-thousand sheets today."

"You just said all things are possible."

"And they are…just not possible today. Let me get on the phone and see what the inventory is looking like." He walks back into the office and takes a seat behind the desk. He scribbles on a pad as he dials numbers on his cell phone. The man scribbles some more onto his pad before ending the call. "I can get you around ten-thousand sheets today, between me and my partner. Give me a week and I can get the rest. Is that okay?"

"Actually, no," Maurice says. "But if that's how we have to do it then we have no choice."

"How soon can we get the first order?" Maurice asks.

"By the end of the workday today," the Mexican replies.

"Ok, cool," Maurice says. "We will go grab some lunch and then check on some of the properties. Hopefully by the time we done we will be hearing from you." Maurice taps the desk before turning around and walking away. Tony and Twelve Play follow right behind Maurice.

The Mexican man then looks to Umar. "Did you tell them what else we talked about?"

"Nah, I really didn't have the chance to yet," Umar explains. Umar slyly shakes his head at the Mexican as to say not right now.

"You said they're cool, right?" the Mexican man asks. Maurice, Tony and Twelve Play stand around curiously, wondering what the man is talking about. "I got the other sheetrock too. If you know what I mean."

"What you mean?" Maurice asks.

"You know," the Mexican man says. He makes a square shape with his hands. "Everything ain't for everybody but Umar said y'all are good people. Just throwing it out there just in case you know anyone in need of them."

"I am Attorney, Tony Austin, CEO of Austin Enterprise and this is my partner Maurice of Brick City Development. We are a developmental group and we are here for the purchase of sheetrock and we want nothing to do with anything illegal," Tony says loud and clearly.

"Oh, sorry, sorry," the Mexican man says apologetically. He looks to Umar. "I thought they were cool."

Umar's eyebrows connect with rage. "I said they were cool to sell them sheetrock, not coke."

Something tells them that Umar knew all about this but is pretending he doesn't because of how of how they reacted to it.

"Come on," Tony says as he taps Maurice's chest. "Let's get out of here."

"Wait, what about the sheetrock?" the Mexican asks.

"Don't worry about it," Maurice replies. "Deal is dead."

Maurice and Twelve Play walk behind Tony who is speed-walking out of the building. Umar runs behind them. Once they're in the parking lot, he cuts in front of Twelve Play. "Akhi, I'm sorry about this. Wallahi, I didn't know he was going to come at y'all all crazy like that. He's my man but he's fucking retarded. He think everybody black with money is drug dealers."

Tony slides around to Umar's blindside. He doesn't notice Tony creeping behind him. Twelve Play and Maurice see Tony but have no clue what he's about to do until he does it. With all of his might, he draws back and fires a picture perfect, straight right that connects on Umar's chin bone. Umar falls on his butt in a sitting position while Tony stands over him in rage. "Motherfucker, you walked me into a fucking drug deal?"

Umar shakes his head twice to ease the dizziness. Right after the second shake, he pops up on his feet and with the quickness his gun appears in his hand under his waistband. "Nigga, you got me chopped!" Umar says with anger bleeding from his eyes. Before he can draw, both Maurice and Twelve Play have already beat him to it. They aim at his head from both sides. Umar removes his hand from his gun and holds his hands in the air. Twelve Play uses his free hand to snatch Umar's gun from his waist.

Umar looks to Twelve Play. "Akhi, I gave you my Wallahi that I didn't know he was going to do that. I wouldn't do y'all like that," he says with sincerity in his eyes. Twelve Play looks at Umar and in his heart he believes his words to be true. Umar has proven to be honorable in the short time they have been around each other. He believes him but still he has to roll with his team.

Maurice and Tony walk toward their vehicles, leaving Twelve Play standing there. He lowers the gun to his side and stares at Umar. Umar lowers his hands slowly. He's trusting of Twelve Play for they have built somewhat of a bond.

"Akhi, as a Muslim, all I have is my word," Umar says. "You just came home from a twenty piece. I would never lead you back to prison. From the start of me and you meeting, I've done nothing but tried to help you eat. I offered you a plate every time I ate, all off halal money at that, Sheihk.

He see three black dudes from *New-ark* making big moves and he automatically assume it's dirty money niggas playing with. I think deep down inside you know I'm not lying. Just do me a favor and talk some sense into your folk's head. They don't know me. You do. Talk to them for me Akhi. That's all I ask."

Maurice rests on the horn angrily. Twelve Play steps backward, still looking at Umar. "Akhi, I think I proved to you I'm a man of men," Umar says with sincerity in his eyes. "I need you to let them know I'm honorable, Insha Allah."

Twelve Play gets into the truck with Maurice. Tony peels off furiously. Maurice speeds off right behind him. Umar stands there looking like a sad puppy as he watches them until he can see them no more.

64

LUNATIC HOLDS HIS head up to the shower nozzle, allowing the water to refresh him. At the door he has two of his men watching his back. With all the dirt they do, they can't even take a shower without worrying that they will be attacked by the enemy. With them always on point it's hard for the enemy to even get close. That is unless it's worked from the inside.

The two men on guard leave their post as a familiar face approaches. The young man tiptoes across the shower. Lunatic turns around, wiping the water from his face. He opens his eyes and he's greeted by a knife just inches away from his face. Too late to get out of harm's way, the knife is plugged into his neck.

Lunatic backs up with his hands guarding his face but the next strike is at his chest. He tries to grab his attacker but the attacker pushes him back against the wall. Lunatic is then poked in the stomach. Like a tire that has been punctured, his wind seeps slowly. Lunatic curls over and the attacker commences to poking everywhere that he finds an opening, shoulder, back, side, kidney, neck, arm. The attacker pokes away relentlessly until Lunatic is no longer breathing.

This man came here with a job to finish and he doesn't stop until the job is finished. When all is said and done, Lunatic lays in a fetal position in a pool of bloody water. The attacker stands up and conceals his bloody knife. He exits the shower as if nothing has happened.

As he walks away he is sure the tape will be played back and he will be charged with the murder but that's a small thing to him. He looks at it as him being a step closer to his end game. That end game is the G status that Smith has promised him in exchange for the what he's done for him. He's sure he may never see the streets again but at least in jail he will have the status that he's dreamed of. He's sacrificed his freedom for the G and he's cool with that because In jail or on the streets that G status holds the same value. That status will give him the power and notoriety that he's always wanted. Today he feels that he has become a made man.

MEANWHILE

A Dodge Charger tinted loose creeps into Applebee's parking lot. The Charger zips into the parking spot right next to Pebbles' Range Rover. The passenger door busts open and a man hops out, leaving the door wide open. He peeks around quickly before bending over. He reaches under the Range Rover and fumbles around for seconds before standing up and getting back into the car and closing the door behind himself.

The man sits in his seat, scrolling through his phone. He presses a few buttons activating the GPS tracking system. Once the system is activated and he finds the Range Rover's location enabled, he looks over to the driver. "Let's go." The Charger cruises out of the parking lot unnoticed.

Lunatic may be out of the picture, but unfortunately for Pebbles, her problem is not over. Even with Lunatic out of the picture her problem still exists. The line has already been thrown out to the wolves and the light has been shone on Pebbles. She's already on their radar. With or without Lunatic the show will go on.

With the GPS tracker their job will be easier. They will not have to follow her around physically. They can sit back and watch her moves and track her whereabouts from the convenience of their phones. Once they put all the pieces together they will determine the right time to make their move. Pebbles may not know it but she's just gotten one step closer to danger.

65

5:48 A.M.

AS TONY STANDS in the mirror brushing his teeth, Jane Doe crosses his mind. Strangely out of nowhere he thinks of her. He hasn't heard from her in weeks. He's been busy putting everything together for the case. He told her 45 days but it looks like he will be ready sooner than that. He makes a mental note to call her and update her today.

MEANWHILE IN NEWARK

Jane Doe steps out of the door of her Mausoleum, dressed in her everyday disguise. It's a beautiful day as the sun is shining and the birds are chirping. She wakes every morning and follows the same regimen. After her morning coffee she takes a walk around the graveyard. She calls it the Awakening of the Dead Tour.

In this tour she walks around the graveyard and picks random plots to visit. The graves she chooses are of those who have been neglected the longest and she can tell no one has visited in a long time.

She reads the tombstone and starts a conversation based on what she's read. As she talks to the person in the grave, she tidies up around the plot, by removing the garbage around it, or plucking the weeds that have grown over it. Strangely, talking to the dead makes her feel alive.

Jane Doe stops in her tracks and rubs her ear. The burning in her ear, she knows to be an indication that someone is thinking about her. She's very superstitious and believes in that wholeheartedly. With not many family members or loved ones, there aren't many she would think would be thinking about her. The only person she can think of would be Tony. They haven't touched basis in weeks. She has been leaving him alone and allowing him to do what he needs to do to prepare for their case. She makes a mental note to call him today and check in.

Jane Doe walks along, humming a tune as she looks around casually. She suddenly misses a step, almost tripping over her feet. She quickly gathers herself. She inhales a deep breath as she takes another few steps. She exhales slowly before raising her hands high in the air, staring upward into the beautiful blue sky.

She slowly lowers herself onto her knees, arms wide, hands still high. The sun showers her face, blinding her yet she stares at it boldly. She drops her head back, lowering her hands close to her head, as if she's washing her face with the sun beams. With her head dangling and her arms wide she gathers all the rays that she can grasp. She reaches for the rays greedily as if this will be her very last encounter with the sun. She freezes as stiff as a statue.

She turns her head slowly to the left and while peeking through her peripheral she speaks. "You can come out of hiding," she says loudly. "I see you back there." She lowers her arms and places her hands onto the back of her head. "All of this for little, old, me?" She smiles as she scans the area. The sniper that she noticed hiding behind the tree is not the only one present. She now sees them hidden all around the cemetery, behind her, on the sides of her and in front of her.

She always knew this day would come. She's envisioned it so many times and the strange part is she pictured it going down just like this. With more than ten snipers dressed in tactical gear, with assault rifles aimed at her yet she kneels in total peace. Her sense of peace comes from the fact that she's succeeded in getting her story and all of her information into the right hands. She always feared them finding her before she could do so. Now all she can do is hope and pray that Tony carries out their mission, even without her. She has no doubt in her mind that he has all he needs to carry it out successfully.

"Please do me the honors of looking me in the eyes when you do this. Don't hide like the cowards that you are. America, such a strong force yet you kill your victims cowardly. For once I ask Uncle Sam to stand up like a man," she says as she gets up slowly. She turns around to face the sniper. From across the cemetery, a couple thousand feet away she can see him itching to pull the trigger. She smiles underneath the mask. "I'm ready when you are."

The cap on Jane Doe's head is knocked off by an invisible violent force. That force being a slug from an M16 assault rifle. Not only has the slug knocked the cap off her head, the mask has been knocked off as well. She topples forward, landing on her face. Blood seeps from the back of her head slowly, as she lays there lifelessly.

She stood up to face her killer like the courageous woman she was but the man she faced isn't the one who pulled the trigger. The real killer wasn't man enough to show his face. Instead, standing behind a mausoleum a few thousand feet away, a sniper stands, still holding his rifle aimed. He's prepared to take another shot if need be, but it's obvious there is no need. The sniper stakes the butt of the rifle into the dirt next to him and gives a head-nod across the cemetery. Immediately after, three men dressed in masks and tactical gear run in from different sides and like vultures they swarm in on Jane Doe.

The three of them together lift her body from the ground. An all-black van comes around the track at full speed. As the truck approaches, the side doors are slid open. The van stops and they throw Jane Doe's body inside the van with no compassion for the dead, whatsoever.

The van speeds off and the men rush inside the mausoleum. It takes all of ten minutes before they exit, carrying a file cabinet, and two crates. They stand for a mere 30 seconds before another black van pulls up. They jump in the van and it speeds off.

66

THE POWER-DRILL SOUNDS off as the mechanic takes the tires off of the Ford Taurus that is raised in the air. In the bay next to that another mechanic has his head underneath the hood of a Nissan. In the third bay a mechanic is on the ground lying underneath a Buick Enclave. In the waiting area, the owners of the cars sit patiently.

Swan stands in front of a woman. "I will get you right in after the Nissan is done," he says.

Suddenly the front door busts open, startling the peacefulness of the shop. A 9-millimeter with an extended clip is raised in the air and the masked man holding it squeezes the trigger. A series of shots rip through the ceiling. The occupants in the shop all stand frozen in fear as two other men rush inside, gripping handguns as well. The patrons scream as they attempt to run away. One mechanic dives onto the floor, the other runs to the back, while the third one lies underneath the car, stiff as a statue, hoping not to be seen.

Swan takes off for the back door as the female customer backs into a corner, face against the wall, hands over her ears in fear. BLOC-KA! BLOCKA! BLOCKA! Swan's body is forced against the wall before it ricochets and tumbles over a few chairs. He lands on his back, staring up into the barrel of the .40 caliber. BLOCKA!

MEANWHILE

Jubilee sits behind the counter inside of his Variety Store. He's multi-tasking. He counts money, while eating and in between he peeks back and forth at the television that's on the wall over the door. The young man, his employee is behind the counter on the opposite side of the room. The employee, with a closed fist, extends his hand over the glass counter to the man on the other side. He drops the pill in the man's hand as the man hands him cash in exchange.

They call this store a Variety Store because of the various items that are sold of course. From hair products, to socks, to hats, to house cleaning products to used video games. It can be compared to a .99 cent store except nothing in here costs .99 cent. Of all the various things sold in here, the drugs are the real money makers. A1 dope and coke is sold here for the old school addicts while the weed, pills and syrup are on sale for the new school addicts. The other items are just the front to disguise their drug dealing activity. The doors are revolving as customers run in and out, like an illegal pharmacy.

A young woman walks in and the employee knows exactly what she's here for. She's a regular, who never changes up. He walks to the back to retrieve her weed, while she makes her way to the counter. The door chime sounds off right behind her as a masked bandit comes flying through the door.

Jubilee looks up and sees the bandit running inside behind the girl. Jubilee ducks low behind the counter as he grips his gun from the shelf. He stands up, gun aimed and he squeezes. BLOCKA! BLOC-KA! The masked gunman sends a few back of his own. BOC! BOC! BOC! The young woman dives onto the floor and tries to crawl away for safety while the back and forth gun battle takes place over her head.

Jubilee has been hit. Some of the fight has been taken out of him. He ducks low for cover and the couple seconds of him not firing back has granted the bandit the access of getting closer to him. The bandit fires consecutively as he runs toward Jubilee. Jubilee has no time to aim and fire. He just sends a shot in the air to back the bandit up but it doesn't work. The bandit hurdles over the counter and lands directly over top of Jubilee. BOC! BOC! BOC! BOC!

The bandit hops back over the counter and makes a break for it. The young woman is crouched in the middle of the floor. She looks up to him screaming with fear. The bandit leaps over the woman. Once the gunman is out of sight, the young woman gets up and runs out as well.

The employee comes out of back slowly. He peeks around nervously. He's sure somebody has been put down, just not sure who. He gets his answer of who when he looks to his right where he finds his boss, his big bruh, on the floor, twisted up like a stiff pretzel.

A FEW MILES AWAY

Skelter runs through the house hurriedly. "Come on," she shouts to Helter. "Let's roll."

"I'm coming," Helter shouts as she runs through the house with her baby in her arms. In her baby's bag she has all of her and the baby's important paperwork. Skelter told her not to worry about packing because they have limited time. Later they can sneak back in and get her things but right now they have to get themselves as far away from danger as they can.

She just got the calls that the moves were executed on both Swan and Jubilee. Vito sent his men to handle the situations at the same time. She's sure right now guns are being loaded up and men are preparing for war. In 20 minutes or less the whole city is about to be set on fire, looking for revenge.

Skelter grabs the baby's bag from Helter and runs to the door. She holds it open for Helter. The huge Suburban EXT rental is at the curb awaiting them. Both of Skelter's Godsons are inside. Two duffle-bags filled with money and all the work that she has left are packed in the back of the truck.

Once she pulls off from here she has no reason to ever come back to Trenton. With the mess that she's made and all the enemies she now has, she knows she will never be welcomed here again. Bringing out-of-towners in to handle Trenton beef is like a cardinal sin. The fact that the out-of-towners are from Newark makes it all the worse. The Trenton, Newark beef is one that starts from the prison. It's not a personal beef, but more of a 'whose city is harder' beef. Skelter is sure if the word got out that she teamed up with Newark to go against her own city, she would lose the love of even the ones who have a little love left for her.

A part of her feels like she is being run out of her own city but she thinks about what Manson told her about pride and ego. She's decided to take her show on the road and move up to North Jersey. There she will get a new start. She tells herself that maybe that is what is needed anyway. Maybe she needs new surroundings and new people to reach new levels.

Bruh in Law comes running out of the backroom with several pieces of Louis Vuitton luggage. Skelter stops him in his tracks. She stands in the doorway so he can't pass. "Where you going?" Bruh in Law stops with confusion. "You ain't going with me," she says sternly. Helter steps back into the hall. She looks to Skelter with the same confusion as Bruh in Law. "He not going with us," Skelter says.

Bruh in Law stands here looking like a sad puppy, waiting for Helter's defense. "What you mean? That's my daughter's father. I'm not leaving him."

"Listen, either you leave him here, or I will leave him here," Skelter says as she pulls her gun from her waist. "It's up to you. This nigga the weakest link and he ain't gone be the cause of motherfuckers figuring out where we at and we got to continue this war. He's not fucking going. So are you leaving him or am I leaving him?" Skelter walks toward Bruh in Law with a determination in her eyes that reassures him that she's ready to do it if she has to.

"Yo, I will stay," he says in order to save himself.

"No, the fuck you ain't," Helter shouts. "If I'm going, you going!"

Skelter aims the gun at Bruh in Law's head. Helter cuts in between them, turning her and her baby into human shields for her lover and daughter's father. She defends him for the sake of love.

Skelter is steaming right now. She hates that her sister loves him so much. She bites down on her lip to contain her rage. Slowly she lowers her gun and tucks it back in her waistband. "Come the fuck on."

Skelter turns and jogs out. Helter and Bruh in Law follow behind. Once they're all in the truck, Youngest Godson pulls off. North Jersey here they come!

67

BABBS GENERAL HAULING

THIS IS ONE of the top trucking companies in the country. In this plant there has to be at least 150 trucks on this parking lot. A tall and brolic, bald man drags across the lot, exhausted but still he keeps his head up, chest out. His backpack hanging on his shoulder feels like bricks are in it. His arms are so tired from driving 12 hours straight. A week and a half of driving to Las Vegas and back has him worn out.

The man hits the button on his keyring and the lights of the Cadillac Escalade shine brightly before the engine starts up. Tony gets out of his Mercedes and walks across the parking lot to meet the man. As he's approaching the man and he notices the man's aggressive demeanor he's having second thoughts. He's not sure if this is a good idea but being in the dark about this all is getting the best of him.

"Attorney Tony Austin," the man says in a cynical manner.

Tony is shocked that he knows who he is yet he plays it cool. This man is the husband of Tony's friend, Jasmine from the FDA. Tony wasn't aware that he knew anything about him. Now, he realizes he truly had no business coming here.

"The man I've been wanting to see for a while now. Hopefully you're coming to me as a man so you can get these hands," he says as he holds his clenched fists up to his face. "You coming to admit to me that you fucking my wife?"

He snatches his backdoor open and wiggles the bag from his shoulder. "My arms tired from driving but I still got some gas in the tank for a few rounds." After he drops his bag, he pulls his jacket off and his t-shirt. Wearing only a tank-top, his superhero physique is now exposed. He looked muscular in his clothes but in the tank-top his muscles are more like mounds and boulders.

Tony pretends to be clueless. "Excuse me? I'm not understanding."

The man slams his door shut and stomps toward Tony with his fists clenched. "Well, let me help you to understand, then." He stops short and looks around the area. He displays a calm look on his face yet his clenched fists and tense body indicates that he is not calm. "Matter of fact let's go around the corner so I don't lose my job."

Maurice notices what's going on and gets out of Tony's truck. He speed walks over to them. He stands shoulder to shoulder with Tony but the man continues on as if he doesn't even see him. He wants Tony so badly that he only sees him.

"I can't believe you got the audacity to come to my job. Are you here to tell me that you and my wife creeping around?" The man forgets all about his fear of losing his job and starts walking toward Tony. "You got to get these hands, bruh." The look on his face is as if he doesn't want to do this but he has to. His pride won't have it any other way.

Maurice steps in front of Tony. "Come on man, ain't nobody about to fight over no chick."

"Nigga, this ain't about no regular ass bitch," the man snaps. "This about my motherfucking wife! Anyway, mind your business before you get dragged into some shit you don't have nothing to do with. If you want some of this ass whooping, I will give you some after I give him his."

Maurice is somewhat huge and the man towers him. This would be the perfect fight, a battle of the biggest. A few years ago Maurice would have accepted the fight with no hesitation but now he's old. He realizes his best fighting days are behind him. In no way would he ever let Tony scrap with this man. He really has no plans of him even scrapping with the man. He discreetly places his hand closer to the gun that's hidden in his waistband. He would really hate to have to splatter him on his job's parking lot but he will if he has to.

"Dig man, all that tough caveman talk ain't gone get you nowhere but in a bad spot," Maurice says with stone cold eyes. He's not one for arguing, never has been. He's fighting back the urge to give the man what he wants him to have.

"Aye man, listen, I've been in bad spots all my life. Nine months down Jamesburg, eleven months down Yardsville, fourteen months down Annandale, two years down Bordentown, five years down Northern State, and twelve years down Rahway State," the man says with pride. Ask about me. Anyway this ain't your beef," he says. He turns his attention back to Tony. "You like fucking niggas wives, huh?"

"Fucking your wife?" Tony asks as if he has no understanding of what the man is saying.

"Yeah, you got to be fucking her," he replies. "That's the only way I can see her willing to lose everything behind you. You know a bitch go crazy over new dick," he says with a smile. Inside his heart is burning.

"Bruh, I'm not fucking your wife," Tony says with sincerity.

"Then why else would she put it all on the line for you?"

"Put what on the line for me, bruh?" Tony asks. "I'm confused."

"You really gone play stupid, huh? You really gone do this bruh?"

"Bruh, I promise you I don't have a clue of what you're talking about," Tony claims.

"I'm just as confused as to why my bitch protecting a nigga who she claim she ain't fucking. Secret Service motherfuckers come to her job and embarrass her by escorting her out of there. They force her to resign from her job that she only have a few years left on before retiring. They told her she could get her job back if she just tell what you have planned. And what this dumb ass bitch do? She tells them she don't know."

Tony's heart is sprinting right now. "So, they know she was in contact with me?"

"No, motherfucker! I know she was in contact with you because she told me. I was ready to go tell them everything but I ain't no fucking rat. I still live by the code. She don't live by no code though so I can't figure out to save my life why she won't tell on your ass. I wonder why my bitch so loyal to you."

"Bruh, trust me it ain't what you thinking. Me and her got history. We go back to our college days."

"Yeah, she told me all that. Fuck that college shit though! Fuck y'all got going on today?" Tony is speechless. He really has no answer for the man. "Exactly," the man says. "That's the same dumb ass look that she had when I asked her that question."

The man leans his head back and blows some steam in the air. "Got Secret Service motherfuckers all in my shit, questioning me about shit I know nothing about. I've been on my job ever since I came home." He blows steam from his nose.

"Almost ten years on that job and I never had a problem. Right after I told them Secret Service motherfuckers I don't know nothing, all of a sudden HR call me in the office. All of a sudden they got to cut me lose because of my jacket. Ten years later! I know that's behind whatever the fuck y'all got going on."

Tony feels horrible, knowing that he's caused all these problems for them. The man shakes his head with pity. I've been with this job for three weeks and something tells me they gone give me the same problem because of my jacket once that background check come back. Bruh," he says as he looks in Tony's eyes. His look is stern and genuine. "I ain't no rat bruh, but I'm telling you this right here to your face. If I lose this job, I'm sending the Secret Service to your office. You ain't gone fuck up my life behind whatever you and my sneaky ass wife is up to."

Tony disregards all he's said. "Can I ask where Jasmine is now?"

"Your guess is as good as mine," he says with his eyes bulging. "Bitch got tired of them people coming to the house and bounced. I told her when she get back I won't be here. I already bounced. I'm just waiting for a buyer for the house."

Tony feels beyond horrible right now. The fact that he has his good friend in a position like this breaks his heart. "Aye bruh, you're making a big mistake. Me and your wife are not having an affair. If we were I wouldn't be in your face. Bruh, I urge you to get your wife back. She's a good girl. I promise you, once the smoke clears, I will fix all this for y'all."

Tony looks deep into the man's eyes for reassurance. "You got my word on this bruh. I will replace everything y'all lost monetarily and situate y'all wherein neither of you will have to work ever again. I apologize for all of this from the bottom of my heart. I'm gone fix this but in the meantime, go and get your wife back bruh."

Tony and the man shake hands. The man felt the sincerity in Tony's words and that's the only reason they can shake hands like men. Tony's words were sincere though because they currently are not having an affair. The affair they had was many years ago so technically he didn't lie. It was a bad time for him and the woman and he hates that it happened but it did.

Tony pulls out of the parking lot slowly. His mind is all over the place. He can barely see straight. Through his peripheral he sees Maurice staring at him from the passenger's seat. Tony looks over and the smile on Maurice's face irks the hell out of him. "What's funny?"

"Boy, you talked your ass smooth out of that ass whooping," Maurice says before falling out in laughter. "You were on trial like a motherfucker, representing yourself." Maurice can barely get the words out due to him laughing so hard. "Got damn, I never saw you talk so fast."

Tony looks at Maurice without cracking a smile. He's too twisted right now to find humor in it. "Yo, not right now. I got some real serious shit going on right now. Save those jokes for later. Shit is more serious than you know."

68

THE ONLY SOURCE of light in the room comes from the New York City Skyline that peeks into the windows. The sound of Jay-Z's 'Picasso Baby' blares through the Bose Surround System. The song plays crisp and clear like a Live concert. The bass jumping out of the speakers is deep enough to cave the windows in.

The King-sized bed is covered with over a quarter of a million dollars in dirty bills. Drowning in the bills is Skelter's naked body. The money is the last of Vito's obligation to her for the 10 kilos she fronted him. As he promised, he put a kilo of cut onto a kilo of cocaine, turning 1 kilo into 2. He shook the 20 birds in record breaking time and is now waiting for her to hit him again. Skelter is amazed how fast he was able to give her a half of a million in cash.

Tonight is just one of those nights. As Skelter was counting through the money, she and Vito smoked through a few blunts. They were just building mentally, and trading some of their war stories, pretty much just getting to know each other a little better. One thing led to another and neither of them have yet to realize that they have crossed forbidden land.

Skelter backstrokes, trying to get away from Vito who is literally sucking her soul out of her body. Her arms fanning behind her, grasping onto bills to keep herself from drowning. She gasps for air as he tries to suck the life out of her. She doesn't get far away from him before he catches up to her and traps her off, pinning her against the headboard.

Since there's nowhere for her to run she figures she should at least take control of the situation. With his head in between her thighs, she palms the top of his head, dictating how much of her he can have. He slows up his flow and feasts on her more passionately and less forceful. Now that she can finally catch her breath she rides his wave. She takes the control away from him again and starts force-feeding herself to him.

Vito stays down, not coming up for air. He caters to every crevice of the kitty, paying special attention to the love button. He flicks it with his tongue, driving her crazy. It's not long before his licking evolves into sucking. He forms his mouth like the letter O, with his lips smothering hers. He gives the kitty mouth to mouth while using his tongue to make fast and ferocious strokes around the button.

Skelter loses all control and her body reacts with a mind of its own. Her body jolts and quivers as her heart races uncontrollably. Vito slows up his pace allowing her to catch her breath. She rocks her hips to the beat of the song that plays in the background. *"Let's make love on a million, in a dirty hotel with the fan, all for the love of drug dealing. Marble floors, gold ceilings, Oh what a feeling, fuck it I want a billion."*

Vito pries himself from between her thighs only to take off the wife-beater that is glued to his torso. He flings it into the air before diving back in between her legs. He plants a soft, wet kiss on her kitten before pulling away. She lays back, yearning for more. The anticipation builds as he slowly inserts two finger inside her. With a slow and passionate stroke he two fingers her into ecstasy. *'The come here'* stroke he exerts inside her is enough for her to come to him.

She lifts herself slightly from the bed and props herself in midair, giving him easier access to her. The two-finger stroke coupled with the figure 8 motion of his tongue on her love button drives her insane. She bucks like a wild horse, pumping away at his mouth.

Slow and passionate has never been her twist. She's too much of a dominant to lay back and submit and be controlled. With a strong thrust of her body she throws him off of her and he lands on his back. She rolls over and the kitten lands precisely on his face. On top where she feels she belongs she commands the kitten to glide all over his face. She smears her wetness all over. His face, his beard, his eyes, his nose, his mustache, his lips are all coated with her sticky juices and he loves it.

He lifts her slightly in the air and slides from underneath her. He ends up behind her. She's propped in a doggy style position, while he's in a froggy style position behind her. They are like two animals in heat. Just as he's about to insert himself inside her, he stops. He debates with himself for seconds before backing off her.

Skelter looks back at him and is confused. She wonders if she's done something that has turned him off.

"What's wrong?" she asks.

He shakes his head, dropping his face into the palms of his hands. He looks at her with guilt. "This ain't right."

"Huh?" she asks. "What you mean?"

"We not supposed to be doing this." He gets up from the bed and walks away.

"Fuck you mean?" Skelter asks.

He's hesitant to tell her this but feels she deserves an answer. "I gave bruh my word." She looks at him even more confused. "He asked me not to do this and I gave my word that I wouldn't."

She's getting angrier by the second. "Y'all talked about this? What type of shit you on? Is this a game y'all playing?"

"Nah, mama, no game. I want you. Bad," he adds. "But I gave my word."

She's now livid. "You gave a motherfucker your word about me and my pussy? Y'all had a conversation about my pussy? Wow!" A cheesy grin stretches across her face. She shakes her head in disbelief before her grin transitions into a frown of fury. "He don't fucking own me!"

"It ain't about owning you. It's about him trusting me with you," Vito says calmly. "And trusting that I can deal with you without doing that to you. I gave him my word."

"I'm a grown ass woman! He can't tell me what the fuck to do! You know what? Fuck this shit!" She gets up from the bed and quickly gets into her clothes. Vito watches her lustfully. He can't believe that he's allowing her to get away from him as badly as he wants her. She rakes the bills from the bed and the floor and dump them into the bag where they belong.

Vito sits on the chair across the room from her watching without saying a word. She steps into her sneakers and throws the duffle-bag over her shoulder. She storms to the door and just as she's about to exit, he snatches her from behind. He pulls her close to him, with his arms wrapped around her waist.

"I want you," he whispers into her ear. "I want more than just your body for one night, though. I want you, want you," he whispers. "But we have to make this right with bruh. I gave him my word. My word is everything to me. Let me talk to him about this before we go any further."

She turns around to face him. She stares into his eyes. "No need to talk to him. Keep your word. Pretend this never happened. It should've never happened anyway. Let's just keep it business," she says with attitude.

She walks toward the door and just before making her exit she turns around. "As far as that goes, anything that it could have been will never be. I slipped but I didn't fall. Now let's get back to the money." She stomps out of the room.

"Wait, Shorty...I mean, Skelter. Hold up!" The door is closed in his face just like he's sure the opportunity has.

69

ROSEVILLE CEMETERY

TONY STEPS CAREFULLY through the cemetery, skipping over tree branches and stepping around garbage. As he gets close to Jane Doe's mausoleum he slows his stride and peeks around suspiciously. Once he finds the coast to be clear, he cuts over quickly and taps on the door. After tapping on the door, he hops off the step and stands in the front looking around, feeling weird. He doesn't want anyone to see him knocking on a mausoleum door.

A sharp whistle catches Tony's attention. Tony looks to his right where he finds a man throwing trash into a huge garbage bag. The man waves Tony on. Tony walks over rather nervously.

The baggy faced old man is dressed in overalls. His bugged eyes make him look spooky. His wrinkled old pitch-black skin looks like death itself; just with his eyes open. Tony is surprised to see him here working after Jane Doe explained to him that no one takes care of the cemetery. It all plays out like a scene from a scary movie.

"She ain't in there," says the old man. His large soup cooler lips hang to his chin.

"You know where she's at?" Tony asks.

"Nope," he says. He continues to throw the trash in the bag. He looks up slowly. "They took her away from here. Right there," he says as he points a couple hundred feet away.

"Who took her away from here?" Tony asks.

"I don't know. Look like ninjas. Dressed in all black. Didn't hear no gunshots or nothing. She just dropped to the ground. It was a sniper over there," he says as he points far left.

"Caught her from the blind side. She never saw it coming. The black van pulled right up and took her body away. Then another van pulled up and some more ninjas ran inside and came out with her computer and all her important papers."

Tony looks around, feeling like maybe he's being watched. Maybe all this is a set-up. "Who are you though?"

"Me, I'm nobody. I'm just a homeless motherfucker that Jane Doe took in and took care of me like I was a no-good brother of hers. I've been sleeping here in this cemetery for years, long before she got here. I helped her move in and I always watched her back around here.

She was like a white sister of mine. She loved this place and she tried her best to take care of it. Every day she sent me out here to clean up a little more of the place. She said the dead should be resting in peace and ain't no peace here. She was determined to help everybody in this place get their proper rest in peace."

Tony listens to the man speak and he has an epiphany. To hear how much Jane Doe cared for the dead amazes him. She was a true humanitarian. The fact that she spent her last years trying to help the dead rest in peace is such a selfless act. Her compassion for the dead makes him question his own life.

Tony follows behind the man, listening to the man tell him more great things about Jane Doe. Before he realizes it, the man is standing in front of another mausoleum. He invites Tony inside, yet Tony rejects the offer. The man steps inside and returns holding a box in his hands. Tony recognizes the box immediately. It's the box that her watch collection was stored.

"She told me if anything ever happened to her to give this to you." He hands the box over to Tony. "It's like she knew something would happen to her." Sadness covers his face. "She made sure that everything would be ok if something ever happened to her."

Tony cracks the lid and there he finds every watch in the same place where he saw it. All of this is really starting to freak him out. "I thank you, Sir. I have to go now. Is there anything I can do for you?"

"No, I don't need anything. I have more than I need. She made sure of that," he says before flashing a wink. "I'm only here, carrying out her mission of cleaning this place up. She paid me to do the job and I won't stop working until my job is done. I don't know what y'all business was because she never said but all I hope is that you carry out whatever business y'all had. As men all we have is our word, remember that."

Minutes later and Tony sits in his car, still parked in the same place. He's heartbroken right now. He tries to picture how it all went down. He thinks of her words to him on how she's sure they will kill her for all that she knows. He also thinks of the constant warnings she gave him. He's torn right now, and not sure if he should stop while he's ahead or carry out the mission. He kind of believes that he may have already crossed the point of no return.

The murder of Jane Doe is confirmation of what extent the Government will go to protect their secrets. It hurts his heart that he's dragged Jasmine and her husband into his mess. He wonders what they have planned for him. Suddenly a thought crosses his mind that he can't shake. He nods his head as it all seems to make sense now.

After pondering on that thought for minutes, his mind then soars in a different direction. Suddenly, he thinks of the money Jane Doe gave him. He wonders if the Government has put a stop to it. He's almost sure they have but he won't know until he checks. He pulls out his phone and hits his banking app. His heart pounds as he logs in. His nervousness is not about the money itself. If they've frozen the transfer that means they are on his heels and thinks are about to make a turn for the worse for him.

To his surprise and his relief the funds are still there. He leans back in his seat in deep thought. For the first time he worries about his career and his future. He thinks of all that is before him right now and he starts to question if this is really what he wants. He somewhat doubted the severity of all Jane Doe was saying. A part of him believed she was overreacting but now he sees that she wasn't. He thinks maybe he should just back off while he still has the chance.

70

DAYS LATER

INSIDE THE MAILROOM the concierge hands Dre box after box and he stacks them neatly onto the dolly. In total he stacks 5 boxes. "Thanks," Dre says. "I will bring the cart right back to you."

"No problem," the concierge says.

Dre knows just what is inside the box. He's eager to see the finished product. He rushes though the lobby and gets onto the elevator. He gets off at the 8th floor and damn near runs through the hall dragging cart behind him.

He busts through the door. Lil Mama stands in the kitchen, totally uncovered. She's so happy that Dre is now her husband and she no longer has to cover in front of him. She's so happy, that she hasn't worn a stitch of clothing around him since they got married. She walks around all day and night naked and free.

She stands on her tippy toes to put something in the cabinet and Dre can't help but to enjoy the view. Her high yellow, low rider as he calls it, just rests on her thick thighs. On her tippy toes, she still can't quite reach the top shelf so she jumps, causing the low rider to bounce like it's on hydraulics. She looks over her shoulder at Dre, hoping he isn't missing the show she's putting on for him. Her mission is to drain him every day and she's been doing that.

Dre turns away, realizing that she's trying to reel him in. He rips open the box on the top and there he finds a blue suit folded up in a plastic bag. He pulls the bag out the box, and as he walks he pulls the suit jacket from the bag. He breezes by her on his way to the bathroom.

Close to 30 minutes pass and Dre's silence peaks Lil Mama's curiosity. She tiptoes into the bathroom where she finds Dre bent over the Jacuzzi. She steps closer to see what he's doing. From over his shoulder she sees the suit-jacket drowned in a tub of water. Clunks of a jet-black, gooey, pasty substance float around in the water. Dre bobbles the suit-jacket in the water over and over and more substance appears.

Lil Mama is baffled as to why he would put a brand-new custom-made suit in water. The pasty substance that is coming off the suit confuses her even more. Dre turns around to face her. "You know what that is?"

"Uh, no," she says. "Should I?"

"Mexican Mud," says Dre. Lil Mama shrugs her shoulders, still not knowing. "Heron in its purest form," he further explains.

Her face drops in sadness as she shakes her head from side to side. As disappointed as she may be at this moment, she can't help but to stare at her husband with admiration. Back when they were making moves years ago, it wasn't just the physical that she was attracted to. It was his mind that she first fell in love with. When he would share his thoughts with her she would be captivated. Here it is all these years later and his mind and his thought process still amazes her. For him to put together a scheme like this is genius in her eyes.

For Tony it was all about a suit. He saw it as a steal getting a $2,500 suit for 10% of the price. Dre had no interest in the suit at all. His only use for the suit was the amount of dope it could hold. The $200 suit was merely the vessel to carry close to a million dollars worth of heroin.

Javier has put Dre in a position that a hustler can only dream of. He brought Dre in like a brother, showing him love that Dre never expected. He fronted Dre 5 bags of Mexican Mud at the value of $40,000 a bag. Each bag of Mexican Mud makes 1 kilo of heroin in its purest form. So pure it can be stepped on 14 times. In that case, 1 bag of Mexican Mud makes 1 kilo that can be cut 14 times and turned into 14 kilos. Five bags of Mexican Mud is approximately 70 kilos once they are cut and mixed.

In total Dre ordered 25 suits and 5 of those suits, the blue suits, have the heroin soaked into them. Javier and the suit-maker worked together in having the liquid heroin impregnated into the suits, using a special technique. Once the suits are dry the heroin is soaked into them and ready to go. This process is known to drug smugglers as 'The Drip-Dry process.'

In this process, a chemical is added to the Mexican Mud in its original chalky, brick type form and it converts the heroin to liquid form. Then to extract the heroin the clothes are soaked in another liquid chemical, which evaporates and the liquid dope bleeds from the clothing. The dope is then put under infrared light and turns it into a dry paste. The final step of the process transitions the paste back into the powder form.

Now that Dre has the suits, he will go to someone who Javier recommended who will extract the dope from the suits and complete the process. Once he has the dope back to the powder form he will then add his Special mix and turn 1 kilo into 14 kilos. Overall, the $200,000 Dre owes Javier is a mere drop in the bucket to the money he will gross.

With kilos of heroin going for $65,000 on up to $70,000, he can serve even the biggest dealers at $60,000 a unit and still gross out at almost 5 million dollars. Dre and Javier will bust the profit bag down the middle as. Unfortunately the entire 5 million isn't profit though. Everything costs. He has pay to have the dope extracted from the suits, have it cut and prepared and ready to be sold on the streets. That could easily take one million dollars away from his profits. Even with such a hefty chunk of his earnings going into production cost, they still make a profit of over 4 million dollars, over 2 million dollars apiece. Could be more, depending on the expertise level of the mixer that Javier has assigned to the job.

In Dre's Block Party days he's done well and back then he thought he was at the top floor of the game. That was his ceiling and he had no clue there were so many floors of the game on top of them. What they were doing back then was the basement level compared to the situation he now has. Back then they bought the kilos already cut. Today he's getting it uncut from Javier who gets it straight from Afghanistan, pure as driven snow. He could never ask for a better situation than this. Javier has granted him a life changing opportunity.

Dre looks to Lil Mama as he wraps his arm around her shoulder. Sadness covers her face, yet she tries to hide it. Her dream of living an all Halal lifestyle is over before it really got started. Dre pays notice to the look on her face. "Talk to me. What you thinking?"

Lil Mama shakes her head and looks into the tub where the globs of what looks like slime, float around. The more she stares at it, the more she sees it as dollar signs. The more dollar signs she sees in her mind, the more her sadness vanishes. She now stands here facing her reality.

"Lil Mama, we are back."

She nods her head slowly in agreeance. "Yes we are," she says. This is the first sign of a flame that he's seen in her eyes since she's been home. The humility that she's had in them has disappeared until now. Dre notices something else too. For the first time since she's been home, he called her Lil Mama and she didn't correct him. Maybe they are back, just like the old days.

"This calls for a celebration," she says. Her eyes light up with horniness. "Let's have sex."

Dre slaps his hand across is forehead and shakes his head in despair. "Damn, Halimah." He realizes he's married to the sexual energizer bunny. "I'm trying to get out here and get this money," he says with popped eyes. "You ain't gone sex me to fucking death."

Lil Mama drops her head sadly and Dre feels sorry for her. "Come on yo!" Her face lights up instantly. She grabs his hand and drags him to the bedroom. And they're off!

71

HOURS LATER

DRE STEPS INTO Tony's office with a spark in his eyes that Tony hasn't seen in years. His walk and his demeanor is like he had in the past. "Hey, man, I was just about to hit you," Tony says. "Got my suits in. Amazing! He's the best kept secret."

"Got mine in too," Dre replies. "That's what I came to rap to you about." Dre's expression changes. "I got a problem."

"With what, the suits?"

"Yeah, something like that," Dre replies. He hates to even talk about this to Tony but he needs his help. "First thing I want to say is don't judge me, bruh."

"Never," Tony replies with sincerity.

"Second thing is I need you to know all what I'm about to tell you was put in motion before we got back here and you told me about the trust funds and accounts." He pauses for a second giving himself time to choose the perfect wording. "You're no idiot so I'm sure you know why I linked up with Javier."

Tony nods and shrugs. "I knew you had something up your sleeve. I just didn't know what."

Dre is careful what he tells Tony out of the respect that he haves for him. Every now and again he will tell Tony something that he thinks he owes him the courtesy of knowing. Other than that, he keeps him out of anything illegal. The less he knows the better.

"I know you said in close to four months the money will start coming in and I'm cool with that," Dre says. "My only problem is before you told me that I already made a commitment with Javier. A major, major commitment. I'm already both feet in. I ain't gone lie, last week my problem was no work and no line. This week my problem is no network."

Dre hesitates before continuing. Tony can sense that he's in heavy thought. "I need your help big bruh."

Tony side-eyes Dre, hoping Dre's question will not be something that will compromise their brotherhood. "What's up?" Tony asks. He's really not sure if he's ready for this question.

Dre digs into his pocket and pulls out four documents. Tony instantly recognizes the documents because he's had them in his possession for over years. "Two hundred and fifty-thousand, apiece " he says as he slides the documents over to Tony one by one. "In four months, you can take the money as it comes in. What I need from you in exchange for the million is every contact you have in that phone," he says as he points to Tony's 'money phone' as he calls it.

"I need every contact you have from the top dogs on down to the bottom feeders. Anybody that you think I will have use for I need to link with them. You have money dudes in that phone that you have represented from all over the country. You know who is who and who ain't who. You know who got it and you know who need it. And most importantly you know who stood up during trying times and who rolled."

"Not one motherfucker in this phone has rolled," Tony interrupts. "If they rolled, they wouldn't be in this phone."

"I believe it," Dre says. "You got them all from the suppliers down to the ones who need to be supplied and I need them. I've been out the game for years and I have no network. I need your help."

Tony is not so quick to reply. He sits back, choosing his words. "First of all, if I take your money I could be considered a criminal by involving myself in criminal activity. But if I let a friend hold my phone and that friend goes behind my back and steals all the contacts in my phone, that is something entirely different." Tony flashes a sly wink of the eye. He reaches over and grabs his phone. "You're my friend and my brother. Of course, you can use my phone.

As my brother and my friend I could never tell you no." He hands Dre his phone. Dre sighs relief. He had no idea how Tony would react to his proposition. "But as your brother and your friend I'm not understanding how you could put me in a situation like this. How could you force my hand and involve me in something that goes against all I stand for?"

Dre lowers his eyes like a guilty puppy. Tony continues on with the verbal lashing. "As I said, I would never tell you no," Tony says with sincerity. "So, go ahead, go through my phone and any contact that you believe you can use, I will connect you with. A friend just doing for a friend in need."

Dre has no words of reply. He looks up into Tony's eyes as he hands the phone back to him. "No, thank you."

"But thank you," Tony replies.

"I apologize," Dre says with sincerity. "I'm just in a tough spot right now and I have to get through this."

"I beg you not to drag me into that tough spot with you," Tony says. "I've fixed your biggest problem and yet you have managed to create another one for yourself. I've been by your side like a brother, fighting battle after battle with you for the past decade. This battle here, please fight without me."

Dre extends his hand and they shake hands firmly. "I hope what I have just asked of you hasn't tarnished our brotherhood."

"Not at all," Tony says as he grips Dre's hand tighter. "But had you accepted that phone you would not have tarnished the brotherhood... the brotherhood would be no longer."

Dre stares into Tony's eyes. "Overstood and respected."

72

ONE WEEK LATER

UMAR STANDS AT the desk in front of the cute, brown and petite secretary. The secretary is dressed quite fashionably in expensive designer clothing from her shoulders down to her feet but her head is covered in hijab modestly. The huge wedding ring on her finger and all of her other gleaming jewelry pieces have nothing modest about them.

Umar holds a stack of papers in his hand as she prints out more documents for him. "The email just came in a few minutes ago," she says. She not once looks up from the printer. She hands him the document and he reads it over quickly.

"Bet. Let me go and run this over to them right now, Insha Allah" he says as he makes his way toward the door. "I will be home early tonight, Insha Allah" he says as he pulls the door open and takes one long glance. "As Salaamu Alaikum!

"Walaikum As Salaam!" the woman shouts back in reply before the door is closed in her face.

Umar steps lightly down the small flight of stairs as he continues to read from the paper in his hand. He doesn't look up once for his eyes are glued onto the paper. As he steps foot on the ground, a van pulls up, cutting him off. The double doors open and two Chinese men hop out. With the element of surprise on their side, they are able to snatch him into the van. The van speeds off, burning rubber.

The door of the building swings open wildly. The secretary witnessed it all from the camera in the office. She watches as the 'Edible Arrangements' van rips out of the parking lot. She pulls out her phone and starts to dial. She's so in shock that she can barely remember the numbers to dial.

MEANWHILE IN SHORT HILLS, NEW JERSEY

Tony sits on the corner of the desk in his intern's office. Traces of worry are smeared all over his face. These last days have been stressful for him. So much has happened that he's having a hard time getting it together.

Maurice and Twelve Play stand before him listening carefully to every word he says. "The reality is this," Tony says. "I don't know if the hit was for me or if it was for you," he says pointing directly to Maurice. "But it most definitely was a hit. The Feds were out to get us."

PHILADELPHIA

Umar lays on his back on the cold floor of the old and empty warehouse. He's sweating pellets of imported oils so loud and pungent that the fragrance is unbearable. His wrists are tied together behind him and his ankles are tied together as well. He's been stripped of all his clothing and is stark naked.

The fear of the unknown has erased the shame of being naked. Both of his eyes are swollen shut from the pistol whipping he received in the van at the beginning of his capture. That abuse was nothing compared to the beating he received once he got here. His body is aching with lumps, bumps and bruises all over as a result of the baseball bat beating he got an hour ago. When they were escorting him into the warehouse he put up some resistance. That resistance earned him a nice beating.

The pain from his cracked ankle pounds harder than the pain in his cracked ribs. He can feel his heartbeat through his swollen lips. The baseball bat to the mouth literally knocked a few teeth down his throat. The pulsating heartbeat from his lips and the pain from his aching and bleeding gums create a rhythm of their own. All in all, he's never been in this amount of pain in his life. In his lifetime he's been shot on three different occasions and neither time was he in this much pain.

A dozen and a half little Chinamen pace around the room with their eyes on their latest assignment. These Chinese men are not your average Chinamen behind the counter at the local Chinese store. They may look like the average but these men are hardened criminals, all part of Philadelphia's Chinese Mafia. These men are a part of a group that runs a great percentage of Philadelphia's underworld, from drugs to gambling to extortion.

Umar lays in pain, wondering what is next for him. He also wonders what the reason for such punishment is. He tries to think hard about what could have landed him here in this position. He's never had a run-in with the Chinese. He's asked them several times what it's all about. Him asking questions is what got his whole top, front row, balcony section of his teeth knocked clean out.

Umar watches fearfully as the most wicked Chinaman of them all walks toward him. In one hand he holds a huge container and in the other he holds a big wooden spoon. Umar's heart pounds with fear, not knowing what is next on the menu of torture for him. The Chinaman digs the spoon into the container and the spoon is pulled out with a huge gunk of peanut butter stuck to it. He flings the peanut butter onto Umar's chest. He uses the spoon to smear the peanut butter evenly all over. He repeats the process over and over until Umar's entire body is covered in peanut butter.

"Yo, what the hell did I do?" Umar asks with fear of the rest of his teeth being knocked out. He wonders if they even understand English because not only have none of them ever replied to him, he's heard not a one of them speak English. This makes him feel like anything he says will fall on deaf ears. How can he talk them out of what they're doing or convince them of his innocence of whatever it is they think he's done, when they can't understand English?

Umar spots one of the men coming back into the room, holding what looks to be a black bodybag in his hand. It's then that Umar loses his mind. "No, please, no," he pleads. The men wrestle with him and try to hold him down in order to place him inside the bag. He yells at the top of his lungs and it does him no good. He flips and he flops and wiggles and attempts to kick as it takes all of them to lay him inside the bodybag.

As he lays in the bag his life flashes before his eyes. All the treacherous things that he's done in life that he thought he got away, plays before his eyes like a movie. He thought he got away with it all but today he sees differently. He was told that taking his Shahada and becoming Muslim would wipe away all of his sins and maybe it did but it could be the sins that he has piled up after Shahadah that he's paying for now. He believes today just may be his Judgement Day.

Two Chinamen are at his feet tying bricks to his ankles. He has no idea of the science behind it. With the sides of the bodybag overlapping his ears, his peripheral is obstructed but what he hears is a familiar sound. The sound of a pack of rats squealing loudly is what brings the first tears from his eyes. "No," he cries. "Please, no," he cries. He finally realizes what the purpose of the peanut butter is.

He tries to fight his way out of the bodybag which is now zipped up to his chest. The bag is snug against his body, limiting his movement. Ankles tied together with bricks attached and his wrists tied, while trapped inside a body bag is a nightmare for any claustrophobic, which, by the way, he is.

He looks upward and what he sees is a cage full of rats, of all colors, black, white and grey and the size of squirrels. The Chinaman stands over him, dangling the cage over his face. "We hear that you like to run your mouth," the Chinese man says in perfect English. "A tattle tale," he says with a huge smile.

"You have a problem keeping your mouth shut but we are going to fix that for you right now. We are going to make it where what you see," he says as he pokes Umar in the eye. "And what you hear," he says as he slaps Umar's ear. "Can never ever come out of your mouth," he says with wickedness in his eyes. The man signals for his men to come over and assist him. "First, we are going to fix that mouth of yours."

The oldest Chinaman of them all walks over holding a pair of surgical scissors. Umar starts to shake his head from side to side just thinking of what is next to come. He tries to keep his mouth shut until the blunt force of a gun knocks out another three of his teeth. It takes three men to hold his mouth open, while the man with the scissors reaches inside for his tongue. He snatches the tip of his tongue with a firm grip and snip…snip…snip. He holds Umar's tongue in his hand for Umar to see. Blood seeps from his mouth. The man tosses his tongue into the body bag with Umar.

"So, from here on out will be no way for you to tattle tell. Apparently, what you saw," he says as he lifts a sharp screwdriver into the air. "You ran back and told. So, let me fix that problem for you," he says as he drives the tip of the screwdriver into the pupil of Umar's left eye. Umar whines like a wounded puppy. The man then drives the screwdriver into his right pupil with even more force. Umar's shriek is ear piercing.

His eyes and his mouth leak profusely. "I also heard that you ran back and told some things that you heard. So, I will fix that for you too in one minute. Right now I'm going to open this cage and place these rats in there with you. You're a rat and so are they. Rats deserve each other. When dealing with a rat or a pack of rats there is no loyalty, no honor, and no integrity amongst them. It's every rat for himself and a rat will eat another rat alive to preserve his own life. Just as these rats will do with you. They are going to eat you alive," he says with a wicked smile.

With no further delay he snips Umar's left ear like he's a Doberman Pinscher. Umar whines and he whimpers. At this point death is better than the pain that he's living through. The cage is opened and the rats are dumped in the bag. They immediately get to feasting as the bag is zipped. They squeal and move around busily all throughout the bag.

The rat party begins. The biggest rat of them all Harlem Shakes as the rats eat at his body. Their little teeth pricking away at his skin in multiples places at one time makes the pain a compilation instead of feeling the separate bites. His flipping and flopping, wiggling, squirming and crying means nothing to the rats for they have no compassion. They eat away with no sympathy for the job of the Rat is to destroy and eat one alive.

SHORT HILLS, NEW JERSEY

"If you really think about it, he never looked me in my face," Tony says. "It was like he always avoided eye contact with me. From the first time I saw him, he looked familiar to me, I just couldn't place the face. Then one day while sitting in my car it hit me." Tony hands two papers to Maurice. On the paper there's a mugshot of a man. Tony has drawn a big beard on the mugshot. "I printed it out and drew the beard on him and boom, there it was."

Maurice looks at the picture of the man with the beard and the picture of the man without the beard. His heart skips a beat. The man looks so much different with the beard. Maurice studies the man's face for he looks somewhat familiar.

Tony continues on. "I did some homework and found out that he has been traveling state to state working with the people. I also found out the lil Mexican works with the DEA. That situation had set-up written all over it. Only a fool would have fallen for such a trap but it happens every day though. Oh, and the Management Company he kept suggesting," Tony says. "That company belongs to him and his girlfriend. They are a team. Like Mickey and Minnie Mouse."

Maurice and Twelve Play look at the picture speechless. Maurice is terrified that the Feds were that close to him without him knowing it. Twelve Play feels like an idiot for letting Umar in. It finally hits Maurice where he knows the man from.

Now, he wonders if the brief encounter he and the man had some years ago is the reason for all of this. Maybe this is some form of revenge. Maurice wonders if it's really him they want. Who else could the hit have been for? He can't understand why they would be after Tony.

"Listen, I'm not going to keep you in the dark," Tony says. "I think I've stepped in some shit that could be detrimental to my life. I have two major cases against the United States Government. This isn't co-incidence. I was warned that the case could be life altering for me. Meaning they would try to fuck my life up. I went forward with it anyway. So, I'm not sure if that was a warning shot of what is to come or not. If this hit was for me, I apologize for bringing you into it. We have a lot of business in the making and I may have to fade to black and detach myself just so our business isn't destroyed."

Maurice thinks of all the business they have in process as well as their plans for the future. This is the absolute wrong time for any trouble. They have come too far for it to stop here. "So, now what? Are you going to take the warning shots and fall back? You see they are not fucking around with you. I say you just pull back from the cases and we get this money."

"I can't fall back now. I've been paid by a client and heftily at that," he says with emphasis. "Furthermore, this is personal now. If I stop now they may still attempt to destroy my life. I already stepped in this shit. But once I expose their secret in front of the world, I put myself in the forefront of this thing. They won't be able to destroy my life because the world will be watching me. Even if I didn't want to, at this point I have to."

"Makes sense, I guess," says Maurice.

"So, from here on out, I'm still with you but only in private. Silent partners. I don't want the smell of my shit to get on you. I have a war to fight!"

TWENTY MINUTES LATER

Tony's office looks like a movie production studio. Cameras, cameramen, news anchormen, anchorwomen and make-up artists flood the office. Every news channel locally and across the country has a representative here in the office. Even CNN anchorman Victor Blackwell is here, ready to make news history. Tony requested him specifically because he wanted to help him make a career building report.

Tony is dressed dapper as usual but today he's gone a step further. A regular suit just wouldn't do it for such a big day. Today he's dressed in all black in mourning of Jane Doe. He's dressed in the double-breasted tuxedo jacket straight from suit-maker in Honduras.

Tony has to admit; the man's needle is on another level. The tuxedo is tailored to perfection, fitting him more like a strait jacket. The tapered cut makes it look as if he has no waist at all, just all shoulders. There he stands at the podium in the middle of his office, looking like a GQ magazine cover model. His young male and female interns stand on opposite sides of him. Both of them are extremely fashionable as well.

Lights from the cameras flash non-stop. He stands there in silence for a couple minutes to allow everyone time to get ready so they don't miss a word of what he says. This is where it all counts. The impact of this press conference has to be groundbreaking. He has to start off strong and keep hitting them stronger. This move he's making right now will be revolutionary in his career. This is history in the making.

Everyone stands around with curiosity, wanting and needing to know what the special announcement is. The female intern raises her hand in the air to silence the crowd. They hush immediately and Tony speaks. "Dear People, I thank you all for coming out," Tony says.

"I've invited you all to be present as my witnesses as I file a complaint, internationally for the whole world to view. Today I wage a war against the biggest corporation in the world. This corporation, we will address as the defendant. The said defendant is guilty of more murders than we can count. I'm talking millions of murders. We can rightfully call this defendant, a serial killer. Or a hitman, murdering for business," he says dramatically.

"I have proof that the defendant has poisoned with deadly medicine to kill off hundreds of thousands of innocent victims. I also have proof that the defendant uses prison inmates as guinea pigs to test out the poisons before they unleash it onto the world. With the motive and intent of poisoning even more people. Today at," he says as he looks at his watch. "At 4:12 P.M. I, Attorney Tony Austin, am filing a complaint against Uncle Sam, the United States Government.

I'm making this complaint a worldwide public spectacle so there is no doubt in the people's minds if anything happens to me after this point, it's indeed another form of Uncle Sam's antics to hide his corruption. Here in front of me, I have a current copy of my health records that shows a clean bill of health, no sickness or disease whatever. This means any sickness that derives any time soon is another one of Uncle Sam's crafty tactics. I have no enemies, which means there is no reason I should be shot down as some of the others who have attempted to wage this type of war. I am strong and healthy and prepared to fight against Uncle Sam, the serial killer! At this point, I will be answering all questions you may have."

"Mr. Austin! Mr. Austin! Mr. Austin!" they yell as they all wave their hands, waiting to be picked to ask their question.

Feds are planted all over the room disguised as cameramen and news reporters. They all watch with anger. They knew he had the balls to go all the way with it, but they hoped he was smart enough not to. Now that he has waged the war and struck, it's their turn to strike back and make sure that it counts. With the spotlight now on him, they will have to be very crafty in their attack.

PHILADELPHIA

The van which reads 'Live Lobster' along the side, speeds around the ramp of the Schuylkill River. Right before the exit, the van stops and the doors bust open. Five Chinamen hop out of the van, carrying the body-bag full of rats.

Most of the movement in the bag comes from the rats picking away at any meat that is left on the bones of their victim. Their rats have damn near eaten him to death. Every so often his body jerks, signaling to the men that he still has some life left in him.

The lead Chinaman unzips the bag, just enough to peek inside. Through the tiny opening he can see Umar's right eye which the lid has been chewed and gnawed on. The blinking of his eye is indication that Umar is still conscious, barely, but he's still living.

The Chinaman smiles from ear to ear as he peeks into the bag. Umar's one good eye is fixed on the Chinamen. His eye shifting from side to side tells the Chinamen that he's alert enough to understand what he's saying. "Smoke, when you get to hell, tell the Mayor that Tony sent you."

It's then that Smoke realizes the game has caught up with him. All the snitching and double-crossing has come to an end. Him posing as Umar, a Philadelphian Muslim is just one of the many assignments that he has taken on. In each assignment he has played the role to the maximum. Some of his roles were Oscar worthy, how he was able to get into character and reel his marks in. It was nothing for him to study the gangsters of a city and teach himself to move and think and even talk like them.

As for the Umar role, Smoke went as far as to taking his Shahada and studying Islam. He also persuaded Jada, Manson's son's mother to take Shahada. He married her and they worked as a team. He learned the religion in and out just so he could use it to get closer to his marks and it worked.

He's sure if he had waited a little while longer before he and the Mexican made their move, they would've been able to lock in Twelve Play and Maurice, but the Feds were rushing him to get in there and seal the deal. Their plan was to bait Maurice and Twelve Play into buying cocaine. Having Tony down as Maurice's business partner would've dragged Tony right in with them. The plan was a good one had he not had the pressure of the Feds on his back. A little more time is all he needed and he would've added three more to the list of people's lives that he's twisted.

The Chinamen swing the bag in the air. "On the count of three. One…two…three." They toss the bodybag over the railing. They watch as the bag descends in the air. The weight causes the bag to drop at a rapid speed. The bag hits the water causing a huge *SPLASH!* The bag floats around for seconds before it disappears under the water. Now, the question is, do Rats die and go to heaven?

The Chinamen hop into the van and before the doors are shut, the driver looks into the rearview mirror. What he sees gives him a panic attack. A State Police car races behind them at full speed. The Chinamen speaks a few words in his language and he steps on the gas before they can get the doors closed.

The sirens are now roaring and the lights are flashing as the car has gotten closer. The Chinamen are frantic. They're all screaming for the driver to drive faster but it's not much faster a van can go. They notice a string of police cars now behind them. Only one car is glued to their bumper. The rest of them have a ways to go.

The lead Chinaman grabs his gun from his waist. He draws his arm back and busts the glass out of the back window with his elbow. He aims and he doesn't hesitate to fire. BOC! BOC! BOC! BOC! He watches as the windshield of the police car caves in. The car swerves and bangs into the railing. With the lead car out of commission and hopefully for them the cops as well, it gives them time to get away.

Up ahead a string of about ten cars are coming toward them. The driver notices a string of five cars cutting across from their left. With no other alternative, he's forced to make a sharp right turn. A sharp turn around the bend at 70 miles an hour is a recipe for disaster. The van tilts over, rolling on two wheels while the driver nervously keeps his feet on the gas. The van rolls over on its side.

The Chinamen scatter as they try to bust the doors to get out. One man gets the driver's door open and he climbs out of it. He reaches back to help the second man. Now the leader and the driver are the only ones left. As the driver is attempting to climb out the leader pulls his leg and drags him down. He then climbs out. He looks back and is tempted to blow the driver's brains out for getting them into this mess. The only thing that saves him is the sirens that are coming from everywhere.

In seconds, police have them trapped. To their right, their left, their front and their back, they are blockaded by police cars. Guns are aimed at them from every direction. To do anything besides submit would be like committing suicide. All four of the men raise their hands in submission.

The police swarm in and tackle them to the ground. They are all put into separate cars and driven back to the scene. The highway is blocked off as police are parked from end to end. Helicopters fly overhead and boats fill the water as a group of scuba divers pull the body-bag out of the water. The Chinamen watch as freedom as they know it, comes to an end.

73

ARCH STREET, PHILADELPHIA/HOURS LATER

THE CHINAMAN IN charge sits in the interrogation room alone. He's the last one to be questioned. There's really not much his men could have said, other than he's the lead in charge, which is true. They know nothing else. In most of the work they do they hardly know the underlying details. All they know is what they need to know.

The leader always felt it was better that way just in case of a situation such as this. The less they know the better off it is in the end. They can't tell the details if they don't know the details. Only thing in this matter, even without knowing the details the authorities have all they need to send the Chinese men up the river forever.

Only two people in the entire world know all the details of this situation and that is the man in charge and Attorney Tony Austin. Tony and this man came in contact many years ago when Tony represented him. The man was fighting a variety of charges but the charge that held the most weight was a triple homicide where the man allegedly shot three men executioner style before setting them on fire. Thanks to Tony, he beat every charge.

That was just the beginning though. Over the years Tony has been their representative for every case members of their organization has had, from small to large. He could call on Tony for anything at any hour of the night. That is why the one time that Tony called on him, he was honored to come running.

The Special Agent comes walking in the room. He closes the door gently and almost glides across the room. His demeanor is mild and meek. He paces around the room with peacefulness as he keeps his eyes on the floor. Finally, he stops and backs against the wall with his hands clasped over his belly.

The Chinaman sits back looking unbothered. His hands are cuffed yet he holds them on the back of his head. He leans back in his chair, rocking back and forth. The look on his face shows no emotion.

"Listen," the agent says. "I'm not one for a long song and dance so we are going to get right to the point. I spoke with your men and none of them were really much help. They really know nothing. The translator says they don't know the man that was tortured and murdered or even why he was tortured and murdered. I'm going to be completely honest with you," he says as he steps away from the wall.

The Chinaman takes his hands from behind his head and places them in front of him on the table. He twiddles his fingers with a cocky expression on his face. The agent comes closer and stops in front of the man. "I didn't even really put my pressure on them yet and I can tell you that once I do, they will crack. Based on them not knowing nothing, I'm sure they will all put it on you."

The agent sits down next to the Chinaman. The Chinaman stares at the agent with his lips snarled. One thing he hates is a cop. "I'm going to give you a chance to save yourself now before they drown you," the agent speaks in his most calm voice. "If you can tell me what I need to know now, I won't have to go in there and pressure them. If I do, they will all go against you. If you make me work and have to squeeze them to roll on you there's nothing you will be able to tell me to get me to help you or take it easy on you."

He zooms in closer to the Chinaman. "Me and you can deal with this right here right now and it could be as easy as pie. Or we can take the scenic route and in the end you will wish you made it easy on yourself." He stands up. "This is what we are going to do, ok? I'm gone lay some facts on the table and then I will allow you to lay some facts on the table. Okay, ready?"

The Chinaman lays his head on his folded arms as if he's napping and not interested in the conversation at all. The agent still continues. "Fact one, we identified the body of the man that was tortured and murdered and found out he was a Federal Informant. He was one of ours, working with us since 2010. Murdering a Federal Informant in the state of Philadelphia is grounds for capital punishment, the death penalty. We won't even add in the torture, the drowning, and the shootout with police because in the end the death penalty is the death penalty."

The Chinaman lifts his head up and for the first time in this interview. He's now quite attentive. "I see the mention of the death penalty piqued your interest, huh? And it should. But I know of a way that can save four lives. The four of you could die old and possibly be free to take your grandchildren to the park and eat ice cream or whatever else you would like to do with the rest of your life."

The agent looks at the Chinaman with a false sense of sadness. "I hate that you're in this mess. It's so much bigger than you. You have no clue of what you have been brought into. It's not fair that you were not even warned but hey we are here.

We have to deal with the facts and move accordingly. So, now I'm going to lay fact number two on the table and then I will give you the chance to lay your facts on the table. Then hopefully we can go from there and work out a deal that helps you out of this mess that you were so unfairly dragged into. Are you ready?"

The Chinaman doesn't reply but his tough edge has softened. He's all ears. The whole thing the agent said about it being bigger than him and him being dragged into this without being warned makes him question it all. He wonders if it's true or just a mind game. Either way he is now listening with his divided attention.

"Okay, here it is. Fact two," the agent says. "We know you were hired by Attorney Tony Austin to murder the informant. He selfishly dragged you into this knowing how risky of a move it was. It's a dog-eat-dog world. No one cares about you and he's proven that. Which is why you must save yourself. Listen man, don't die for that motherfucker. Admit that he hired you to murder our informant and save yourself from the death penalty."

The agent sits on the edge of the table. He looks down at the Chinaman who looks back at him fully attentive. "So, what are we going to do today? Are we sacrificing one life to save four or are we letting that one life go free and sentencing the other four to death?"

The Chinaman's thoughts flicker rapidly like the numbers on the screen of the Wall Street Stock Market. The agent sees him ready to roll and decides to force his hand while he has him. "Come on, I'm about to clock out for the day. My partner isn't as understanding and compassionate as me. He won't be so willing to work with you. Tell me what we doing."

The Chinaman leans his head back and rubs his hands over his eyes. He shakes his head in deep thought. The thoughts trample over each other in his mind. The mind game the agent is playing is working.

The Chinaman looks in the eyes of the agent. The agent can see the weakness in them and he feels like he has him on the ropes. He loves the feeling of victory. Nothing makes him feel more in power than breaking a man, crushing his manhood and having him roll over.

"Talk to me, man," the agent says very cockily.

The Chinaman opens his mouth slowly. "I wish to speak to my attorney, Tony Austin."

The Saga Continues...

ACKNOWLEDGEMENTS

FIRST LET ME take this time to thank each and every one of you whom have taken the time to sit down and read my work. In a time like today where readers are becoming more and more extinct, I am thankful for those who still take out the time to do so. I appreciate your support and I bear witness that without you, there would be no me.

Many readers say that I inspire and motivate them but truthfully my inspiration and motivation comes from my readers. It's because of readers that I now have 17 years in the business and 15 novels to date. When I first wrote No Exit, I had no idea that this is what I would be doing 17 years later. No Exit was never written to sale or publish. It was simply me, writing to prove that I could write a book if I chose to, and also prove that I could write a better, more realistic street story than the ones that were on the shelves at that time.

I'm grateful to have a reader base of individuals who prefer realness over fantasy because that is all I know how to bring. My goal is to shine the light on issues that many pay no mind to while making the story entertaining as well. All in all I appreciate you allowing me to share my vision and my thoughts with you.

Last but not least, I would like to thank my target audience, the inmates that populate the federal and state prisons all across the country. As I always state, from day one of this writing journey my target audience has always been behind the prison walls, for many reasons. One of the main reasons being, with me writing from a more realistic stance, I knew, only certain types could relate or even appreciate that stance, and most of those certain types would be people who actually played the game that I write about. I knew that certain things may go over the heads of folks that may have never witnessed these things that go on. I write for those that fully understand.

Secondly, I chose the prison population as my target audience because for years I walked that same tight rope that could have resulted in me spending the rest of my life in prison. I understand the trials and tribulations that come with that life. I also understand what is to be addicted to fast money and the lifestyle. I know the mindset that comes with it and the thought process. Thank God I never spent anytime in prison but for years I jailed on the streets. In prison just minus the bars. From being dirt broke in it to being all the way up top floor with it. From being stabbed to being shot down two summers in a row. I played on every Ievel of it.

I understand the game but the older I get I don't respect the game. Just in the past few years I started to realize the game is an illusion. It's a trick that we fall for, most out of desperation. We all had dreams of making it out of the game with a big bag of money but the reality is the game wasn't designed for us to walk away into the sunset with a bag of money. It was designed for us to lose our lives on front line or to lock us away and keep us enslaved forever.

As I evolve in life and my perception changes I try to bring my readers with me. Through my books from the first to this one here, a person can read the books and see the changes in tone of the streets. From earlier books we saw when the game was about the money and the women. Then we saw in Block Party 1 where the dope took over and because the stakes got higher the murder rate increased as well. Then we saw how gang life crept in and in later books we saw how gangs took over. Now, today, we see where nothing in the game is sacred. Friends killing friends in the comfort of their homes and cars. We see used to be stand up dudes now tattling on each other to save their freedom. Any honor or integrity that may have been in that game is no longer. From my later works if you take nothing else from them, I hope you get that.

I know some of you are waiting for the day to make your exit from prison and have plans on getting out here and getting back what you may believe the game owes you but please take it from me, there's nothing left out here. The rats, the informants and dishonorable took it all! Know that! For the rest of your bids I urge you all to take the remaining time to put another plan in place because that other plan is a trap. There are millions of ways to make a million dollars, choose another one! In closing, I urge you to find another way. I thank and appreciate you all for the continuous support. Salute to the honorable! True 2 Life Forever!

BOOK ORDER FORM

Purchase Information

Name: _____

Address: _____ City: _____

State: _____ Zip Code: _____

Books are listed in the order they were written and published

$14.95-No Exit _____
$14.95-Block Party _____
$14.95-Sincerely Yours _____
$14.95-Caught em Slippin _____
$14.95-Block Party 2 _____
$14.95-Block Party 3 _____
$14.95-Strapped _____
$14.95-Back 2 Bizness (Block Party 4) _____
$14.95-Young Gunz _____
$14.95-Outlaw Chick _____
$14.95-Block Party 5k1 Volume 1 _____
$14.95-Block Party 5k1 Volume 2 _____
$14.95-Heartless _____
$14.95-Block Party 666 Volume 1 _____
$14.95-Block Party 666 Volume 2 _____

Book Total: _____

Add $7.00 for shipping of 1-3 books
Free shipping for order of 4 or more books

Mailing Address:
True 2 Life Publications
PO Box 8722
Newark, NJ 07108
Make Checks/Money Orders payable to: True 2 Life Publications